The Books of Nancy Moser: www.na...

Historical Novels

Where Time Will Take Me (Book 1 of the Past Times Series)
The Pattern Artist (Book 1 of the Pattern Artist Series)
The Fashion Designer (Book 2 of the Pattern Artist Series)
The Shop Keepers (Book 3 of the Pattern Artist Series)
Love of the Summerfields (Book 1 of Manor House Series)
Bride of the Summerfields (Book 2 of Manor House Series)
Rise of the Sumemrfields (Book 3 of Manor House Series)
Mozart's Sister (biographical novel of Nannerl Mozart)
Just Jane (biographical novel of Jane Austen)
Washington's Lady (bio-novel of Martha Washington)
How Do I Love Thee? (bio-novel of Elizabeth Barrett Browning)
Masquerade (Book 1 of the Gilded Age Series)
An Unlikely Suitor (Book 2 of the Gilded Age Series)
The Journey of Josephine Cain
A Patchwork Christmas (novella collection)
A Basket Brigade Christmas (novella collection)
Regency Brides (novella collection)
Christmas Stitches (novella collection)

Contemporary Books

The Invitation (Book 1 of Mustard Seed Series)
The Quest (Book 2 of Mustard Seed Series)
The Temptation (Book 3 of Mustard Seed Series)
Crossroads
The Seat Beside Me (Book 1 of Steadfast Series)
A Steadfast Surrender (Book 2 of Steadfast Series)
The Ultimatum (Book 3 of Steadfast Series)
The Sister Circle (Book 1 of Sister Circle Series)
Round the Corner (Book 2 of Sister Circle Series)
An Undivided Heart (Book 3 of Sister Circle Series)
A Place to Belong (Book 4 of Sister Circle Series)
The Sister Circle Handbook (Book 5 of Sister Circle Seri(
Time Lottery (Book 1 of Time Lottery Series)
Second Time Around (Book 2 of Time Lottery Series)
John 3:16
The Good Nearby
Solemnly Swear
Save Me, God! I Fell in the Carpool (inspirational humor)

Children's Picture Books

Maybe Later (Book 1 of the Doodle Art Series)
I Feel Amazing: the ABCs of Emotion (Book 2 of the Doodle Art Series)

THE SHOP KEEPERS

ISBN-13: 978-1-7339830-1-3

Published by:
Mustard Seed Press
10605 W. 165 Street
Overland Park, KS 66221

This story is a work of fiction. Any resemblances to actual people, places, or events are purely coincidental.

All Scripture quotations are taken from The Holy Bible, King James Version.

Cover design by Mustard Seed Press.
Photograph: Fashion by Amy, Linker, & Co. 1914
Photograph: Félix

Printed and bound in the United States of America

THE
SHOP
KEEPERS

Book 3 of the Pattern Artist Series

~~~

NANCY MOSER

Mustard Seed Press

Overland Park, Kansas

DEDICATION

To my grandfather,
Lester C. Young
who fought in the great war.
And my grandmother, Almeda,
who waited for his return.

To my grandparents, George
and Ruth Swenson
who married in 1920.
Grandma's dress inspired the
wedding dresses of Unruffled.

CHAPTER ONE

Late July 1919
New York City

"All this black. I want to see color again!"

Annie Culver had meant to say the words to herself — she thought she *had* only thought the thought — until her six-year-old daughter responded.

"Me too, Mama. I like pink best." Victoria pulled a pink ribbon from a box of trim Annie kept under the counter of their dress shop, Unruffled. She wrapped it around her finger.

Victoria's younger sister shook her head.

"What color is your favorite, Alice?" Annie asked.

She scanned the box, then chose her favorite. "Red!" She waved the short length in the air, then stood, skipped around the dress racks, and began to sing, "'Pack up your troubles in an old kit-bag and smile, smile, smile. While you've a lucifer to light the flag, smile boys, that's your style.'"

Victoria joined her sister and Annie grabbed a green ribbon and joined the parade as they sang together. "'What's the use of worrying? It never was worthwhile. So pack up your troubles in an old kit-bag and smile, smile, smile!'"

They ended with flourish and very off key. Yet the laughter was a much-needed balm, a ray of emotional light among the racks of mourning clothes they'd been forced to sew. For not only were there countless widows of the World War, but there were many who had lost loved ones during the influenza epidemic. The latter hit close to home. Annie had friends who'd lost loved ones. Mr. Sampson, the dear husband of Annie's friend and benefactor, Eleanor, had succumbed early on. Even one of their seamstresses, Gert, had lost her husband. Nearly every family on the block had lost someone. Death was greedy and hit rich and poor alike.

The bell on the door announced a customer. Annie put on a smile. "How may I help you today?"

A middle-aged woman scanned the store. "I'm looking for a new best-dress — not black."

Exactly.

❦

Edna Holmquist took the short walk from her apartment building on Leroy Street to the tenement across the street. Unruffled now had two sewing workshops there.

The newer one-bedroom space used to be Annie and Sean's apartment until the birth of Victoria and Alice forced them to find a two-bedroom in the same building. Instead of letting their old flat go, they'd adapted it to a second workshop. In the throes of their 1913 success, Unruffled had needed four seamstresses working at the two workshops *and* a half-dozen working in a small factory space. But then the war came. A wave of melancholy and fear descended over the country. The United States had been late to the fight, joining the cause when the suffering of Europe was too much to bear. War brought devastating repercussions that surged and broke like a wave as millions died.

As had their business. Not completely, but enough to close the factory and let most of the seamstresses go. Now there were only three. Edna called them her Three Gs: Ginny, Gert, and Gela.

Edna stopped at Annie's old apartment first and found two of them at work.

Gert looked up from her machine. "Morning, Edna."

"Where is Gela?"

"I'm sure she'll be here — be here late." Gert glanced at Ginny, who nodded.

Gela Ricci's tardiness was a continuing problem. But Edna set that aside to commend the two workers who *were* here. "We appreciate your hard work, ladies." She nodded toward the stacked tables, chairs, and sewing machines that filled the front room, waiting to be used again. "I know this is awkward having all these stored here."

"I'm just happy to still have a job," Ginny said.

"Me too." Gert checked a hem on a sleeve, and finding it satisfactory, continued to sew.

Edna was moved by their loyalty, for they were two of the original seamstresses.

Ginny sat at a machine and pinned a seam for sewing. "Surely with the war over, women will be buying dresses again."

"That's our hope."

"If I see one more button that says, 'I am making my old clothes do', I'm going to scream."

Edna agreed, though didn't say so. "It's admirable that people stood together and made sacrifices for the war effort."

"And we won," Gert said.

"And we won." It was telling that none of them smiled at this fact. Yes, the war was over. Yes, the Allies had been victorious. But at what cost?

As if reading her thoughts, Gert asked, "How is Steven?"

Edna's son Steven had returned from the war, whole in body, but not in spirit. "He's glad to be home safe with Henrietta and the boys."

"We should pray for all the soldiers who've come home," Gert said.

Edna thought about Sean. "And those still missing."

"So no word on Mr. Culver?" Ginny asked.

Edna shook her head. "It's hard on Annie and the girls not to know, but they still hope."

"Hope is a good thing," Gert said.

Sometimes, it was the only thing.

Gela Ricci stood in her bedroom, sucking in her mid-section so she could hook her corset. She let herself breathe, then moaned. "This is ridiculous."

Mama must have been at the door because she cracked it open and said, "What's ridiculous?"

"Wearing a corset."

Mama slipped into the room and shut the door. "Now is not the time to argue, Angela. We're going to be late for work. Get dressed. Quickly now."

Gela shook her head and unhooked the clasps. "I'm done with it."

"Don't be silly."

She removed the corset and tossed it on the bed. "Our motto at Unruffled is "Fashion for the unruffled, unveiled, unstoppable woman. I want to add 'uncorseted' to the list."

"Don't be ridiculous."

"That's my word, and you can't use it." Why didn't Mama understand? "We claim to be the patrons of fashion so shouldn't we be on the cusp of being modern and new? Corsets are old fashioned torture."

"I can't disagree, but why don't you just loosen your stays at the end of the day like the rest of us?"

"What does that accomplish? Partial rather than full pain? I want no pain."

Mama retrieved Gela's corset. "Fashion is making progress, but for now, be a proper young lady and wear your —"

"So you'd rather stay stuck in the style of your mother's time, or *her* mother's?"

"Of course not. At Unruffled we're making great strides providing more comfortable clothes: shorter hems, looser sleeves, lower waists."

"We need to start from the inside out," Gela said. "Unruffled needs to carry the new brassieres. I was talking to a friend and she says there's such a thing as a side-lacer that would —"

"Not now, Gela," Mama said. "Since you were only ten when we opened the store, I don't think you get a say in how it's been run. Leave that to Annie, Edna, Henrietta and I."

"So my opinion means nothing?"

Mama put a hand to her forehead, a familiar gesture. "Please, Gela. Get dressed."

Gela knew she was being peevish, but she couldn't help herself. "I don't want to go to work. At all." She plopped onto the bed. Realizing the action might make her look even more childish, she stood.

"Nonsense. You have a responsibility to Unruffled."

"A responsibility, but not an opinion?"

Mama's face grew red, a warning sign — that Gela ignored.

"We don't even have a factory space anymore. I don't like working in the workshop. It's just an apartment."

Mama stood in front of the mirror and tucked a stray strand of hair. "Why does location matter? The work is the same."

Gela regretted bringing it up, and knew her mother wouldn't understand how work was tolerable when it was in a real factory, but seemed lesser when done in an apartment close to home. How the former made her feel older than her sixteen years, while the latter made her feel like the token daughter of Maude Ricci, one of the owners.

She glanced in the mirror. "I also want to bob my hair."

"Cut it off?"

"All the girls are doing it."

"A very few girls are doing it," Mama said. "It's a fad. It won't catch on."

Gela shrugged, hoping that the diversion into the subject of hair would make Mama give in regarding the corset.

"Maude? Gela?" It was Papa, calling from the parlor. "Don't you need to leave?"

Mama pressed the corset into Gela's hands. "In two minutes I'm leaving without you." She left the room.

Gela made a quick decision. She tossed the corset on the bed and put on a blouse and skirt. The skirt was a little tight in the fastening without the structure of the corset to pull her in. But Gela adjusted the hooks and it was fine. And more than fine, it meant she could breathe.

She joined her mother, grabbing her straw hat and going out to the hallway before Mama could notice her lack of a corset. "Come on, Mother. We don't want to be late, do we?"

~

Maude and Gela climbed the stairs of the apartment building that held both Unruffled workshops. Gela turned to enter the one on the second floor.

"Have a good day," Maude said.

"Hmm."

Maude pointed at her. "Tomorrow a corset. Understood?"

Gela shrugged and went inside.

Maude kept going to the third floor, to the original Unruffled workshop. Gela made her feel weary before the day even began. When Maude Nascato had first married the widowed Antonio Ricci six years earlier, she had become mother to Angela, age ten, and her brother, Matteo, nine. Blessedly, the children had accepted her as Mama, giving Maude the family she could never have on her own. God was very good.

But in the past year, Gela had left "Mama" behind and had started to call her "Mother" — at least to her face. That, in itself wasn't alarming, for she had grown from a child to a young woman. But it foreshadowed more changes. Sweet, vibrant Gela had grown argumentative and moody. Although Maude knew those traits often accompanied Gela's age, it didn't make it any easier to handle. If Maude mentioned the sky was blue, Gela would argue it was slightly gray. Today's argument about the workshop . . . Maude knew the girl didn't particularly like to sew and would have rather worked elsewhere, but during the war, with Antonio off to fight — without his wages — the family had needed the income. Antonio's real estate company had been put on hold until his return. That lack of income, added to the low sales at Unruffled, had caused Maude more than one night wide-awake with worry. She'd even considered returning to her old job as a pattern artist at Butterick Pattern Company. Unfortunately, they weren't hiring.

As she reached the door of the workshop and used her key, she recognized her dark mood growing darker and tried to divert it by thanking God for her husband's return. Many families weren't so lucky. Which bought to mind Annie, who had no idea if Sean was alive or dead. She shook her head quickly. "Enough, Maude. 'Be strong and do the work.'"

She opened the windows wider to catch every breeze. At this time of year the summer heat never left them completely, only teasing them with temperatures that were less oppressive at night. She placed her hat on the rack and turned toward the cutting table that dominated the main room. Two bedrooms held two sewing machines and supplies.

Absently, she picked up fabric scraps from the latest cutting and placed them into the trash bin.

But then, she stopped. She stared at them as if seeing the fabric for the first time.

"It's all black."

She looked around the room at the bolts of fabric they'd recently used. Although it was summer, there wasn't a light or cheery color in the bunch. Even if the dresses weren't black, they were somber, even discouraging.

The sound of people on the stairs interrupted her thoughts.

Maude set aside her musings.

For now.

≈

Henrietta Kidd Holmquist sat at the kitchen table of her family's apartment on Leroy Street, the ledgers for Unruffled spread open before her. A stack of bills demanded to be paid. Somehow.

The sound of blocks falling—a tower of toys falling upon the wood floor—caused her to look up.

"You broke it!" four-year-old Lennie yelled.

"Stop yer belly-aching," older brother Willie said. "We'll build it again." He turned to their father, sitting by the window. "Will you help us, Papa?"

Steven kept staring out the window, giving no indication he'd heard either the fall of the blocks or the invitation from his five-year-old son.

Henrietta felt bad for them. She set down her pencil and knelt on the floor beside. "Let's see how high we can build it this time."

As the boys focused on the task, Henrietta let herself worry about their father. He'd been back from the war six months now, and they had celebrated his safe return. Yet it many ways it was as if he was still absent, for he showed little interest in the doings of family life, and had rejected Henrietta's suggestion he go back to teaching. "Not yet" had been his reply to that suggestion. And all the other suggestions. He spent his time sleeping or sitting at the window, staring at what, she had no clue.

What had he seen on the battlefields? What had he experienced? What memories held him captive?

Most importantly, how could she bring him back?

The last block was placed on the tower and both boys clapped with glee. "We did it!" Lennie said.

"Look, Papa!" Willie said.

Steven stared out the window, unwavering. Henrietta went to her husband's side, putting a hand on his back. "Look at what the boys built."

Steven turned his head, seeing but not seeing. She watched his facial features struggle to smile. Yet he *did* smile. A bit. And even said, "Good."

"Let's knock it down!" Lennie said.

Willie nodded vigorously. "Together on three. One. Two."

"Three!" Lennie swiped a hand at the middle of the tower, sending the blocks clattering all over the room.

Steven started. His shoulders raised. His hands covered his ears.

Henrietta wrapped her arms around him. "It's all right, darling," she whispered. "It's all right."

But it wasn't.

CHAPTER TWO

"It's mine!" Victoria grabbed the pink ribbon out of her sister's hands. "You chose the red one."

Alice tried to grab it back. "But *I* like pink today!"

A scuffle ensued, leading both girls to the floor.

"Girls!" Annie pried them apart. "No fighting."

"But I want the pink one," Alice said.

Victoria held the ribbon close to her chest. "You can't have it, it's mine."

Alice grabbed at it, and more fighting ensued.

Annie separated them and held out her hand. "Give it to me."

"But it's mine."

Annie let her eyebrows raise. Victoria handed it over. Annie saw the glimmer of a smile on Alice's face. *Oh, no you don't.* She extended a hand in her direction. "The red one, please."

"But Mama, we weren't fighting about the red one."

"Now."

Alice plucked the red ribbon from the floor and gave it up. Annie wrapped them around her hand, then placed them in the top drawer of the bureau in her bedroom. "If you can't share, if you fight, you both lose."

"But—"

She waved a hand at them. "Finish your breakfast. Grandma will be here any moment and I want the dishes cleared by then."

The girls went back to the table, muttering under their breath.

"I heard that!" Annie said.

Annie sat on the bed and began to put her shoes on. She let out a deep sigh and then—as often happened—she put her hand on the bed. On Sean's side of the bed. Funny how she kept sleeping on her side, even after nearly two years apart. *Seven hundred twenty-four days to be exact.* Victoria had been Alice's age when Sean left to fight in Europe. And Alice had been but a toddler. If Sean came back, would Alice even recognize—

She clapped a hand over her mouth. Not *if*. When.

Tears came and she angrily swiped them away. It did no good to cry. She had daughters to raise and a business to run. And it wasn't just about her. Where *was* he? Was Sean suffering in some prisoner camp, or in some unknown hospital? Was he wandering through the debris of fallen European towns, unable to find his way home to them? Or was he dead, buried in a mass grave, forever lost to her?

"Annie?"

She looked up to find her mother-in-law in the bedroom doorway. Annie busied herself with tying a shoe. "I didn't hear you come in. I'll be gone in a minute."

Vesta came into the room and closed the door behind her. She sat on the bed and put her arm around Annie, drawing her upright. Then she gently pulled Annie's head against her own, two women, sharing the heartache of loss. For even though there wasn't confirmation Sean was dead, there was loss just the same. And Vesta had the worst of it. She had lost her husband Richard three years previous. Not from the war but from a heart attack. Grief then, and grief now.

They were two women, confronting life alone. They clasped hands and found a common rhythm in their breathing.

୶

Maude entered Unruffled with four dresses draped over her arms. "Four more for the racks."

One of their clerks, Birdie Doyle, rushed to take them.

Maude saw Annie speaking softly with a customer, a hand to the woman's back, as the woman nodded and used a handkerchief. They stood before the racks of mourning dresses.

Another day, another widow.

With Annie and Birdie occupied, Maude helped a woman who was looking to buy an everyday dress. Maude smiled. She said all the right words. But her heart wasn't in it. Would her heart ever be in it again?

When the woman left with her purchase, Maude scanned the store, remembering the joy of its inception in 1913 and the outdoor fashion show that had brought such pleasure to the entire neighborhood. Their pleasure was short-lived. Everything began to change a year later.

In June 2014, Austrian archduke Franz Ferdinand and his wife were assassinated by a Serbian radical while riding in an open car. It was a handy excuse for Austria-Hungary and Germany to declare war on Serbia and Russia. Then France and Britain joined in on the Russian side.

The war news had been confusing and harrowing, and was the main topic of conversation at every get-together with friends. Antonio, Steven, and Sean spoke of going off to fight. The women admired their bravery, but took comfort in knowing it would remain just talk. The United States wasn't involved. It was a European war.

Until it wasn't. Until it became their war. Until the men left to fight.

From the beginning they all witnessed the effects of the war. Many New Yorkers were but a generation away from those warring countries. Familial roots were at odds with those of friends and colleagues. As countries in Europe took sides, so did New York. Many, as proud citizens, sent aid back home. The thoughts and interests of most women rightly veered away from fashion. Fashion was frivolous. Caring about fashion was irresponsible. Almost disloyal.

And Maude had agreed. In part. When the United States entered the war in 1917, sewing dresses with pretty fabrics or accessorizing them with a perky hat or a matching coat seemed wrong.

She sighed deeply. "When will it end?"

"When will what end?" Annie said, coming back from the fitting rooms where the widow was probably trying on some widow's weeds. At least heavy veils were out of style.

Maude didn't have to answer, as the bell on the door chimed and one of their seamstresses walked in with an older woman.

"I'm not sure we have any alterations for you, Gert," Birdie said.

Gert shook her head. She was beaming. "I'm not here for that." She drew the woman forward. "Mother, you remember the ladies of Unruffled. Ladies, this is my mother."

Annie shook her hand. "So nice to see you again, Mrs. Cody."

"Nice to see you too. Gert's always talking about the ladies at work, but with the bakery, I haven't had time to come shop much."

"Until now." Gert beamed. "Is Henrietta here?"

"Not today," Annie said. Gert looked disappointed. She and Henrietta had grown close and had even shared a flat when the latter had first come to New York.

"I wish she was here," Gert said. "But . . ."

Something was going on. "You look positively chuffed," Annie said.

"If that means proud and happy, yes, I am." Gert bobbed twice on her toes, then held out her left hand where they saw a ruby ring.

Did it mean . . . ?

"Simon proposed. I said yes!"

The ladies embraced Gert with hugs and congratulations. Maude was very happy for her. Gert had once suffered under a husband who beat her. She'd left him years ago, and more recently he'd died of the influenza. A bad end, but it had left Gert fully free. Maude had heard she was being courted by a man named Simon, a fish monger down by the docks. That it had come to this was marvelous.

Annie asked, "When is the happy occasion?"

"Soon," Gert said. "I wasted too many years with Frankie. Simon and I aren't getting any younger."

"It's never too late for love," Maude said.

"Truth is, we're tired of waiting."

"Waiting *is* hard." Maude glanced at Annie.

Gert must have seen the direction of her gaze. "Oh, Annie. I'm sorry. I know you're *very* tired of waiting — for a different reason."

"Yes, I am," Annie said. "But today is not about me." She took Gert's hands in hers. "You will need a wedding dress."

"Well, yes. I know we've occasionally made some and I was hoping . . . Papa said he wants me to have a fancy dress to celebrate our new life."

"We can design you one," Maude said. "It will be our pleasure. Anything to work on a dress that isn't —"

"Black," Annie said in unison.

"I knew you could design it." Gert said. "I can do the sewing."

"There's some fancy fabric in the back," Birdie said. "Bolts and bolts of it."

And there it was. The answer to Maude's creative melancholy. She linked her arm with Gert's. "Let's go see what treasures we can find."

و

Gert and her mother oohed and ahhed over the bolts of luxurious fabric that showcased a pallet of autumn hues: greens, blues, coppers, and ivories. "I'd forgotten about these. We've had many of them since the beginning, haven't we?"

Maude fingered a sea green batiste. "We have."

"Why haven't you used them?" Mrs. Cody asked.

Maude explained. "Our original investor, Mrs. Sampson, wanted fancier designs than those we'd envisioned for our business. At first we bowed to her wishes and agreed to make them out of these fabrics — after all, money is money, and we had little of our own. But Annie stood firm. She put us back on our path, toward our original direction, providing fashion for working woman, mothers, teachers . . ."

"Fashion for the unruffled, unveiled, unstoppable woman," Gert recited.

Maude laughed at the mention of the store's motto. "These fabrics didn't fit that mold. But the ivory ones can be used for wedding dresses." The light was dim in the storeroom. "Let's take these out into the showroom to see them better."

Each woman carried a long bolt into the main room, the size of the bolt nearly as tall as the petite Mrs. Cody. They set them on the front counter. Annie and Birdie came close.

"I'd forgotten about these," Annie said. Then she added, "Birdie, go fetch the box of trims that's in the same area. To the right, I think."

"Mrs. Sampson's fancy trims!" Maude said. "I'd forgotten about them. Wasn't there some Chantilly lace?"

"I believe there was."

Birdie returned with the dusty box, untouched for six years. They made room for it and removed the lid.

Maude's eyes immediately fell upon the lace. She unwound a yard of it, setting it upon the ivory fabrics.

"Oooh."

They laughed at their communal reaction.

Gert put her hands to her chest as if containing the beat of her heart. "These are exquisite. Perfect." Her eyes glistened. "You're willing to use these on a dress for me?"

Maude put an arm around her shoulder. "Who better than you?"

"Now then," Annie said, taking up a sketch pad. "Tell us what you'd like in a dress."

⨞

Edna examined the work of the seamstresses. Her gaze stopped when she spotted some wavy seams. *Oh dear. Not again.* "Gela?" she called out. "Come here, please."

She could hear the girl's exasperated sigh before she came out of the room. "What did I do wrong this time?"

"Don't play the martyr, it's unbecoming." Edna pointed to the stool beside her, letting the dress fall upon the cutting table. "Tell me what's wrong with this seam."

Gela gave it a cursory glance. "The machine is testy today."

"That's not an answer, that's an excuse."

Gela shrugged, let out a puff of air, and said, "It's crooked."

"And?"

"The edges don't meet up straight."

Edna handed her the dress. "Did you pin it?"

"No."

"Taking the time to pin saves time in the long run. Do it over, please."

Gela stood. "Yes, ma'am."

"Do your best first."

"The truth is, factory or no factory, I don't really like sewing." She rolled her eyes. "At all."

She could be such a child. "Many people don't like their jobs. But they still do the work and do their best. People need to earn a living."

"But Papa is back now. He's starting up his business again."

Edna was frustrated. "Isn't your brother working? Making deliveries?"

She rolled her eyes. Again. "Matteo likes *his* job."

Edna had no experience dealing with 16-year-old girls. Her son, Steven, had always been selfless and giving. He'd been a gifted teacher — until he'd come back from the war.

But that was another subject for another moment. How could she get Gela to think beyond herself?

Then she got an idea. "I was going to go to a place called Port Refuge tomorrow. Saturday. I've never been before, but have heard they can use volunteers to help those in need. Would you like to come with me?"

Gela made a face. "And do what?"

"Talk to people who have fallen on difficult times. You're very personable, Gela." *When you're not complaining.* "You could help them forget their troubles."

Edna could see the girl's mind working. Finally, she nodded her head once. "I'll go. What time?"

~

Henrietta finished a letter to her mother in England. *I haven't heard from you in far too long, Mamma. With Papa gone I worry about you. I need to know you are all right. I've written Adam and he says you are, but I know he is consumed with his new duties as viscount and being lord of the manor. Besides, we both know he isn't one to be attune to what others are feeling. For that, I need to hear directly from you. Please, Mamma. Ease my mind!*

She signed it, addressed the envelope to Crompton Hall, and sealed it with a red-wax H. If Henrietta didn't hear from Mamma soon, she would send a cable, demanding a swift answer. Or maybe she would contact her cousin May at nearby Summerfield Manor. It wasn't like her mother to be silent so long.

She suffered the inner question of why she hadn't sent a cable already. The answer was known — and simple — the last time she'd dealt with a cable was when she was informed of her father's death during the war. Although Father had been too old to be a soldier, he rode with a supply truck and was killed when it overturned. It was just like her father, volunteering. Yet selfishly, Henrietta held it against him. War was bad enough without choosing to be in harm's way.

It was hard to mourn while she was so far away from her childhood home. Her first instinct to sail home had been met with wartime travel restrictions. Everyone remembered the sinking of the Lusitania. Actually, that was another case where people purposely put themselves in harm's way. The passengers had been warned of German submarines in the Atlantic before they booked passage. The company was warned. The United States had been warned. Twelve-hundred lives lost.

She closed her eyes against the thoughts of danger and death. What was done was done. The war was over. Her brother had become the Viscount Newley, and his wife, Theodosia, was the viscountess.

Theodosia. What a ridiculous name.

Henrietta recognized her unfair peevishness but allowed herself the thought.

And yet . . . Mamma was the dowager now, living as second fiddle at Crompton Hall. It was in her nature to be kind and helpful. Surely Theodosia and Adam appreciated her many abilities and care. They'd better.

Henrietta gathered the boys. "Come now. We need to post a letter to your grandmother, then stop at the workshop." She helped Willie tie a shoe. "Steven? We'll be back in a few hours. All right?"

He gave a feeble nod, but kept staring out the window at the sky.

As she walked down the hall, she mourned that there was nothing more she could say to him. She'd cried, shouted, ignored, and pleaded, but no matter how she tried to communicate, Steven would only acknowledge her with a nod or the scantest of words.

Henrietta needed advice. She was closest to Annie, for it was Annie who'd inspired Henrietta to come to New York in the first place. But Annie was busy dealing with the floundering business, her daughters, and the constant worry regarding Sean's fate.

Maude, on the other hand, had Gela-issues. How lucky she was that Antonio had returned from the war. He limped, but Henrietta would much prefer that physical weakness over Steven's emotional and mental incapacity.

Which left Edna. As Steven's mother, surely she would know what to do.

࿐

The boys rushed into the workshop and into their grandmother's arms, ignoring the dress she was hemming. "There's my boys!" Edna set aside the dress, her needle and thread, and kissed them each on the head. They jostled each other for seating on her lap. "Sit still now," she said. Only then did she look up at Henrietta. "Are you off on an outing?"

"Actually . . . I need to speak with you. Do you think it would be an imposition if I asked Vesta to watch them for a bit since she already has the girls?"

Edna looked concerned. "All you can do is ask. It *would* be a fine chance for the children to play together."

Henrietta held out her hands to gather her sons. "I'll be back after I drop them off."

She took the boys to a large two-bedroom flat where Annie and Sean had moved. She heard the girls singing inside. So did Lennie, for he called out, "Alice!"

The door opened and Vesta smiled. "How nice. You've come to visit?"

In a way. "Could you keep the boys for a short bit?"

Vesta cocked her head. "Is something wrong?"

Henrietta shook her head. "I want to speak to Edna without . . ."

"Of course." Vesta opened the door wider. "Come on in, boys. We're learning a new song."

"Thank you," Henrietta said. "I'll be back soon."

Vesta reached out and touched Henrietta's hand. "How is Steven?"

She didn't like that everyone knew, and yet embraced that same fact. In England such personal deficiencies were hidden under a dome of propriety. New York was different.

"He's the reason I need to talk with Edna."

Vesta squeezed her hand. "Take as much time as you need."

When Henrietta got back to the workshop, Edna met her at the door. "By the look on your face I assume you want privacy?"

"It is preferred."

"Let's go to the roof."

The women went up to the fourth floor, then through a door that led to another set of stairs. They wove their way through clothing hung on lines, finding two chairs someone had set at the far side.

Once they were settled, Edna asked, "What's on your mind?"

"Steven."

Edna sighed. "He's on my mind too. Always. Any better?"

Henrietta shook her head, letting it hang low to mask her tears.

"Now, now," Edna said, rubbing a hand on her arm. "Tell me everything."

Henrietta retrieved a handkerchief and dried her tears, grabbing a new breath. "He seems fine of body. I see no physical infirmities at all."

"Which *is* a blessing."

"I know it is. He's *here*. With *us*. Yet he's not with us. He sits by the window and stares. He rarely even moves his head from right to left. It's like he's not seeing anything at all."

"Anything *here*, you mean."

"What?"

"Perhaps he's reliving some moments from the war. Perhaps they dog him. Haunt him."

"I've asked him to tell me what's wrong and he shakes his head."

"He may not know what's wrong. You and I weren't there. We don't know what horrors he saw or experienced. He's like my Grandpa Floyd."

"How so?"

"Grandpa came back from fighting the War between the States a changed man. Where he'd been happy-go-lucky before, he was sullen and moody."

"Quiet?"

"Sometimes. And sometimes he'd yell about the stupidest things. I remember a time when me and my cousin started marching around playing a fife and harmonica we'd found in the attic. Grandpa sprung out of his chair and grabbed them away from us. 'No!' That's all he said, but my mother explained that it was probably because the sounds reminded him of the battlefield."

"Steven has reacted like that. I'd almost welcome *that* versus not reacting at all."

Edna smoothed her apron over her dress. "You've come to me for answers, unfortunately I have none."

Henrietta felt deflated. If his own mother didn't know how to reach him . . .

"Does he respond to the boys?" Edna asked.

"Very little. Perhaps an occasional smile."

"Does he . . . have you . . .?"

It was awkward to speak of such things to her mother-in-law. "He lets me hold him at night, but that's all. He doesn't sleep well. He has nightmares."

Edna looked out over the sea of rooftops and chimneys. "Perhaps if he talked to Antonio about it?"

"If he'll talk at all."

Edna nodded. "Be there for him. Love him. He experienced a world turned upside down. Be his rock. His safe place."

"I'll try. I'll ask Maude to ask Antonio if he'll talk to him. And I'll pray."

"And *I'll* pray. Even if we don't know what's going on with Steven, God does."

If only He'd let me in on it.

Edna stood and drew Henrietta to her feet, embracing her with a hug that was always a comfort.

CHAPTER THREE

"So you'll talk to Steven?" Maude asked her husband as they got ready for the day.

Antonio stopped tying his tie and lifted Maude's chin with a finger. "Do I have a choice?" He gave her a kiss on the nose.

"You imply that I'm pushy and need to get my way."

He smiled and raised his eyebrows.

"But you love me anyway?"

He winked. "I do. I'll go to their apartment on one condition."

"Name it."

"You come with me."

"Won't it be awkward with me there?"

"It would be more awkward for me to simply show up alone. If we're visiting as a couple, then you and Henrietta can find a reason to busy yourselves, leaving me alone with Steven."

She slid her arms around his waist. "You're very smart."

"I married you, didn't I?"

He held her close and gave her a proper kiss.

"Ugh," Gela said from the doorway of their room. "Stop it."

"We will not." Antonio gave Maude another kiss for good measure.

"Then don't do it in front of me."

Antonio spread his arms to encase the room. "If memory serves, this is our bedroom. You are a visitor."

Gela rolled her eyes, an action that was getting to be a habit. "I'm leaving."

"It's Saturday. Where are you going?"

"To some charity place. Edna invited me."

Maude hadn't heard about this. But if Gela was with Edna, all was well. She followed her into the parlor. "When will you be back?"

Gela was already at the door. "I dunno. Bye."

Matteo was tying his shoes nearby. "I'm leaving too. Lots of deliveries to make today."

Antonio joined them, putting on his suit coat. "Your work ethic is commendable, son."

"We need the money."

Maude knew Antonio wanted to disagree, but didn't. Couldn't.

She went to the kitchen and retrieved the food she had packed. "Don't forget your lunch."

Matteo took it and left.

"He's so grown up and responsible," Maude said.

"I leave a boy behind and come home to a man."

Maude thought of Gela. "And a woman."

He shook his head. "Woman in body, petulant child in action."

"I was that way at her age."

"I doubt that."

"You shouldn't. I just wish I knew what to do about it."

"Maybe some time under Edna's motherly wing will snap her out of it." Antonio collected his hat. "Are we going, or not?"

❧

Annie knew the girls would enjoy some time out of the apartment. Truth was, she could use the outing herself.

They took the elevated train to Central Park and she let them run ahead, rolling their hoops, skipping, hopping, chasing birds and rabbits. Where did they get their energy? Although it was morning, Annie felt as tired as she used to feel at bedtime.

She drew in a deep breath, willing the air to rid her mind of the cobwebs that threatened to muddle every thought. Just strolling down the mall was an effort. *If only Sean were here.*

"Mrs. Culver?"

She turned around and saw someone she had known before the war. "Guy Ship. How nice to see you."

He rushed forward to greet her, kissing her on the cheek. "It's been a long time."

She thought of the last time she'd seen him at Unruffled — at least two years ago. He used to be a fabric salesman. She assumed he'd gone overseas. "I'm glad you're back ."

"Me too."

Though in some ways he looked different — more wan and pale — he still had a mischievous glimmer in his eyes. "You have a mustache."

He stroked it. "I'm trying to have a mustache. My light hair makes it look more like a caterpillar strolling across my upper lip."

It felt good to laugh. "Are you back in your old position?"

He raised a finger in the air. "Olivet Fabric and Supplies: Distributing all your sewing needs. At your service." He gave her a smart bow. "I was planning to call on you at the store at your convenience. Pardon me for asking, but *is* Unruffled still open for business? So many retail establishments have closed."

"We are open." *Barely open.* "And we'd like for you to call on us."

"I will wait for your call."

Victoria and Alice called to her from up ahead. "Mama! Come on!"

"I am being summoned."

"They have grown into lovely girls."

"Thank you."

"You and your husband must be very proud."

"I am — we are. Were."

He paused and put a hand on her arm. "I'm so sorry. How thoughtless of me. Did your husband . . . ?"

"Actually, I don't know what happened to him." She hastened to add, "Still waiting to hear."

"Waiting is difficult."

She looked at the ground. "That, it is."

"If there's ever anything I can do, please let me know."

"Thank you." She extended a hand for him to shake. "I will see you soon."

"You will. But . . . may I walk with you? It's a lovely day for a stroll."

She couldn't think of a reason to say no. Having a little company brightened the day.

৵

Annie and the girls returned home from their Central Park outing. "Race you up the stairs!" she told the girls.

They won — of course. "We won, we won!"

"You did. You're both very fast." She unlocked the door and went inside, removing her hat.

"You seem happy, Mama," Victoria said. "You weren't before, but now you are."

"I am?" *I am?*

"Did that man make you happy?"

Did he? The thought was slightly unsettling. "I am happy because I got to spend the morning with both of you."

When she tickled them, their laughter covered up the hidden part of the truth.

৵

"That's it?" Gela asked Edna as they approached a dilapidated building that Edna called Port Refuge.

"You were expecting a palace?"

26

"Of course not, but . . ." Gela had never been inside such a ramshackle building, or visited such a rundown neighborhood. She placed the back of her hand to her nose, trying to block the foul smells that competed for worst-smell-ever. She stepped over a wet spot on the sidewalk. Who knew what *that* was.

They reached the entrance. "Make their day better with a smile," Edna said.

Smile? About what? Gela tried her best, but the sight inside made her want to turn around and leave. There was one large room filled with tables and chairs — most occupied. There were dozens of men with stooped shoulders and dingy clothes, nursing a hot drink or chewing on a sandwich as though the act took all their energy. And some were missing appendages. One man had his trouser leg pinned up at his knee. Arms, hands, legs. Gone. Papa had shown her his leg wound — now healed, though leaving behind a limp — but she'd never thought about having a leg cut *off*.

"Don't stare," Edna whispered.

"Sorry."

Edna approached a woman who was carrying a tray of sandwiches. "Good day to you. I am Edna Holmquist and this is Gela Ricci. We came to help."

The woman's face washed with relief. "We's glad for every hand." She scanned the room, then looked at Gela. "You good with children?"

"Maybe."

"We could use some help corralling the ones in that room over there."

Gela looked toward a room that was overflowing with children, some playing jacks, some pretending to shoot each other, some wrestling. Young voices rose as if there was a contest to see who could be the loudest. Babies cried. Two women held wee ones, bouncing them up and down, trying to get them to stop.

"I don't know anything about babies."

"You can learn, can't ya?"

Gela glanced at Edna, wanting to be saved. "I suppose."

"Good. Introduce yourself. And Mrs. Holmquist, we could use some help serving the soup." She pointed toward a kitchen area, then went back to serving the sandwiches.

"Can we leave?" Gela whispered to Edna.

"You'll survive. They're just children."

There was a loud scream from the room. "They don't seem to be *just* anything."

"Go on now. Remember, you're doing a good thing here."

"That remains to be seen." She looked toward the children. "Are they orphans?"

"I don't think so. There are orphanages for them. I was told this is a day nursery, that these children are here so their mothers — usually widows — can work and earn a living. Without a husband to provide for them, the families are in dire straits."

Gela remembered her own family's predicament while Papa was away.

You can do this. They're just children. "Very well then. Here I go." She approached the room with trepidation. A stray ball rolled out of the doorway. She rolled it back.

"Thanks," said a boy of about eight.

One woman was comforting a child who kept rubbing her head. "It's all right. He didn't mean to bonk yer head."

"Yes, he did!"

From Gela's experience with a little brother, she could support the girl's view of it. "Bonk him back."

The woman looked up, her forehead furrowed. "That is *not* good advice."

Gela shrugged. "I came to help?"

"I'm not sure we can use your kind of help."

"I'll be happy to leave."

"No!" The woman stood, sending the girl back into the fray. "We need hands. You have hands?"

Gela held up her hands. "Two at last count."

"Just enough to feed this one."

The woman transferred a fussy baby from a makeshift crib into Gela's arms and handed her a bottle. Gela couldn't remember the last time she'd held a baby, much less an unhappy one. She found a chair and tried to get comfortable. She rearranged the squirmy child in the crook of her arm. "Here you go. Bon appétit."

The baby sucked on the bottle as if her life depended on it. "There now. Drink it all down." The little girl looked up at Gela, studying her face as she drank. Her eyes were deep brown with hazel flecks. "Your eyes look like mine."

The woman checked on her. "She likes you."

"What's her name?"

She scratched her head. "I can't keep track very well, but I think that's Gladys."

"Eww," Gela said. "What a horrible name."

"Actually, her mama calls her Glad. That better?"

"A little."

"By the by, what's your name?"

"Gela, short for Angela."

"I'm Dorothy. Nice to meet you." She pointed to Gladys. "You need to hold her upright against your shoulder and burp her every few ounces or she'll spit it up."

With a little finagling, Gela got Gladys up against her shoulder.

"Pat her back. Nature will do the rest."

After only a few pats, Gladys gave out a hearty burp, making the two women laugh. "Good one, Glad."

The little girl smiled and drank the rest of the bottle. Gela was surprised that Glad made her very . . . glad.

≈

The children got antsy. It was like a bucketful of pebbles had been thrown into the room, skittering around, causing them to bobble and fall and run into each other. Which, of course, made them snipe and argue, with pushing involved.

Finally, Gela had enough. She set a dozing Glad in her crib, and broke up a skirmish between two boys. "Come now," she told them. "Let's play a game." She took one of the boy's hands and raised them to form an arch. "Now, all of you, walk in a line under our bridge."

The children looked confused, but they soon made a line. Gela began to sing, "'London bridges, falling down, falling down, falling down . . .'"

The children beamed and walked under the arch. On "my fair lady", Gela dropped their arms around a little girl, capturing her. She was quickly let go, but as Gela sang other verses, the children marched faster, not wanting to get locked up.

When they were done, the children laughed and clapped. "More!"

"Yes, miss. More," said a middle-aged man in the doorway. "You have a fine voice."

"Thank you."

"You know any songs we all can enjoy?" He pointed towards the main room. "I'll play the piano for you."

Gela was taken aback. Although she sang hymns at church and an occasional tune while sewing, she'd never sang for an audience.

She looked to Dorothy, who waved her away. "Go on then. We could all use a pretty song."

Gela followed the man into the main room. "I'm Mack McGinness," he said over his shoulder. "And you are?"

"Gela Ricci."

He reached the piano and grinned. "If you ask me, that's a grand name for the theater."

Gela didn't have time to react, for he pointed at some music. "You know 'Greensleeves'?"

"I do."

Bert sat at the piano and opened the sheet music. "Sing it out and make 'em happy." He played the introduction of the song.

Gela's stomach fluttered with nerves. But not for long. Once she began singing, the nerves left her. "'Alas my love, you do me wrong, to cast me out discourteously. For I have loved you well and long, delighting in your company.'"

She saw Edna sitting at a table, beaming—as were many others.

It must not sound too bad.

For the chorus, Gela ventured away from the piano and strolled among the tables. 'Greensleeves was all my joy. Greensleeves was my delight. Greensleeves was my heart of gold, and who but my lady Greensleeves.'"

As she continued with the other verses—she was surprised she knew them by heart—her thoughts seemed to separate from what her body was doing, as if there was no need for her to think while she sang as it came out as naturally as breath leaving the body. She was able to fully see the joy on the faces of her audience, to note how some closed their eyes with a wistful smile upon their lips, and others swayed with the rhythm. Their reactions fed her as much as the song fed them.

She touched shoulders, smiled a smile, and sang from her heart. She captured every ear, for even the children stood bundled together in the doorway, being still, as though enraptured. Dorothy held little Glad in her arms, and the baby was happy.

When Gela sang the final chorus, she raised her hands, encouraging all to sing along. The sound that filled the room made her shiver in awe and delight. *Surely, this is heaven.*

When the last note faded away, there was a moment of silence. A man touched her hand and whispered, "You've warmed me heart today, lassie."

The applause began. It was a new phenomenon for Gela, and she wasn't sure how to deal with it. She nodded her thanks, and hurried back to the piano. Her cheeks were warm. "Now what?" she asked Mack.

"Now, you sing another one."

❧

Edna checked the time. She and Gela had been at Refuge for five hours. Maude and Antonio were probably worried.

She approached the piano where Gela was speaking with the piano player about more music. "Gela? We should go."

"Why?"

"Because it's late."

"What time is it?"

"A quarter past three. Your parents will be worried."

"I had no idea of the time." Gela turned to the man. "Thank you so much for playing—and for urging me to sing."

"You enjoyed it then?"

"More than anything."

The man looked at Edna and stood. "She's got a talent, this one does."

"She does. An unexpected talent."

"You her family?"

"Nearly," Edna said. "Her mother and I work together."

"What sort of business?"

"We own a store, Unruffled, that sells women's —"

"Dresses. I know of it. I bought my late wife a dress there once."

"I'm sorry about your loss."

His eyes scanned the room. "There's a lot of that going around."

"Indeed."

He cocked his head. "You a widow?"

That's a very personal question. Yet she answered him. "A widow of long-standing." She held out her hand. "Edna Holmquist."

He shook her hand. "Mack McGinness, at your service."

Edna felt herself blush, and quickly looked away. "Nice to meet you. Gela, we need to go."

"Will you come again soon?" Mr. McGinness asked.

"Probably not until next Saturday."

He gave her a small bow. "Until Saturday then. Good day, ladies."

As they walked to the exit—to many exclamations and thanks for Gela's music—Gela slipped her arm through Edna's.

"Edna has an admirer," she said in sing-song.

Edna felt another blush come over her. "You're the one with the admirers."

They went outside. "You could, you know. Have a beau. It's allowed. Even at your ancient age."

"Don't be silly."

And yet . . .

It was nice to be noticed.

Henrietta greeted Maude and Antonio as if nothing was amiss.

The boys ran to the couple and were given hugs and kisses. Steven —who sat by the window in the parlor—did not react to the activity.

"Steven? Look who's come to visit."

He stared out the window.

Henrietta went to his side. "Come now, Steven. Come sit with us and have a chat."

He didn't look at her. Didn't acknowledge he'd even heard.

Henrietta looked to Antonio, pleading with her eyes. *Please help him.* The two traded places.

"Nice to see you, old chum," Antonio said with a hand to Steven's shoulder. "What do you see out there?" He knelt beside the chair in order to see what Steven saw. "Sky. You like to look at the sky?"

After a brief moment, Steven nodded.

He nodded!

"I used to stare at the sky for hours when I was stuck in those hellish trenches."

For the first time since they'd arrived, Steven turned his head. "Clouds kept me sane."

It was the first full sentence he'd said in six months! Henrietta began to rush toward him, but Maude pulled her back, leading her into the bedroom. "But . . ." Maude shushed her and gathered the boys. Then she closed the door, keeping it open just a crack. With a finger to her lips Maude quieted them all.

Henrietta stood at the door, peeking out. She was thrilled to see that Steven had turned around in his chair. Antonio had pulled his own chair close. They spoke in low tones, Antonio doing most of the talking.

"I want to know what they're saying," she whispered.

"You will. After the fact. We need to leave them alone. Don't disturb the moment." Maude closed the door all the way.

Henrietta knew she was right. She sank onto the bed.

"Can we play with your jewelry, Mama?" Lennie asked.

"Go ahead."

The boys took the jewelry box off the dressing table, set it on the rug, and began digging through it. "I hear Steven talking. I wish he'd talk like that to me."

Maude put an arm around her shoulders. "Comrades in arms have a bond like no other."

"More than the bond of a wife and husband?"

"Different."

"But I need more than the occasional word from him."

"It will come. The barrier has been broken."

Henrietta felt peevish for thinking it, but she was sad that *she* hadn't been the one to break the barrier.

The women played with the boys, putting a bracelet on Lennie, and a necklace on Willie. Henrietta welcomed the diversion.

The bedroom door opened suddenly.

Antonio said, "Maude, we should go. It's very nice to see the four of you, Henrietta."

It had only been fifteen minutes. "You're leaving so soon?" She peeked around him to see Steven, still staring out the window.

"Why don't you see us outside?" His eyebrows rose, implying more.

"Of course."

She turned to the boys. "Play nicely. I'll be right back." She repeated the latter to Steven. He did not respond.

Henrietta followed Antonio and Maude out of the building and stopped on the stoop to talk. Antonio pointed upwards at the open window of their flat. They moved away, so their words wouldn't reach Steven's ears.

Henrietta began. "I heard him say that clouds kept him sane. And you mentioned you liked the sky too. In the trenches?"

"Surely you know about the trenches?"

"A little. From news reports." She tossed her hands in the air. "But Steven hasn't spoken about any of it. What happened out there?"

Antonio watched a produce truck drive by. "It wasn't a normal war fought in the fields of battle. We were stuck in trenches that were muddy, stinky, and full of rats and disease. Between us and the enemy was a few miles of open field we called 'No Man's Land'. It offered no cover. And on the other side, past barbed wire, were the Germans in *their* trenches. We would shoot artillery at them, and they would do the same. Once in awhile we were ordered to storm forward, where we would get slaughtered by their machine guns. Victory was measured in inches."

Henrietta put a hand to her chest. "How could you stand it?"

He pointed upward. "By looking at the sky. The trenches were foul and dark and dirty. The sky was blue and fresh and reminded us of home and better times."

"Why didn't Steven tell me that? Explain it to me."

"It's hard to climb out of hell."

Hell?

Henrietta began to cry and Maude held her close. "There, there. He'll get better."

She felt embarrassed and stood erect, brushing the tears away. "When? How can I help? For six months I've tried everything I can think of to reach him, to help him. But then you . . ."

She let the sentence die, but Antonio finished it for her. "Then I come in and he speaks."

"Well . . . yes. Shouldn't he talk to me? I'm his wife. I love him more than words can say."

Antonio put a hand on hers. "He knows he's less than whole right now. He wants to be normal again."

"He said that?"

He nodded. "He told me he's trying. I've heard it called shell-shock."

"What's that?"

"He spent months being afraid that his life would end at any moment. The sound of artillery and guns was torture. He can't get it out of his head."

Henrietta remembered his reaction to the blocks falling. She tried to understand, but she had nothing in her life remotely close to Steven's experience.

Maude had a question. "Why didn't you suffer from it?"

Antonio looked at the sky, then back at them. "I don't know."

"Steven is an English teacher," Henrietta said. "He likes silence. And order."

"In the trenches there was little order, and when there was silence it often was the wrong kind: the silence of fear and death."

Henrietta's heart broke to think of her sensitive husband subjected to such anxiety and tension.

"Life experiences probably come into play," Antonio said. "I lost a wife and was left with two young children. I've been through agony and helplessness. Perhaps the war was Steven's first exposure to pain and despair."

Henrietta thought about Steven's past. He'd lost a father — after he was grown. She didn't know of any other life crisis he'd been forced to endure.

Antonio looked back toward the stoop. "I don't know if it's important to understand the whys of how we reacted to the war differently, only to acknowledge that we obviously did. Do."

"What can I do to help him?" Henrietta asked.

"Talk to him. Don't get angry. Keep him a part of your lives even when he doesn't seem to notice. Ease him back into this world."

"He *will* come back?"

She didn't like his hesitation.

"I believe he will." He sighed. "Maybe he could talk to a doctor."

"Aren't those mind-doctors quacks?"

"I honestly don't know."

Maude squeezed her hand. "We'll pray for him. And you."

Henrietta thanked them and went back to the flat. She paused at the door and listened to the boys talking inside. They were back to playing with their blocks.

She bowed her head, said a quick prayer, then entered with a smile. "Such good boys. Would you like a treat?"

"Yeah!"

She got them a biscuit and brought two for Steven, setting them on the window sill. She took the seat nearby and put a hand on her husband's knee. "The sky is beautiful today, isn't it?"

Steven slowly turned his head toward her. And smiled.

Henrietta had hoped for something more when they retired that night. Nothing drastic, but perhaps Steven could hug her?

Yet as they lay down, he turned his back to her — as was his new habit.

She fought back tears, not wanting to add her pain to his own.

But then he lay his arm on the top of his side, and turned his hand over, as though wanting her to take it.

When she did, he pulled her arm around himself, drawing it to his chest. She snuggled against his back. "I love you, Steven," she whispered.

He squeezed her hand.

Chapter Four

Antonio was quiet. He hadn't eaten a bite of breakfast.

"What's wrong, Papa?" Matteo asked.

Gela and Maude exchanged a glance. Then Gela said, "You can't just sit there and not eat."

He looked up. "I believe I can." He shoved the bowl of oatmeal toward her. "You want it?"

She got up from the table and stormed to the door. "Eat or don't eat. I'm going to work at a job that I absolutely despise. Ta ta."

After the door shut, it took a moment for the room to settle.

"Don't mind her, Pa," Matteo said. "But something *is* bothering you."

Antonio pulled the bowl close again and took a bite. "It's complicated."

Matteo looked to Maude for help. She remembered something she'd heard as a child. "Shared joy is double joy; shared sorrow is half sorrow."

Antonio sighed. "You can't help."

"But I can listen." She nodded toward Matteo. "We can listen."

Her husband stood, taking a place by the window. "I got a new client yesterday. He owns a building with ten apartments. He wants me to rent them out for him."

"That's marvelous," Maude said.

"I brought him a tenant."

"That's good too," Matteo said.

"He won't rent to the man because he's . . . he's German American."

They'd all witnessed persecution of such people during the war. But now? "The war is over. Your landlord needs to move on." She knew it wasn't so easy.

"The family who wants to rent the apartment has been here for two generations. But their name is Kraus."

Matteo nodded. "A German friend of mine at work changed his name from Schmidt to Smith."

"No one should have to do that," Maude said.

Matteo shrugged and finished eating the last bite of his oatmeal. He took his bowl to the kitchen. "What are you going to do about it, Papa?"

"If I tell the landlord I won't abide by his restrictions, I lose a lot of business. But if I let him deny a good family a home, I . . ."

Maude reached across the table the touched his hand. "You know what you have to do."

He nodded. "But we really need the income. I didn't think I'd have such trouble getting my business going again."

Although she was as worried as he, she touched his arm. "The right thing is always the right thing to do."

"Another proverb from your youth?"

"A timeless truth."

He took her hand and leaned toward her. They kissed across the table.

_ə_

Annie saw Henrietta enter Unruffled, carrying a ledger. She'd come to dread money-news. It was rarely good.

"So," Annie said as soon as their only customer left. "How are our finances?"

"Fair to middling."

"Which means . . .?"

"We've earned enough to pay bills, but . . ."

Annie asked the question that had been looming for some time. "Do we have enough to buy new fabric to sew new designs?"

"And wedding dresses," Birdie added, joining them at the counter. "That's what Maude wants us to add."

Annie nodded toward the storeroom. "We have more of the ivory she's using for Gert's dress. Isn't that enough?"

"Not all women will want the same sort of dress," Birdie said.

"Brides don't want to look like other brides," Henrietta said. "I think that's the main problem. We'll need a half dozen styles to choose from."

Annie pressed her fingers to her forehead, a gesture that had become all too common in the past few years. "We need the dresses in all sizes. I hate to waste expensive fabric on wedding dresses that may or may not sell."

"It's not fiscally sound," Henrietta said.

"But it's what Maude suggests," Birdie added. "And I do like the idea of it. I have friends whose beaus have come back. They want to marry sooner rather than later. They want to start their new lives _now_."

That settled it. "If we're going to jump onto that bandwagon, we'd better get to it."

Henrietta bit her lip. "But where will we get the money for the fancy fabric?"

Annie thought of Guy. "I think I may be able to work something out."

"How?"

She didn't want to tell them about it yet. And then she had another idea. "What if we make up the most popular sizes in the nice fabric, and make samples in the less popular sizes—using inexpensive fabric. If someone comes in and likes the style but we don't have their size, they can at least try on the dress and then we'll make it up to order. Perhaps promise them the dress in three days' time."

Birdie nodded, but had a question. "Surely it takes special skill to sew the luxurious fabrics."

"It does." Annie thought of Gela. "Perhaps we can designate our most skilled seamstress to sew the wedding dresses."

"Ginny?" Henrietta asked.

"Ginny. She's been with us since the beginning."

"What about the styles?" Birdie asked. "We need the designs right away."

The bell on the front door tinkled, and Maude came in, carrying Gert's wedding dress over her arm. "Good morning ladies." She nodded toward the dress. "I just came from a fitting with Gert and wanted to show you the end result."

They admired the dress. Annie could easily imagine other brides wanting something similar. "Speaking of wedding dresses. We'll need five new designs. Now."

"Now?"

"You want Unruffled to carry wedding dresses, don't you?"

"I do, but—"

"Listen to what we've come up with." The ladies filled Maude in, and then they began to brainstorm dress designs, with Annie sketching as they talked. Within a half-hour they'd come up with five variations.

Annie finished up the sketches, adding the details they'd chosen. "I like these a lot. Maude, will you make patterns for the popular sizes first, and get Ginny sewing on them?"

Maude looked deep in thought. "We'll need more workers than Ginny. We had a few women from the factory who were that skilled — Myrtle. Maybe Mary."

"Can we hire them back?" Annie asked.

"With what money?" Henrietta asked, pointing toward the ledger.

Why did it always come down to money?

"It's said you need to spend money to make money," Maude said. *Money we don't have.*

"Let me talk to our supplier about getting the fabrics at a deep discount," Annie said. "And see if you can talk with Myrtle and Mary about the work."

≈

It only took a phone call. Within the hour Guy Ship arrived at the store, oozing charm.

He removed his hat. "Good morning, ladies! My, what a lovely gaggle of beauties we have here."

Annie noticed the customers blush, even the elderly Mrs. Ravenwood, especially when Guy moved in her direction, and commented on the dress she was considering. Annie guessed — with near certainty — that she would purchase it.

Guy moved to the counter. "My dear Mrs. Culver. For days I have been waiting with bated breath for your call." He bowed gallantly. "I am at your service."

Birdie was watching from nearby, grinning. Annie leaned toward him and said softly, "You are too much, Mr. Ship."

"Actually, I am just enough." He placed his hands, flat against the counter. "Now then. What can I do for you this fine day?"

Annie didn't want to conduct this business in the front of the store, yet to move to the back, where they would be alone . . . There had always been something about Guy Ship that made her a tad nervous. He was *too* charming. She was just about to ask Birdie to accompany her, when a new customer came in, needing Birdie's attention.

"Come in the back," Annie said, "and we can talk about our needs." She regretted the words as soon as she'd said them, and quickly added, "Our fabric needs."

Guy chuckled and let her lead the way. They went to the storeroom where the long bolts of fabric leaned against a far wall, interspersed with shelves of supplies. The light from a lone hanging light bulb was distressingly dim. "We had three older bolts of ivory, and are using one of them for wedding dresses. We might be able to use another one of these, but some women will want pure white." She put one hand behind a draw of the fabric, and stroked it against her palm with the other hand. "We need something similar to the feel of these, but —"

Guy reached out and stroked the fabric too, his fingers skimming hers. She pulled her hand away and let the fabric hang free. "Very nice," he said.

"Very well then," she said, moving to return out front.

"Hold up, Mrs. Culver," he said. "How much would you like to order?"

She paused right before the door — which she had purposely kept open. "Can you bring by samples of four different fabrics? We'll probably need a bolt of each. And hopefully, we'll need more."

"How soon do you need these?"

"As soon as possible."

"Very good. I'll come back this afternoon."

"I'll make sure the pattern designer is here to give her approval."

He cocked his head. "Safety in numbers?"

Annie hated to feel herself blush.

He motioned toward the door, but she had one more subject to broach.

"Since this is a new line for us, we . . . we need your very best discount."

"I'm sure something can be arranged."

That's what I told the ladies. "And I also need for you to extend us credit — beyond the usual terms."

His eyebrows rose. "You ask a lot."

"I do. But since our chance meeting in the Park — "

"Who says it was chance?"

She didn't like the idea of him arranging such a thing. She'd only had contact with him *in* the store, and that was years earlier. "I . . . how . . .?"

He laughed. "It was totally by chance. You fluster too easily, Mrs. Culver."

"You enjoy my fluster too much, Mr. Ship."

"I won't deny it."

Annie was unnerved by the way he looked at her. "Our extended credit? Can it be arranged?"

"Anything can be arranged." He offered her a bow. "Until this afternoon."

He went into the showroom and left. Annie stayed in the back a few moments to collect herself, trying to calm the beating of her heart.

Even more unnerving was the fact that she wasn't sure it was beating because she enjoyed the attention of an attractive, attentive male, or because she was afraid of enjoying the attention of an attractive, attentive male. One thing she knew for certain: she would make sure there were no more private meetings with Guy Ship.

&

"I wish Mr. Ship would show up," Maude said as she straightened a display of accessories that didn't need straightening. "I have things to do."

"The samples he's bringing are bridal fabric," Annie said. "It's essential you're here to help make the choices."

Maude sighed deeply. "I trust you to make the final decisions."

"Please, Maude."

At the plaintiveness in Annie's voice, Maude's dark eyebrows rose. "What aren't you telling me?"

Annie glanced around the store, and turned her back so customers — and Birdie — couldn't hear. "He makes me nervous."

"In what way?"

Annie didn't want to mention the man-woman way, because it wasn't exactly that. *Or was it?* "He's slick. He always says the right thing, but not in a normal way. There's always a hint of suggestiveness to it."

Maude nodded knowingly. "So he's the same as he was before the war."

"Worse."

"He *is* a gifted salesman."

Annie's thoughts tumbled to a halt. "A salesman. Yes. That's exactly what he is. That's the source of his flirtatious talk. Of course."

Maude looked at her sideways. "With Sean away so long, have you forgotten what it's like to have male attention?"

Annie pressed a hand to her cheek — which was warm. "I suppose I have." She took a new breath. "I feel better about him now. Forget I said anything. Nervous? I was being silly."

"So I can leave?"

Annie's confidence wavered. "I'd rather you stay."

"Either he's just a salesman or he's not," Maude said.

Annie's uncertainty made her feel weak. "I need you to stay to make the fabric choices."

"Very well. If that's all it is."

Annie wasn't sure that *was* all there was to it, but thanked her. And just in time too, for in walked Guy carrying a leather portfolio case. "Ladies!" he said with a smile to Annie. Turning to Maude. "Mrs. Ricci. How nice to see you again. Lovely as usual."

"Oozing charm as usual," she said back.

"I charm to disarm, not to harm." He set the case on the counter and unbuckled its strap. "I have brought for you today the most delectable, delightful, and delicious wedding fabrics you will ever see." He pulled out a bound sample book and opened it to the proper page. "Voila."

Annie and Maude stood shoulder to shoulder and looked at the six by six-inch swatches of three different luxury fabrics.

"Each is available in colors from White Ice to Indian Ivory. Enjoy."

Maude and Annie exchanged a bemused look. Guy was in full salesman form.

"I like this one," Annie said, pointing to a snow white charmeuse. "But I wish I could fully feel it, check its drape. I choose by the feel as much as the appearance."

"Don't we all," Guy said.

Annie gave Maude another look. *See?*

"I agree," Maude said. "We need larger samples."

With his case on its side, he carefully slid out nine neatly-folded one-yard samples, each wrapped in tissue, held with a gold seal.

"Impressive," Maude said.

"Luxury deserves a fine presentation."

"Show me the white charmeuse," Annie said.

He set a packet in front of her. "You may do the honors."

She hated to admit it, but she appreciated his extra effort that heightened the choosing experience. She carefully broke the gold seal. The tissue fell to either side as if an active participant in the presentation. Annie picked up the fabric. "Ooh."

"Exactly," Guy said.

"Feel the weight of it, Maude." Annie handed it to her friend. "It will drape beautifully."

"That it will." Maude tested the fabric's free hang and flow over her arm. "Our first choice."

"Very good," Guy said.

Yes, it was. The choices were made, the yardage ordered, the amazingly good price agreed upon—with extended credit, and the delivery arranged.

Guy packed up his samples. "I thank you for your business." He offered a bow. "And so I bid you adieu. I will see you soon." He looked directly at Annie, winked, and left.

"Gracious," Maude said. "It's going to take me a minute to calm my ego. Such flattery."

"I told you."

"And I told you," Maude said, gathering her hat and reticule to go back to the workshop. "He's a salesman, saying anything and everything to get the sale."

Annie looked at the copy of their order. "He did charm us into buying more than we planned."

Maude spread her hands. "My point is made." She secured her hat with a hatpin. "I wouldn't worry about Guy Ship. I think he's harmless."

Annie agreed. It felt good to let one worry fall away.

◈

Edna tided up the workshop for the day. "Good work, ladies," she told the Three Gs.

Not surprisingly, Gela was the first to leave her sewing machine. "Edna, are you going to Port Refuge this evening?"

"It's a work night. I wasn't planning on it."

"Oh."

Her pout was pathetic—but effective. "I suppose I could go, if you'd like to join me."

"Yes," Gela said, her countenance changing to the joy that came with getting her way.

"You need to ask your mother. She may have plans for your family this evening."

"We have no plans. We never have plans. Every night it's the same: we have dinner, clean the dishes, read a little, and go to sleep. It's utterly boring."

Edna chuckled. "What do you think most families do in the evenings?"

Gert and Ginny put on their hats. "That's what me and Simon do," Gert said.

"Same with me," Ginny said.

Edna could see that Gela came close to stomping her foot. "That doesn't make it better."

The other seamstresses shrugged it off, said goodbye, and left.

Gela turned to Edna, "So can we go?"

"What did I tell you?"

"Fine. I'll be right back." Gela left to go upstairs to the old workshop to ask her mother. Edna adjusted her hat just so. She'd been looking forward to a quiet evening—boring or no. At age fifty-nine, she was *done* by the end of a work day.

She heard Gela's feet running down the stairs. She burst into the door. "She says it's all right, as long as we stick together coming home."

"Wise advice. Women should not walk anywhere alone in the evening, much less in such a questionable neighborhood."

With a cursory nod, Gela said, "I have a new song I want to sing. I hope Mr. McGinness knows it."

Mr. McGinness. *He* was far from boring.

Gela was only a little bit disappointed that most of the children had already been picked up from Port Refuge, or were eating a meal with their families at one of the long tables.

Yet she wasn't there for them. She was there to sing.

She scanned the room for Mack and was nearly disheartened, when she saw him walk in. She ran to him. "Mr. McGinness. You're here."

"That I am, lass." He greeted some men standing near the door. "I'm glad to see you back again. Did you bring Mrs. Holmquist with you?"

"Yes, yes, she's here." Gela pointed to Edna, who was helping serve dinner. "I thought of a new song to sing. Do you know, 'Beautiful Dreamer'?"

"Of course. Shall we?"

She nodded her head emphatically and they moved to the piano. Along the way, they received many shouts of encouragement. *That's* what Gela longed for.

There was a stack of sheet music on top of the piano, and after a little searching, Mack took out the song. He played the introduction and Gela began to sing, "'Beautiful dreamer, wake unto me, starlight and dewdrops are waiting for thee. Sounds of the rude world, heard in the day, lull'd by the moonlight have all passed away! Beautiful dreamer, queen of my song, list while I woo thee with soft melody; Gone are the cares of life's busy throng, beautiful dreamer, awake unto me!'"

There was applause, and Gela curtsied. She noticed many of the people were crying. She turned to Mr. McGinness. "They're crying."

"It's a poignant song, Miss Gela. It's a serenade to a woman who may actually be dead."

"It is?"

He nodded once, then dug through the music a second time. "Here. This will cheer them up."

The song was "Alexander's Ragtime Band." Gela had never sung it, but she'd heard it on the family's Victrola.

Mr. McGinness began to play the raucous introduction. People who hadn't been listening, took notice. Gela began to sing. "'Come on and hear, come on and hear Alexander's Ragtime Band. Come on and hear, come on and hear 'bout the best band in the land . . .'"

Before they reached the next stanza, people got out of the seats and began to dance. Soon the entire room was filled with couples dancing wherever there was space. The non-dancers clapped — and sang along until the entire room vibrated with the joy of it.

When the song finished, someone yelled, "Again!"
One more time!

≈

"I would have sang that song a hundred times if they would have let me," Gela said as she, Edna, and Mr. McGinness walked to the streetcar stop.

"Your voice lasts longer than my fingers. They were beginning to cramp up," he said.

Gela took his hand and they did a little fox trot down the street. When Edna laughed, Mr. McGinness gave her a turn. A passersby smiled.

"That's the key of it," Gela said, pointing to a mother and boy who'd smiled. "That song made everyone happy. My first song made them cry."

"There's a time for that too," Mr. McGinness said. "But from what I've seen, right now people want to listen to happy songs that make them forget the war and the flu, loss and hardship."

Edna nodded. "Everyone at Refuge is going through difficult times."

"Then happy music it is," she said. "When can we sing again?"

"Gracious, lass. You *are* enthusiastic."

"I am. I love every minute of it."

"Very well then. I'm there every night and on Saturday afternoons. You come and we'll make music." He looked at Edna. "You too, Mrs. Holmquist."

Gela turned to Edna, grabbing both of her hands. "So can we?" Gela asked. "Go every evening?"

"I doubt your parents will approve."

Gela's head dropped. Unfortunately, she was right. Then she got an idea. "I'll invite them to come with us and see what a good place it is. Then they'll approve."

"It's worth a try," Edna said.

≈

After work, Henrietta and the boys stopped at a fruit stand before heading home. The boys devoured their pears, with juice dripping down their chins. She took out a handkerchief and dabbed at them. "You're a sticky mess."

They seemed unconcerned.

As they neared their building, Henrietta looked up to the window—Steven's window of choice. She didn't see him there.

"Where's Daddy?" Willie asked, following her gaze.

"He's probably taking a nap. Let's be quiet when we go in, all right?"

But when they got inside, he wasn't in the parlor. Nor the bedroom or bath.

"Steven?"

"Shh. You said to be quiet, Mommy."

She stood in the middle of the parlor, turning around slowly, trying to see some clue that would tell her where he was. If he went out, wouldn't he leave a note?

Yet beyond the *where* was the fact he had not left the house in six months. Ever. He didn't go to dinners at his mother's, or to church, or even for walks in the park so the boys could run and play. His life revolved around the windows, the bedroom, and the bath.

"Boys, go wash your hands and faces, then play. I'm going to go downstairs to your grandma's."

"But where's Daddy?"

"He's probably there. Stay put. I'll be right back."

On the way out, she looked at the key nail by the door. Their spare key to Edna's was where it always was, which meant if she wasn't home, he couldn't get in. She grabbed the key and raced downstairs.

She tried the door knob. It was locked. She used the key, going inside, calling his name.

Nothing.

Which could only mean he was out on the street somewhere. She rushed down to the stoop and looked up and down the street. She didn't see him. She wanted to search, but the boys . . .

She went home and gathered them. "Where are we going?" Lennie asked.

"Out. To find Daddy."

"Daddy doesn't go out," Willie said.

Exactly.

❧

Gela and Edna got off the streetcar near Gela's house. "This isn't your stop," she said.

"I promised your mother I would get you home safely. It's getting dark."

46

Gela huffed, but Edna wouldn't budge. They walked the two blocks to the Ricci residence. "Do you want me to come up and talk to your mother about coming to Refuge with us?"

"No," Gela said, skipping up the steps of the stoop. "I can do it." She paused at the door. "The real question is, who's supposed to get you safely home?"

"I'm a tough old dame."

Gela smiled. "Not always so tough. You'll be all right?"

"I will. I'll see you at work in the morning. On time."

"Yes, ma'am."

Edna walked back toward the streetcar stop, but decided to just keep walking. It was only four blocks. The summer evening was cool — for once. It seemed safe enough. There were a lot of people sitting on their stoops, chatting. They exchanged greetings as she walked by. There was no danger here.

But when she turned the corner she saw a crowd of people ahead, gathered around something. She hurried forward, just as curious as they were.

"Come on, you git. Stand up. We don't abide bums sleeping in our doorways."

"He's tetched in the head," someone said.

"Don't hurt him, Ollie," said another. "There's obviously something wrong with him."

Edna craned her head to see who they were talking about. And then, with a break in the crowd, she saw him. Saw Steven!

She rushed forward, pushing people aside. "That's my son! Let me through!"

He was crouched in a doorway, his knees to his chest, his hands over his head. She knelt before him. "Steven, it's mother. I'm here now. Everything will be all right."

He peeked out from beneath his hand. "Mama?"

She gave him a smile even though her heart was breaking. "That's right. It's me. Let's go home now, all right?"

He nodded. With the help of a bystander, Edna got Steven to his feet. His head hung low, his eyes were focused on the ground.

"What's wrong with 'im?" someone asked.

"The war," Edna said. "Let us pass."

The crowd parted and Edna led her son toward home. They didn't talk. Talking would come later.

When they reached their building, Edna began to lead him up to the third floor, to his flat.

He pulled back, shaking his head.

"I need to get you home. Henrietta is probably worried sick about you."

He pointed toward her apartment.

"You want to come in with me?"

He nodded.

"All right then. For now."

They went inside. Steven stopped in the parlor as though he didn't know what to do next. "Would you like to go lie down in your old room?" Edna asked.

He didn't even nod. He just walked into the room and lay upon the bed, pulling a pillow to his chest.

All righty then. Edna closed the door and expelled a deep sigh. She needed to go upstairs to tell Henrietta he was all right.

She tiptoed out, and hurried upstairs, knocking on their door. No one answered. She returned home, wrote a note, and backtracked to slip it under their door.

It was all she could do for now.

Once inside her apartment she put her ear to the bedroom door and listened. There were no sounds. She carefully opened the door, expecting to find him asleep. Instead, he was sitting in a chair by the window.

"Steven?"

He didn't acknowledge her.

She knelt beside him, putting a hand on his arm. "What happened?"

His forehead furrowed but he didn't look at her. "I tried outside."

"That's good."

He shook his head and returned his gaze to the window.

Please, Father. Help my son.

❧

Maude was washing the dinner dishes when she heard Gela come in. "You missed dinner."

"I ate there," she said.

"You didn't have as good a dinner as we did," Matteo said as he polished his boots. "Ma made beef stew and we had fresh peaches with cream."

"I ate well enough."

Antonio looked up from reading the newspaper. "You didn't come home alone, did you?"

"No," she said, "though I could've. Edna saw me home."

Thank you, Edna. "Come wipe these dishes."

Gela sighed as though the task was beyond bearing, but took up a towel.

"So how was your night? Tell us about that Refuge place you go to."

Gela cut to the chase. "I want you to go with me and see it yourself."

Maude stopped washing a glass. "Why?"

"Because what happens there is wonderful." She set down the towel, letting her excitement take over. "Mr. McGinness—he's a man who likes Edna. She pretends she doesn't care, but she really does. He plays piano. The first time I went there he heard me singing 'London Bridges' with the children, and asked me to sing to everyone. So I sang 'Greensleeves'. And this time I sang, 'Beautiful Dreamer', but the slow song seemed to make people sad, so Mr. McGinness played some ragtime and suddenly everyone was dancing and laughing, and . . ." She took a fresh breath. "The music made people happy and I was a part of it."

Maude risked a glance to Antonio—whose eyebrows were raised.

"I'm very happy for you," Maude said.

"You do have a pretty voice," her father said.

Matteo strolled across the room, holding a boot to his chest, "La-di-da, di-daaaaah!"

"Stop it," his sister hissed.

Maude agreed. "Stop."

Gela went to her father's side, kneeling beside him like Maude had seen her do a hundred times. "Please, Papa. Come see."

"Well . . ."

Gela stood. "I want to go every evening after work."

"That's too much," Antonio said. "You'll be exhausted."

"But I'm not." She put her hands to her chest. "I'm not tired at all. I'm invigorated." She looked at her father, then at Maude. "I'm . . . I'm filled up."

Matteo returned to his chair. "That's just weird."

Gela slapped him on the arm.

"Oww!"

Maude stepped between them. She pointed at Matteo, "That was rude." Then at Gela. "That was unnecessary."

"So you'll come tomorrow night?"

"I can't," Antonio said. "I have a meeting with a client until late." He looked at Maude. "I'll be home late for dinner."

Maude saw Gela's shoulders slump in disappointment. Perhaps this was a way to bond with the girl. "I'm free. I'll go with you."

Gela took Maude's hands, her face glowing. "You will?"

"We'll leave from the workshop at six."

Gela kissed her cheek. "Are there any more peaches?"

Maude's cheek felt warm for a long time.

&

"I'm tired," Willie said as they reached home. "We walked a million miles."

"Almost." *And no Steven.*

"I'm hungry," the boy said.

As am I. Henrietta carried Lennie up the stairs to their apartment, each step testing the limits of her legs and back.

"I'm hungry too, Mama," Lennie said.

"I know. Just a few more steps and I'll get you something to eat."

Willie ran ahead, and called at the top of the stairs. "Look, Mama. There's a note outside the door." He waved it at her.

From Steven? She set Lennie down and rushed up the last few steps, reading the note: *Steven is at my place. Edna.*

"Come on!" She hurried down the stairs.

"But we're hungry."

"Papa is at Grandma's."

They followed her downstairs. Henrietta knocked, but didn't wait for a response before going inside. The parlor was empty. Edna was in the kitchen, putting a kettle on the stove. "Where is he?"

Edna put a finger to her lips and came close. "He's in his old bedroom."

"He came here? Where has he been? Why didn't he come home?"

"He didn't come here. I found him on the street, cowering. He wasn't himself. I brought him here." Edna led her to a kitchen chair, and pointed to the kitchen. "There's cookies in the tin, boys."

Once they were occupied, she leaned toward Henrietta. "I was coming back from Refuge when I saw a crowd looking at something. They were looking at Steven, huddled in a doorway, covering his head."

"What happened to him?"

"I asked, and he simply said he tried to go out."

Henrietta glanced toward the bedroom. "He didn't say anything else?"

Edna shook her head. "He's in there, staring out the window."

Frustration spurred Henrietta to pace. "That's all he does at home too!"

Edna held out her hand, urging Henrietta back to her chair. "He tried. That's progress, isn't it?"

She forced herself to see the hope of it. "I just wish he would have let me go with him."

"Maybe he wanted to do it on his own to make you proud."

But he failed.

"I need to talk to him."

"Go ahead. I'll keep the boys busy."

Henrietta's heart beat double-time as she stood outside the bedroom door. She knocked gently, but receiving no response, opened the door. As expected, he was sitting by the window.

She went inside, closing the door. "Steven. Darling. I heard you went on an adventure today."

He shook his head.

"Can you tell me what happened?"

He shook his head again.

"I'm proud of you for trying. I'd love to go with you next time."

No response.

She moved to face him, blocking his view. She leaned down and took his face in her hands. "I love you, Steven. We *will* get through this."

His eyes were heavy with pain.

She kissed his forehead, then held out her hand. "Let's go home now. The boys and I are famished. I'm sure you are too."

He ignored her hand and looked away. "Stay."

"Stay? Here?"

He nodded.

"That's not right. You need to be at home — at our home."

He shook his head.

Her voice rose. "Don't be ridiculous! You can't stay here! Get up this minute and come home with us!"

Edna opened the bedroom door, her face concerned. She motioned Henrietta into the hall.

"He wants to stay here," Henrietta whispered.

"He certainly can."

"That's not the point. He should be with us."

Edna bit her lip. "Let him stay here tonight. He's had a hard day."

"And we haven't?" Henrietta put a hand to her chest, trying to keep her voice low. "I come home and find him gone and spend two hours dragging the boys around New York, looking for him? *That's* a hard day."

Edna cupped her cheek in her hand. "Small steps. He *tried* to go out."

Henrietta walked away, feeling utterly dejected. Steven wasn't the only one who felt like a failure.

She returned home and somehow got the boys fed and to bed. She retired soon after.

In bed, Henrietta turned on her side and faced the empty place where Steven should be. She placed her hand on his pillow. "Father, please. Show me how to help him and make him whole again."

She cried herself to sleep.

CHAPTER FIVE

Edna was glad to hear movement inside Steven's room. "Come out for breakfast, Son."

She went to the kitchen and finished making the oatmeal Steven loved as a child.

A few minutes later she heard him in the bathroom, and when he came out to the kitchen, he was fully dressed. And shaved. Hope took hold.

"Good morning."

He nodded.

"Did you sleep well?"

He shrugged.

"Pour us some coffee."

She was relieved when he did just that and took a seat at the kitchen table. She felt the need to make small talk as she took up their breakfast. "Do you see this double-boiler here? I got it directly from the people at Quaker Oats. A few years ago they had a promotion where I sent a cutting of the man on the front of the box along with a dollar, and they sent me this pan. I've used it ever since. Don't you think that was a good offer? On their part, and mine?"

He nodded.

I need to stop asking him yes or no questions.

Edna spooned the oatmeal into two bowls and brought him a pitcher of cream and some brown sugar. "Would you like raisins?" She chastened herself for asking another yes-no question. "Maybe you've never had raisins. I didn't discover them until after you and Henrietta were married, but I quite like them." When he didn't respond, she put a small dish of them on the table, then sat.

Then she took his hand, bowed her head, and said grace. "We thank you Lord for happy hearts, for rain and sunny weather. We thank you Lord for this our food and that we are together. Amen." She had hoped he would join in with their family prayer. He only bowed his head in silence.

But he did try the raisins.

೨

Henrietta knocked on the door of Edna's apartment and heard, "Come in."

She and the boys went inside. She was happy to see that Steven was up, eating breakfast — anything but sitting at a window.

She went to his side and kissed his cheek — which was freshly shaved. "Good morning."

The boys stood near the door, uncertain of what to do. "Come say good morning to Papa."

They hugged him — and he hugged back. Then Lennie asked, "Why are you staying here? Don't you like us?"

Steven's forehead furrowed. "I love you."

"Then come home."

Henrietta nodded to Willie. The little boy approached his father warily, bringing him two of his favorite things. "Look, Papa, here's some crossword puzzles." He fumbled in his pocket, "And some Life Savers — cherry. Your favorite."

Steven stared at the gifts as if unsure of what to do with them. "Thank you." Then he rose, giving Henrietta hope — until he walked to the bedroom and closed the door.

"Mama?" Willie said, frowning.

She put her hands on his shoulders. "It will be all right. Papa isn't feeling well."

"But when —?"

"All in good time. Come now," she said. "Let's get you over to Annie's. The girls are waiting to play with you." To Edna she said, "I'll come to the workshop after."

"I'll see you there."

&

After washing the breakfast dishes, before leaving for work, Edna checked on Steven. She found him by the window. "I'm going now."

No response. Which incensed her.

She moved in front of him, blocking his view. "If you were a child and were acting like this you'd get a spanking. You're an adult and I know you're going through hard times, but so is your family. You came home alive, Steven. That's more than millions of other men can say. I'm probably doing the wrong thing by calling you on this, but as a mother I can only coddle you so long. You need to be a man, Steven. Be a husband. A father. And if you don't feel like you have the strength to do that, then pray God gives you the means to do it."

She leaned forward and kissed his forehead. "You know where I am — you can see the workshop from here. If you need me, come get me."

As she crossed the street she looked up to the window and saw him as she'd left him. She climbed the stairs to the workshop and prayed aloud, "Father, help him."

"Amen to that." Henrietta was coming out from Annie's apartment. They went inside the workshop.

"How is he?" she asked.

Edna was glad the seamstresses weren't there yet. "I yelled at him."

"You what?"

She took out some sewing, needing the focus to move to anything beyond her bad behavior. "I told him I knew he was going through something difficult, but he is lucky to be alive. Many aren't." She began to thread a needle.

"Nearly every family we know lost someone."

The next part was harder to share. "But then I told him to be a man. Be a husband. And a father."

"Oh."

"I told him to pray about it." She let the needle fall on the table. "Was that too harsh?"

"Maybe," Henrietta said. "But it's what I've been wanting to tell him." She sat on a stool as though unable to stand any longer. "How do we reach him?"

Edna had no answers.

❧

The four children played happily. Vesta was so good with them. It was a blessing Henrietta's two boys and her own two girls got along. Although technically, they weren't related, they were growing up as close as cousins.

But Annie let their happy sounds of play fade into the background. As she finished with the last hairpin at her dressing table, she saw the letter she had received yesterday from Congressman Baines. Once again she warred with herself about whether to open it. *You contacted him. You need to open it. But if you do —*

"Annie?"

Vesta stood in the doorway.

She stood. "I'm leaving."

"It appears you've already left. You weren't . . . here."

Annie sighed deeply and pointed at the letter.

Vesta moved to pick it up, but hesitated. "May I?"

"I wish someone would because I'm too much the coward."

Vesta took the letter and read the return address. "A congressman? Why is he writing you?"

"I wrote to him, asking if he could try to get some information about Sean's whereabouts."

Vesta swallowed deliberately. "We want to know, but —"

"But we don't."

Vesta stared at the letter while putting a hand to her mouth. "If it's bad. If he's dead . . ." She shook her head violently. "We would have felt something, don't you think? Sensed something?"

"I don't know about that sort of thing." Annie rose. "I wrote the letter because I'm tired of waiting, even though I know that waiting with hope is better than knowing . . ."

Vesta let out a huff. "I'm opening it. All right?"

Annie nodded and braced herself.

Vesta took out the letter. A crease formed between her eyebrows. But she wasn't crying . . .

"What's it say?"

She handed the letter to Annie. "*Thank you for your letter, Mrs. Culver. I did make inquiries about your husband, Sean Culver, but came up empty. There is no record of him as injured or deceased, or taken as a prisoner by the Germans. I'm afraid I have no better news. I can only offer my sincere appreciation for his service, and for your sacrifice. Sincerely, Congressman Harold Baines.*"

Annie sat upon the bed, the letter still in her hands. "So now what? We don't know any more than we did before."

Vesta sat beside her. "That's not true. He made inquiries. All records were checked. Sean isn't dead or injured."

Annie sprang to her feet. "Not dead or injured that they know of! The war's been over for nearly a year. Steven and Antonio have been home for months and months. Where is Sean?"

Vesta took her into her arms.

But then, out of nowhere, Annie glanced at the calendar hanging on the wall. And then, she noted the date and gasped. She stepped away.

"What's wrong?" Vesta asked.

"It's July thirtieth."

"Yes . . ."

"Sean left on July thirtieth. He's been gone two years today!" She saw a photograph of Sean on a shelf, rushed toward it and hurled it across the room. It hit the wall and fell to the floor. Glass scattered.

She immediately sank to her knees, picking up shards in her hand. "I'm so sorry, so sorry. So sorry. . ."

Vesta knelt beside her, putting a hand on her back. "Annie. It's all right."

Annie emptied her hand of shards, letting them drop to her lap. Sobs overtook her. "He's gone! He's really gone!"

"Shush now." Vesta handed her a handkerchief. "Don't say that. We don't know that."

Annie nodded. "Yes, we do. He'd be back by now if he was coming back." She gazed into her mother-in-law's eyes. Suddenly, she remembered Vesta's pain. "You lost Richard, and now Sean. We're both alone!"

Vesta stood and drew Annie to her feet. She faced her, squeezing her hands. "We are not alone. We have each other, the girls, and our friends."

Annie felt bad. Selfish. "I know it's not just us. Millions are mourning."

"All over the world."

Annie stared at the shattered glass. "Sometimes I want to go to my room, lock the door, and never open it, no matter who knocks."

Vesta nodded. "I wanted to give up. I wanted to run away and hide. And I was extremely mad at God."

Annie agreed. "How could He let the war happen? And influenza? If God loves us, how can He let us suffer and die?"

Vesta shook her head. "I don't know. You'll have to ask Him." She smiled wistfully. "I have."

"What did He say?"

Vesta looked toward the windows as if trying to find a way to describe God's words. Finally she looked at Annie. "He didn't tell me anything. I don't understand now and I never will. But I chose God anyway."

"Chose Him . . .?"

"Trust Him, no matter what."

Annie wasn't sure that was possible. "How?"

"One step at a time. Tell Him you trust Him and choose Him as your God. Acknowledge . . ." Vesta nodded once, found her purse, and removed a folded piece of paper from it. "Here."

Annie unfolded it and read aloud. "'Trust in the Lord with all thine heart; and lean not unto thine own understanding. In all thy ways acknowledge him, and he shall direct thy paths.'"

"Proverbs three, verses five and six," Vesta said. "They sum up what we're supposed to do, and sum up what He will do if we trust Him. I have it written on a note in the kitchen, in the parlor, and in my bedroom. And in my purse, so I have it with me everywhere I go."

Annie stared at the words, reading them again. And again. There was power there. Hope. Strength.

"Here," Vesta said. "Let me make you a copy." She found a piece of paper in the desk, and copied the verse, reading it aloud as she did. Once finished, she handed the note to Annie. "Now it's yours."

Annie stared at the verse. "You act like this is a sort of talisman, that will magically make everything better."

"It's not magic at all. Prayer works. That's a fact." She shoved some paper toward Annie. "Go ahead. You write it down a few times more. Get it to stick."

Vesta left Annie alone and went to play with the children. Annie took up a pencil and began to copy the verse three more times. Certain words stood out: trust, lean, understand, acknowledge, direct . . . *Help me follow this verse, Lord. Embrace it.*

Once finished, Annie distributed the notes around the apartment, just as Vesta had done.

"Do you feel better?" Vesta asked.

Annie pulled her into an embrace. "I do. Thank you."

"Thank Him."

۶

Annie was helping a customer choose between two dresses when Guy came into Unruffled. She nodded to Birdie, who took over the sale.

"Good afternoon, Mr. Ship."

"Oh, it's a very good afternoon, Mrs. Culver." He went to the door and waved at someone. Immediately, a stream of men paraded in, each carrying multiple long bolts of fabric. Four bolts had their protective brown paper removed and were tied with satin ribbon. Guy directed the men to lay those bolts on a table near the counter and take the rest of the dozen to the storeroom.

Guy looked around the store and clapped his hands. "Ladies! Come close! Come see the luscious fabrics that will soon be used in new fashion creations at Unruffled!"

There were six customers in the store, and all gathered round. With flourish, Guy untied two pink ribbons from the first bolt and unrolled it enough that he could display its drape. "Feel it, ladies," he said, drawing out the first word like a caress. "Who wouldn't like to feel this sumptuous silkiness next to their skin."

Each of the ladies took his bait and stroked the fabric, letting it drape over their arm or slide over their hand. There was a general consensus expressed in one word. "Oooooh."

"Indeed," Guy said. "Anyone bound for the altar?"

"My niece is planning to wed come Christmas."

"Perfect!" he said. "I'm sure you can imagine her in a lovely ivory gown made out of this luxurious fabric."

The woman nodded, taking his bait.

Another woman raised a hand. "I'm getting married."

Guy lured her close. "As a bride you should indulge yourself." He turned to the group. "Shouldn't she, ladies?"

"Oh, you should."

"You will be a gorgeous bride."

"My niece will love these fabrics," said the first woman. "I know she will."

The bride kept her eyes on the satin, stroking it. "I would love a dress out of this." She tore her gaze away and looked at Annie. "Will it be expensive?"

Annie wished Maude were there. They hadn't really talked about the price yet. But she did know most of the fabrics were a dollar a yard — with some a bit more. A dress would take from five to seven yards, plus trims, interlinings, thread, closures, and labor . . .

They were waiting.

"We have not completed any dresses yet but — "

"But we certainly can abide by your schedule," Guy said. "When is the wedding, Miss . . .?"

"Branson."

"Though you won't be 'Branson' for long."

The girl blushed. "Jimmy just got home in June and asked me. We haven't set a date yet. But soon. I'd like the wedding in the fall."

"I'm sure the expert designers and seamstresses at Unruffled can make that happen."

"But . . . how much?"

Annie didn't want to discourage her, but also didn't want to be locked into an unfeasible number. "Though I cannot give a fixed price as yet, I would think we could create a beautiful dress for around $20."

The girl bit her lip. "What about a headpiece and veil?"

"Just a few dollars more."

Guy rushed to close the sale. "Where are the sketches of your bridal designs, Mrs. Culver?"

Birdie piped up. "I'll get them."

A minute later Annie spread the designs on the counter and the ladies — even those long-married — gave their opinions to Miss Branson.

"This one has a nice neckline to show off your long neck."

"I think this skirt length would be good for your small frame."

"I was at a wedding last month and the bride had the most luscious headpiece dotted with real pearls. It had tulle hanging all the way to the floor."

Annie wanted to nip in the bud any mention of real pearls. "We can get that effect with faux pearls."

Miss Branson sighed. "I need my mother here."

"Indeed you do," Annie said. "Perhaps you'd like to make an appointment?"

The woman with the niece also chose a time. The appointments set, the ladies went back to perusing the day dresses.

The delivery men came out of the storeroom, one asking about the four bolts on the table. "Do you want these back there too?"

Although Guy looked to Annie, he answered for her. "We will keep these out front to tempt the next bride."

Guy paid each man a few coins and they left. He rushed to the window. "Perhaps we should create a display of the fabrics here, where everyone can see. We can add some tulle and a few headpieces."

Annie hated to agree with him, but agree she must. "Good idea. Birdie and I will work on it later."

"Why wait?" He lugged two bolts to the window area and began to undress one of the dress forms.

"We want that dress in the window, Mr. Ship. We have a good supply we need to sell."

"Very well." He buttoned up the blue cotton dress and pointed to the other one. "Is she available?"

"I suppose. But let me undress her. If a passersby sees a man . . ."

He put an offended hand to his chest. "So scandalous."

"You have no idea how easily some people are scandalized." Annie removed the pink frock and laid it on a nearby chair.

"You have personal experience with scandal?" he asked.

"I most certainly do not."

"Just checking."

She retrieved a pin cushion, pulled some yardage from the ivory bolt, and began draping it over the mannequin.

"Do you have lace in the back?"

"We do. I'll—"

"I'll get it."

Guy returned with three different laces—and some tulle. He studied her work. "Almost looks like a dress."

"Hardly, but thank you anyway." She created some shape with pins, and draped lace around the neckline.

"Why don't you have the other three fabrics draped over a table, hanging to the floor?"

It was a marvelous idea. "You've done this before?"

"Not at all."

She gave voice to a question, even though she knew it would lead to flattery. "Do all your customers get such special treatment?"

He wrapped a length of lace around his hand and stared at her, becoming serious for a moment. "Not at all."

Oh dear. She chastised herself for encouraging the exchange. *Stop it, Annie.*

He pinned the end of the lace to secure the hank. "If I'm not being too forward — even if I am — I would like to take you to dinner sometime, Mrs. Culver. You work far too hard."

"I do, but . . . I'm not sure that's proper, Mr. Ship. I'm a married woman."

"Who has the world sitting heavily on her shoulders." He gathered the supplies together. "We told Miss Branson she deserved to indulge herself, so I tell you the same thing. You need an evening that doesn't involve work and family. Pamper yourself."

It did sound enticing.

Her face must have shown acquiescence, for Guy said, "Very good then! Tomorrow night? At Delmonico's."

She was impressed. "That's an expensive place, Mr. Ship. I don't want you to spend so much."

"I assure you, I am good for it."

"I didn't mean to offend, it's just that — "

"Have you been there?"

"Only once, six years ago, when Henrietta and Steven celebrated their engagement. Her parents, Lord and Lady Newley, invited all of us." She remembered the tuxedoed waiters, the silver trays, the white linens amid sparkling chandeliers.

"It's high time you went again. I won't take no for an answer."

She gave in, excited about the prospect, despite her misgivings.

≈

"Edna, you simply must go with me tonight. Mama agreed to go with us."

"I'm sorry, Gela, but my family needs me."

Although Gela was totally consumed with her disappointment, an inner nudge spurred her to ask, "What's going on?"

Edna seemed hesitant to say anything in front of Ginny and Gert. "I don't want to get into it now. Just know that I would if I could. Besides," Edna said with a flick of Gela's nose. "You don't need me. This is your show. Your mother will be very proud of you."

Maybe. "I'll tell Mack hello for you."

"As you wish."

❧

After work, Maude sat next to Gela on the streetcar. "I didn't realize Port Refuge was so far."

"It's in Little Italy. It doesn't take *that* long. Ten minutes." She pointed ahead. "We're the next stop."

Maude looked out the window. The buildings were far more deteriorated than those in Greenwich Village. The windows and sides of the buildings were sooty, their steps littered with trash — and people. She saw a man sleeping in a doorway, making another man step over him to get inside.

How could this place give her daughter joy? And Edna too? Where Gela was naïve, Edna was a wise woman. She knew what was what — and where was where. She knew that a young girl like Gela shouldn't even *be* in a neighborhood like this. Yet she brought her here anyway? Maude closed her eyes and prayed for strength she did not have. *Help me give Gela what she needs so we'll grow closer. And keep us safe.*

The streetcar slowed and they exited. Maude was immediately assailed by the smell of excrement, urine, and rotting food. She began to cover her nose but fought through it. Gela didn't seem to notice any of it, but took her hand and pulled her ahead.

"Over here."

They stopped in front of a building whose door was on street level. Above the door was a hand-painted makeshift sign: *Port Refuge. All Are Welcome.* Somehow, the "all" was not comforting to Maude. Who knew what sort they'd encounter inside.

They went in and Gela was greeted by many of the people milling around or seated at tables. They were a disheveled mix of men in old uniforms, many missing a leg or an arm; elderly people bent over a bowl of soup or playing cards; mothers bobbing babies in their arms; and others hunched over with heads down, in their own world. Despite their greetings, a wave of despair rode as a wave around the room. Such need. Such pain. Such hopelessness.

Then do something about it.

"Is Mr. McGinness here?" Gela asked a man.

"Last I saw, he was getting a cup of coffee."

Gela turned to Maude. "You'll love Mr. McGinness. He's a great piano-player. He's the one who first got me to sing."

Maude had heard this description many times on the way here.

"There he is!" Gela rushed toward a short middle-aged man with a face that looked like it had seen too much wind and sun. His smile changed him from tough to gentle. His blue eyes twinkled.

"There she is. Our very own nightingale."

Maude caught the reference to Jenny Lind, the Swedish Nightingale. Gela had a pretty voice, but to make such a lofty comparison? Maude didn't like men who employed flattery.

Gela was quick to make introductions. "Mother, this is Mr. McGinness, Mr. McGinness, this is my mother, Mrs. Ricci."

"Nice to meet you, Mr. McGinness," Maude said with a nod.

He tipped an imaginary hat. "And you, Mrs. Ricci. Have you come to hear your daughter sing?"

"I have." She glanced around the room. "And to see the place that has captured her interest."

Gela took her hand. "I'll be over to sing in a minute, Mr. McGinness. I want to introduce Mother to the children in the day nursery. I do hope some are still here."

Maude was led into a room where a half-dozen children immediately ran toward Gela, squealing with glee. Some wanted her to hold them. The older ones wanted her to play.

"Let's sing 'London Bridges' again."

"Play blocks with us, Miss Gela."

"Perhaps later. I'd like you to meet my mother."

The kids hesitated a moment, but then one of them hugged Maude's legs. The others followed until she had the full contingent all around her. "Oh, darlings. How sweet. Hello to you too."

Maude was shocked by the children's affection. She wanted to embrace each one.

"Now, do you understand?" Gela asked.

Maude's throat was tight as she nodded.

Gela lifted one blonde beauty into her arms, telling the others, "I'm going to sing with Mr. McGinness now. You can all listen, all right?"

She kissed the blondie on the head as she put her down, then went back to the main room.

"You have quite a following," Maude said. "I didn't know you liked children."

"Neither did I." She found a chair for Maude and moved to the piano. After a short piano intro by Mr. McGinness Gela sang a familiar

Stephen Foster song. "'Mid pleasures and palaces though we may roam, Be it ever so humble there's no place like home . . .'".

Maude was dumbstruck. Although she'd heard Gela sing while sitting in a pew with her, she hadn't heard her sing by herself since she was a child. She was very good. More than good. Talented. And totally at ease. *Why didn't I know?*

Two other songs followed, one fast, and one slow. After her last song, Gela came to Maude, her face awash with joy — and hope. "Did you like it?"

Maude took her hands. "You were amazing. I didn't know you could sing like that."

"Actually, neither did I."

"It's like with Annie. Another hidden talent come to life."

"Annie can sing?"

"Not a whit — as far as I know. But talent-wise . . ." Maude looked around the room. "You made many people very happy."

Gela's eyes misted over, and she fell into Maude's arms. Maude held her close, realizing how stingy she'd been with praise for the girl.

Mr. McGinness joined them. "Did I overstate the nightingale reference?"

Maude stroked a stray hair from Gela's forehead. "You did not."

"You coming here today . . . this is God's doing," he said.

Maude glanced at him. "Why do you say that?" Maude asked.

"Just some news. Shall we sit?"

Maude and Gela exchanged a look. The three of them sat at the nearest table. Maude pushed some dirty dishes toward its middle.

"You don't know this, Gela," he said. "But a very important man heard you sing yesterday. He's an old friend — we served in the war together and I'm going to work with him in a new musical. We talked and he wants you to try out for one of the 'debutantes' in the play. Long story, and the roles were already cast, but last week, someone bowed out, so they're in need of a replacement. Though there are actresses aplenty wanting work, he wants to take a chance on you."

"A play? Where I'd get to sing?"

"And act. And dance."

"And wear costumes?"

He smiled. "Yes indeed."

Maude was skeptical. " Out of the blue . . . Why is this man giving her this chance?"

He shrugged. "Explainable or not, it *is* a chance."

"What's the name of the show?" Gela asked.

"'Irene.' It's about an Irish girl who works in a music shop with her widowed mother. She falls in love with an aristocrat." He stopped and looked at Maude, as if gauging her interest. "Shall I continue?"

Maude loved such stories. "Go on."

"The rich man's cousin is backing a fashion designer —"

"Mama! A fashion designer." She looked at Mr. McGinness. "Mother and her friends design clothes and have their own store."

"I know. Mrs. Holmquist told me."

"Continue with the story, Mr. McGinness."

"The designer tries to pass himself off as a famous couturier when he isn't anything like that, and there's a scheme to have Irene pretend to be a socialite to generate sales. She doesn't like that the rich man wants her to continue the ruse, and there's . . . well there's mistaken identity, arguments, pain, heartache. But it all ends happily."

Gela's sighed deeply. "It's a real show . . ."

"The lead is Edith Day."

"I've never heard of her," Maude said.

"Neither have I," "Gela said. "But we don't go to shows much. Is she famous?"

"Mr. Starling thinks she will be. She's already been in three Broadway shows, and two silent films."

"A movie star? Like Mary Pickford?" Gela's voice dripped with awe

He laughed. "Not as famous as that. Yet."

Gela grabbed Maude's arm. "Can I, Mama? Please? It's like a dream come true."

She looked sideways at your daughter. "I have never heard you mention wanting to be on the stage. Not once."

"Because I didn't think it was possible. This is like a dream I didn't know I had come true."

Maude held back a smile. "Appearing on stage is hardly a reputable experience for a young lady." She looked at Mr. McGinness. "I've heard stories about illicit lifestyles and . . ." She lowered her voice. "Debauchery."

"What's that?" Gela asked.

"Bad behavior," Maude said. "Mr. McGinness?"

He nodded — which did not give Maude comfort.

"Are those stories true?"

"Yes, and no."

"This does not encourage me, sir."

He took a moment — to gather the right words? — which made her even more wary. She would take whatever he said with a large dose of skepticism.

"It *is* true that the life of an actor is unconventional. We work in the evenings. When other people are done with their work, we begin ours." He paused. "And temptation *is* present — as it is in any line of work." He smiled at Gela. "But I promise to be Gela's personal protector."

"She will need protection?"

He made a face, clearly regretting his choice of words. "I have the feeling no matter what I say, you will keep your present opinions."

He was right. "Above all else, I want my daughter to be safe."

"But I would be safe, Mama. Safer than — "

Maude filled in her sentence. "Safer than here?"

"That's not what I meant."

"I think it was exactly what you meant."

Gela's expression turned to a pout. "I'm sixteen now. I'm not a child. You and Papa agreed I was through with school. You put me to work, sewing." She looked at Mr. McGinness. "This is a paying job, yes?"

"Not a lot of pay, but you will be paid."

"See?" Gela said. "You know I hate sewing, and beyond that, I'm not good at it. Ask Edna. She's constantly having to rip up my work."

"Then do a better job."

"I want *this* job!" Gela had raised her voice. She lowered it again. "I love to sing, Mama. Like you said, it was a hidden talent which is now found. Would you have told Annie not to sketch and design after she discovered *her* talent?" She hurried to answer her own question. "No, you wouldn't. You didn't. You encouraged her and she encouraged you until you all gave up your other jobs and opened Unruffled. You took a chance. I want to take a chance too. Don't deny me this chance to shine."

Maude took a cleansing breath. "Gracious."

Mr. McGinness winked at Gela as if saying, *well said.*

It *was* well said. Despite her doubts, Maude was inclined toward allowing her the job — until she remembered the next hurdle. "We will have to ask your father."

Gela took hold of her hand across the table. "But *you'd* say yes?"

"I am leaning in that direction." She nodded at Mr. McGinness. "Although I *would* like to speak to this Mr. Starling, and would count on you to protect Gela from bodily harm *and* protect her innocence."

He raised a hand as though taking an oath. "I will do my very best to protect her as I would protect my own daughter. In all ways."

Gela looked at Maude, her face hopeful.

"As I said, we will have to ask your father for the final say."

Gela flung her arms around Maude's neck. "Oh, thank you, Mama! Thank you! I'll make you proud, I promise."

Maude closed her eyes and soaked in the moment. They embraced far too seldom. And when was the last time she'd seen Gela so happy?

"Very well then," Mr. McGinness said. "I will await your answer — but the sooner the better. Mr. Starling will not wait."

"When would rehearsals start?" Maude asked.

"On Monday, August the eleventh. We will rehearse Monday through Saturday, noon to seven. Opening night is November the eighteenth."

"How long is the run?"

"We never know. If people like it, a show can go on indefinitely. I've heard good things about the production. And Miss Day is very talented, so I am hopeful of a long run."

Maude wasn't sure if she hoped the show would be a hit or not. But the fact it *could* be emphasized the crossroads. If she and Antonio said no, Gela's future would go left, toward the status quo — where she was *not* happy. If they said yes, Gela's future would go right, leading her into a life of theaters, performing, singing — a world that was totally foreign to all of them. One road was safe. One was risky.

As was your road from Butterick to Unruffled.

Gela popped out of her chair. "I want to sing some more. Come on, Mr. McGinness."

The two of them went to their places, and Maude turned her chair around to watch.

But when she did so, she saw someone. A man. A man whose face was etched into her memories.

She gasped, putting a hand to her mouth. Her heart beat in her throat.

No. It can't be him. It's been thirteen years.

Gela began to sing, but Maude barely heard the song as her attention was focused on the man standing against the side wall. He was watching her daughter. Smiling at her daughter.

No, you don't! Don't you dare look at her!

People began to clap. The man began to clap. Maude glanced at Gela who gave her a questioning look.

Maude clapped and managed to give Gela a smile. But her heart continued its wild rhythm. She stole glances at the man, wanting to be sure.

His hair was coal black but was longer and more disheveled then when she'd seen him last. He had a distinctive widows peak and one continuous eyebrow spanning dark eyes and a hooked nose. Suddenly, he looked her way, and in that split second—there was a flash of recognition on his face.

It is him! As she watched her daughter sing, Maude's mind swam with questions about what to do next. Was there a policeman in the room? Or outside? Should she make a scene and accuse him in public? She was unfamiliar with the neighborhood. Was there a precinct nearby where she could report him?

She looked back at him. He was gone! She saw movement and saw him hurrying to the door. She wanted to jump to her feet and shout, "Stop that man!" But the moment passed.

The song ended. Applause.

Gela came over to her. "Are you all right, Mama?"

Maude nodded, but stood. "We need to go."

"Now? It's too soon."

She thought fast. "You want to ask your father, don't you?"

"I do! Let me say goodbye to Mr. McGinness."

While she did, Maude looked toward the door. The man was gone. For how long? Forever?

Mr. McGinness came over to say his goodbyes. Maude took advantage of the chance. "I saw a man standing by the wall. He looked familiar. Long black hair, widow's peak, bushy eyebrows and hooked nose? Do you know him?"

"Not really. Though I know who you're talking about. Last name is Varner, I believe. And I've heard him called Dock."

"As in doctor?"

He shook his head. "I don't think so. By the looks of him, I think he's worked on the docks."

"Does he still?"

"I don't know. I'm not sure he would come in here for free food if he had a paying job."

"How do you know him, Mama?"

She couldn't say. "We met many, many years ago."

Gela's eyebrows dipped in concern. "You don't act like it was a happy meeting."

"It wasn't."

Mr. McGinness nodded toward the door. "He's pretty quiet. Keeps to himself mostly. I've never gotten the impression he was a bad sort."

"You don't know!" Maude was surprised by the hatred in her voice. She'd gained the gaze of others at the table. "Come now, Gela. As I said, we need to go."

"Is there anything I can do to help?" Mr. McGinness asked.

She shook her head and they left.

"Mama? What was all that about?"

Gela wanted to be an actress? Now was the time for Maude to show her own talent in that area. She pasted on a smile. "Nothing that concerns you." She put an arm around her daughter's shoulders as they walked to the streetcar.

But her eyes scanned the street as they walked.

✺

"So, Papa? Can I take the job?"

Antonio looked at Maude for guidance. They'd talked their way through it, front and backwards, side to side.

Maude was weary from the day, her thoughts still tainted by seeing the man called Dock. She didn't have the strength or inclination to discuss Gela's job another minute. "I say let Gela try. She has talent. Let her use it. This isn't a life-long choice, just a chance."

Gela nodded vigorously. "Aren't you always saying that God opens a door and it's our responsibility to walk through it?"

"Our choice to walk through it." But then Antonio sighed deeply — a familiar sigh he offered when he was about to give in to the women in his life. "Go ahead and try, Gela. But your mother and I would like to meet with Mr. Starling when it's convenient for him."

Hugs and kisses and shouts of joy.

At least someone was happy.

✺

Maude lay in bed and stared at the dark. What if Dock *was* the man from her past? What if he wasn't? After years of struggling to forget him and all the details of their encounter, and after six years of being successful in forgetting him while she was happily married to Antonio, here he was again. Making her remember.

She turned on her side and closed her eyes. *Chances are it isn't him at all.*

But then her eyes shot open as she remembered the moment their eyes had met. *He* had remembered *her*.

This wasn't nothing.

Maude knew it would not go away on its own.

Antonio put a hand at her waist, and snuggled close. "You're not sleeping."

"No."

"What are you thinking about?"

She thought of telling him, but decided against it until she knew more. "I'm thinking about tomorrow. Sleep, my love."

She would try to do the same.

CHAPTER SIX

It was awkward.

For the second time, Henrietta stopped at her mother-in-law's to visit her husband. Willie tugged at her skirt. "Will Daddy come home today?"

"I don't know, sweetheart. Let's hope so."

She knocked. But just as Edna opened the door, the neighbor from across the hall opened *her* door.

"Good morning, Mrs. Hutchins," Henrietta said.

"'Morning, Henrietta. Ed —"

The older woman stopped her greeting and looked through Edna's opened door. Steven stood there with his shirt untucked, his hair tousled from sleep.

Edna quickly drew Henrietta and the boys inside, looking to the neighbor, "Have a nice day."

Immediately Steven retreated back into his room and shut the door.

Henrietta sighed. "Well that's a scandal.".

Edna diverted the boys by getting them each a scone. "I'd say don't worry about it, but we both know what a gossip she is."

Henrietta poured herself a cup of coffee and warmed Edna's cup. "I wish there was a logical explanation for my husband sleeping at his mother's, but there isn't. She'll think we're having troubles in our marriage."

"Which you're not."

They sat at the table and Henrietta felt the weight of the situation fall upon her. "Technically not, I suppose. But it sure seems like trouble to me." She pointed toward the bedroom door. "He's obviously not any better."

Edna shook her head. "I tried to get him to talk last night, but didn't get very far. Though I did apologize for yelling at him."

"He deserved your ear-bashing. And more." Henrietta immediately felt guilty for her attitude. "I want to help him, but I don't know how."

"I could ask Pastor Mannington to come speak with him."

Henrietta had already thought of that idea — and dismissed it. "This isn't a spiritual issue. This is a war issue. Antonio tried to reach him. You've tried. I've tried."

Edna took Henrietta's hand and bowed her head. "Help him, Lord. Make him well again."

⁓

By the time she got to work, Gela was out of breath. She was glad Edna wasn't there yet.

Ginny and Gert were just setting up. "What's wrong with you?" Ginny asked. "You're sweating like a field hand."

Gela got out the dress she was sewing. "I had to get up early and run a note over to a friend." *All the way to Port Refuge – and back.*

"Oooh," Gert said. "A friend?"

"Not that kind of friend. Mr. McGinness is old."

"A man's a man," Ginny said. "I could do with a man – old or young."

That's not going to happen. You're ugly as a mud fence. Gela felt guilty for thinking it – even if it was true – because Ginny was very nice.

She sat at her machine, wanting to be hard at work when Edna showed up because Edna would not like what she had to say.

She didn't have to wait long. "Well now," Edna said, taking a quick scan of the flat. "This is a happy sight. All three of you, hard at work."

Gela wanted to talk to her, right then and there. But she chickened out. She would wait for Mr. McGinness. He would get her note, honor her request for a meeting, and come to the workshop. His presence would give Gela the strength to take the next step.

⁓

Every time the door of the workshop opened, Gela looked up, only to be disappointed it wasn't Mr. McGinness. When would he come? She had no idea when he usually went to Refuge. She saw him in the evenings or on Saturday. But she couldn't wait until then. He'd said the director needed an answer. Plus, her stomach couldn't take the nervous knots much longer.

As they were eating their lunch, he finally walked in.

He glanced at their food. "Do I know how to time an entrance, or what?"

Gela sprang to her feet, dropping half a sandwich to the floor. "Mr. McGinness."

"You summon me, I come," he said with a little bow. He looked at Edna. "Good afternoon, Mrs. Holmquist. Nice to see you."

72

"And you, Mr. McGinness." Edna tucked a stray hair into her bun. "To what do we owe the honor?"

There was a moment of confusion, but he quickly covered. "Miss Gela left me a note, asking me to come." He spread his arms. "And so I am here." He looked at the other girls. "Ladies."

They giggled.

Gela didn't want to talk in front of them. "Can we go outside and talk?"

"Of course."

He held the door for her. Gela turned back and said, "Edna, would you come too?"

Her eyebrows rose, but she followed Gela downstairs and out to the street.

"What's all this about?" Edna asked.

She took a deep breath, hoping it would provide enough air to say what she had to say. "Mr. McGinness has offered me the chance to audition for a part in a Broadway play, as a singer."

"I'm playing the piano for the production."

Edna looked confused. "That's very nice for both of you. You are very talented."

"The thing is . . . rehearsals will be during the day. And so . . ."

"You're quitting?" Edna asked.

"I am."

"Do your parents know about this?"

"They do." Gela couldn't hold back a smile. "They agreed to it."

"I find that hard to believe."

Gela didn't like her words. "Don't act like I'm lying to you. Because I'm not."

Edna nodded. "I'm sorry. I believe you, but you must admit it's extraordinary."

"That, it is," Mr. McGinness said. "The rehearsals begin Monday, August fourth."

"That's only five days away," Edna said.

"Sorry," Gela said. "It happened fast."

Edna looked up toward the workshop window. "We're just getting busy again. Yet I suppose there *is* the chance you won't get the part."

How rude! "I'll get it!" Gela said. "Mr. Starling already heard me sing at Refuge. He *asked* me to try out."

"That's true," Mr. McGinness said.

"You will work tomorrow," Edna said.

It wasn't a question. And though Gela hated to stay, it was the right thing to do. "All right."

"Bravo," Mr. McGinness said. "When the show opens I want you, Mrs. Holmquist, to come as my guest."

Edna blushed. "Of course I'll come to see Gela perform."

"Very good then." He checked a watch in his vest pocket, then looked at Gela. "You wanted me to say hello to your mother?"

"Yes. Please. She's in the other workshop." Gela glanced up and saw Ginny and Gert standing at the second-story window, eavesdropping. "Stop it!" she said. They disappeared inside.

Mr. McGinness opened the door for them, and they walked up the stairs. "Thank you for supporting me in this, Edna," Gela said.

"It's not up to me to support you. I'm still surprised by the whole thing."

"As am I. A wonderful surprise."

They left Edna at the workshop. "Will I see you soon, Mrs. Holmquist?" Mr. McGinness asked.

"Will you continue to sing at Refuge?"

"As long as the schedule allows."

She seemed pleased by his answer and went inside. Gela and Mr. McGinness walked up one more flight to the larger workshop.

☙

Maude set pattern pieces on the lovely ivory fabric. Although she was always careful before cutting, she was especially diligent today because of the cost of the satin, which, even with Guy's discounts was more expensive than any fabric they'd used before. They could not afford mistakes.

The door to the workshop opened, causing a breeze to come through the opened windows. A pattern piece fluttered to the floor.

Mr. McGinness retrieved it, "Hello again, Mrs. Ricci."

She had pins in her mouth and quickly stuck them into a pincushion. She was surprised to see him. "Obviously Gela made quick work of telling you we said yes."

He grinned at Gela. "That she did. She is very eager. As she should be."

"Hmm."

"I understand your wariness. You wish to protect your daughter from unfamiliar influences and harm."

"Harm?" *I know about harm firsthand.*

"I overstated. Unfamiliar influences — which will mostly be of a positive nature."

Mostly?

Gela bounced on her toes. "I'm so excited."

Of that, there was no doubt. Maude loved seeing Gela enthusiastic about something, but knew she was naïve. It was Maude's job to be wise. "When can we meet with Mr. Starling?"

"I know he and the director are going to be at the theater tomorrow. Gela should come then." He turned to the girl. "You will have to sing something to prove yourself."

"I can do that."

Maude admired her confidence. And gumption. And her total faith that everything would turn out perfectly. Oh, to be young.

"Would you like to meet Mr. Starling then?" he asked Maude.

"I would. We would."

Gela's eyes lit up. "Papa too?"

"I think it would be best." Besides, Maude needed the support and another set of eyes and ears to fully understand the situation. Above all else, she wanted to make sure Gela would be safe—though the theater seemed safer than letting Gela continue to go to Port Refuge. That man was there. He was a regular. *He* was not safe.

Mr. McGinness took a piece of paper out of his pocket. "The address of the Vanderbilt Theatre is 148 West 48th Street. Meet me outside the theater at a quarter to ten." His business accomplished, he looked at the fabric on the table, and stroked its edge. "Lovely. Perhaps you should consider making costumes for the theater, Mrs. Ricci."

"Oh, Mama! That would be so grand."

Maude raised an eyebrow. It was an interesting idea. "One step at a time, m'love," Maude said.

Mr. McGinness's suggestion was ten steps up a very steep road.

✍

Maude approached Unruffled with three finished dresses over her arm. As she walked past the display window she was surprised to see a portion of it draped with bridal fabric. When did this happen?

She went inside and asked Annie just that.

"Guy delivered the fabrics yesterday. Actually, he helped me create the display."

"That is a bit above and beyond."

"It is." Annie busied herself straightening stacks of gloves. Her cheeks were flushed, and she was smiling.

Something was afoot. "You're not sharing the full story."

Annie scanned the store. Birdie and their other clerk, Sara, were helping customers. "Let me show you the fabrics he brought in."

They went into the back room. The sight of the gorgeous fabrics pleased Maude, but also sent her into panic. "I didn't know they'd come in so soon. I just hired Myrtle and Mary."

"When do they start?

"Tomorrow."

"Good timing then."

She looked at the bolts. Bolts and bolts and bolts. "Guy should have delivered them to the workshop. That's where I need them. Now we have the extra step of getting them from here to there. Why didn't he ask?"

"We'll work it out." Annie gave her a pointed look. "Are you all right?"

Was she? "I have a lot on my mind. I just cut out Gert's dress and now you say Miss Branson wants one, and you're advertising the fabric, which means there will be more sales and more pressure, and — "

"More sales are needed."

She forced herself to calm down. "Of course. And I *was* the one who wanted to expand into wedding dresses."

"Which was a very good idea."

Maude nodded, but her thoughts were not on sewing at all.

Annie noticed. "What's wrong?"

So much. "First off, Gela quit her job with us and is going to — "

"Quit? When did this happen?"

"This morning. She's going to sing in a Broadway production."

Annie pressed a hand to forehead. "What are you talking about?"

Maude told her the entire story of Port Refuge, Mr. McGinness, the children, the songs, and her daughter's delightful voice. "It's an amazing opportunity."

"You and Antonio agreed to it.?"

"I went to Refuge and heard her sing. I never knew how good she was. Knowing that, I just want her to have the chance to use her gift like we've been given the chance to use ours." *Argue with that one, Annie.*

"I'm not arguing with you."

I'm arguing with myself. Maude retied a ribbon around a bolt. "There's another reason I'm letting Gela sing in the show."

"What's that?"

"It will get her away from Port Refuge."

"That's a charity. She was helping people there."

"People . . . "

Annie cocked her head, studying her.

Maude looked away. "Don't look at me like that."

"What aren't you saying?" She pointed at Maude's face. "You can't hide things from me."

The decision whether to tell Annie everything didn't take long. "I saw the man who raped me."

Annie's mouth gaped open. "Where?"

"At Port Refuge."

"Are you sure it's him?"

She hesitated. "No."

"Then how—?"

"Our eyes met and . . . he recognized me. The next thing I know, he's rushing out of the building. Why would he do that if he isn't the one? If he was a stranger?"

"What did Antonio say about it?"

Maude paused. "I haven't told him."

"Whyever not? You have to tell him. He knows about the attack, doesn't he?"

Maude sat on a crate as the weight of the situation grew too heavy. "He knows in general. When we were courting I told him what happened. He knows the assault is the reason I can't have my own children." She looked up at Annie. "Antonio married me and changed my life. He made me the mother of two wonderful children. He gave me the life I never thought I could have."

"Yes, he did. You *share* a life, which means you need to tell him."

She nodded, but looked to the floor, at a stray piece of twine. "Even if it is him, I'm not sure I want to dredge it all up again."

"Was he ever arrested and charged?"

"No." *I never reported it.*

"So he's been out there all these years? It's more than likely he's committed more crimes, has hurt others like he hurt you."

"Should I go to the police?"

Annie looked taken aback. "What else would you do?"

"Do a little investigating on my own?"

"No!" Annie said. "Absolutely not. If it's truly him, you want to stay away from him."

"If it isn't?"

"Do *you* want to be the one to accuse an innocent man, who's obviously down on his luck?"

It was a good point. "I suppose not."

Annie spread her hands, laying out the point.

"All right," Maude said. "I'll go to the police."

"After telling Antonio about it."

She wasn't sure about that.

"Maude . . ."

"Let me report it. If it goes somewhere I'll tell him. If not, I won't."

"But—"

"That's the only way I'll do this, Annie."

"Let me go with you."

Maude didn't have to think long. "I'd like that."

"When?"

Maude thought about her busy day. She'd missed being with Antonio and Matteo at dinner last night. Plus, Gela was arranging a meeting with the higher-ups at the theater. There was only one logical time. "Now? I won't be of much use until this is settled one way or the other."

Annie nodded. "Let's check out the front of the store, and if we're not busy, we'll go now."

Maude took Annie's hand. "Thank you."

"Of course."

As they walked toward the front of the store, Maude realized she hadn't asked Annie about what was going on in her life that had made *her* act a bit strange. "I actually came back here to ask about *you*."

"We'll talk about me later."

※

Maude and Annie entered the nearest police station. Maude's stomach tightened as she approached the officer at the front desk.

"Yes, ma'am? How can I be of assistance?"

"I'd like . . . I'd like to report a crime."

His bushy eyebrows rose. "What sort of crime?"

"An assault. On me."

Annie leaned forward and whispered, "A rape."

The officer drew in a breath and reddened. "Oh. My. Come with me. I'll take you to Sergeant Ramsey."

They were led to a small office. A sixtyish man stood as they entered. "Do you have a minute to speak to these ladies about a crime, Sergeant?"

"Of course." He offered them the two chairs in front of his desk. He took out a piece of paper and a pencil. "Now then. Tell me what's happened."

Suddenly Maude had doubts. No matter how well-intentioned, this man couldn't help her. Too much time had passed. She began to stand. "I'm sorry to trouble you. I need to go."

Annie pulled her back to the chair. "Just tell him. Start with the man you saw."

Perhaps that was the better place to start. "I was at the Port Refuge charity."

"A good place, that's doing good work."

"It seems to be just that. But when I was there I saw a man —"

"*The* man," Annie added.

"*The* man who assaulted me."

"Raped her."

Maude hated that Annie had used that horrid term twice in so many minutes. But since there was no denying it, she added, "He did. Rape me."

"I am sorry for your pain, Miss . . .?"

"Mrs. Ricci. Maude Ricci. Though my last name was Nascato then."

He seemed confused. "Then?"

"Thirteen years ago."

He froze, then let out an awkward laugh. "You're reporting this again, now?"

"Actually . . . I never reported it. Then."

He huffed. "Why not?"

Her reasoning seemed very lame. Juvenile — though she *had* been a juvenile. "I was living with my mother and aunt. We'd had an argument. I was mad and went for a walk alone after dark. It happened and then I . . . I was ashamed."

He pointed a finger at her. "That wasn't wise to be out alone after dark."

Annie shook her head, incredulous. "So she deserved it?"

He cleared his throat. "I'm not saying that. It just wasn't wise."

Maude pressed a calming hand in the air. "I agree. But that doesn't negate the fact it happened." She took a breath. "Or the fact that I saw my attacker yesterday."

The Sergeant leaned back in his chair. "A person's looks change a lot in thirteen years."

"They do. But I know it's him."

Annie prodded her arm. "Tell him the other part, about him recognizing you."

"Our eyes met and he recognized me," Maude said. "As soon as he did, he rushed out of the building."

"Innocent men don't run," Annie said.

"Maybe you spooked him. Maybe you looked agitated. Maybe you scared him."

It was possible.

"What's his name?"

Maude was glad she'd made inquiries. "Dock Varner."

"Doesn't ring a bell."

It seemed a thoughtless statement. "So you know all the criminals in New York City by name?"

He balked. "Of course not. But I haven't heard his name before. It's an odd name. I would have remembered it."

"I need you to find him and speak with him. Interrogate him."

"About something that happened in . . ." He looked to the ceiling, as if doing the math.

"Nineteen-aught-six," Maude said. "May twenty-third. In Chelsea."

"That's not our precinct."

Annie tossed her hands in the air. "So the year doesn't suit you? And neither does the location? My friend was a victim of a vicious crime that has affected her bodily person in very permanent, tangible ways. You could at least try to give her some justice."

Maude wished Annie wouldn't have mentioned her injuries. Yet what did it matter?

Sergeant Ramsey wrote a few things down, then looked up. "Port Refuge is in another precinct but I will send a note to Sergeant Abrams over there and ask him to look into it."

Progress. Maybe. "Should we go talk to the other sergeant?" Maude asked.

"That's not necessary. I've got all the information written down here."

Annie pointed at the page. "Don't you need contact information for Mrs. Ricci?"

"Of course." He looked to Maude, who gave him her address at home and at the store.

"Unruffled is your property?"

"It is."

"My wife bought a dress there. Very pretty and the price was reasonable."

The conversation seemed out of place. "I'm glad she liked it."

He stood and led them out. "Someone will be in touch with you, Mrs. Ricci. I am very sorry for your pain."

That his words exactly mirrored those of the officer at the desk, diluted their concern.

The ladies left the precinct and headed back to work. "That was pointless," Maude said.

"I bet a year's worth of dresses he will never contact the other precinct."

The chances did seem miniscule.

Annie slid her hand around Maude's arm. "We can check back in a few days."

What else could they do?

&

On their way back to the store Annie and Maude noticed a large crowd near the arch at Washington Square Park. "What's going on?" Annie asked a woman on the outer edge.

"It's a victory parade for the First Division, just returned. They say General Pershing is here too."

They heard a band playing. The ladies stepped onto benches to see over the heads of the people lining Fifth Avenue. Rows and rows of uniformed soldiers marched in sync, wearing their flat brimmed trench helmets and jodhpur pants, carrying guns over their shoulders. They could have easily been going off to war as coming back from it.

Annie put a hand to her chest. "I can feel the rhythm of their marching in my very soul."

"It's a victory march, Annie. We won the war."

But lost the battle. Where is Sean? He should be here, marching with the others. She wanted to jump off the bench and rush into the marching men, shouting, "Did you know my husband? Sean Culver? Where is he?" She'd be restrained and bodily taken aside. People would look at her and stare. Even if they empathized, they'd be embarrassed by her hysterics.

The moment to follow through with her impulse passed as the soldiers marched on. Annie felt herself sinking to the edge of despair. She was done. She couldn't go on. If Sean was dead, she didn't want to live. Her body wavered and she nearly toppled off the bench.

Maude caught her arm. "I know what you're thinking. Seeing all these soldiers . . . Don't give up. He's out there somewhere. I know it. We have to believe it until we're told not to."

It was a simple instruction: Hope until there was no hope.

Not so simple. At all.

CHAPTER SEVEN

Gela couldn't sit still. As the elevated train jiggled and jawed its way north to the Theatre District, her stomach threatened to do something nasty.

She felt Papa's hand on her knee. He offered her a smile. "*Canterete splendidamente, cara ragazza.*"

"I heard the word 'splendid'," Mama said.

"I said, 'sing splendidly, dear girl.'"

"I know you will," Mama said.

Gela wanted to believe them.

"And don't be nervous," Mama said.

"How can I not be? This might be the most important day of my life."

Mama shook her head. "You will have many important days."

She hated how Mama diluted things with logic. "Then it's the most important day of my life so far. Does that make you happy?"

"Gela . . ." Her father drew out her name, showing his displeasure.

"I'm sorry. I'm just —" She crossed her arms and looked out the window.

"Nervous," Mama said. "And I shouldn't nit-pick. It *is* an important day." She put a hand to her midsection. "In fact . . . I'm feeling a bit nervous *for* you."

Misery loved company.

❧

"There's Mr. McGinness!"

Maude and Antonio let Gela rush ahead to the front of the Vanderbilt Theatre. There were three double doors with two-story, embellished arches rising above, marking the spot to enter and be entertained. A double-marquee would soon announced "Irene" — her daughter's show. She was surprised by the pride she felt. A daughter on Broadway had never been a goal, or even a glimmer of a notion. What had Gela aptly called it? 'The dream of a dream'?

Mr. McGinness looked up from Gela's exuberant chatter and shook their hands. "I'm so glad both of you could come. Mr. Starling is waiting inside."

They entered through the center door into a beautiful lobby lit by bronze sconces with dangling prisms.

"Pretty nice, eh?" Mr. McGinness said. "It was opened just last year."

"It's lovely," Maude said.

"How many does it seat?" Antonio asked.

"Seven hundred and eighty." He winked at Gela. "We hope every seat is filled every night, don't we, Miss Gela?"

She nodded enthusiastically.

Maude was unexpectedly taken by the fact he called her *Miss* Gela. It showed respect.

They moved into the main auditorium. The seats were upholstered in red velvet, with two aisles leading to the stage. There was a large balcony embellished with carved medallions. On either side was a grand half-circle box that had its own arched entry with brocade curtains. This was where the wealthy patrons sat. The walls reaching from the balcony to the tall ceiling were decorated with *trompe l'oeil*, braided swags with dangling tassels. Across the top of the stage was a scalloped valance, with massive velvet curtains sitting ready on either side.

"Oooh," was Gela's response.

"Glad you like it. Sit in the front and I'll tell Mr. Starling you're here."

They walked toward the front row. "Oh, Papa, isn't it grand?"

"That, it is. No wonder people like going to the theater. It's like entering a perfect, posh world." He glanced at Maude. "We should go more often."

"Maybe we will," she said. "Now that we've a reason to." She loved seeing how her words made Gela beam.

Mr. Starling and Mr. McGinness came out of the wings, and stepped down to the audience level. "Welcome," Mr. Starling said, introducing himself. Shaking their hands. "Please be seated." He leaned against the edge of the stage, facing them. He was totally at ease — the exact opposite of Maude.

"Mack told me you have some concerns?"

Maude looked to Antonio to answer. "This will be our daughter's first show, and — "

"Hopefully not my last," Gela said.

Mr. Starling smiled. "Hopefully not your last." He leaned closer, "From my experience, once the theater bug bites, there's no going back."

Gela nodded. It was clear she'd already been bitten.

Antonio continued. "We just want Gela to be safe. She's only sixteen. Taking the El alone, at night . . ."

Mack raised a hand. "I live in Chelsea. I'll see she gets on the train safely." He looked to Antonio. "Perhaps you could meet her at the station every night to walk her home?"

"That's a keen idea," Antonio said.

"A solution," Gela said.

"A solution to the transportation issues," Maude said. "But there are also the issues of morals and influences . . ."

Mr. Starling nodded. "The life of an actor is unique. They are asked to pretend to be someone else, to take on *their* traits and mannerisms from speech to dress to emotions. In order to do that, the actors themselves tend to be a . . ." He searched for the word. "An exuberant and demonstrative bunch. They are asked to step beyond themselves into another world. It's an exhausting experience, so when they are allowed to just be themselves, they . . . celebrate."

"That's what we worry about," Antonio said. "The temptations of celebration and exuberance."

"I am not a child, Papa," Gela said with a pouty voice — which only proved she *was* one.

"You are not grown either," he said. "The expanse of your world has been very limited. You don't know what's out there."

"I want to know."

Maude jumped on her answer. "That's what worries me. That you'll be tempted to try things that the adults in the company . . ."

Mr. McGinness interrupted. "I won't allow her to drink or smoke."

Mr. Starling nodded. "A cast that includes younger members is generally respectful of them, keeping the boundaries of modesty and vice."

Modesty? Maude hadn't even thought about the fact the players would be changing costumes during the show. She put a hand to her forehead. They were nervous about the known commodities, but there was so much they didn't know. Couldn't know.

Mr. Starling must have seen her dismay, for he spoke directly to her. "Mrs. Ricci, Mack and I will do our best to make the Irene-experience a safe and fulfilling one for your daughter."

Maude nodded her thanks. There was nothing more he could say. He would do his best, but the brunt of the situation would fall on Gela. Was *she* strong enough for it? Unfortunately, there was no way to find out except by letting her do it.

She had one more question — a delicate one. "If I may ask . . . why Gela? Why an unknown, with no experience?"

Mr. Starling considered this a moment. "My answer mirrors that of many businesses: the war and the flu changed everything. Many actors served and were killed. Many died of influenza."

"Some theaters closed during the epidemic, didn't they?" Antonio asked.

"Some hole-in-the-wall theaters closed, but most were told to avoid overcrowding, ventilate well, prohibit smoking, and not admit children under twelve. Actually, I was rather shocked they *didn't* close us down. We were actually told to stay open—within the Board of Health conditions—to show people the proper way to gather, and to avoid hysteria. And provide a diversion."

"I suppose closures would send an end-of-the-world type of message," Maude said.

Mr. Starling nodded. "But with these world crises affecting so many . . . many survivors moved on, starting fresh elsewhere. And so we start fresh with new faces. Miss Day has marginal experience but represents the essence of optimism. As does your daughter."

Gela nodded vigorously and Maude knew if this man said the moon was purple she would heartily agree.

Mr. Starling slapped his legs. "Now then. How about we finalize this transaction by letting Gela sing a song?"

"Yes, oh yes!" Gela said.

Mr. Starling took a seat beside Maude. "The stage is yours, my dear," he said.

Mack led Gela up the side steps to the stage. He pushed a piano closer to the front. "What's your pleasure, Miss Gela?" he asked.

"'Beautiful Dreamer.'"

Mack nodded and played an arpeggio, then gave her a few chords of introduction.

Gela stood center stage and sang. There was no hint of nerves and she kept her head high, singing to the back of the balcony. Her voice soared over their heads, flying back again to surround them with its pure tone.

Maude felt Antonio's hand on her knee. She glanced at his profile. He was enraptured. Then she realized he had never heard his daughter sing like this. His forehead crumpled and she could see a glistening in his eyes—which made Maude's eyes fill with tears.

At the end of the song, Mr. Starling applauded, giving Gela a standing ovation. "Bravo, my dear! An angel come to earth indeed." He looked at her parents. "Gela . . . does that stand for Angela?"

"It does."

"Angela, who sings like an angel. For the program you will be Angela Ricci."

Gela beamed. "So I have the job. For certain?"

"For certain," Mr. Starling said. "That is, if your parents approve."

Maude and Antonio exchanged a glance, then Antonio said, "We approve."

Gela and Mr. McGinness returned to the audience level. She threw her arms around her father's neck and then Maude's. "I've never been so happy! Thank you for letting me do this."

Suddenly, there was applause from the back of the theater. A woman with bobbed hair covered with a pink cloche walked down the aisle toward the stage. "Bravissimo."

Mr. Starling greeted her by kissing the air above her cheeks. "Edith, come meet the newest member of the Irene company. Miss Angela Ricci. Angela, this is Miss Edith Day, our star."

Gela's eyes were large as she exuberantly shook Miss Day's hand. "I'm so glad to meet you, Miss Day."

The woman covered the handshake with her other hand. "And I you, Miss Ricci."

"Gela. My friends and family call me Gela."

Miss Day winked at her. "Then I shall call you Gela too."

Gela's face glowed like she was meeting Ethel Barrymore or Gloria Swanson. She looked toward Maude, as if saying, *See this, Mama? I'm meeting a star!*

Miss Day turned toward Maude and Antonio. "You are the parents of this talented girl?"

They both stood. "We are," Antonio said, introducing themselves. "So nice to meet you, Miss Day."

Maude wasn't sure what to say, so stated the obvious. "Gela is excited for rehearsals to begin."

"Enthusiasm and hard work will take you far, Gela." She noticed Mr. McGinness. "Hi there, Mack. Are you a friend of the family?"

"I am now." He too kissed Miss Day on both cheeks. "In fact, I am quite willing to take credit for discovering Gela's talent."

She flicked his chin. "Thatta boy. We performers know that credit is everything."

"Did you come to speak with me, Edith?" Mr. Starling asked.

"I did. If you have the time."

"We're just about done here." Mr. Starling took a piece of paper from a valise, handing it to Antonio. "Here is the contract. It's standard, I assure you. Take it home and look at it, but I need it back as soon as possible. Two copies. Signed and dated." Then with a smile to Gela, he said, "Welcome to the show, Angela Ricci."

He left with Miss Day the way he'd entered. "Nice to meet both of you," Maude called after them.

"And thank you!" Gela added.

On their way out of the theater, Antonio grabbed Gela's hand, turning her towards him. He lifted her chin, peering into her eyes. "Why didn't I know you could sing like that?"

She shrugged. "I didn't know myself."

"A star is born!" Mr. McGinness said.

Would this job lead to others? To a career? Maude didn't know what to think about that.

Mack held the door open for them. "I would love to take all of you to Barbetta's to celebrate, but alas it is too early. They have the most delicious risotto. And porcini mushrooms that the owner Mr. Maioglio hand-picks in the Connecticut woods."

"That sounds delicious," Antonio said with a smile. "And familiar, as my family is from Italy."

"Of course. Ricci. Perhaps another time?" Mr. McGinness said.

"Yes. Please," Gela said. "Are you going to Refuge tomorrow?"

"I'll be there. Will you come?"

Gela looked to her mother. "Can I?"

Maude's thoughts turned shadowy as she remembered Dock Varner. She needed to find out more about him and the best way to do that was to see him again at Refuge. "I believe I'll come with you."

Gela beamed. "You'll do that for me, Mama?"

For me. Though she truthfully added, "I'd love to hear you sing some more."

Antonio stood on the sidewalk, looking at the contract with a furrowed brow.

"It's as bad as it looks," Mr. McGinness said. "Basically, the actors have no rights, and profit rules."

"That doesn't sound good," Maude said.

"Tis the way of the theater."

She suspected this would be a reoccurring excuse.

❧

Edna was washing dishes when she heard singing. She stopped and listened. It was coming from the front of the apartment. Was it Steven?

It didn't sound like Steven. In fact . . .

Steven came in the kitchen and pointed outside. "A man . . ."

She went to the parlor window and looked out. It was Mr. McGinness.

He looked up at her and waved, and began again. "'My wild Irish rose, the sweetest flow'r that grows, you may search ev'rywhere, but none can compare with my wild Irish rose . . .'"

Edna stuck her head out the window and Mr. McGinness continued singing another verse. He had the attention of everyone on the block, which initially embarrassed her. But when she saw their smiles, she let herself enjoy it. It felt good to have a beau.

I have a beau?

The song finished and the impromptu audience clapped. He bowed, then called up to Edna. "Come out and let's take a walk."

"Who is he?" Steven asked.

"A friend." She called down to Mr. McGinness. "I'll be right there." She caught Steven's disapproving look. "You may choose to ignore your life, son, but I choose not to ignore mine. I won't be gone long."

She checked her hair in a mirror, then gave herself a nod. "It's just a walk."

Then why was her stomach all a'flutter?

Mr. McGinness tipped his hat to her. "Good evening, Mrs. Holmquist."

"Good evening to you, Mr. McGinness. Thank you for the song."

"You're quite welcome. By the by, I do know you're not Irish, and considered singing, 'my wild Swedish rose' but then thought that you might have Norwegian roots or even Danish, so left it alone."

She chuckled. "Swedish is correct, and I enjoyed the song as-is. You have such a lovely voice—and you play the piano too. What talents you have."

He offered her his arm and they began to walk. "What can I say? My parents were in vaudeville, a singing duo, the Merry Macs."

"Did you ever appear with them?"

"From the time I was five. But enough about me. How did you come to be involved in a dress store?"

It's more than a dress store. "I owe it all to Annie Culver, a dear friend. She and I worked at Macy's—I sold sewing machines there for decades. She became my boarder and I discovered that she could sketch fashion. Sean, her husband-to-be, worked at Butterick, and got Annie a job there. That's where she met Maude, who designed patterns. After gaining some experience Annie got the idea to open a store. Then Henrietta showed up from England—she's Annie's former mistress, and—"

"Mistress?"

"Annie was a maid in a grand hall in Summerfield, England, working for Henrietta and her mother. Henrietta showed up here – again, because of Annie's inspiration for going after her dreams – and we found out she was good at numbers. So everyone has a place, a job, a purpose."

"The Unruffled name is a bit unusual."

"We wanted it that way. We knew most stores were named after the owners: Macy's, Bergdorff-Goodman, Lord & Taylor, Bonwit-Teller."

"Tiffany's and Brooks Brothers."

She nodded. "Male names. We wanted something more unique. Do you know our motto?"

"I do not."

Edna swept a hand through the air. "Fashion for the unruffled, unveiled, unstoppable woman."

"That's very descriptive," he said. "And even inspirational."

"We thought so." They turned onto Bleecker Street, heading toward Washington Square Park. "We opened the store at just the right time – or so we thought. We focused on fashion for working women. Then the war broke out and even more women were called into the work force. They needed – and deserved – fashion that was affordable, pretty, and functional."

"I approve of the shorter skirts."

"Really."

"Not for the reason you think – or not only for that reason," he said. "Obviously I enjoy a nice turn of ankle, but it never seemed logical to have women's skirts dragging on the ground, through dirt and . . . muck."

"We are finally free of brushing mud off the hems of our skirts, and mending them because they are ragged and worn."

"The war forced everyone to make wiser choices."

"If it wasn't so totally wrong, I'd say the war was a good thing."

"You're not totally wrong," he said. "The war stopped some very bad people from doing very bad things. That good could come from it is a relief."

"Good overcomes evil. It's God's way."

"Eventually."

Edna turned the subject back to something lighter. "There used to be so many fashion rules: skirt length, sleeve length, how much skin could be shown, which gloves to wear, when. And clothes were so heavy – the physical bulk of all those layers weighed us down. It's like women were forced to focus on such mundane matters as fashion do's and don'ts rather than the matters that really . . . mattered. Now women can improvise their fashion as well as their lives."

He laughed. "That's the way it is with music too. Ragtime is full of joy and delight, and jazz is all about improvising, letting the music take us where it will."

"As we let fashion take us where it will."

"It seems we have much in common, Mrs. Holmquist."

❧

Annie knelt beside her daughters. "You be extra special good staying at Grandma's flat this weekend. Eat what's put on your plate and no fuss about bedtime."

"We'll be good," Victoria said, while Alice nodded.

She gave them each a hug, then stood. "You don't have to do this," she told her mother-in-law. "It's just a dinner with a salesman." She hadn't told Vesta the dinner was at Delmonico's.

"It's good for you to go out," Vesta said. "Besides, I haven't had the girls come and stay at my place for far-too-long. Plus, it's just across the street now, not back in Brooklyn."

Vesta and Richard had lived in a lovely home in Brooklyn until his death. Vesta could have stayed there, but had chosen to move close to Annie and Sean. When a flat had opened up in Edna and Henrietta's building, she'd taken it. Annie loved having her close by.

"Actually," Vesta said, "I thought the girls and I would spend Saturday night at a friend's home, back in my old neighborhood. The girls will think it's a lark. I'll bring them home Sunday afternoon."

"Whatever you'd like," Annie said.

Victoria looked up at her grandmother. "Can we still try on all your jewels, Grandma?"

"We'll be at my apartment tonight, so yes, you may try on my jewelry."

"If you're careful," Annie added.

Alice took Vesta's hands and drew her toward the door. "Let's go!"

"Have a good time and don't worry about a thing," she said.

And then they were gone, the girls' exuberant footfalls on the stairs fading into silence.

Silence.

Annie stood in the parlor, holding her breath as the silence slipped around her, filling every space like water flowing around a stone.

She sat on the window seat that overlooked an open atrium area. There wasn't much privacy. She was able to see into the back windows of people who lived in the building on Morton Street, behind her. Although she'd been in New York for eight years, sometimes she missed the lush English countryside around Crompton Hall. Although she'd been just a maid, she'd enjoyed the fresh air and the utter space of it all. There was little space in New York that wasn't filled with people and noise.

There's green in Washington Square . . .

Maybe tomorrow she'd take a walk. But now she needed to get dressed for dinner at Delmonico's. She went into her bedroom and perused the dresses hanging in the armoire. She remembered the snooty looks she'd received the last—and only other—time she'd dined at Delmonico's. Lady Newley had downplayed the discrepancy in Annie's clothing and that of her friends, compared to the attire of other diners. This time she was wiser and knew what to expect.

She chose a yellow silk she'd made for Easter. It was a maize-colored silk chiffon with embroidered medallions in the same color. It fell into three ruffles at the bottom, had elbow-length sheer sleeves, a scoop neckline, and a wide satin cummerbund She'd wanted a pretty dress to wear when Sean got home—for she'd expected him in May. Or June. Or . . . and now it was August.

Perhaps it wasn't appropriate to wear a dress she'd wanted to wear for her husband to go out to dinner with another man. She let the notion linger a moment, then fade away. A pretty dress always made her feel better.

و

"I am determined to enjoy myself," Annie said softly.

Guy sat beside her in the Yellow Cab. "Are you saying this to yourself, or to me?"

She hadn't realized she'd spoken aloud. "Both," she said honestly. "This is all rather strange to me. I have never ridden in a taxi."

"Why not?"

"Because they charge fifty-cents a mile. When I worked at Macy's I earned six dollars a *week*."

"But now you own a successful business. You've come far."

She didn't want him to know how they had struggled—were still struggling. "How far is it to Delmonico's?"

He shrugged. "Two or three miles."

"So if I took a cab to get there and back it would cost me half a week's wages."

He chuckled. "Your Macy's wages."

She shrugged. "Wages are wages. It's expensive."

"I didn't know you were adept at math."

"As a business owner I am adept at economy and spending wisely."

"Then we shouldn't be going to Delmonico's."

She'd gone too far. "Please don't take offense, Mr. Ship. I am not disparaging how you spend your money, just explaining how I spend mine."

"No offense taken. And please call me Guy. In truth, I take great pleasure in spoiling you."

Her defenses rose. "I assume you get reimbursed for all this by Olivet? After all, I am a customer."

He touched her arm. "As I told you when we created the window display, I do not give all my customers special treatment."

She looked out the cab's window. She'd let herself be charmed by him beyond common sense. She never should have come tonight and was just about to ask him to turn the cab around, when he pointed out the left window.

"Look, there's Macy's. Your humble beginnings."

A thousand memories assailed her. Eight years ago — just eight years ago — she'd been a nineteen-year-old British maid who had nothing but ambition and gumption. And now . . . now she had a family, good friends, a business, hope for the future — and a gaping hole in her heart because Sean wasn't with her.

"I . . . I need to go home. Please turn around and take me home."

"Nonsense. We're almost there."

She looked at his face — which was far too close as they sat shoulder to shoulder in the cab. "This is too much, Mr. Ship."

He looked into her eyes. His eyes were incredibly brown. She looked away.

"You have to eat, Mrs. Culver. Tis a physiological fact. I have the reservations, and have asked for a nice table and hors d'oeuvres to be ready when we arrive — which will be momentarily. Two business associates sharing a meal. I ask no more than that."

The carriage turned onto Forty-fourth Street. It would be incredibly rude not to follow through. He *had* backed off from the flattery, thereby diluting his degree of familiarity. "I suppose you're right. I have to eat."

"Marvelous."

Annie hoped she wouldn't regret it.

❧

Oysters. Some kind of broth with mushrooms. A meat pate on bread. Guy had called it *foie gras* and said it was a fancy name for duck liver.

Annie was full already, and her steak — her Delmonico steak — had just been served.

"Oh my," she said, staring down at the huge piece of meat with a globe of herbed butter oozing down its sides. "I could eat off this for a week. We could have shared it."

Guy shook his head. "One does not share a meal at Delmonico's. It would be gauche."

He took a bite of his Lobster Newburg, another Delmonico creation. He closed his eyes. "Mmmm."

Annie sliced a bite of her meat. "Moaning at one's food is not considered gauche?"

"It is an involuntary reaction. Go ahead. Let's see how you react."

She took the bite of steak and immediately closed her eyes. "Mmmm."

They shared a laugh.

"Have some potatoes," he said, nudging the dish of cheese-encrusted potatoes in her direction. "I heard President Lincoln considered these a favorite."

Eating the food of presidents . . .

To be polite, Annie spooned a small amount onto her plate, though she was uncertain where she would find the appetite to try it.

"Tell me about yourself, Mrs. Culver."

She didn't want to share more than she already had. "Not tonight, Mr. Ship. You know far more about me than I do about you. Your turn. Tell me about your beginnings. And the war. I'd like to hear about your experiences in the war."

His left eyebrow rose. "I would think that would be the one thing you wouldn't want to hear about, considering your husband . . ."

"What you experienced, maybe he experienced."

Guy shook his head. "War is hell. That's all I'll say."

Annie was disappointed, but understood. "You only recently returned — at least recently returned to your position at Olivet's?"

"That is true. Actually I got out — returned from the war — in May, but spent time with my family in Boston before coming back to New York."

"Were you raised in Boston?"

"I was. My father was a banker. My mother did charity work."

"What was your first job?"

He enjoyed another bite of lobster and potatoes. "I was a runner."

"Runner?"

"A delivery boy, if you will. Taking goods from stores to homes."

"Macy's hired boys as runners."

"You don't say."

"Have you always had an interest in fabrics and laces?"

He grinned. "I believe so. Mother always wore the most gorgeous clothes and she'd make me go to the dressmaker's to help her choose the designs. Apparently, I have an eye for it."

"You do. The window display is netting results. We've had half a dozen women come in, interested in bridal."

"There you go. Mother always said, 'Take advantage of the chances that come your way.' Which is what you have done with your business opportunities."

"It was never just me, alone. I had the other ladies. And Sean. And generous financial supporters."

"Really?"

"Mr. and Mrs. Harold Sampson. More Eleanor than Harold. She saw something in me when others did not. Mr. Sampson is the name behind Sampson Shoes."

Guy was silent, suddenly interested in his fork.

"Do you know them?"

"I haven't had the pleasure." He nodded toward her plate. "You've not tried the potatoes."

≈

Annie slipped into bed. She'd been relieved when Guy had been a gentleman and had seen her to the door, and had not assumed more to the evening. And it *had* been a wonderful evening, a rare time when she'd been able to think past responsibilities and duty.

But now, the silence of the apartment threatened to drown Annie alive. Yes, she'd noticed it when Vesta had taken the girls for the weekend, but that pause-of-commotion was nothing compared to this utter stillness, this lack of noise and motion, lack of life. This was not just a lack, but a nothingness. And with that nothingness came the yoke of loneliness. With her busy life Annie had always appreciated solitude, but in the dark of the night, alone in her bed, the solitude was an affliction she found hard to bear.

For the umpteenth time, Annie turned over, trying to find a position of comfort — in body *and* mind. She reached across the bed — to Sean's side, and imagined him there, safe and warm and loving. "Darling, I miss you so. Come back to me."

She focused on sleep and repeated her nightly prayer: *Father, lead Sean back to me, the woman who loves him.*

❧

With difficulty Sam Colyer turned over in his tiny bed in a rooming house in London. He closed his eyes and once again saw the mental image of a women with dark hair and perfect skin. A woman who smiled at him and said, "Darling, I miss you so. Come back to me."

If only I could. If only I could remember who you are. Who I am.

As he did every night when the image assailed him, he shoved it aside. He needed rest because his job at the garage was exhausting.

He focused on sleep and repeated his prayer: *Father, lead me back to the woman who loves me.*

CHAPTER EIGHT

Sam Colyer was glad for summertime when the sun woke him early and took away any chance of being late for his job at the garage. Even though he couldn't remember his past, he had the notion that he always rose early — sun or no sun.

He got dressed and used the shared bath down the hall. Using the facilities first was another reason he liked to arise early. Sharing with four other men often stretched his patience and made life a bit . . . uncomfortable.

Back in his tiny room he set his shaving kit on the dresser and smoothed the covers over his bed. Yesterday's shirt was draped over the back of the room's only chair, and he checked it for dampness. It wasn't dry yet. With the heat and humidity of summer rolling in through the opened window, it took a long time to dry, but would be ready by this evening when it would be replaced by the washed shirt he now wore. He didn't mind the never-ending routine. At least he had two shirts. At least he had a job.

With one last look in the cracked mirror above the dresser, he swiped his blonde hair back, grabbed his cap, and went down for breakfast. Only one other boarder was seated as the landlady brought in a plate of sausages and stewed tomatoes.

Sam took his place and set his napkin in his lap. "Good morning, Mrs. Birch."

"Good morning to you, Mr. Colyer." She pointed to the cut on his cheek. "In need of a new razor?"

"The old one will do." *It's all I can afford right now.*

She handed him the tray. "Eggs are on the way."

Sam took half of what he wanted to eat, and passed it to Arnie, who said, "You can eat more. We pay plenty enough for the room."

"I don't want to take advantage."

Arnie shook his head and took Sam's desired double-share. "Suit yerself. More for me."

Sam was ravenous. Although his room and board included two meals, and he paid a few pence more for Mrs. Birch to pack him some bread and meat for lunch, he was always hungry. The work at the garage was strenuous and he hadn't fully regained the use of his left arm that had suffered shrapnel wounds during the war. His arm wasn't the only casualty. Apparently, he'd been blown completely out of a trench and had lost consciousness, along with the hearing in his left ear. He'd awakened in a British army hospital. They'd patched him up — which made him very thankful. The trouble was, he couldn't remember his name, and his dog tags were gone. He became Soldier Twelve.

The nurses had been so kind to him. When it became clear that his memory was lost, they suggested he choose a name. He'd been drawn to the initials S and C for some reason, and so chose to be Sam Colyer. It was as good a name as any. The name of a hardworking man.

He'd made his way to London, where he remembered that he'd taken care of vehicles in the army and knew something about engines. Dougal's Garage gave him a job, which he enjoyed well enough. Again, at least he had a job. And a room at Mrs. Birch's.

Things could be much, much worse.

Every time he had a flash of the pain and devastation of war, he shut his eyes and prayed God would take it away. Then he added a prayer that he would remember who he really was, and more than that, who he belonged to. To be without a name was bad enough, but to be without family and memories of family put him in a purgatory that had no end.

He twisted the wedding band on his ring finger.

"You do that a lot," Arnie said.

Sam glanced at his ring. "Habit I guess."

"You'll find her someday. Or she'll find you."

Mrs. Birch came in with the eggs. "Who will find who?" she asked.

"Sam will find his wife."

She nodded and passed the eggs. "True love will bring you together."

Sam wasn't so sure. "I don't even know her name. Or mine."

Mrs. Birch dug her fists into her ample hips. "You saying yer situation is too much fer the Almighty to handle?"

"No, it's just . . . it seems impossible."

"Nonsense," she said, rearranging what was left of the other platter. "You remembers the verse I taught you, eh?"

"Matthew seven-seven: 'Ask, and it shall be given you; seek, and ye shall find; knock, and it shall be opened unto you.'"

She nodded approvingly. "Until you have full memory, you ask, seek, and knock. He'll do the giving, the finding, and the opening of the exact right door at the exact right time."

Sam winked at her. "Did anyone ever tell you that you were a good and wise woman, Mrs. Birch?"

"Wise? A few times. Good?" She wobbled her hand.

Laughter made the food go down easy.

＆

Without the girls to worry about, Annie went to the large workshop as soon as the sun came up. She wanted to get a lot done before the seamstresses came in at nine—a later start seeings how it was Saturday. She was glad Maude had talked Myrtle and Mary into coming back to work. Their skill put the wedding dress orders in good hands.

Maude had a dress ready to cut out on the large table in the main room, but Annie didn't dare do the cutting. Maude often adjusted something *as* she cut. Instead, Annie organized the fabric and supplies, cleaned up the scraps and swept the three rooms.

After the sewers arrived, time was spent going over the details of the dresses. All that settled, the other ladies got to work, and Annie took a basket of rubbish down to the bin.

Before returning inside she looked up at Edna's apartment windows across the street. She spotted Steven sitting at the window and waved.

He didn't wave back.

She tried not to take offense, but still found it annoying. He was home. His family *could* be with him if only he'd snap out of it. Her attitude made her feel guilty. Which made her think about Sean. Which made her think about how they often spent their Saturdays taking the girls for a walk in Washington Square.

On a whim she set the empty basket next to the front of the building and walked toward the park. A few blocks from home, as she turned onto 4th Street, she started noticing disapproving looks from other women—and some men.

She realized the reason. She wasn't wearing a hat. She and her friends were used to crossing Leroy from each other's apartments, and going to and from the workshops without worrying about hats. But Annie couldn't remember a single time she'd ventured to Unruffled on Bleecker Street without her head being covered.

She was tempted to go home and call the outing over. And yet . . . She didn't.

With chin held high—pretending that going hatless was what she intended all along—Annie continued toward her goal, which suddenly gained an extra level of importance.

It was strange walking to the park without the girls, which made Annie realize how seldom—if ever?—she'd gone there alone. At least not recently.

When she and Sean were courting they'd often strolled through the park. But after the girls were born, their times there alone — or anywhere alone — had been few and far between.

Maybe that's why I feel such regret.

Regret?

I feel regret?

She was so stunned by the thought that she nearly stopped walking in the middle of Sixth Avenue. Not a good idea if she wanted to live another day.

She dodged traffic, hurried beneath the elevated train, and continued on 4th toward the promise of the park. Purposely, she kept her thoughts at bay until the canopy of green trees and grassy lawn drew her in.

She walked along a path toward the fountain in the middle, but was distracted by too many people noticing her bare head. So she took a sharp turn toward the northwest, away from the crowds. What she really wanted was to sit down, but surprisingly for the early morning hour, most benches were occupied. When a woman with a pram got up to leave, Annie rushed to take her seat. "Good day to you," she said.

The woman's eyes skimmed her head, then nodded and hurried away with her child — lest the child be corrupted by the sight of Annie's bare head? She was done with it. She had more important things on her mind.

And so she sat, ignored the man reading a newspaper at the other end of the bench, and let her thoughts go where they wished.

Unfortunately, they returned to the word "regret". *I have regrets about Sean and I.*

They'd been in the midst of a sour spot when President Wilson had sent the country into the war. Delicate and painful memories stepped forward, making Annie remember the many times — too many times — she'd resented Sean's unwavering certainty that he knew what was best in every situation. Even when he didn't. He really didn't.

When they were first married she'd welcomed his opinions. But as the years passed and her own confidence grew, patience had turned to annoyance. Unfortunately, she didn't hold her tongue as often as she should have, which had caused hurt feelings on both sides, as well as arguments that made the girls scurry to their bedroom and close the door.

I hated when we argued. It reminded me of Ma and Pa. Annie didn't like anything that reminded her of her parents. There were no fond memories of her family life back in Summerfield, only cringe-worthy memories of her father who'd beaten her brother to death, and her mother who had a similar predisposition of inflicting pain for pleasure. Annie and Sean never hurt each other physically. Yet emotionally?

There are so many should-have-saids, even during his final days at home.

Annie felt tears threaten and crossed her arms to help hold the emotions inside. She looked at her lap, not wanting anyone to see her pain. *I could have prevented most of the arguments if only I would have listened more than talked. If only I hadn't been so independent and . . . and right all the time.* They'd argued away a good portion of his last night together — over nothing important. *Father, please bring him home. I've learned from my mistakes. I'll love him as I should, and be patient and kind and . . . please bring him home to me.*

Annie stifled a sob, immediately wishing she had a handkerchief.

But then one appeared. She looked up and saw Guy standing before her.

She wiped her eyes, feeling completely embarrassed. "Where did you come from?"

"The stork brought me." He offered her his arm. "Shall we walk?"

She nodded and rose, letting him lead the way back toward the fountain and the arch.

"Would you like to tell me what's wrong?" he asked.

"No."

"Then perhaps we should talk about what's right." He pointed to the sky. "Look at that sky. Have you ever seen such a shade of blue? And those clouds . . . that one looks like a brown bear."

She glanced at the sky and had to laugh. "A white cloud looks like a brown bear?"

"It got you looking, didn't it?"

That it had.

"I know what would cheer you up. Ice cream." He led her past the fountain and south to the edge of the park. There she saw an eyesore of an establishment that she and Sean had heard gossip about. Surely Guy wasn't taking her there.

"Have you ever been to Grace Godwin's Garrett?"

"No, I can't say I've had the pleasure." Pleasure was the wrong word. The building on the corner of Washington Square South and Thompson looked as though it should be torn down.

"Instead of ice cream, we could go upstairs and have tea or if we wait long enough, perhaps a spaghetti dinner. It's a very unique place."

"Full of Bolsheviks and artsy types," Annie said. "I've heard the customers draw on the walls and Mrs. Godwin sings with a guitar."

"I believe she does."

"So you've been upstairs?" Annie asked.

"A few times. She does attract an interesting clientele." He patted her hand. "You're an artsy type. You might enjoy it."

"Not that type of artsy."

"How do you know?"

As they drew closer Annie felt uncomfortable. The street level *did* advertise ice cream and Coca-Cola, and had a sign saying "Oasis of Washington Square". Annie loved ice cream, but had no wish to enter the building.

A middle-aged woman appeared at the second-story window, leaning out against its sash.

To Annie's dismay, Guy called out to her. "Heya Grace!"

"Well I'll be. How ya doin', Guy?"

"Fairly well."

She looked at Annie, then said, "I'll say. Bring your lady friend upstairs. I'll make you something special."

Annie realized she was a woman with a bare head, walking with a man. What kind of woman did Grace think she was?

Annie applied pressure to Guy's arm. "Not today, please. I need to get home."

"Another time," Guy called.

They turned west and walked away.

"Did something offend you?" Guy asked.

"No, it's fine, but I want to get home."

"Where are the girls?"

Annie didn't dare say they were staying the weekend with Vesta. "Edna has them. I'm due to pick them up." After crossing Sixth, Annie let go of Guy's arm. "It was nice seeing you, but I can make it from here."

"What kind of gentleman would I be if I didn't escort you home?"

She realized there was no way to handle this politely, and so she faced him. "Mr. Ship, I need to part ways right here. My friends and family are expecting me. I've been gone too long."

He glanced back toward the park. "Why were you there – alone – in the first place?"

"Good day to you, sir. I'll see you at the store soon."

She hurried away, nearly running. She only glanced back once and was put off to see Guy was still standing there, watching her. *At least he's not following me.*

Once she turned the corner and reached Leroy, Annie ran the last block, into her building, and up three flights to her apartment. She'd left it unlocked but now locked it behind her.

Her chest ached from the unusual exertion. She leaned her back against the door, letting herself slip to the floor.

Where she cried.

For so many reasons.

⤻

"You're going with Gela to Refuge, again?" Antonio asked. "Why?"

It was a complex question, which required a complex answer that wasn't clear even to Maude.

"She wants to hear me sing again," Gela said as she tied her shoes.

Matteo put on his cap, ready to go to work—even on a Saturday. "Don't go singing around here."

"Why not?"

"You'll make the neighbor's dog howl."

Gela started to respond, then saw his wink. Instead she turned to her father. "Papa, why don't you come with us? I'm going to tell everyone that I got a part on Broadway."

"I'd like to, *cara,* but I am showing a client some properties."

"Some of us have to bring in the money," Matteo said.

Gela put her hands on her hips. "I'll be making money too."

He gave them a salute goodbye, then left. They heard him singing on the stairs in an overly dramatic, off-tune voice, "'Let me call you sweetheart, I'm in love with you. Let me hear you whisper, that you love me . . .'"

They heard the front door close.

A dog howled.

Maude laughed. "Not totally bad."

Gela shook her head. "It was awful, but the song . . . I know that one. I'll sing it at Refuge today. I'm sure Mack knows it."

"Oh it's Mack now?"

"He said I could call him that, now that we're working together." She kissed her father on the forehead then headed to the door. "Come on, Mama, let's go."

⤻

Mack knew the song, and Gela sang "Let Me Call You Sweetheart", getting everyone to join in.

But Maude wasn't interested in everyone. Only in one person.

She sat at a table and angled her chair to see Gela while still being able to glance at the door to check each and every person who entered. *Come on, Dock. Get here.*

Maude found it unnerving to want her attacker to show up, while cringing at the very thought of him. She acknowledged a definite stirring inside, as though new elements had been added to who she was, making her someone different. Different good or different bad was yet to be determined.

The song ended and Maude applauded with the rest. Then Mack stepped away from the piano and put his arm around Gela's shoulder. "Ladies and gentlemen, you who have enjoyed the singing of this lovely young lady, I want to inform you that she is not just any singer, but recently became a professional performer on Broadway."

There were happy murmurs and shouts of congratulations.

"What show?"

"'Irene,'" Gela said, beaming. "Opening night is November the eighteenth."

"You get us some free tickets and we'll fill the house!" a man said.

Gela looked to Mack. "Can we do that?"

"We'll see what we can do. Meanwhile, want to hear another one?"

Of course they did.

After an hour Maude was getting antsy. She excused herself from the table where she'd been sitting with an elderly couple who slurped their soup something awful, and strolled around the room. A mother holding a baby on her shoulder dropped a blanket. Maude retrieved it for her, and when she looked up . . .

There he was. Just coming in.

Their eyes met. Then Dock Varner turned around and fled.

Maude hurried through the crowd, toward the door. She went outside and saw him walking down the street, on the brink of a run.

She went after him, walking as fast as she could. "Pardon, pardon," she said as she stepped around people on the sidewalk.

He looked over his shoulder and saw her. He dashed away.

Maude had no choice but to run. She held her side, her corset fighting against her expanded lungs.

"Ma'am, is something wrong?" a man asked.

"I'm fine," she said as she ran, then immediately wondered if she should have stopped and asked for assistance.

She kept her eye on Dock's black bobbing head, and saw him turn left into an alley. She reached it and —

He stepped in front of her.

She took a step back.

His eyes were intense. "Get away from here," he said. "Go back where you belong."

It was hard to breathe. Hard to talk. "I want to speak with you."

He pushed her away. "Go!"

Maude felt the gaze of many eyes from the street, the alley, and from the windows above. She had no choice but to leave. But as she began to walk, she turned toward him one last time. "Admit it. You remember me from another alley in Chelsea thirteen years ago."

He hesitated just a moment and his forehead furrowed. "Go on! Git!"

Maude hurried away, ignoring the curious looks of those she passed.

Eventually her heart returned to a normal rhythm, but her mind and emotions ran full speed. What had she been thinking, running after him? Running into a dangerous situation?

I know he remembers me. I know he does.

She paused outside the door to Refuge, hearing her daughter singing inside. She took a deep breath, and with difficulty, transformed herself from Maude, the victim into Maude, the mother.

CHAPTER NINE

"Yummy, Mama."

Alice licked her fingers, making an awful noise, but Annie didn't chastise her. Not this morning. Not after having the girls gone from Friday night to Sunday after church. She'd missed every noise they made.

Victoria unpeeled a large bit of her Chelsea roll, picking the currants out of it, popping them into her mouth separate from the bun.

"Why do you do that?" Annie asked.

She shrugged. "I like to count how many I get. I'm up to nine."

Alice pouted. "I want to count too, but mine's all gone."

"Would you like another one?"

She looked surprised. "Yes, please."

Annie put one on her plate and set a second one on Victoria's plate too. "Help your sister count."

They proceeded to make quite a mess, plucking out the currants as if on a treasure dig. On a normal day, Annie would have forbid them from playing with their food, and would have never given each girl a second sugary bun. But as she watched them count the fruit, her heart softened and she felt a warmth that had been hiding the past few months. The reasons for her discontent were logical and could even be forgiven. She missed Sean. Greatly.

But after getting her coveted time alone — and spending some disconcerting time with Guy — she'd had enough. She'd spent Saturday afternoon tidying up the apartment, and Sunday morning counting her blessings in church. At the sound of their footfalls on the stairs, her heart had beat double-time in anticipation. She'd thrown open the door and had taken them into her arms with a grateful heart, full of joy that they were back.

Victoria broke through the memory. "You seem different, Mama. What happened?"

Annie flicked the tip of her nose. "I was sad without you, and now I'm happy you're back."

Alice shook her head. "We didn't have time to miss you, Mama."

Well then.

"Sixteen!" Victoria shouted, pointing to her plate. "I have sixteen currants and Alice has twelve. I win!"

We all win.

Annie had a late morning with her girls before Vesta came over to watch them. Henrietta's boys were added, allowing Annie and Henrietta to walk to Unruffled together. When they entered they expected to see Birdie and Sara running things. Edna's presence was a welcome surprise.

But her face was glum. "Unfortunately, you come in time to hear bad news." She nodded to Birdie. "Tell her, dear."

Birdie Doyle, always tiny in stature, looked like a child as she turned toward Annie, her head down, her hands keeping each other company. "I'm so sorry. It wasn't my doing."

Thoughts of torn dresses or missing money came to mind. "What happened?"

"Nothing really happened, it just . . . oh dear."

"Gracious, Birdie," Edna said. "Tell her."

Birdie took a fresh breath. "Johnny's pa died."

"I'm so sorry. If you need time off for the funeral and such, then by all means—"

Birdie shook her head. "We're moving to the family farm in Dutchess County. His ma needs our help running it."

Annie was stunned. She could have handled torn dresses or money problems, but losing Birdie? "You've been here since the beginning," was all she could say.

She nodded. "You hired me after Johnny stole two dresses and I brought 'em back and asked for a job." Her eyes scanned the room. "I loved working here. You were always so kind, even giving me time away when I had Little John."

Birdie looked on the verge of tears, so Annie held her close, for her own sake as much as Birdie's. "We're going to miss you."

She stepped back, wiping her eyes. "I'm sorry to leave you in a lurch like this, but we're leaving today. The funeral, and then moving in with his mother . . ."

Birdie looked miserable. The women added their own hugs, and Annie asked if she wanted to choose one of the black dresses for the funeral. She did.

What a bittersweet goodbye gift.

Not fifteen minutes after hearing the news, Birdie was gone.

"Now what?" Henrietta asked.

"We need a replacement," Sara said. "Business is picking up again."

Edna was already creating a "Clerk Needed" sign. She set it in the window. "If this doesn't work, we can place an ad."

Almost immediately a sturdy-looking woman came in the door and snatched the sign out of the window. "You hiring?"

"That was fast," Edna said under her breath.

Annie stepped forward to greet her. "We are indeed. And your name is . . .?"

"Tildie Pruitt."

"Nice to meet you, Mrs. — "

"Miss."

"Miss Pruitt. Let's step over here so we can chat."

They moved away from the main part of the store, and Annie gathered two chairs from the fitting room area. "Now then. Tell me about your work experience."

Miss Pruitt scratched the back of her head. "During the war I was a conductor on a streetcar — took up for men who left to fight."

"I've seen women in that position," Annie said.

"Saw."

"Saw?"

"We were forced out by the law."

Annie had no idea what she was talking about. "What law?"

Miss Pruitt set the Clerk Wanted sign on her lap. "The one that limited the number of hours women could work."

Annie smiled, enjoying the woman's spunk. "I'm afraid I'm not familiar."

The woman set the sign on the floor to free her hands when she talked, her bag dangling wildly from its handle around her wrist. "Everything was hunky-dory until the men came home and wanted their jobs back. We women workers put up a stink and most of us kept our jobs — for a while. But then they passed that stupid law limiting the hours we could work because they didn't want us standing so long, saying it was a detriment to our health. Ha! Sakes alive. So our legs are different than men's? Sitting all the time ain't good for a person anyways; it doesn't exercise your muscles. Ain't the law ridiculous?"

"It is." Annie had to make a valid point. "You would be on your feet many hours at a time while working here."

"Exactly. So I's ready to do it."

Annie wasn't sure whether *she* was ready to have Miss Pruitt represent Unruffled.

The woman wasn't done with her complaints. "Then the law insulted us more, saying we were only earning money to buy candy and orchids." She tossed her hands in the air. "Talk about outlandish. I need money for rent and food like everybody else."

"Pardon me, but if the companies would let you stay on in spite of the law, how exactly did the law hurt you?"

"Shorter hours, don't you see." She sighed deeply, ending it with a loud sniff. "The companies need us to work more hours, but after the law we women can't. It says we can't work more than nine hours per day between the hours of 6 a.m. and 10 p.m. and no more than six days each week. I was willing to work as many hours as they gave me. I don't have a husband or children. I loved my work. I got to meet lots of people. But they didn't care. They let us go and hired men who could work whatever hours the company wanted them to." She calmed herself with a fresh breath. "There were 1600 of us women working the cars, and I tell you this, we're not going to take it. We're looking to get the law repealed."

Her passion was . . . so passionate.

"Until then, I's looking for work. I was walking past and saw your sign and decided *why the fiddle not?* and came in." She looked around "What exactly do you sell? I didn't pay much attention."

"We sell ladies dresses and are expanding our line to include bridal."

"Wedding dresses and such?"

"Yes . . ." Annie didn't quite understand the question.

Miss Pruitt stood, retrieved the sign, and gave it back to Annie. "This ain't for me then 'cuz I hate men."

Annie felt herself gawking. "You do?"

She nodded. "Never saw much need fer 'em. And if you ask me," she leaned forward confidentially, "the troubles of the world are caused by men, and they've proved over and over they aren't able to fix what they mess up. So long ago I determined I don't needs them."

"Hopefully women will get a chance to vote next year. Then we'll have a voice."

"I looks forward to it." She extended a hand for Annie to shake. "Nice talking to you, ma'am. Sorry it didn't work out."

Annie was left speechless, as if she'd had the wind knocked out of her. Edna and Henrietta came to her side. "I take it she wasn't hired?" Edna asked.

"It wasn't up to me. Turns out she didn't want the job."

"Then why did she come in?"

"Long story. Let's just say she wasn't a good fit."

She set the sign back in the window.

❧

Maude checked in at the workshop and found Myrtle and Mary hard at work. She answered their questions, knew she should stay and cut another dress, but told them she would be back soon.

She took a streetcar back to the Refuge neighborhood, and with the asking of a few questions, walked to the local police precinct.

"May I help you, miss?"

"I already spoke to Sargent Ramsey over in the Village, and he said he was going to contact someone here about my complaint."

"Which is?"

There were a lot of people in the lobby. She didn't want to say it aloud. "It's a bit sensitive. Could you please go ask the officers here if they've spoken to Sargent Ramsey about Mrs. Antonio Ricci?"

He gave her an annoyed look, but left his desk and went in the back. She heard voices, and soon he returned, shaking his head. "Sorry, miss. No one knows anything about it."

She was struck dumb.

"Now, if there's nothing else, other people are waiting."

Maude started to turn around, then turned back. "There is something else. I need to make a report. Here. Now."

He hesitated, as if sizing her up. She gave him her most determined, I'm-not-leaving look.

"Come with me."

Maude followed him into a large room with many desks manned by officers. A few nodded, a few smiled, and a few looked away as though not wanting to be bothered.

She was brought to the desk of a man who had a nameplate: Sargent Wilkerson. He stood.

The desk officer introduced her. "This here is . . ."

He'd already forgotten. Maude took over, extending her hand to Wilkerson. "My name is Maude Ricci."

He shook her hand. "Thank you, Sargent," he told the officer.

Maude heard him muttering as he walked away. "She never said her name was Maude. I would have remembered 'Maude', my sister's name is Maude."

Sargent Wilkerson chuckled. "Have a seat and tell me how I can help you."

She liked him immediately, and found new hope that justice could finally be done. She went through the same information she had given Sargent Ramsey, adding, "Last week I followed him from Refuge to where he lives." She repeated. "Dock Varner. I want you to go arrest him."

"I know him," the Sargent said.

"You do?"

"He's a vagrant. Used to work on the docks but got the influenza and missed enough work they let him go. He's not all *there*," he said, pointing to his head. "But he's harmless."

Maude had trouble processing her thoughts. "He's far from harmless. He raped me and hurt me enough that I can never have children."

The Sargent looked down. "Oh. Dear. I am sorry for that, ma'am. But it seems far removed from the Dock we all know. He's not a violent person."

She'd stood and raised her voice, causing other officers to look in her direction. "Not now, maybe. But he was!"

"Sit down, Miss Ricci."

"Mrs. Ricci."

He corrected himself. "I'd like to help you, but there's no evidence to convict him for a crime thirteen years ago. Especially since you didn't file a police report which might have provided a description of your assailant. Although I doubt it would match the Dock we see today."

"*I* recognized him." She thought of something else. "And he recognized me. That should count for something. He ran when he saw me looking at him."

"Perhaps he was frightened by the intensity of your gaze. Vagrants can be skittish."

All hope slipped away and hid under a desk, never to be found again. "So you're not going to do anything?"

"There's nothing I can do."

"You could at least talk to him."

"I have talked to him. He's spent a few nights in jail when he was found passed out from drink." Sargent Wilkerson sat back in his chair. "He's a broken man, Mrs. Ricci. Dragging him in here for questioning, or locking him up for a crime that can't be proven against him, will only make his life worse. Is that what you want?"

"What about my life?"

He clasped his hands on his desk. "You're married. From your clothes I would say you live a life of comparable ease in a nice home, yes?"

That was beside the point.

"Your husband provides well for you?"

"He does, but I also work. I'm a partner in the store Unruffled on Bleecker Street."

"I'm afraid I don't know it."

"We sell women's dresses."

He shrugged. "I'm sorry you and Mr. Ricci can't have children, but—"

She drew in a breath. "Actually, he was a widower when I met him and had two children."

"Who have become your children?"

I never should have brought them up. "Yes. They are my children."

He spread his hands, finalizing his point. "I am very sorry for your past suffering, Mrs. Ricci, but I suggest you leave it in the past, enjoy the life you have been given, and count your many blessings. Dock Varner has none of those blessings. *If* he was your attacker, he has suffered beyond the law in ways I wouldn't wish on an enemy."

She couldn't argue with him. She wanted to. But couldn't.

~

Gela sat beside her brother on the El, heading to her first rehearsal. He whittled a piece of wood, letting shavings fall to the floor.

"You're making a mess."

He glanced around the train car. "It's not the cleanest place."

"That doesn't mean you should make it worse."

He moved the shavings together with his feet, picked them up, and dropped them in his pocket.

"That's better."

He shrugged.

She felt bad for getting after him. "Thank you for taking me to rehearsal. I know it's out of your way."

"Papa and Ma say it's necessary."

"I'm not sure it is."

He stopped whittling. "You've never been to the area, have ya?"

"I have," she said proudly. "We went to the theater on 48th for my audition."

He shrugged again. "Then you know it is necessary. It ain't the best place for a girl to be."

"*Isn't* the best place."

"Like I said."

Gela *did* realize that. With the dark created by the elevated train, and the older buildings, Gela knew it was best to walk briskly, with conviction.

The train slowed for the 50th Street Station. They both got out and walked down to street level. Matteo began to walk south on Sixth with her, but Gela stopped him. "You need to get to work. You don't need to walk with me. It's just a few blocks."

"But I promised. And *I* want you safe."

She was touched by his concern — and theirs. "You got me this far the first day, and I appreciate it, but I don't want you going with me every day. It's unnecessary."

He kicked a newspaper that was fluttering around their feet. "I'll walk you all the way today. After that, you can work it through with our parents."

Agreed. She took his arm and they walked toward her future.

෴

Mack met Gela in front of the theater. She was relieved to see a friendly face as her stomach was in knots.

She introduced him to Matteo. "Now there's a nice brother," Mack said.

"Yes, he is. But I told him he didn't need to be my chaperone after today."

"No, he doesn't," Mack said. "Cuz I'll be. Like I told your parents, I take the El home myself. We'll take it together."

Gela felt great relief. Not that she was afraid of the daily travel to and from, but Mack's presence would get Matteo off the hook with her parents.

"I best be going," Matteo said. "Nice meeting you, Mr. McGinness."

"Mack. Everybody calls me Mack."

Matteo walked back toward the station and Mack showed Gela to a side door. "This is the way you come in for rehearsals."

It was certainly a lesser entrance than the front where she'd entered with her parents. Inside it zigged and zagged to the back of the stage area. There, two dozen people engaged in lively chatter. *My castmates.*

Mack drew her front and center, clapping his hands. "Everyone! I'd like to introduce you to Gela Ricci, one of the debutantes."

A pretty blonde stepped forward and took her arm. "I'm Maggie. Stick with me, Gela. You're one of us now."

What a glorious thought.

෴

Gela had never felt so completely and utterly filled up, as if one more teaspoon of happiness would make her spill over. She was relieved she could read the music fairly well, and learned from her mistakes quickly. Other than in church she had never sung with a group, and found the mixture of male and female voices pure pleasure.

As the rehearsal progressed she lost track of time. When the director broke for lunch she wouldn't have been surprised if someone had said an hour had passed.

Lunch? She'd never thought about bringing a lunch. But then she noticed no one else had brought a tin with them either.

Edith Day must have noticed her look of confusion. "Come, Gela. Let's show you the wonders of Gold's Delicatessen."

"I . . . I didn't bring money for lunch."

"Not to worry. It's on me, today, since this is your very first production."

The whole group walked a block away and entered Gold's en masse. They swarmed over numerous tables in a corner by a window, as if this was their usual spot. A waitress came over and actors began barking out lunch orders.

Edith raised a hand and said, "Gela and I will have the pastrami on rye. Two pickles each."

Gela was grateful, but said, "I've never had pastrami."

"Then you haven't truly lived."

After the first bite, Gela agreed.

❧

Henrietta waited outside Steven's room while Edna was inside, softly coaxing him into their outing. *Please, God . . .*

She was surprised when the door opened and Edna came out with a smile and a small nod.

"Papa's going?" Willie asked.

"Papa's going," Edna said.

The boys burst into his room, chattering happily. Henrietta took advantage of the distraction and asked her mother-in-law, "How willing is he?"

She shrugged. "He's going. That's the important thing."

A few minutes later, Steven emerged from the bedroom, buttoning his jacket. He avoided Henrietta's gaze, but she decided to act normal — as much as that was possible. She kissed his cheek. "It's a lovely day to go to the park. Not as hot as it has been."

Talking about the weather? Really?

"I'll carry the picnic basket," Willie said.

"I want to help," Lennie said, trying to grab it away.

Henrietta opened its lid and removed a small tablecloth. "Would you carry this, Lennie? I'm afraid it will get wrinkled in the basket."

He carefully draped the tablecloth over his arm, smoothing it. "I'll be careful, Mama."

"Then we're off."

Henrietta saw Steven give his mother a doubtful look. More than doubtful, fearful. *What have I gotten us into?*

The boys led the way outside. Henrietta took her husband's arm and they walked up Leroy toward Washington Square while the boys skipped ahead.

Henrietta found herself tongue-tied. She and Steven had always had an easy way of it, and their conversation always flowed. But since he came back . . . She raked her mind, trying to find something to talk about. Gela's new adventure seemed the most interesting, so she prattled on, giving too many details, eager to keep the monologue going. Steven gave no response at all, though he did seem to be listening.

When they reached 4th and Sixth and had to cross the busy street, Lennie wasn't paying attention and began to walk when he shouldn't have.

"Stop!" Steven said, pulling him back to the sidewalk.

Henrietta waited for him to say more, to explain the dangers of not being careful, but Steven simply put a hand on the boy's head as they waited to cross together.

Being a Monday, the park wasn't busy, and they easily found a long bench to have their lunch. "Look at the sky, Steven," she said, pointing to the clouds above. "You like the sky."

He looked up, and his gaze stayed in the heavens. Meanwhile, Henrietta spread the tablecloth on the seat and began removing the sandwiches.

"Let's sit on the grass," Willie said.

Lennie nodded. "I want to use my table cloth on the grass, not the bench."

She looked to Steven for a nay or yay. "There are fences to keep us on the bench side. I don't think they'd like us ruining the grass."

"We wouldn't ruin it, we'd just sit on it," Lennie said.

That was true. Henrietta was just about to say yes, when Willie added, "Let's go sit under the Hangman's Elm."

Henrietta was alarmed. She'd never mentioned the infamous tree. "We will not. And how do you know about it?"

"Some friends told me. They said people were hanged there."

"That's just a story people like to tell," Henrietta said. "I don't think it's true." She turned to Steven. "Is it true?"

His body was tense and he gripped the seat of the bench. His eyes flit left and right, toward the fountain, toward the bus stop, to two women riding by on bicycles, to some men having a discussion as they smoked cigars.

"Steven?"

Suddenly, he stood up from the bench. "No talk of death."

Before she could stop him, he bolted down the walk, heading toward home.

"Steven!"

He didn't stop. He didn't look back.

"Where's Papa going?"

Henrietta gathered the picnic supplies, took Lennie's hand, and followed him.

"Did I say something wrong?" Willie asked.

Apparently.

"What about the picnic?"

Henrietta stopped. They were right. What about the picnic? Steven was probably headed home. He would run upstairs and close himself off in his room whether she went after him or not.

"Let's have our picnic. On the grass."

"By the Hangman's Tree?"

"On the grass."

Steven would be there when they got home.

Edna wasn't home when Henrietta and the boys stopped by after the picnic. She knocked, but when no one answered she used her key. The door to Steven's room was closed and Henrietta called through it. "Steven? Are you all right?"

No answer.

"Steven?"

"I'm fine."

"We kept some lunch for you."

"No thank you."

"All right then. We'll be upstairs if you need us." *We need* you.

Back in their flat, Henrietta got the boys interested in some tin toys, then sat at the kitchen table and wrote a letter to her mother. She began by mentioning that something had happened to Steven and she was worried, and he was staying at his mother's, and —

She stopped writing. Her mother didn't need Henrietta's problems added to her own. Europe had more to deal with after the war than America did, for they'd been in the war nearly three years longer than the United States. She had no idea the number of soldiers killed but knew Europe's portion had to be incrementally more. During the war Mother's letters always included news about some acquaintance or friend who had died, and some deprivation of food or supplies. Daily life had been altered — and still was. Plus, Mamma was still grieving.

I can't tell her about Steven. He's here. He's alive. He'll be fine. Eventually.

And so Henrietta spoke of light and pleasing subjects: the boys and Unruffled. Once again she ended with her plea: *Please come visit soon . . .*

&

Edna felt a bit foolish balancing a fruitcake on her lap on the elevated train. A few passengers gave her the eye and more than one made a comment about it smelling tasty. She hoped so. She hoped Mr. McGinness would like it.

She got off at the 50th Street stop and walked back to 48th. The area was not friendly like the streets of Greenwich Village. Garbage was scattered and piled, and people sat in doorways. They all put out a cap or cup, asking for money.

I bet they'd enjoy the cake.

She walked faster. The cake was for Mr. McGinness — and the cast, or whoever he wanted to share it with. The idea to make it came last night. She'd felt a bit like a schoolgirl trying to please a beau, but had continued with her plan. What would it hurt? He'd come to sing for her, she could bring him a cake.

She reached the Vanderbilt Theatre, and wasn't surprised the front doors were locked. She went around the side and found an entrance. She slipped inside, and let the voices lead her through the dimly lit halls. She didn't hear Mack's voice, but a mixture of people talking at once, and some singing, like there were many groups rehearsing at once.

Suddenly she realized she hadn't fully thought this through. She couldn't barge in and bring him treats. It was totally inappropriate. *What was I thinking?*

Then she heard some giggles off to the right. "Oooh, Mack. You naughty boy."

Then his voice, low and sultry. "You have no idea . . ."

When she heard kissing sounds she turned on her heels and left the way she'd come, out the door, down the sidewalk, past the beggars —

She stopped. "Here." She handed one of them the fruitcake. "Enjoy."

She heard his thanks, and strode toward the El, chastising herself for opening herself up to a man.

Edna kept herself busy at Unruffled, putting stray items back where they belonged. It was nearly closing time and they had been especially busy since Birdie's departure. Too busy to worry about the likes of Mack McGinness. And too busy to worry about Steven and Henrietta's picnic. She hoped it had gone all right. Getting out into the world, into "normal" should help him. Shouldn't it?

Then Edna got an idea. Maybe having friends around would also help her son.

As she watched Annie count out the money drawer, she shared her idea. "Why don't you and the girls come over for dinner Thursday. I'll invite Henrietta and the boys. And Vesta. And of course, Steven is there."

"Thursday? We'd love to. Any special occasion?"

Actually . . . "It's my birthday."

Annie blinked. "August the seventh. It is! I'm so sorry, I nearly forgot!"

She heard the bell on the door open. "I'd say I'm too old to remind you, but I guess I just did. You'll come then?"

"Of course. But you shouldn't have to cook for others. It's your day."

"I don't mind a bit. My apartment works well for our gatherings."

"That it does. At least let me bake you a cake," Annie said.

"Cake, you say?" came a man's voice.

Edna turned around and saw Mr. McGinness, standing nearby, hat in hand. Her anger flared. "May I help you, Mr. McGinness?"

"I'd really like if you called me Mack."

She ignored him.

Annie piped up. "You're Mr. McGinness?"

He chuckled. "You've heard of me?"

Edna flashed Annie a look—which she caught. "Edna and Gela have spoken of you, of your playing at Fort Refuge."

"Port," he said. "As in 'port in a storm'? Port Refuge."

"Of course."

"You must be Mrs. Culver."

"I am." They shook hands. "Very nice to meet you."

"And you." He grinned at Edna. "Back to the cake . . . I love cake."

Again, Annie answered. "I'm baking Edna a birthday cake."

"The best kind," he said. "As I said, I love cake."

Annie looked between them, then said "Edna?"

She was backed into a corner. "I'm having a dinner party Thursday."

"I'd love to come," he said.

They all turned when Sara pulled down the shade on the door.

"You're closing."

"We are."

"I will see you on Thursday then," he said. "What time?"

Edna wished she hadn't invited him, but it was too late now. "Seven."

He swept his hat into a bow like a gallant. "I will be there."

He moved to the door. Edna felt a nudge and called after him. "May I speak with you a minute, Mr. McGinness?"

"Of course."

She led him away from Annie and Sara. "I saw you today. Or rather, I heard you."

"You did?"

"I came to the theater." She didn't mention the fruit cake.

His forehead furrowed, but for only a moment. "I didn't see you."

Her anger stirred. "Actually, I didn't *see* you either, I heard you. Kissing someone. I believe the woman — girl, by the sound of her voice — said, 'Oooh, Mack. You naughty boy.'"

There was the slightest flash of panic in his eyes, then he shook his head. "I don't think so. I play piano during the rehearsals. Did you hear music?"

"Well, yes, I heard singing."

"There you have it. Whatever you think you heard . . . it wasn't me."

The possibility of his innocence opened, then closed when she remembered, "She said your name."

"You must have misheard." He tried to take her hand, but she pulled it away. "Edna . . . you should have made your presence known. I would have loved to see you and introduce you to all the cast." Then his eyes widened. "I bet you heard someone talking with Max, who works with the props. He's quite the ladies man."

Mack? Max? It *was* possible.

He must have seen she was wavering, for he touched her hand again. This time she didn't pull away.

"I came here to see you, dear lady. And I thank you for coming to see me. I just wish you wouldn't have let an odd incident scare you off."

"It didn't scare me off. I . . . I just thought you were . . . and I didn't like it."

"Of course not. *If* it had been me. Which it wasn't." He tilted his head and gave her a smile that melted away any doubt. "It's closing time.

I should go. I look forward to seeing you Thursday." He tipped his hat and left.

Sara locked the door behind him.

Edna sighed deeply.

"He's a charmer," Annie said.

"Almost too much so," Edna said.

Sara brought the key back to Annie. "A man can't have too much charm."

Annie and Edna both replied at once: "Oh yes he can."

Edna was pretty sure Annie wasn't talking about Mack.

~

Sam Colyer liked getting his hands dirty at the garage. He was good at it, though oddly, he had the impression his skill was recently learned. He wished he could remember. He had the bonnet of a truck open and was adjusting the carburetor when a man came in the garage.

"Will it live?" the man asked.

Sam laughed and wiped his hands on a cloth that lived in his pocket. "I believe so. Vulcans are good vehicles."

The man put his hand on its fender. "Up until now this one's been a good workhorse for my carpentry business."

"What do you make?"

"Furniture, cupboards, whatever people need."

"Business picking up?"

"It is." The man held out his hand. "Timothy Billings."

"Sam Colyer. Nice to meet you."

"You asked about business. It's doing well enough that I could use another lorry, so I just bought one."

"What kind?"

"A 1914 Leyland S-type. Dropside."

Sam nodded. "You'll like that feature. Makes loading and unloading easier."

"That's my hope." Timothy took off his cap, ran a hand through his unruly gray hair, and said, "But here's my issue. It's an RAF type, used as a mobile workshop while fixing planes. After the war, the Leyland company bought most of them back from the government to recondition and sell."

"I heard that. The government was auctioning them off and the company didn't want their good reputation sullied by lorries that needed work so they bought them and fixed them themselves."

"All except this one, I'm afraid. It needs more than a reconditioning."

"I can fix it."

"You're confident."

Sam shrugged. "Haven't found one I couldn't fix."

"Capital. I'll bring it by tomorrow."

He turned to the Vulcan. "This one will be done for you by then."

"Very good." Timothy turned to leave. "You're American."

"I am."

"You were a soldier?"

"I was."

"You stayed here. You find a good English lass to love?"

Sam cocked his head.

Timothy pointed to Sam's ring. "You're married."

Sam twisted the ring. "I am. But not to someone here. At least I don't think so."

Mr. Billings' eyebrows rose. "You have my interest."

"I lost my memory. I woke up in a British army hospital with no identification."

"You said you were Sam Colyer."

"The nurses told me to choose a name until I remember my real one."

Timothy chuckled. "You're in an odd spot then."

"That, I am."

"Since you can't remember, maybe you are married to a British girl."

Sam shook his head. "I don't think so. I'm here, but I don't belong here."

"How are you going to find out where you do belong?"

Sam snickered. "You tell me that one, and I'll do it." He pointed to the truck with his screw driver. "Until then, I work, and wait for God to make me a miracle."

Timothy nodded. "He's known to do that on occasion. You *are* alive."

"I am. One miracle done. And hopefully one more coming."

"Until then, you'll fix my trucks?"

"That, I will."

CHAPTER TEN

Edna opened her eyes. It was still dark. Moonlight lit the clock on her dresser: half-past five. And then she remembered . . .

Happy birthday to me.

She was glad Steven was still asleep for she needed some quiet time to let her birthday sink in. For it wasn't just any birthday, it was her sixtieth. "I'm an old woman," she whispered.

She sat up in bed, letting the covers fall away. The night wasn't hot, but the breeze fluttering the curtains was welcome. Edna liked to sleep with fresh air coming in, even in winter—for as long as she could stand it. More than once she'd awakened to a cold nose and snow on the floor.

Ernie liked the cold as much as I did.

She smiled at the thought of her late husband, who'd been gone for twenty years. He'd indulged her in so many ways. He always bought her the most modern kitchen appliances. "I'm doing it for me. I'm selfish. I love your cooking." Same with the open window. "I'm doing it for me. I'm selfish. The cold makes you cuddle with me."

Ernie was the most unselfish person she'd ever known. His unselfishness had killed him.

Edna loved fish—shad to be more particular. Decades earlier, in early May, Edna had told Ernie she had a hankering for fresh shad. Though a boney fish, she especially loved the roe as the fish headed upstream to spawn. She remembered saying it in passing. But as often happened, Ernie embraced her whim as a cause, and stepped forward to make it a reality. He went with a friend to the Hudson River where they boarded a rowboat and set out to get Edna some dinner.

Neither one of them had expected the freakish lightning storm or the high winds and heavy rain. The friend later told Edna that when the boat capsized he had repeatedly tried to dive down to find Ernie. But all he recovered that day (for Ernie did wash ashore later) was Ernie's brown bowler hat.

Yes, indeed, Ernie was an unselfish man, dying in pursuit of Edna's supper.

She hadn't eaten fish since.

Edna tried to rationalize the tragedy, remembering how much Ernie enjoyed fishing, and enjoyed pleasing her, but to little avail. Dead was dead. Knowing it was an accident, that the weather had surprised everyone that day, didn't help. It wasn't anyone's fault, but somehow that made it harder to accept. She wanted to blame somebody and so she blamed herself. If only she hadn't mentioned her love of shad.

After months of beating herself up to the point of surrender, it had been Steven — almost sixteen — who finally pulled her out of the pit. He'd found her sitting on the side of her bed, head down, shoulders slumped, holding Ernie's bowler against her chest.

He'd quietly walked into the room and said, "Pa was going to get me my own bowler for my birthday."

"He was?"

Steven had nodded. "Can I have Pa's hat instead?"

Edna put the hat on her son's head and was surprised that it fit. She'd always thought of Steven as a boy, but he wasn't. He was grown. And yet . . . at that moment Edna shoved aside her selfish melancholy. He needed her *here*, engaged in this and every moment of his life.

Together they'd moved past the pain, grief, and blame. Together they'd stepped into the new century side by side.

She was proud of how she'd encouraged Steven to go to college, to move on, away from home — even though a good part of her had wanted him to stay. She had continued to sell sewing machines at Macy's, rarely missing a day. She'd found a way to stay in their apartment plus pay for Steven's education, all the while supplying him with a safe haven at home, with happy memories, old and new.

God had helped, more than a little. For as she and Steven traveled through hard times, their faith had grown. They'd both held tight to that, and she could honestly say that she and the Almighty were on good terms.

And yet . . . on days such as today, when faced with one of life's milestones, she missed Ernie with an ache that threatened to crush her.

She let the tears come. After a good cry she wiped them dry and got out of bed. She had a birthday party to think about.

And then, with a laugh, she decided what they'd eat for dinner.

≈

Henrietta didn't have her head on straight.

It started when Lennie spilled his milk on the table where she'd been working on the books for Unruffled.

Panicked, she accidentally shoved all the bookkeeping paperwork onto the floor trying to save it.

Lennie cried and *she* wanted to cry as she dabbed at the soggy pages, despairing of ever getting everything in the right order again.

Then, while getting the boys dressed, she handed Willie Lennie's shoes. "These aren't mine, Mama. They're too little."

She brushed the error away. "They used to be yours. Hurry boys, we're late."

Henrietta put on a hat and slipped the soggy stack of papers into her briefcase. As she went to close the door, she noticed a strange, metallic smell. She looked to the stove. A burner was still on under the tea kettle! She rushed to turn off the gas, and found the kettle had burned dry.

"You don't have time for more tea, Mama," Willie said.

"I never had tea." To skip her morning cup was unheard of. Suddenly, the implications of what might have happened if she'd left with the stove on made her shudder. *Thank You for letting me see it.*

With one final scan of the apartment, she herded the boys out.

As they passed Edna's door, she contemplated checking on Steven, but because she was late, she didn't.

The boys stopped on a stair. "What about Papa? We want to see Papa."

But Papa doesn't want to see you. "Not today," she said.

"But I want to see him!" Lennie whined.

She did *not* have time for this, so she grabbed him by his hand and pulled him down the last flight and out the door, with Willie running after them.

By the time they crossed Leroy, both boys were crying.

People were looking.

She let go of Lennie's hand and slowed down. "Morning," she said to those on the sidewalk.

Their greetings contained a hint of wariness, and there was disapproval in their eyes.

"My shoe's untied, Mama," Lennie said.

She pointed to a step and he sat.

"Tie it," she told him. "You know how."

He began fumbling with the laces, making the loop, bringing the other lace around, but failing to get it in the right place.

"Here! I'll do it."

She set down the briefcase, then stooped to tie his shoe like she was tying up evil.

It was then she heard the women's voices. A trio stood close by — she knew each one of them. Snippets of their exchange reached her — on purpose?

"Yes, they are still living apart," said Mrs. Collier.

"There has to be something wrong with the marriage," said Mrs. Dupeau.

"For Steven to live with his mother . . . I wouldn't let my husband do such a thing," said Mrs. Hutchins. "It's not healthy."

You have no idea what I'm dealing with!

Henrietta was about to bring the boys inside to Annie's, when she heard Mrs. Hutchins add one more barb.

"Word is, Steven isn't right in the head."

That did it. Henrietta strode toward the women, causing them to expand their circle. "What gives you three biddies the right to judge *my* life?"

They looked at her aghast.

She moved close, wanting to yell directly in their faces. "If I'm not mistaken, Mrs. Collier, your daughter has been fancying around with a boy who's been caught stealing — more than once."

The woman put a hand to her chest.

"And you, Mrs. Hutchins? Didn't your husband get let go from his job?"

She looked away.

One more. "And you, Mrs. Dupeau, the leader of this little triad of cutthroats, I hear that your husband has been seen staggering home at the wee hours, having spent too much time and money at O'Malley's."

Mrs. Dupeau grabbed the arms of the other two and scurried away.

So there!

Henrietta's heart beat in her throat as she turned back to her boys. But they were not alone. Two other neighbors were with them, their arms around their shoulders. *Sheltering them. From me?*

And then, as the topper of all toppers, Henrietta glanced up and saw Steven looking down at her from his window.

Oh, Father, what have I done? She wanted to melt into a puddle.

She gathered the boys with a brusque, "Excuse us" and entered Annie's building.

She paused in the foyer, trying to calm her breathing. Her face felt on fire.

"Mama, are you all right?" Willie asked.

No, I'm not. She knelt down and drew them close. "I'm so sorry you had to see that. I was upset and said mean things to those ladies. It wasn't right."

"They said mean things about you and Papa."

"They did." She felt slightly vindicated. But only slightly. "We're supposed to turn the other cheek when wrong is done to us. Not return wrong with wrong."

Willie looked toward the front door. "That's hard."

"Yes, it is. And I failed." She ruffled their hair. "I will apologize to the ladies later." She kissed them and followed them up the stairs. *At least they've moved on.* She still felt out-of-step.

Vesta greeted the boys, who forgot all about their mother's drama and started playing with Victoria and Alice.

Henrietta turned to leave. "Thanks again, Vesta."

Vesta put her hand on Henrietta's arm. "Not so fast."

Reluctantly, Henrietta faced her, though she avoided eye contact.

"What's wrong?" Vesta asked.

Henrietta looked to the window. "You heard?"

Vesta shrugged. "Windows are open."

She dropped her briefcase to the floor with a thud. "I shouldn't have done that. It won't make things better. Everything they said was correct, but to hear them chittering about our lives when theirs are less than perfect . . ."

"Their gossiping has stabbed almost everyone in the neighborhood. But . . ."

Henrietta filled in the blank. "But I was wrong to snap at them."

Vesta smiled. "You didn't just snap at them, you eviscerated them by stabbing back."

She felt her remaining energy evaporate. She needed to regroup. "Do you have any water on for tea? I boiled my pot dry."

Vesta chuckled and gave her a hug. "You *have* had a day."

"I need a new one."

"A new teapot or a new day?"

"Both."

"Then make your day new. Come have a cup and start over. Where there's tea there's hope."

Henrietta sat down, and Lennie crawled into her lap. Henrietta stroked his hair. "It's been one thing after another lately. I'm making all the wrong choices, which just makes things worse."

Vesta sat in a nearby chair and Lennie climbed off Henrietta's lap into hers. "I have found a remedy for such times."

"Poison?"

Vesta gave her a look. "An antidote. Do something nice for someone else."

Henrietta didn't feel very nice at the moment.

"Didn't you tell me one of the Cohen brothers has been sick?"

The elderly Abel and Aaron Cohen lived with their sister, Berta. Henrietta had met them when she'd stupidly entered their jewelry store while it was being robbed. "You're right. Abel was sick."

Vesta spread her hands.

I've been meaning to visit. "I'll take him some flowers tomorrow."

"Do you feel better?" Vesta asked.

"Actually . . . yes." But then she felt an uneasy stirring and knew what else she needed to do. She stood and kissed Vesta on the cheek, hugged her boys, and set out.

❧

Two down, one to go.

Henrietta knocked on the door to Mrs. Hutchins' apartment. The older woman cracked the door, peering out.

"What do you want?"

"I wish to make amends. May I come in a moment?"

The woman hesitated, then opened the door. Henrietta stepped inside. The place was tidy, with simple furnishings. She suddenly worried that Mr. Hutchins was home. She glanced toward the bedrooms.

"He ain't here." She wiped her hands on her apron. "I don't rightly know where he's at. Looking for work, I hope."

Which led perfectly to her apology. "I am so sorry for what I said about him. It's none of my business. I was having a difficult day and hearing you ladies . . . I snapped. And so I apologize."

Mrs. Hutchins blinked. "That's mighty kind of you. Considering."

Considering?

She pointed to a chair at a table. "Have a sit down, Mrs. Holmquist."

When they were settled, Mrs. Hutchins said, "Me and the others were wrong saying what we did about you and your husband." She sighed. "We get caught up in things, and when one starts stirring the pot we all dive in, and . . ." She wiped her hands against her legs. "We know it's wrong. That Commandment . . ."

"'Thou shalt not bear false witness against thy neighbor.'"

"That's the one."

"I appreciate your words, but honestly, what you said wasn't false." Henrietta didn't go into details.

"Honestly, what you said wasn't false either."

They shared a silence. Then Mrs. Hutchins said, "But that doesn't mean we should say it aloud, does it?"

"It does not." Henrietta pressed a flat hand on the table between them. "These are private issues that cause our families pain."

Mrs. Hutchins didn't say anything, but her forehead furrowed. Then she lowered her head and began to cry.

Oh my! Henrietta rushed to her side, putting an arm around her shoulders, leaning close, cheek against hair. "I'm so sorry. He'll find another job soon."

Mrs. Hutchins nodded, and dug a handkerchief from her apron pocket. "I know. This isn't the first time. Matthew is a good man. He works hard when they give him a chance and have a little patience with him."

Henrietta didn't ask more. *These are private issues . . .*

Mrs. Hutchins recovered, shoved her chair back, and stood. "How would you like a cup of tea? Where there's tea there's hope."

Henrietta smiled. "I'd love a cup."

❧

Lila Kidd looked at the box sitting on her bed at Crompton Hall. It was a nondescript box: brown cardboard with a lid, the size of a hat box. And yet it represented upheaval, change, rejection, and discord. In that respect it was stuffed to its brim.

Considering the burden of its contents, why open it at all? Why not carry it to her dressing room, shove it under a row of hanging dresses, and hide it beneath their skirts never to be found again.

She sat next to it, not daring to touch it, like two youngsters sitting warily beside each other on their first foray into courtship. Nervous. Looking straight ahead. Wishing it were over. Lila caught a glimpse of herself in the full-length mirror and realized how idiotic she looked. *This is ridiculous.*

She carried the box to the small secretary that had been brought into her bedroom, placed to the left of the large window. She set the box on the floor, took a chair, and lowered the lid on the desk to reveal the cubbyholes—what few there were. There was just one drawer which was only accessible if the lid was closed. It was not enough room.

Lila opened the box and began removing her writing supplies, old letters, fresh paper and envelopes. She paused to open her box of wax sealing supplies that included the burner and wax spoon, a drawer for the wax, and a brass stamp emblazoned with the letter N. How many letters had she sealed with this set? Letters as Lady Newley, Viscountess Newley, and to close friends and family, just Lila Kidd.

I'm not a viscountess anymore.

She glanced back at the bed she had shared with her husband for thirty-five years, a nearly scandalous arrangement, when most noble husbands and wives slept in separate rooms. Theirs had been a true love, a one true love of a lifetime.

Her heartache throbbed anew, missing Joseph, feeling as though a part of her had been carved out and left empty.

She'd kept herself sane by thinking of their son, Adam and his wife, Theodosia. They had been thrust into their titles, into being Lord and Lady Newley. Adam grieved his father — Lila had no doubt of that — but he soon became focused on the present and the future of the family estate. Crompton Hall was centuries old and there was an unwritten charge that it was his responsibility to help it continue and thrive for centuries more.

The thriving was the difficult part. During the four years of war, prices has doubled in England. The monetary stress was nearly overwhelming as the workers on the estate needed to be paid, and the substantial expense of maintaining Crompton Hall was never-ending. The Kidds were not extravagant people. Lila and Joseph were homebodies, traveling to visit family more than traveling for pleasure. Traveling to visit Henrietta in New York . . .

Lila found Etta's last letter. *Please come for a visit. I miss you beyond words.*

She held the letter to her chest, feeling the same emotions. She and Joseph had visited Etta twice in New York. The first time to meet Steven and the second to celebrate their wedding. But that had been in 1913. Although they'd wanted to visit again, the war had prevented such travel. Especially with the sinking of the Lusitania, and the presence of German U-boats in the Atlantic. It wasn't safe. So they had stayed at Crompton Hall. Adam had gone to fight and had returned safe. Joseph had gone to help, but had not.

Etta hadn't even been able to come back for her father's funeral. And none of them had ever seen little Willie and Lennie in person.

Lila took out the newest photograph of the boys, her arms aching to hug them, her ears longing to hear their voices for the first time.

She carefully folded Etta's letter and added it to the rest, slipping them all into their own cubbyhole. The war was over. She *could* go visit. But Adam, Theodosia, and eight-year-old Robbie needed her during the difficult transition. That is why Lila had given up her desk in the morning room — *her* morning room. As viscountess, Theodosia needed a place for her correspondence. Lila had volunteered to have her papers moved to her bedroom. In truth, she had expected Theodosia to refuse her offer. That the girl had accepted had caused this newest feeling of unease and regret.

Actually, Theodosia had jumped into her new role with vigor and an almost ruthless glee as though being viscountess had been her life's goal.

"I'm being unfair." Lila had come from humble roots, from being a shopkeeper's daughter. Theodosia was the daughter of a baron. Becoming a viscountess was a step up for both of them, one they had both embraced. Lila had been grateful, while Theodosia acted as though it was her due.

It's almost like she's glad Joseph was killed.

Lila shook her head vehemently. Such thoughts were rude, unconscionable, and of no good worth. "Move on, Lila," she told herself.

And so she filled the desk as well as she could, and returned the unhappy overflow to the box.

❧

Maude brought three wedding dresses into Unruffled—three different designs.

Annie and Sara rushed to see. "These are beautiful."

Sara turned the second one to the back, noticing the curve of the train. "I love the drape of the silk." She looked up. "Can we afford silk? I know it's out of the realm of my business, but . . . this is gorgeous."

"We can afford it," Annie said. "Mr. Ship gave us a good discount."

"Where is Mr. Ship?" Sara asked. "I haven't seen him in more than a week, since he brought in the bolts and helped create the window display."

Annie thought about Delmonico's and him showing up when she was at the park on Saturday. "I don't know where he is," she said honestly.

"That's fine with me," Maude said.

Annie was taken aback. "Why do you say it that way?"

She shrugged. "There's something about him that doesn't . . . fit."

"Fit what?"

"Fit the traits of a gentleman."

Annie knew he wasn't *that*. But he wasn't bad either. Was he?

Maude and Sara were looking at her. "You're quiet."

"If you can't say something good about someone . . . "

Their eyes brightened. "What do you know?"

"Stop it." She turned to the dresses. "Let's arrange these in a display, put one on a mannequin, and make a sign that says other sizes can be made to order." She looked at Maude. "Samples of other sizes will be ready soon, yes?"

"Yes."

"You're not convincing."

"We're working as hard as we can."

129

"Can't ask for more than that."

"I'll put prices on them." Maude moved to the counter and got out the hang tags.

They heard the bell on the door. Guy came in, sought out Annie, and removed his hat with flourish "Annie, how good to see you."

Annie glanced at Maude, then said, "Mr. Ship. Did we have an appointment?"

"We did not, and I can only stay for the briefest moment, and then, I will not see you for a short while. Olivet is moving and I have been called upon to help." He gave her a piece of paper. "I came to carry out one of the necessities of business."

It was a bill for the bridal fabric — showing a hefty discount. "Thank you for your generosity with the price. I will have Henrietta pay you immediately."

"Very good." He pointed at the bill's header. "Please have her note the new address. We don't want your payment lost in the mail."

"Consider it done."

With that accomplished, he offered her a little bow and left.

Maude came close. "He's a whirlwind."

"Always that. Sometimes more of a cyclone." She handed Maude the bill. "See the discount he gave us?"

Maude looked at it. "Very generous."

At that moment Henrietta came in, a bit flushed. "Sorry I'm late. I know you need extra help since Birdie left."

Annie was concerned. "You are rarely late, if anything, early. Is something wrong?"

Henrietta put her satchel of ledgers behind the counter and removed her hat. "Let's say I was delayed by a life lesson."

"Oooh," Maude said. "Sounds interesting."

"Only to me." Henrietta set her hat on a shelf beneath the counter. She took a fresh breath. "There now. I'm ready to work." She noticed the wedding dresses. "Oh, Maude, those are lovely."

✍

The door of Unruffled opened and in walked Eleanor Sampson. The air of the room vibrated with her entrance.

"Hello, ladies!"

Everyone in the store turned in her direction. Annie rushed to greet her, kissing each cheek. "It's so nice to see you."

"And you, my dear." Her eyes scanned the store. "Business is picking up, I see?"

"A bit slowly, but yes, it is."

Eleanor strolled between two racks, touching the dresses hanging there. "Zippers. I'm so glad you've become modern and are using zippers. They are amazing inventions." She sighed deeply. "I told Harold — bless his soul — that one of my deepest regrets is parting ways after funding your store."

"It is my regret too," Annie said, though she didn't mean it. Mrs. Sampson had wanted Annie's designs to appeal to her wealthy friends, where Annie, Maude, and Edna had wanted to appeal to working woman — which was the right choice.

Sara and Henrietta went back to helping customers while Eleanor and Annie talked near the counter.

"How are you faring without Mr. Sampson?" Annie asked.

"Not well. For such a strong man to succumb to influenza is beyond my comprehension."

"He is missed."

Eleanor stopped perusing some necklaces on a stand. "Speaking of missing husbands . . . any word on Sean?"

"None."

She put a gloved hand on Annie's arm. "Oh, my dear girl. In some ways my knowing Harold's fate is easier than you not knowing Sean's."

"You could be right."

"But there's still hope."

"I will always hope."

With a flick of her hand, Eleanor changed subjects. "I see you have a 'Clerk Needed' sign in the window."

"One of our long-time clerks moved away." Annie noticed a woman standing by the front door. "Excuse me a moment, while I help a cus — "

"No need." Eleanor motioned toward the woman. "Eudora? Come join us."

The young woman tentatively stepped forward. She was very pretty, with small features and lovely hair that had been bobbed in the latest fashion. The rust color of her ensemble brought out the hues of her hair. Her slight build was evident even while wearing a loose sheath that formed a knee-length overskirt, covering a straight skirt beneath. A long string of pearls draped down to her midsection over a self-tied belt.

"Hello," she said.

Annie noticed the short sleeves and overskirt were edged in a wide ruched trim that spoke of couture. The girl wore a gold asymmetrical hat, sweeping high on the left, and dipping low over her right ear. This woman did *not* shop at Unruffled.

Eleanor stepped forward. "Annie, I would like to introduce you to Eudora Mitchell, your new clerk. Eudora, this is Annie, the owner of this fine establishment and a talented fashion designer."

It took Annie a moment to collect her thoughts. Although she was used to Eleanor's willful ways, today she'd been surprised. She quickly took back the control. "You would like to apply for the position?"

Eudora looked at Eleanor with an expression of concern. It was apparent Mrs. Sampson had told the girl she already had the job. "Yes, I wish to apply."

"Very good then. Let's sit." Annie led the two ladies to chairs near the fitting rooms. They each took a seat while Annie stood. "Do you have experience selling dresses?"

Another flit of a look to Eleanor. "No . . . but I like dresses."

"I can see that. Your ensemble is very stylish."

She smoothed the skirt across her lap. "Thank you. Mother ordered it for me from Worth."

A Paris designer. Which increased Annie's curiosity. "We are a store that sells off-the-rack dresses to middle-class women. Although we have the occasional special order, even most of our wedding dresses are made from a sample."

Eudora looked panicked. Eleanor stepped in. "Here is the situation, Annie. Eudora is the daughter of a dear friend of mine. She and her family live on the North Shore."

Annie had no idea where that was.

"Of Long Island?" Eleanor said. "Oyster Bay? Nassau County?"

Annie shook her head.

"Teddy Roosevelt lives down the street from them."

Eudora piped up, "Sagamore Hill was the summer White House."

"I wasn't in the country when he was president," Annie said. But she caught the drift of what they were saying: Eudora's family was wealthy.

Mrs. Sampson continued her story. "Eudora was betrothed for a time."

From the look on her face, Annie could tell that was no longer the case.

"I . . ." Eudora searched for the words. "I did not act in a ladylike manner—and the man in question was no gentleman. My parents are angry at me. I need a job."

And there it was.

Eleanor spread her hands. "It's complicated and there's no need for details at this time. But I would take it as a personal favor if you would hire her."

"That's possible, but you live so far away, I'm not sure it's feasible."

"She lives with me now, God knows I have the room. It's just a hop, skip, and a jump from Fifth to Bleecker Street."

Eudora's face softened. "Mrs. Sampson has been very kind to me. I don't know how I will ever thank her."

Eleanor reached over and touched her knee. "I'm glad to help. Your mother and I have known each other for over twenty years."

Which led to a question Annie wasn't sure she should bring up. "Excuse me for asking, but if her parents are so angry at her, doesn't taking her in cause trouble between you and her mother?"

"Yes." Eleanor left it at that. "But Eudora is my goddaughter and in this case I choose her over her mother."

The girl smiled gratefully, her eyes misty. "I do want to get my own place. For that I need a job."

Annie admired her gumption. "Yes, then. You're hired."

Eudora sprang from her chair and shook Annie's hand. "You won't regret it."

Time would tell.

❧

Gela felt like skipping to rehearsal, yet she knew it would look far too childish, so she contained her exuberance and walked from the El to the theater. She must have been smiling because people smiled when they saw her. She greeted them with "Good morning" and received a tip of the hat or a "Good morning" in return.

I never felt like skipping when I went to my job at the workshop. Never. Ever.

She was able to make such a declaration because of her certainty that she was called to perform. Gela wouldn't be sad if she never sewed another stitch—except sewing her own costume, which she'd been told she would have to supply herself. *That* would be fun.

She swung her drawstring bag around her wrist, enjoying the tug of it.

Suddenly, she let it fall slack. Up ahead, she saw all the cast gathered in front of the theater. Something was obviously wrong.

She ran to join them. "What's going on?" she asked Mack.

"We're on strike."

"Who's on strike?"

"Actors."

"Why?"

"Attention! Attention everyone!" Walter Regan, the man who played the lead in "Irene", stood on a step.

People quieted and turned toward him.

"I know this is a shock."

"Will we still get paid?" someone asked.

"Payment is part of the reason the Actor's Equity Association called the strike. Actors have not been paid what they're due. I don't know about all of you, but I've been in many productions where we've been asked to do extra shows and received nothing for it."

"Me too!" said many.

"None of us pursue acting as a hobby. We are professionals. We need to be paid as professionals."

Cheers rang out.

"We need to be paid for rehearsal time and shouldn't have to provide our own costumes."

"Hear, hear!"

"The producers shouldn't be able to fire us on a whim, without grounds or representation!"

Applause.

"We need to have standardized contracts for all!"

"Yes!"

He pumped a fist in the air. "Until our terms are met, the theaters will be dark!"

More cheering and applause. It was all very rousing, but Gela wasn't sure exactly what it meant. "So how does this affect us?" she asked Mack.

"The show's shut down."

Her heart sank. "No rehearsals?"

"Not until the producers agree to the union's terms."

"But I'm not a member of the union. I *want* to work."

Maggie, one of the other chorus members spun toward her. "You live with your parents. You don't care what you get paid. But I have a son at home. I need to get paid enough to pay the rent, buy food and clothes and—"

"I'm sorry. I shouldn't have said anything. I'm with you. I was just enjoying the rehearsals so much that I don't want them to end."

Maggie's face softened and she took Gela's hand in hers. "I know how excited you are. We all love what we do. But there are times when one has to take a stand." She looked to Mack. "Some famous person said, 'Those who stand for nothing fall for anything.'"

"I think that was Alexander Hamilton."

"Is he an actor too?" Gela asked.

They both laughed.

"He was one of the founding fathers," Mack explained.

"Of the Actor's union?"

More laughter made Gela feel very stupid. Mack put his arm around her shoulders. "I'm glad you're with us."

"You're officially one of us now," Maggie said.

Gela felt better but she was still confused. "What happens next?"

"We wait."

"For?"

"For the producers to give in."

"And if they don't?"

Mack sighed and looked down the street of theaters. "It's going to be rather quiet around here."

❧

Gela burst in the door of Unruffled.

"Gela," Annie said. "How nice to see you."

Maude could tell something was wrong.

"You don't look happy," Henrietta said.

Maude knew her daughter's face. She was more than unhappy, she was mad. Had she been fired? "Why are you here? Didn't you have rehearsal today?"

The news about the strike spilled out of Gela.

At least she wasn't fired. "Shutting down the show doesn't seem fair," Maude said. "You just started."

"The existing contracts don't sound fair," Henrietta said. "You signed one?"

Gela glanced at Mama. "I did. Mama and Papa said it was all right."

"As far as we knew," Maude said. "And Mack said we should sign it."

Annie had the clearest head. "It sounds like all the contracts were bad for the performer."

Gela nodded. "That's what they say. But I want to work. This is my big chance."

"Strikes end," Henrietta said. "Don't they?"

"They do end." Maude's thoughts sped to the next logical step. "Until then you can go back to sewing. We need your —"

"No!" Gela's face was red. "I am not a seamstress. Never was, never will be."

"What are you going to do while you wait it out?" Henrietta asked. She scanned the store. "Is Edna here?"

"Not yet." What did Edna have to do with anything?

"I'm going to go to Refuge and volunteer. Sing. Help with the children. Whatever they need."

Maude's "No!" screamed inside, but no one else heard. "I . . . I don't want you spending that much time there." *Not when Dock is around.*

"Why not? They always need help."

She wasn't sure how to counter this logic.

Henrietta helped. "That's not in a very good part of town. You'd be going there by yourself."

"That's right," Maude said. "Your father would never approve."

"What if I got Mack to go with me?"

Everyone looked to Maude. It *was* a solution. But not a solution she could live with. "We'll talk to your father later."

Maude stopped Gela's pout. "Girls who pout like a child will be treated like a child."

She could see Gela fight her mood, and was rather proud of her for lifting herself out of it.

"We could use your help here," Annie said.

Gela shrugged. "Just for today."

And hopefully longer.

≈

Edna handed Annie a stack of plates. "They'll be six of us at the dining table. I thought the children could sit at the kitchen table — if you think they'll behave."

"They will giggle and play with their food," Annie said. "But it's our only hope of having adult conversation." She pointed at her daughters. "You and the boys will behave while you sit together, won't you?"

All four nodded enthusiastically. Edna had her doubts.

Vesta put glasses around, and Henrietta set the silverware. Edna could see her studying the table. She guessed her thoughts. "Steven will come out to eat."

Henrietta nodded. "Maybe having Mr. McGinness here — another man — will help."

Mack. Edna wasn't at all sure whether his presence would be a blessing or a disaster.

A knock on the door gave her notice she would soon find out. He came bearing a bouquet — and a song. "Happy birthday, dear Edna, happy birthday to you!"

She felt herself flush and pulled him inside. "I don't want the entire building to know."

"Why not?" he asked.

She took his hat and let him play the room, greeting the ladies and meeting the children. And then she saw him doing something she had rarely seen a grown man do: he got down on the floor with them, and helped build a tower out of blocks. She hated to admit it, but her heart melted a bit.

The ladies noticed too. "Now there's a sight," Annie said.

The blocks fell. The children screamed. Mack started the tower anew.

And then . . . the bedroom door opened. Henrietta rushed to welcome Steven to the party. Instead, his eyes turned toward Mack — who got to his feet.

Edna stepped forward. "Steven, I'd like you to meet Mack McGinness, a friend of ours. Mr. McGinness, this is my son, Steven."

"Call me Mack." He held out his hand, and after a pause, Steven took it. "Nice to meet you, Steven. I didn't know Edna had a son."

Edna smelled something on the stove. "Oh!" She ran to the kitchen and saved the carrots from destruction. Annie came to help. "Just in time. Tell everyone to sit."

Henrietta took up plates of food for the children and got them settled, while Annie showed the adults their places. Edna and Steven sat at the ends. Vesta and Annie sat on one side — with Annie directing Mack to sit nearest the end where Edna would preside, next to Henrietta, who sat near Steven.

Carrots, potatoes, rolls, and . . .

Lastly, Edna brought the serving plate of fish.

"What is it?" Henrietta asked.

"Shad." She looked to Steven, but he didn't seem to understand the significance. "Let's say grace and then I'll tell you the story behind my choice."

They bowed their heads and thanked God. Edna added a silent prayer for a pleasant, uneventful evening.

"So," Annie said, after taking her first bite. "It's delicious. Share the story."

"I haven't had shad since my husband died twenty years ago."

"Why not?" Mack asked.

She told the story of the unselfish Ernie wanting to fulfill his wife's desire to have shad. "His boat capsized in a storm and he died."

Everyone stopped eating. Edna chastised herself. "I didn't mean to state it so bluntly, or to put a damper on the evening . . . oh dear. Perhaps I didn't think this through."

"I'm glad to know the story," Henrietta said. She looked at Steven. "I wish *you* would have told me about your father."

He looked at his plate.

Edna wished she could back up and *not* say anything, but it was too late. She needed to turn the mood around. "I haven't eaten shad since then, but this morning when I woke up—on my sixtieth birthday—I thought it was time to move on, to face the demon once and for all."

Mack laughed and lifted his glass. "To conquering the demon shad!"

They laughed with him and clinked glasses—all but Steven. Edna gave Mack a thankful look. He winked.

"Tell us about your family, Mr. McGinness," Annie asked. "Mack."

He set his fork down. "I also lost a wife—to influenza."

They all shared their condolences.

"Do you have children?" Henrietta asked.

His face changed, like a shadow had passed over it. "I did. My son was killed in the war."

Edna felt bad for not knowing this. She glanced at Steven. Would he say anything?

He continued eating as though oblivious.

Henrietta spoke next. "I'm so sorry. Steven fought too. Didn't you, dear?"

Steven looked suddenly panicked at the attention, pushed back from the table, and escaped to his room like a frightened child.

"He's not been the same since coming back," Henrietta said.

"Many suffered—and many continue to suffer," Mack said.

Annie suddenly began to cry, and excused herself to the bathroom. Vesta ran after her.

Edna hurried to explain. "After two years gone, her husband is still missing. Vesta is Sean's mother. They try to remain hopeful, but no one has any word about him, dead or alive."

The children used this moment to spill milk, drop a plate, and argue about whose fault it was.

Henrietta went to their rescue, leaving Edna alone with Mack.

"I'm so sorry for the evening," she said. "It's not turned out as I had hoped."

"No worries, dear lady," he said, reaching for her hand on the table. "I had no idea about your son and wife. I'm so sorry for your loss."

He nodded toward Steven's empty chair. "Loss comes in many forms."

Vesta and Annie came back to the table with apologies.

Henrietta came back, apologizing for the children.

Steven stayed in his room with the door closed.

Birthday or no birthday, Edna was very tempted to call it an evening. Until . . .

"I know how to change the mood," Mack said. "Let's talk baseball. Giants or Yankees?"

⁌

The apple birthday cake that Annie brought was delicious. The gifts were opened—a new pocketbook from Annie, a book of poetry from Vesta, and a scarf from Henrietta.

The guests had gone. All except Mack.

Edna handed him his hat. "Thank you for the beautiful flowers—and for saving the evening from sure disaster."

"Talking about serious issues does not denote a disaster." He shrugged. "As I said, many suffered, and many continue to suffer." He touched her arm. "But beyond that, many have overcome. As have you, dear lady."

She nodded and felt grateful tears threaten.

He put his hand under her chin. "Chin up now. All will be well. Happy birthday."

Then he kissed her cheek and was gone.

She leaned against the door and thanked God for Mack *and* that the dinner was over. She also made a new vow to never serve shad again.

Steven came out of his room to use the facilities. Suddenly, all the tension of the night poured over Edna, and she rushed to him, stopping him in the hall. "How dare you leave the table like that."

"Sorry."

"Mr. McGinness lost his son! Annie has no idea where Sean is. And here you stand, here, but not here." She took his face in her hands, peering into his eyes. "I don't know what to do to help you, but you have to snap out of it, Steven. What you're doing to those who love you—and to yourself—isn't right."

His forehead furrowed, and he nodded. He put his hands over hers, then lowered them, giving them a squeeze. "I'm trying. Happy birthday, Ma."

She pulled him into her arms.

CHAPTER ELEVEN

Gela knew it wouldn't be easy.

She put on her shoes before leaving her bedroom. Then she put her ear to the door. She could hear the sounds of her family accomplishing their own morning tasks in their bedrooms, but it didn't sound like anyone was in the parlor or kitchen.

She looked down at the note. *It's now or never.* She opened the door and tiptoed out. She placed the note on the kitchen table, grabbed an apple and her purse, and carefully unlocked the front door. She was just opening it when Matteo came out of his room.

"Where are you going so early?"

"Mind your own business."

"Ma!"

Gela couldn't believe he'd done that. She opened the door just as her mother and father came out of their bedroom.

"Stop!" Papa said.

So close!

"Get back here. Now."

For a fleeting moment, Gela thought about leaving anyway, but had a glimmer that running away like that would make everything worse. So she went inside and closed the door lest the neighbors hear more than they should.

Mama stood with the right side of her hair swept up and the left side hanging over her shoulder. "Where are you going?"

"You know where. I told you."

"I said you couldn't go to Refuge without Edna accompanying you."

She didn't want to tell them she'd already gone once on her own to bring a note to Mack. "I'll go with Edna — after today. I need to see Mack and talk to him about a regular schedule at Refuge until the show starts up again."

"I don't want you there."

Gela was confused. "I'm *not* going to sew anymore. I told you that."

"That's not what I meant." Mama looked to Papa for help. "Antonio?"

He balked, then said, "You could come to work for me for a short time. I could use help in the office, filing and helping my secretary with correspondence and paperwork."

"I don't know how to use a typewriter."

"You could learn."

She stomped her foot—and immediately regretted it. "I don't want to sew! I don't want to type. I want to act and sing, but since—" They both looked ready to interrupt. "But since I can't do that, I want to sing at Refuge, and help there." She thought of some additional words that might clinch it. "I want to help people. How can you object to that?"

Mama's forehead furrowed and Gela could see her desperately trying to think of a comeback.

"See?" she said quickly. "You can't think of a reason."

"It's in a bad part of town," Mama said. "It's not safe."

"I know how to be safe. I'm aware of where to go—and not go."

"What if Mack's not there?" Papa asked.

"I know some of the people in charge: Dorothy, Mrs. Sutter, Mr. Gooden . . . You met some of them. They'll be there for me."

"Matteo will go with you," Papa said.

Her brother shook his head. "I need to get to work."

Papa gave him a look. "At least . . . go as far as you can with your sister."

Gela hated that they thought she needed a chaperone, but if it would get her to Refuge, she'd go along with it.

"I still don't like it," Mama said.

Papa put a hand on her arm. "It's a compromise, Maude." He gave her a look Gela had seen before, one that said the subject was closed.

"Can I go now?"

"What about breakfast?" Mama asked.

She held up her apple. "Get one for yourself, Matt. I want to leave now."

He plucked an apple from a bowl and cut off a huge slice of bread. Finally.

They ate as they walked to the El. Once on the train heading south her brother finally asked the question she'd been dreading.

"Why this need to go to Refuge so early?"

"Like I told everyone, I want to help people."

"Baloney."

She knew there was another answer she could share. "You heard them trying to keep me busy. As long as I'm at Refuge they can't ask me to sew or work at Unruffled or help Papa."

"What would be so wrong with any of that?"

"It's what they want me to do."

He snickered. "My sister, the rebel."

She angled in the seat to face him. "You like pleasing them. I don't. Never have made it my first goal."

"Don't we know it."

She swatted his leg. "It's not a bad thing. I just want to be treated like an adult for once, not be at their beck and call. Not be beholden to their choices. I want to make my own."

"You can make your own when you live on your own. Until then . . ."

He was repeating their parents' logic. "Don't *you* want to live on your own?"

"Sure," he said. "When the time's right. I'm only fifteen. I'm making a decent wage so the time will come. I like my delivery job because it gets me outdoors and I get to see different parts of the city."

She shook her head. "I don't like being outside."

"You never have," he said. "We're different that way." He huffed. "Lots of ways."

She thought of their outings to the park as children. Matteo always longed to stay longer, while Gela wanted to go home. "I like to see different parts of the city too. I'm seeing Soho and Little Italy going to Refuge, and I'm seeing a lot more going up to the Theatre District to do my job—all areas I'd never seen before."

He nodded, then glanced out the window. "That's good, but . . . " He looked at her. "I get the feeling that you believe because *you're* in a place, everything is good and right and normal. It's not. There are a lot of people who don't live in a nice house with family who loves them. They don't have a job. They don't have food in their bellies. And they don't think the world is a good place. To them, it isn't good at all."

"I have eyes. I know that," she said. But she did take his words to heart.

&

Henrietta paid the street vendor for a bouquet of flowers, then immediately inhaled their scent. And sneezed. Daisies were not her favorite and didn't smell that good. But they were pretty and lasted a long time.

The street on the Lower East Side seemed more crowded than usual. There were men of Italian descent with their elaborate mustaches and vested suits. And Jewish men who wore a yarmulke scull cap beneath their black hats, and prayer shawls around their waists. She realized that men's fashion hadn't changed much in the seven years she'd known the Cohens. But women's fashions were something else. Gone were apron-clad mamas in their skirts and blouses with shawls around their shoulders. The women wore dresses with low waists and comfortable sleeves. Dresses that could have been purchased at Unruffled. In fact . . . she recognized a maize-colored dress from their spring offerings.

She loved hearing the different languages — or most often a combination of English and some other tongue. She was fascinated by the signs on the storefronts using words — and even letters — she didn't understand. She enjoyed seeing mothers getting after their children, making them behave. It was comforting to know that motherhood issues were universal. She received many smiles as she walked by with the flowers and hoped they would elicit the same reaction from the Cohens.

She reached their jewelry store and went inside. She spotted Aaron sitting at a table behind the counter, leaning over some gem that was lit by a lamp, wearing his jeweler's loupe for magnification.

The clerk — their nephew — greeted her. "Mrs. Holmquist. How nice to see you."

"And you, Levi."

Aaron looked up. His smile made his long silver beard move. With a moan he rose from his seat.

"You don't have to get up," she said. He was in his late eighties, though he was the younger of the two other siblings.

"I do not have to, but I want to," he said. "Come 'round the cases to greet me."

She did, and he embraced her. "*Shalom,* dear Yetta."

"Shalom." She loved the nickname they had given her. They'd told her it meant 'ruler of the household.' It was ironic that life had thrust her into that role.

She held out the flowers. "I brought these for Abel — and you and Berta. How is he?"

"Ornery, which means he is well enough. Go up and see them. They'd love a visit. Plus, you can meet some relatives who've recently arrived from Prussia."

Henrietta went outside, entered a door next to Cohen & Cohen, and climbed the narrow stairs to their flat.

Berta answered her knock. "Shalom, Yetta."

"Shalom to you, Berta. I came to check on Abel. These are for all of you."

"*Sheyn*. Beautiful. Come in."

As usual, it took Henrietta's eyes a minute to adjust to the dim light of the Cohen's flat. Also, as usual she found Abel in *his* chair next to the kitchen table.

He rose to greet her with a shalom, but when he coughed, he sat down. "I sound worse than I feel," he said.

"He's better," Berta said, bringing the flowers to the kitchen. "His cough no longer wakes the dead."

Henrietta noticed another couple sitting in the parlor, who'd also stood when she'd entered. "Hello," she said.

Berta rushed to make the introductions. "Henrietta, meet our distant cousins, Heber and Mara Cudek. They have escaped from Western Galacia — Poland." The couple nodded, though by their expressions it seemed clear they didn't speak English. "Heber. Mara?" Berta motioned toward Henrietta. "Henrietta Holmquist. *Mishpocheh*." She nodded at Henrietta. "You're like family."

Henrietta was honored and touched Berta's arm, repeating the word. "Mishpocheh."

There were nods all around.

"Sit," Berta said, pulling out a chair at the table. "I just poured tea."

Berta poured her a cup and sat at a third chair. She put a hand flat on the table. "Now then. Tell us about your family. How are the boys?"

Henrietta shared a few funny stories about Willie and Lennie, which made Abel and Berta laugh — and even Heber and Mara when their high-jinks were translated.

"And how is Steven?"

She was set to say "fine" until Berta cocked her head and raised her eyebrows. "Not so good?"

"He's not recovered from the war. From battle. From what he saw."

Abel translated and their relatives nodded and moved to the table. Heber began telling a story. Abel and Berta asked questions and Mara added a few words here and there. It was fascinating to hear so much of a language and not understand any of it.

Henrietta *could* translate the emotion behind the words and the dramatic hand gestures. The couple had suffered their own violent experiences.

When they finished talking, Abel said, "Our cousins' village suffered under the Revolution, and then during the civil war between the Red, White, and Green armies."

Henrietta shook her head, having never heard of these.

"That war is still going on. The Red Army consists of Bolsheviks fighting for Marxist socialism under Lenin. The White Army is a mixed bag, but they generally want capitalism and democracy in some form. And then the Green Army fights against them both." He nodded toward his relatives.

"Who will win?" Henrietta asked.

Abel considered this a moment. "The Bolsheviks. They killed the tsar and his family, pulled out of the war with Germany and the United States, and concentrated on taking power for themselves. The White Army can't agree on the color of the sky, and the Green Army hates everyone." He shrugged. "Russia will never be the same."

"Which side are you on?" she asked.

He looked at Berta, his face sad. "We are on the side of peace and understanding, but are fearful those attributes have been killed and buried."

"I'm so sorry."

"Thank you." He looked at his cousins. "They and many others were caught in the middle of the chaos and had no one who would defend them."

"Pogrom," Heber said.

Abel nodded. "Their village suffered a pogrom, a violent purging of Jewish lives in every way, from their homes, their businesses, and their bodies." He looked upon the couple with a pained expression. "Their sons and their wives and children were all murdered. Heber and Mara survived only because they had traveled to visit a sick friend in the country."

Heber said something else, his voice dripping with despair. Mara took her husband's hand.

Abel translated. "They went back to their village to find every Jew dead. All their possessions destroyed. A lifetime destroyed."

Henrietta felt her throat tighten. "I don't understand such hatred."

Abel translated her words and Heber responded. Abel translated for him. "There is no understanding evil."

"We Jews are different," Berta said. "People don't like different."

True, and yet . . . Henrietta pointed outside. "This city is populated by *different* and for the most part, we get along." *Don't we?* She had never witnessed any serious dissent. "From what I've seen, the war brought people from different backgrounds together to fight a common enemy. We eventually stopped being immigrants and became Americans."

"That is a good thing." Abel glanced outside. "You are also right that the evil is less violent here, but it still exists in people's hearts."

Henrietta nodded. "'Thou shalt love thy neighbor as thyself.'"

Abel cocked his head.

He doesn't know this verse? Then she realized it was from the New Testament and that Jesus had said it. "It's a command from Jesus. We are to love God first, then love our neighbors — as we love ourselves."

"It is a good command. Your Jesus seems wise."

Words came to Henrietta's mind and she hesitated to say them, yet felt as if a door had opened that she should not shut. "He was more than a wise man or even a prophet. He was the Messiah — of all men. He's your Savior too, the One you've waited for."

They were all silent. Then Heber said, "*Vas?*"

Abel told him what he'd missed. Heber shook his head adamantly.

Henrietta didn't want to argue with them, and displace the foundation of their faith and their culture. Even though her heart ached because they didn't understand that Jesus was theirs, she felt she'd said enough. For now.

"I didn't mean to upset him. Or you."

Abel waved her apology away. "*Tsvey kluge kenen nit shtimen.* Two smart people can't agree."

Heber smiled and nodded.

Henrietta felt herself relax. Then she remembered something Abel always said at the end of their visits. She raised her teacup and said, "*L'chaim!*"

Abel laughed and said, "To life!"

On that, they could agree.

◆

Maude stood at the parlor window holding the sheer curtain to the side, staring at nothing. Her thoughts provided too many images.

Antonio pointed to Gela's note. "She'll be fine. Matteo is taking her most of the way. Refuge is a place of hope, with people our daughter can help."

"Hmm."

"Why so skeptical?"

She pondered whether to tell him about Dock, but saw him looking at his pocket watch. Any Dock-discussion would be lengthy.

She gave him a kiss and forced a smile. "Go to work. Sell something."

He kissed her back. "You too."

❧

Maude sat on the floor of the workshop, a pincushion in her lap. Gert stood before her wearing her wedding dress.

"Oh, Maude," she said, preening before the mirror. "It's beyond pretty."

"I'm glad you think so."

"Don't you?"

"I do. Of course I do. Let's decide on a length." She turned under the hem. "Here, or . . . here."

"Longer, I think."

"Sure."

Gert touched Maude's cheek. "Sure? That is not a Maude answer. What's gotten into you today? You're distracted."

Maude held out a hand, wanting help up. She sat on the window seat and sighed. "It's Gela."

"Isn't it often Gela?"

Maude chuckled. "Matteo has always done everything that's expected of him, but Gela pushes us. She's always stirring things up, like a caged bee."

Gert sat nearby. "Does she sting?"

"Sometimes."

"She's sixteen, yes?"

"She is."

Gert spread her hands.

"I know. I was spirited at that age too." She thought back to the difficulties she'd cause her mother. Talking back, thinking she knew everything. Thinking she was invincible.

Until she'd learned she wasn't.

"I don't want her to get hurt."

"It's not inevitable."

"She's reckless. She doesn't think things through."

Gert spread her arms a second time.

"She's at Refuge today. All day."

"I heard about the strike. So it affected her play?"

"It did. I wanted her to come back to work here."

Gert raised her hands. "Please no."

Really? "She was that bad?"

"She is a singer, not a sewer."

Maude nodded. "That's what she said."

"Then let her be. She's helping people, yes?"

"Yes."

"Helping others is better than sitting around pouting about the strike."

Maude thought of Dock. Dock who recognized her. Dock who knew that Gela was her daughter.

"There's something else?"

Maude hesitated but chose to share a bit of it. "There's a man at Refuge that I don't trust. He's not a good man."

"How do you know anyone at Refuge?"

"From my past. I recognized him."

"Is he dangerous?"

"Perhaps."

"Have you gone to the police?"

"I have. They know him. They say he's harmless."

"Then perhaps he is."

"I worry. If Mr. McGinness isn't there, she's all alone."

Gert sat a moment, then said, "Go on then. Go see she's all right, then come back."

A wonderful idea.

❦

If it would have been acceptable for a woman to run, Maude would have run down the street from the El to Port Refuge. As it was, she walked fast enough to gain concerned looks from those on the sidewalk. She smiled and nodded, reassuring them she was all right.

But was she?

She reached the building, brushing past a small group that congregated outside.

She was immediately struck by the absence of music. Gela wasn't singing. Mack wasn't playing. She scanned the large room for her daughter.

A woman cleaning a table looked up at her. "You looking for someone?"

"My daughter. Gela Ricci. She sings and —"

The woman straightened with an arch to her back, craned her neck, then pointed. "Over there. Talking to Dock."

"No!" Maude pushed her way through the room to her daughter — who was indeed talking to Dock. She yanked her away.

"What? . . . Mama!"

Maude stood between the two. "You stay away from my daughter!"

Dock's face reddened. "I . . . we were just talking."

Gela stepped out from behind her mother. "He's right. We were just talking!"

Two men stepped forward. "What's going on here?"

"This man was . . . " *Talking to my daughter?* The absurdity of the situation fell upon her.

"Dock, what's going on?" one of the men asked.

"Nothing. I swear." He pointed at Maude. "This woman is crazy. She followed me and now she's accusing me of . . . I haven't done anything wrong."

"Talking ain't a crime," said a second man.

"Exactly," Dock said.

"Exactly," Gela said.

"I was telling her how I've enjoyed her singing."

Gela nodded.

Maude noticed a crowd had gathered. Everyone was listening. *You either accuse him of his past crime or walk away.*

The words Officer Wilkerson said about Dock came back to her. *"He's not a violent person . . . he's a broken man . . . if he was your attacker, he has suffered beyond the law in ways I wouldn't wish on an enemy."*

The memories fell upon her, a heavy weight of confusion. Maude needed to leave. "Excuse me for causing a scene. Gela, come with me. We're going."

Gela shook her hand away. "You go. I'm staying."

The look on her daughter's face told Maude that forcing the issue would only make things worse.

As she walked outside she felt a hundred eyes upon her. She brushed past the group outside, and hurried up the street the way she had come, wanting to get *away*.

Her thoughts ricocheted, making her head hurt and tears threaten. She spotted a church and rushed inside, needing to be alone with her emotions.

It took her eyes a minute to adjust to the dim light. She slipped into the sanctuary, into the back pew. She bowed her head and let the tears come. "I'm so sorry, Lord. I shouldn't have done that. But I don't know what to do. Now I've ruined things with Gela. I've made such a mess of everything."

"Haven't we all?"

She looked up and saw a priest standing in the doorway to the sanctuary. *He heard?*

He took a seat at the pew in front of hers, angling his body to talk to her. "I didn't mean to eavesdrop but you said you'd made a mess of things? I simply said 'Haven't we all?' For I have made more than my share of messes."

"You? A priest?"

He chuckled. "A flawed sinful man first, a priest second." He extended his hand. "Father Roberts."

She shook his hand. "Maude Ricci."

He looked toward the front of the church where a statue of the crucified Christ hung behind the altar. "Only He was without sin. The rest of us . . . " He shrugged. "We struggle."

Maude nodded and found a handkerchief in her bag. She wiped her eyes. "I've become obsessed."

"With . . .?"

How could she word it? "I'm obsessed with someone else's sin. They sinned against *me*. It was a long time ago, but I just confronted him and caused a scene, and my daughter hates me for it, and . . . " She looked toward Jesus. "I don't know what to do."

"You're looking in the right direction. Ask Him." He closed his eyes. "'Trust in the Lord with all thine heart; and lean not unto thine own understanding. In all thy ways acknowledge him, and he shall direct thy paths.'"

The words offered comfort, but also a challenge. "I desperately need direction."

"Then trust Him, lean on Him. Acknowledge Him. He'll show you the way."

With that, Father Roberts left, leaving Maude alone.

With Him.

Maude bowed her head and did what he'd suggested. She trusted. She leaned. And she acknowledged.

But could she forget?

It was in God's hands.

❧

Gela was mortified by the scene her mother had made at Refuge. The two men who had broken it up suggested she sing something. Mack wasn't there yet, so she sang acapella. Her music seemed to calm the room, but her own heart was still reeling. Why had Mama done such a thing? She'd humiliated Dock *and* Gela. He was a nice man. He was down on his luck like most of the people here. What did Mama have against him?

As she finished her third song, she saw Dock making his way to the door. She wanted to talk to him and apologize. As soon as she was through, she hurried outside.

She looked to the left, then the right, and saw him a block ahead. She didn't want to call out but started to follow him. Maybe she could give Mama evidence that there was nothing to fear from Dock . . . Dock what? She didn't even know his last name.

He turned this way and that, and Gela realized she was quite a ways from Refuge. *I can't stop now.* She nearly lost him at a corner, then saw him go into an alley. She hurried to catch up, but as she turned into the alley, she stopped. It was shrouded in shadows. No sun reached its depths. She was immediately assailed by the stench of excrement, rotting food, and misery. There were people living in blanket tents, and shacks made of scraps of wood, cardboard, and stray bricks. She could see legs sticking out of one and some movement in another.

Leave. Leave now.

Suddenly, someone touched her shoulder from behind. She whipped around to find a weaselly-looking man grinning at her.

"Hey there, chickie. You come to visit me?" He glanced down at her bag. "Whatcha got in there?"

"Leave her be!"

Gela turned around and saw Dock step out of the darkness.

The man took a step back. "Come on, Dock. You knows it's first come, first served."

Dock rushed forward and grabbed Gela's arm, pulling her out of the alley.

"Ow!" she said, yanking herself free.

His eyes were intense. "Why did you follow me?"

"I want to talk to you."

"We've done enough talking. You should listen to your ma."

"You know her?"

He looked away, then pointed down the street. "Walk with me."

They walked past a haberdashery and a cigar shop, so there *were* people around. Gela wasn't sure if she should be afraid or not. Then a fruit vendor nodded at Dock. "Want an apple, Dock?"

He shook his head. "Maybe later."

He stopped walking at a small treed area smaller than the Ricci apartment. A man slept on the only bench. Dock shooed him off and offered her a seat. He did not sit beside her.

"How do you know my mother?" she asked.

He paced up and back, shaking his head, muttering, as if arguing with himself.

"Dock?"

He finally stopped and faced her. "I . . . I assaulted her thirteen years ago."

Gela couldn't help but gawk. "Assaulted . . .?" *What does that mean?*

Dock looked in both directions, then sat beside her. She scooted to her end of the bench.

His voice was low. "I raped her."

Gela had no words. Rape? Her mother had been raped? Suddenly, Mama's reactions to Dock made sense.

She stood, needing distance. "I don't understand any of this. You hurt my mother? How could you do such a horrible thing?"

He drew his knees to his chest and held them tight, like a child. He spoke into his legs. "I was bad. Very bad."

He looked so pitiful but she kept her distance. "Yes, you were. That's an awful thing to do. To my *mother!*" She thought of something. "Did you go to jail?"

He shook his head once. "Should have. Expected to." He leaned his forehead against his knees. "So wrong, so wrong. So sorry. So sorry."

His remorse made her feel sorry *for* him. "Have you been living on the streets all this time?"

He lifted his head. "Not all. I worked on the docks some."

Docks. Dock. "What's your real name?"

He cocked his head, as if trying to remember. "Clarence. Clarence Varner. I haven't been Clarence in years."

Gela looked to the small patch of grass, to a pile of human excrement half-covered with trash. "Do you still work at the docks?"

He shook his head. "Got the flu. Nearly died. Shoulda died. Missed too much work."

"They shouldn't hold the flu against you."

He hung his head. "Stole some stuff too. Got sacked. Sold stuff for booze money." He looked up at her. "You got money?"

"Not for alcohol."

He nodded, as if he'd known what she would say. "Refuge is a good place. They feed me and give me a place to go away . . ." he nodded toward the alley. "Away from there."

"It *is* a good place. Don't let Mama keep you from going there." It felt strange to encourage him.

"I don't want to get you in trouble with her."

Gela knew the trouble with her mother was just beginning. If Mama found out that Gela had followed Dock and spoke with him . . . "It's all right. I'll talk to her."

His dirty face looked incredulous. "You'll tell her I'm sorry? You'd do that for me?"

"You said you were sorry." *She doubted an apology was enough to compensate for what Mama went through.* Suddenly, his face crumpled and his eyes filled with tears. "I wish she'd forgive me. I know I don't deserve such a thing, but I wish . . . I've tried to forgive myself too. Spent a lifetime trying to forgive myself." He wiped his tears with his sleeve. "I *am* sorry. I'm not that man anymore. Never shoulda been that man. I only did it once and it scared me so . . ."

"Scared you?"

"Scared me that I could even do such a thing." He looked up to the small patch of sky overhead. "A fellow thinks he's one way, then suddenly he's doing something that's beyond anything. Everything. She was walking by and I . . ." He put a fist to his belly. "I was having a hard time of things, and then I got this urge in me and before I could even think yes or no, I'd tackled her to the ground, and then . . ." His head fell forward like his neck wasn't strong enough to hold it up. "I'm so sorry, so sorry."

Gela put a hand on his shoulder, immediately realizing how odd it was that she was comforting her mother's rapist. "You're not that man anymore." *At least I hope you're not.*

He risked a look. "I'm not. I swear to God, I'm not."

She wanted to believe him. But then she thought of her mother. "I need to get home."

He stood. He seemed so small with his body hunched over in shame, his face hidden behind a curtain of dark stringy hair. "Thank you for talking to me."

Saying "You're welcome" seemed . . . off. "You take care of yourself, Dock. Clarence. And keep coming to Port Refuge, all right?"

"Will you keep singing there?"

"I will. When I can." On impulse, she held out her hand. He stared at it, as if unsure what to do with it. "Goodbye, Clarence," she said.

He tentatively shook her hand. "Goodbye, miss."

Gela walked to the El with her head held high but her heart sunk low. So low.

She needed to talk to Mama.

❧

Although she wanted to go home after her confrontation with Dock and her time in the church, Maude went back to the workshop. There were dresses to cut and sew. She needed to keep busy.

She heard Myrtle and Mary whispering in the sewing room nearby, which meant sewing wasn't happening.

Maude went to the doorway. "Secrets?"

Myrtle blushed. "No secrets, ma'am." She looked to Mary. "We're just concerned about you. You . . . you haven't been yourself for a while now."

"Is there something we've done to upset you?" Mary asked.

She felt awful. "Not at all. You're both doing fine work."

"Is there something we can do to help?" Myrtle asked.

Maude was touched by their concern. "It's a personal matter," she said. "I apologize for letting it be so evident."

Mary nodded. "My husband says I have a transparent face. Whatever I feel shows for all the world to see."

Maude understood what she was saying—from experience. "I think I have one of those myself. It's all right, ladies. No worries."

"Glad to hear it."

They all went back to work. Although Maude didn't remember all of the verse the priest shared, she remembered the first part and vowed to put it into practice immediately.

Trust in the Lord . . .

æ

Gela stood outside the workshop door. She couldn't hear the whirr of sewing machines inside. Was Mama in there? Gela had already stopped at home, only to find the apartment empty.

But then she heard her voice. With a quick prayer for the right words, Gela went in.

Mama and the two seamstresses were standing around the cutting table.

"Gela," Mama said. There was a stiffness in the way she said her name.

"Mama."

Myrtle and Mary retreated to the sewing rooms, leaving them alone.

"I want to talk to you," Gela said. On the way over, she'd decided not to use the word "need" as that would make it sound confrontational. There was enough tension between them without adding to it. She added, "Please? Could we take a walk?"

Mama's forehead tightened, as if in pain, but she nodded.

At least now I know what's causing her pain.

They went downstairs and out to Leroy Street, turning right. They didn't speak until they walked across Bleecker onto Cornelia.

Gela started. "I'm — "

Mama interrupted. "I'm very sorry, Gela. I shouldn't have yelled at you at Refuge. I shouldn't have made a scene. I . . . it has nothing to do with you. I have some things I'm dealing with from the past, and I let them take over and — "

"Dock attacked you."

Mama stopped walking. "How do you know that?"

"I followed him. I talked to him."

Mama's eyes grew large. "You shouldn't have done that! Are you all right? He's dangerous."

She shook her head. "He's not. I know he's not. He told me what happened."

Mama pressed a hand to her chest. "He admitted it? It really is him?"

Gela was surprised she hadn't been sure. She nodded. "He and I talked a long time about it."

"What did he say?"

"He said he'd only done it the one time. He hated that he'd done it and seemed shocked that he'd done it. He told me it scared him."

"It scared me!" She lowered her voice. "And hurt me. He . . . he injured me for life."

"What?"

Mama's face was contorted with emotions. "He hurt me so bad that..." She turned away, wanting to escape the admission. "So bad that I could never have children."

Gela let her mouth gape open. "I didn't know that. Why didn't I know that?"

Mama touched her cheek. "I don't need children of my own. I have you and Matteo. God sent me to your father to give me the gift of *you*. I know it."

Gela couldn't believe what she was hearing. Dock had confessed — and what he confessed to was bad enough — but to hear the lasting impact of his crime made Gela sick to her stomach.

Mama stroked Gela's hair behind an ear. "It's all right now, dear. It was thirteen years ago."

"But still . . . he didn't tell me *that*."

"He wouldn't have known. I had no contact with him afterwards. I didn't report the assault to the police. Nor to my own mother."

"Why not?"

She looked beyond Gela, as if looking at the past. "I was ashamed. And as far as my mother went, I was out walking alone because she and I had argued. I'd been acting selfish and willful and—"

"Like I act?"

Mama smiled. "I was a difficult daughter."

"Like me."

Mama began to shake her head but nodded. "I don't want us to have dissention between us. You father and I are not your enemies. But we're not perfect either. You're our oldest. We've never been the parents of a sixteen-year-old girl before."

"You're doing fine. I shouldn't make things so difficult."

"You shouldn't. But we never should have forced you to be a seamstress when you have other talents. I am still ashamed we didn't realize what a good singer you are."

"You let me audition for 'Irene.' You're letting me sing there and at Refuge. I'm singing in a real theater, mama, if the strike ever ends, that is."

Mama lifted Gela's chin and looked into her eyes. "We've both been difficult. Shall we call a truce and try to be allies instead of enemies?"

"I'd like that." On impulse, Gela wrapped her arms around her.

Mama kissed her hair. "Oh, my dear girl. My dear angel, my Angela."

It felt so good to be held like she used to be held as a child. There was no reason they couldn't embrace like this more often. "I like this."

"I do too."

After a lingering moment, Gela pushed back. "Now I know why you didn't want me to talk to him."

They sat on the steps of a brownstone. "I didn't know if he was still a . . . a bad man."

Gela shook her head. "I don't know for sure, but I don't think he is. But he *is* a very poor man. He's living in a hut made of scraps in an alley. He saved me from a man who was annoying me, suggesting . . . things."

Mama sighed deeply. "I went to the local precinct and they said they knew him. He's been arrested a few times for drunkenness. But the officer didn't think he was violent. He actually acted as if he felt sorry for him."

"I feel sorry for him." Gela got an idea. "I want you and I to go together to see him."

"I don't think that's wise. Or necessary."

The idea gained strong roots. "I think it is. He's been hating himself all these years. He said he's been trying to forgive himself for what he did to you."

"That's not my problem."

"But he's sorry. He wants you to forgive him."

"Me?"

"*Have* you forgiven him?"

Mama looked to the sky. "I don't think so. Otherwise, why would seeing him upset me so much."

"Then maybe it would be good for both of you. Maybe forgiving him would help him forgive himself. Maybe it would be a new start for him, and you."

"You're putting a lot of stock in forgiveness."

"Well . . . yes. It is kind of important."

Mama bit her lip, then nodded. "'Judge not, and ye shall not be judged: condemn not, and ye shall not be condemned: forgive, and ye shall be forgiven.'" She sighed deeply. "I know what I should do, but that doesn't mean I'll ever forget. It haunts me. I still feel the fear and pain."

Gela couldn't imagine what Mama had been through. "Will you go visit him with me? Sometime?"

Mama put her arm around Gela's shoulders and their heads touched. "I will visit him. For you. But I offer no promises of forgiveness."

CHAPTER TWELVE

Annie watched Eudora help a customer. She had good fashion sense, was kind and complimentary, yet tactful when a dress didn't suit.

She was just about to go back to arranging a display of hats, when she saw Eudora striding toward her. She looked ready to cry.

"What's wrong?" Annie asked softly.

"She . . . she wants a wedding dress, and I thought I could help, but I can't yet. I just can't."

"That's all right. I'll help her. Go in the back and have a good cry."

"I . . . you'll let me cry?"

"We all need to now and again." *I've cried my share.* "Just do it beyond the eyes and ears of customers. Go on now."

Eudora fled to the storeroom and Annie went to help the bride.

After showing her a few dresses, the bride commented on the fabric. "It's very chic. The very best quality."

"It is." Annie carried two of the dresses to a fitting room for her. "Would you like assistance?"

"No, thank you. I think I can manage."

Annie stood nearby, ready to help, if needed. The comment about the fabric made Annie think of Guy. She hadn't seen him since he'd brought in the bill last week. It wasn't like him to be absent from Unruffled for more than a day or two. If he didn't have anything new to sell, he came in to schmooze—and, to see Annie. Had she offended him in some way?

She hated caring about it. She didn't want his affection, but she didn't want his ill will either. *It's best he stays away. Your life is easier if he does.*

Edna came in the store juggling a lunch basket and an armload of freshly sewn dresses. Annie hurried to help relieve her of the clothes. Edna checked the sizes on the rack. "We need more tens again? We can't keep up."

"It's a good problem to have."

"It is." She lifted the basket. "I brought lunch for everyone."

"How sweet of you."

"It will have to wait." She pointed toward the fitting room. The bride had emerged.

ᴥ

Edna took her sandwich to the storeroom. She needed to check stock of the green jersey as they were nearly out at the workshop. Women loved the drape of it compared to the usual cottons and wools.

She set her sandwich on a crate and looked through the tall bolts that leaned against the far wall, thinking of colors for autumn. "The light is so poor back here," she said to the air. "We need to add another lightbulb. I can't tell what color a fabric is."

Edna pulled out a gabardine, angling it toward the light. It was a caramel tan color, which would be ideal for an autumn suit. She took the bolt out to the showroom and talked to Annie about it. Annie did a quick sketch and Edna cut off a swatch to bring to Maude for her approval. She loved how easily new designs were created. From idea to sketch to pattern to reality in a few blinks. Each woman had their place in the process. They made a good team.

Edna brought the bolt back to the storeroom and went to fetch her sandwich.

It was gone.

I don't remember eating it.

This wasn't the first time an idea had caused her to get totally immersed, forgetting all else. But it was the first time she'd forgotten that she'd eaten.

⋰

Maude had trouble keeping up with Gela as they walked the last block toward Port Refuge.

"I hope he's there, Mama. He didn't come in Refuge Saturday *or* Sunday."

Maude agreed it was odd that Dock had disappeared since he'd spoken with Gela. Gela had been so disappointed because she wanted Maude to talk with him, to see his remorse.

Maude wasn't so sure. If the man regretted what he did, good. But that didn't mean Maude needed or wanted to talk to him face to face. She could see little good coming from such interaction and had been relieved when Gela had reported his absence.

Yet Maude knew Gela wouldn't let it go. And so today, Maude agreed to go with her to Refuge. Not that her presence there would suddenly make him appear . . . she went along for her daughter's sake.

Gela paused before entering the shelter. "If he's not here, we need to go where he lives."

What? "No. Gela. I never agreed to that."

"We have no choice, Mama. This needs to be finished. You and him, talking it through."

She lowered her voice. "One does not 'talk through' a rape. It's not that simple."

"It could be."

Maude was torn between telling Gela it was over, or going along with her daughter's naïve notions to prove to her that not everything could be made right with a simple "I'm sorry." Yet perhaps it was a life lesson Gela needed to learn. Maude was counting on the train-up Bible verse: "Train up a child in the way he should go: and when he is old, he will not depart from it." Hopefully.

Gela must have seen some sort of acquiescence on her face, because she took Maude's hand and led her inside Refuge. She received hearty greetings upon entering, along with many requests for her to sing.

"Not today. Have you seen Dock?"

No one had.

Gela immediately led Maude outside and began walking down the sidewalk.

"I'm still not sure about this," Maude said. "He wasn't friendly when *I* followed him. And you were hardly welcomed. Maybe he doesn't want to be found."

Gela stopped walking and faced her. "Don't you want this completely over? Finally resolved?"

Maude wasn't sure how to answer. "I'm not sure it will ever be *over*. I've moved on, but it's still *there*." Although she'd pushed the event into a back corner of her mind, it still lurked in the shadows, ready to pounce.

"What happened to forgive and forget?" Gela asked. "Maybe you can't do one without the other."

Her daughter was incredibly naïve. She though a smile and a word would make the world right. And yet . . . maybe it could be made better.

Gela linked her arm with Maude's. "Let's do this. Try this. I guarantee it won't make things worse."

That remains to be seen.

Maude felt great trepidation as they walked down one seedy street after another to face the man who had attacked her. To talk to him. To get to know him. It was going above and beyond what most victims chose to endure. Yet she'd been praying about it for days. The "judge not" verse she had recited to Gela had become a dogged mantra that wouldn't leave her alone. Hopefully today would silence the directive and bring an end to *any* thoughts of Dock Varner.

"Over there." Gela pointed to an alley.

Lord, help me.

They stood at the apex of the alley and Maude peered into the dim. The sun was a stranger. The smell of the unwashed and under-fed assailed her.

Gela stepped a few paces in. "Dock? Are you here? Clarence? It's Gela."

"It's Gel-a," mimicked a man. Others laughed.

Another said, "Clarence? Who's Clarence?"

Maude felt the goosebumps of fear and took her daughter's arm. "Let's leave."

"Wait." A man climbed out of a shack built from trash. He straightened with a groan. "I'm here."

Gela stepped closer, urging Maude along. "I brought my mother. She wants to speak with you."

Not exactly. But Maude didn't correct her. "If you're . . . " her voice cracked and she cleared her throat. "If you're willing," she said.

He nodded once and thankfully led them out to the street. He avoided Maude's gaze completely, looking between and around her. "To the bench?" he asked Gela.

"That's perfect."

They walked to a bench and Dock shoved trash and stray leaves away. He offered them the seat. Maude and Gela sat down.

Under their scrutiny he ran a dirty hand through greasy hair. "Gela told you what I said?"

"You confessed."

He nodded. "Did she also tell you I am appalled at my action. I'm sorry. It wasn't like me and I . . . I've been paying for it ever since."

She was touched by his sincerity — for he did seem sincere — but she needed to say, "So have I."

He was still a moment. "I'm sure you have."

She shook her head. "I don't think you fully understand. Because of what you did to me, how you harmed me . . ." To speak of such things to a man, any man, much less her attacker stretched the boundaries of propriety and feasibility. Yet none of that mattered today. Gela was right. She needed to finish this. "I couldn't have children because of your attack. I don't love like I could have loved. I still experience fear and pain and . . . shame."

His eyes grew large and he began to mouth unheard words before saying, "Because of me?"

"Yes. Because of you." Finally confronting him caused Maude to feel a surge of inner strength. "Because I was unable to bear children I nearly didn't marry, for it wouldn't have been fair to the man I loved."

He looked at Gela. "But she's your daughter?"

Gela answered for her. "My mother died. Mama married my father when my brother and I were small. She's my mother now."

Dock bit a dirty fingernail. "I'm glad for you. Nothing good ever happens to me. God doesn't want nothing to do with me. I've been paying penance all my life. Ain't been able to climb my way out of it." He tucked his fingers under and looked away.

He wanted her to feel sorry for *him*? About what *he'd* endured?

Her heart pounded in her chest. *What am I supposed to do? Help me!*

But then . . . her heartbeat began to slow down one beat at a time as though God was placing a calming hand upon her. *Forgive him as I have forgiven You. You don't need to forget but You do need to forgive. Do it for Me.*

Gela nudged Maude. They were waiting.

It was time to say what she'd come to say. "Maybe you can start that climb today."

He looked up.

Could Maude really do this? Did she want to do this?

Do it.

"I . . . I forgive you, Dock. Clarence."

He bobbled on his feet and took a half-step back as if her words came with a physical shove. His chin quivered. He wiped his nose with the back of his hand. "You do?"

"I do." It was not a strong testament, but it was a start.

He turned his back to them and they saw his shoulders quake. They heard his sobs.

His angst and relief tore through her. *You did this, God. This moment is Yours, not mine at all.*

Then Maude stood and did something she never, ever expected to do. She put an arm around the shoulders of her attacker and told him everything would be all right.

And it would.

❧

After speaking with the Cohens and hearing about their cousins' suffering in war, Henrietta was determined to be more patient with Steven. Although he had seen death, he had not lost his entire life to evil. He had not been forced to flee his homeland and start over in a strange place. He had come home to his family. But . . . the fact he was still struggling deserved Henrietta's compassion and understanding, not impatience and demands.

She and the boys left their apartment to check on him.

"Can we go outside while you see Papa?" Willie asked.

"Don't you want to talk to him?"

He shrugged. "Maybe tomorrow."

His reluctance saddened her, yet she understood. Each time she checked on him made her stomach get tied in nervous knots. "Go outside then and play nicely. I'll be out in a minute and take you up to Vesta."

Willie and Lennie raced down the stairs. Henrietta knocked on the door to Edna's flat, and receiving no response, used her key.

Edna was probably at work. Henrietta went to Steven's bedroom and found him where she always found him: sitting by the window, looking outside. He was never *here*, always somewhere else, as though his mind and body were totally separate entities that rarely connected in the pres —

A scream! It was Lennie's scream!

Henrietta ran to the window and looked out with Steven. Their little boy was lying on the ground next to a delivery truck. Had he been hit?

Before she could move, Steven burst into action. He ran out of the apartment and hurtled down the stairs, out to the street, to Lennie's side, with Henrietta close behind.

Steven cradled Lennie in his arms. "Are you all right?"

Lennie blinked, as if he'd hit his head. There was a gash on his forehead and blood streamed into his hair.

"I was jumping from the back of the truck and fell and hit my head."

Henrietta took out a handkerchief and pressed it against his cut, breathing a sigh of relief. "Silly boy. You know you shouldn't do that."

"I told him not to," Willie said.

"No, you didn't. You did it too," Lennie said.

He tried to sit up, but Steven held him down. "Stay put." He took the handkerchief. "Head wounds always bleed a lot . . ." He stared at the crimson cloth. "Head wounds always bleed . . ."

Henrietta knelt beside them. "You're right, they do. But Lennie will be all right. You saw him and saved him. He'll be fine."

Steven looked at Henrietta, his face drawn. "I wanted to save them all. I couldn't save them." His face crumpled in misery.

Henrietta wrapped her arms around her husband and son.

॰౿

Steven carried Lennie upstairs to their apartment and took charge of cleaning his cut and bandaging it.

"I look like a soldier," Lennie said.

Henrietta cringed at the reference.

But Steven nodded. "You do. A brave soldier who will learn from his mistake and never ever jump like that again. Promise?"

Lennie nodded. Then he studied his father. "Are you back, Papa?"

Steven looked at Henrietta, then at Lennie and Willie. "I think so. I hope so."

Praise the Lord!

ঽ

Edna was on her way out of Unruffled to head back to the workshop when Henrietta rushed in. She was beaming from ear to ear.

"Gracious," Edna said. "What's made you so happy?"

Henrietta didn't say anything, but stepped outside. When she returned, Steven was with her.

"I'm so glad you got out of the house," Edna said to her son.

"There's more to it than that," Henrietta said. "Tell her."

"I'm back, Mother. Really back. I'm myself."

Edna stared at him, unbelieving.

"We just moved him back home."

Edna began to laugh. "That most certainly is *back*." She pulled Steven into an embrace, rocking him. "Oh, dear boy. I'm so glad. We've missed you."

He pulled away to look at her face. "Thank you for never giving up on me. I wanted to break free of the prison I was in, but I just couldn't do it." He swept a hand through his hair. "It made me feel weak and a failure. As you said after your friend Mack came to dinner, many men died. I didn't." He looked away. "I didn't." He extended his hand to Henrietta. "I know you were praying for me, and I was praying too. But today the fog lifted and I could see again. See my many blessings."

Edna was moved by his testimony. "What happened?"

He told her about Lennie's fall and his cut. "My instincts took over."

"You had to help your son."

He nodded, but still looked troubled.

"What's wrong?"

"The blood . . ." He pressed his fingers to his eyes. "The trenches ran with it, became muddy with it. There was no beauty anywhere, just dirt and mud and gray skies and the silhouettes of blackened trees and buildings in the distance. The only color was the blood. And the mortar explosions. The blood pouring out of my friends . . . I couldn't help them. It was hell on earth." He looked on the verge of tears. "Sometimes I wanted to stand up and walk across no-man's land and let the Germans shoot me. Just be done with it."

"Oh, no . . ."

He nodded. "There was no hope there. None. I don't understand war. What's the point? So many good men dead. For what?" He looked directly at both of them. "I'm asking a serious question: what was it all for?"

Edna wasn't sure of the answer. At first. Then she remembered something she'd read. "The war made two empires disappear: the Ottoman and the Austro-Hungarian. Maybe they were too powerful and greedy. Maybe they needed to disappear."

"But the Bolsheviks took over," Henrietta said. "I just visited the Cohens and they have cousins who fled Russia. Their family was murdered and their village wiped out. They're afraid of the future of their country."

Edna nodded. "Two empires gone, and Russia struggling to rebuild. Those are huge far-reaching changes."

"The war showed us all sorts of new ways to kill each other," Steven said. "Tanks, airplanes, machine guns, mortars . . ."

She rubbed his upper arm, wanting his thoughts to move elsewhere. "Time will tell whether it truly was the war to end all wars."

"Surely, wars can't get worse," Henrietta said.

Edna wasn't sure. The perversity and hatred of men could invent all sort of evil methods to kill. She kept such fears to herself and smiled. "You are with us again. Fully back from the shadows. We must remember, but not dwell on the horrors of war."

Steven nodded and pulled Henrietta's arm through his, holding it in place with a pat to her hand. "I am home, fully home. And I am thankful."

On that, they could agree.

≈

Across the ocean, Henrietta's mother walked toward the drawing room of Crompton Hall. She heard female voices and was eager to greet the visitors.

But just as she was reached the edge of the room she heard her name mentioned. Lila stopped.

"Really, Theodosia," said a guest. "You can't mean that."

"I *shouldn't* mean that, but I do. I wish my mother-in-law wasn't here. Then I could have free reign and run this house exactly as I want."

Lila's stomach clenched. *She doesn't want me here?*

"Don't you get along?" someone else asked.

"She's nice enough. Kind enough," Theodosia said. "It's not that. It's just that it's my turn to be the viscountess."

"But it's normal for the dowager to stay on."

"That doesn't mean I like it. More tea, anyone?"

Lila fought back tears, and turned around to walk back the way she had come.

But then she stopped. *Don't run away. Confront her.*

The inner suggestion surprised her and gave Lila its own measure of discomfort. Lila was *not* a confrontational person. Never had been. When she'd married Joseph she'd been forced to become stronger, but her innate tendency to avoid conflict remained.

Do it.

Through the years Lila had learned that such inner nudges — especially if they went beyond her normal thoughts — were not rooted in herself at all. She called them God-nudges. She'd ignored more than she should have, and had found that following through, even when it was difficult, always produced the best results. Eventually.

She took a breath to fuel herself, closed her eyes, and said a prayer for strength — and the right words. Then she stepped into the room.

"Mother." Theodosia looked a wee bit nervous at seeing her.

"Theodosia. Dorothy. Gwendolyn. How nice that you ladies came for a visit."

"It's nice to see you, Lady Newley," Gwendolyn said.

Dorothy nodded.

"Would you like to join us?" Theodosia asked.

"No, thank you. Actually, I think what I have to say is best said standing."

"Have to say?"

"I heard that you want me gone."

Theodosia set her teacup down, making it titter against the saucer. "Whyever would I say such a thing?"

"Something about 'free reign'?"

Theodosia sprang to her feet and took Lila's hands in hers. "I'm so sorry, Mother. I didn't mean it. I was just making small talk."

"Wanting to be rid of your mother-in-law is not small talk."

The girl bit her lip, then turned to her guests. "Would you excuse us, please?"

"Of course."

The women were out the door in record time. Lila could see them hurry away through the large front window, their heads together as they fine-tuned their gossip, no doubt.

Theodosia fell into a chair, her hands to her face, crying. "I'm so sorry. I shouldn't have said any of it. I don't know what got into me. We were talking about family and it . . . it just came out."

"The truth often does."

She sprang to her feet. "It's not the truth! I have nothing against you being here. Honestly."

Lila caught a small distinction. "You having nothing against me being here is not the same as you wanting me here."

"Then . . . I want you here."

Lila decided this was a good place to end the discussion. "I have much to think about." With that, she left the room.

She hadn't expected to feel good about the confrontation. And yet....

She did.

∾

After her confrontation with Theodosia, Lila needed fresh air. She took a walk through the rose garden, cutting blooms for an arrangement. She held a yellow rose to her nose, drinking in the heady fragrance. She knew they all had names, but never could remember them. Mr. Drexel, the gardener would know.

She heard someone behind her. Expecting to see the man, she inquired, "What is this one called again?"

"I'm sure I have no idea. " It was her son, Adam.

"I thought you were Mr. Drexel."

He held up a thumb. "Nope. Not green at all." He looked over the garden. "Under my care they would surely wilt and die."

"Nonsense." She handed him the basket. "Hold this while I cut some more."

He stood patiently and she was glad to let the moment be awkward. She could guess why he was there, especially since he rarely partook of the garden.

"There." She took the basket back. "I think that's enough for a good arrangement for the dining room." Then she looked at him. Pointedly. "You heard?"

When he sighed he looked ten years younger. "Theodosia didn't mean it."

"Actually, I believe she did."

He didn't argue with her. "She's an independent sort. You know that. She likes to have control."

"I believe I have given her control."

He offered her his arm and they began to walk. "You have. You've been very gracious."

"But?"

"But, actually . . . I think I know how she feels."

"You don't want me here, either?"

"I just mean when Papa was alive, I felt like second fiddle."

"You were. He was the viscount. You were his heir."

"In a way Theo is *your* heir. She's taking over your position, except for the fact that . . ."

"I'm still here."

He shrugged, then stopped and faced her. "Will you forgive her? You know she often speaks when she should remain silent."

Don't we all. "Of course I will. But that doesn't — "

He waved toward the far corner of the garden, and Theodosia hurried forward. Her face was serious. Her eyes red. From crying?

She reached them and grabbed his arm, as though for support. "I'm so sorry, Mother. I'm a fickle woman who has much to learn. From you. Will you forgive me?"

Lila felt her throat tighten. She held out her hand and Theodosia took it. Lila gave it a squeeze. "Of course I forgive you."

Theodosia sighed deeply. "I feel better now."

"As do I," Lila said.

They went back to the house, with Theodosia chittering on about the roses Lila had cut. Her flattery and extravagant details were too much, but Lila appreciated her effort.

❧

Sam walked the same way to work every day, past the same buildings, even past some of the same people.

"Morning," he said to Mr. Slivington as he put a collection of hats outside his haberdashery.

"Same to you, Sam." The man fanned himself with a hat. "Goin' to be a hot one."

"That, it is."

The man nodded toward a woman walking by. "Women 'ave it made nowadays. We 'ave to wear the same clothes be it summer or winter. They get to adapt."

Sam watched the woman a moment. "Cooler fabrics like batiste and cotton lawn helps. As do the tea-length skirts and raglan sleeves."

Mr. Slivington gave him a look. "Raglan, batiste, and cotton lawn, you say? Since when does a mechanic know about such female things?"

Sam just stood there. How *did* he know?

He chuckled. "Maybe you should go work at one of those fancy dress stores or over at the Butterick store a few blocks over. I'm sure they'd love to have ya."

Butterick?

Mr. Slivington slapped him on the back. "Don't look so worried. You's a man's man, I can tell. I'm just joshing ya. Even I's been in the Butterick store with me wife."

Sam nodded and was on his way. He'd feel better once he got his hands dirty in an engine.

☙

Sam was glad to see Mr. Billings come into the garage. "It's all done, sir. As good as it can be."

"If you don't say so yourself."

Sam felt himself redden.

"Tell me what you did with it."

Sam explained the truck's repairs, one by one.

"Well done," Mr. Billings said. "I am thankful."

"I'm glad to help."

"Actually, I have one more task—if you are so inclined."

"Another truck to fix?"

"No, no," Mr. Billings said with a laugh. "My wife will think three is one too many."

"Then how can I help?"

"I need to get both trucks back home. And as I am but one driver, I need another. Would you be interested? You could take the train back to London."

The chance to see different scenery was enticing. "I'd be happy to do that. But I'll have to ask my boss."

"I already did. He says you can go. No pay on his part, but I will compensate you for your time."

"I'm not worried about that at all. I'd like a chance to drive in the countryside and get out of the city."

"Agreed. I have a little more business in London, but let's leave Thursday morning at seven? Three days from now?"

"That will be fine."

"Capital. I will meet you here."

Sam thought of something. "Where is home?"

"Summerfield."

☙

Henrietta felt as awkward as a new bride.

She soaked in a leisurely bath, using the time to thank God for His blessings and answered prayers. But she also prayed for this particular night. It would be the first time they'd been together as man and wife since before the war. It felt odd to pray about such things yet hadn't God made them both, man and woman? Didn't He sanctify marriage?

And so she prayed all would go well and they would rekindle their love — which had been sorely tested.

The bath over, she put on her prettiest pink nightgown — purchased for their honeymoon. It was a simple silk sheath with tiny tucks marching up the bodice and delicate lace around the neckline and arm holes. There was a matching dressing gown with a tie at the neck, but moths had gotten to it, making it unusable. It was too hot for a wrap anyway.

She combed through her hair but didn't plait it in a single braid as she usually did. Instead she let it cascade over her shoulders. Steven liked her hair down and despaired that women were not allowed to wear it so all the time.

She gazed at her reflection and stroked a line that had been worn into her skin between her brows. A worry line, though not entirely Steven's fault. The past six years had been full of worry, both personal and for the world. She sighed. "Not too bad for being thirty-six."

She dabbed some perfume to her neck, wrists, and one to the center of her chest. On a whim she'd purchased the new fragrance, Tabac Blond, because it said it was for the emancipated woman. It smelled a little leathery, musky. Not like the lilies of the valley and honeysuckle scents she was used to. It smelled . . . sexy.

And so, with her hair a burnished mantle, her garb a flowing gown, her scent a sultry vixen, Henrietta entered their bedroom where Steven waited. He'd pulled down the covers on her side of the bed. An invitation.

Which she accepted.

God was good. In so many ways.

CHAPTER THIRTEEN

The world was good. Edna couldn't stop smiling. To have her son back and see him laugh and play with the boys made her heart overflow with thanksgiving.

Her joy in him spurred her to find joy in the sewing again, which was contagious, making Gert and Ginny work harder. It had been a very productive five days, with a dozen new dresses ready to take to Unruffled.

Of course, part of Gert's joy stemmed from her upcoming marriage in three days. The restoration of Edna's son and the marriage of her friend . . . new beginnings all around. God was so very good.

Edna hung the new dresses on the racks at Unruffled, chatted with Annie, Sara, and Eudora, then went to the storeroom to get more fabric for the coming week's work. As she neared the rows of bolts in the far back, she spotted some feet sticking out from behind some crates. Child's feet.

She pulled up short, a hand to her chest. *So I didn't eat the sandwich after all?*

A child. Hiding in the storeroom. Or was there more than one?

She took a step toward the front of the store to tell the others, then stopped. If the child knew they were found out, they'd run. Would they find another safe place? Edna could imagine far too many awful fates for a child on the streets. At least they were safe here. As far as she'd seen, nothing was damaged.

In a way, she admired their pluck. And so she decided to keep their secret. At least for the moment.

Edna moved to the bolts and chose the one she wanted, talking to herself about nothing. But then she took a few yards of wool off the end of a different bolt and said aloud, "We don't need this blue anymore. There's not enough to do anything with it. I'll just lay it here on the crate and we'll toss it in the dustbin later."

As she was walking away, she thought of another way to help. "Oh dear. I hate having change in my pocket. I'll just set it on the fabric."

She knew it was an odd — and illogical — thing to do, but she hoped a child in need would accept her farce for its good intention.

Edna left the room, feeling an additional dose of joy.

᪥

Henrietta and Steven strolled through Washington Square Park, with the boys skipping happily ahead of them, tossing a ball back and forth.

"This is good," she said softly.

He patted her hand. "This is very good. Life is very good."

"I'm so glad you've applied for a teaching position again."

"As am I. A different school, different children, a different me."

"A man made richer from his experiences?"

"Hmm. We'll see."

Henrietta spotted someone she knew and called to her. "Mabel!"

The woman turned around. "Henrietta. How nice to see you." She looked at Steven. "I don't believe we've met."

"Mabel, this is my husband, Steven. Steven, this is Mabel Humbolt who works in accounting at our fabric supplier, Olivet."

Steven tipped his hat. "Very nice to meet you."

Henrietta remembered what Annie had told her about Olivet. "How goes the move?"

"Move?"

"Olivet. The offices and warehouse? I was shown the new address on the invoice, where to send payments."

Mabel looked confused. "We haven't moved. We're still in the same place we've been for fifty years. Who told you we'd moved?"

Henrietta's insides tightened. "Never mind. I must have misunderstood."

"We look forward to more business from you," Mabel said. "Has it been slow at Unruffled?"

"Not lately." *What's going on?*

Mabel cocked her head. "You know we always appreciate your business." She saw someone in the distance and raised a hand in greeting. "There's my friend. So nice seeing you, Henrietta, and meeting you, Steven."

"That's odd," Henrietta said after she'd left them. "We've given them a lot of business lately, what with the fabric orders for the wedding dresses."

"Maybe she hasn't invoiced the orders yet and is unaware."

"I just paid a large invoice — and sent it to their new address."

"She says they don't have a new address."

Henrietta felt her stomach grab in a most uncomfortable way. "Something is wrong here."

"Apparently," he said. "One plus one is not equaling two."

Her mind raced and she knew her ability to enjoy the stroll was over. "I need to get home, check the ledgers, and figure this out. Can you stay with the boys?"

He nodded and kissed her cheek. "Don't get too carried away with your thoughts. It's probably a simple mistake."

Her instincts said different.

৶

Henrietta checked the ledgers. One plus one *did* equal two. The math was correct on the billings and the payments to Olivet. It was the address that was in question.

"Where are my payments being sent?"

She had an awful feeling, a deep suspicion. Annie had told her the bill had been hand-delivered by Guy. *He'd* been the one to point out the new address. But she couldn't accuse him of such a deception until she was sure. The first step to being sure was to go to the address on the invoice and see what was there.

Steven came in the door, his face exuberant. He waved a telegram. "I intercepted the telegraph messenger while I was outside with the boys. I got a teaching position!"

She sprang to her feet and into his arms. "It's only been a few days since you applied."

He twirled her around.

The sins of Guy Ship would have to wait.

৶

Sam found driving in the English countryside very relaxing. The rolling expanses of green fields and towering trees were a sharp contrast to London. Yet they were foreign to him, and not just because he knew he was an American and this was England. Being in the countryside seemed foreign to him.

Does this mean I'm a city boy?

It was another clue, another puzzle piece to add to the jumble that one day would hopefully help him remember his life before the war.

He'd lost sight of Mr. Billing's truck around a curve and nearly missed him taking a left fork. Luckily, a herd of sheep had caused Mr. Billings to stop and wait. Sam caught up.

Sheep swarmed around the trucks. An old man with a staff nodded to Sam as he passed. *This* he had never seen. He was certain of it.

They passed the entrance to an estate that had large trees edging a drive. He could spot a many-turreted mansion in the distance. Surely this was the home of some Lord and Lady. Were they called counts or earls? Barons? The whole hierarchy of British titles was totally outside his knowledge.

Viscount.

He mentally started at the word. Vie-count? That was an odd title. And being so, why would it come to mind?

They came to the beginnings of a village, not the first they had passed through, but this time Mr. Billings turned down a small street off the square. Sam saw a sign for Billings Carpentry. He pulled his truck next to Mr. Billings and got out.

"Welcome to Summerfield," Mr. Billings said. "Come into the shop and I'll show you what I do."

The carpentry shop was abuzz with activity and Sam was introduced around. All types of furniture were being built and stained.

Mr. Billings ran a hand along the top of a table with turned legs. "There's nothing like the feel of wood sanded into submission. Feel it."

Sam obliged. "It's like satin."

"And that's before the stain and varnish—five coats, lightly sanded between each one."

"That's very labor intensive."

The older man nodded. "I know it's the old-fashioned way to do it as people can buy furniture made in factories now, but this is the way I was taught, and this is what I've based my reputation on. I can't do it any other way."

"Nor should you." Sam stroked the table again and could imagine a family around this table, sharing a—

Suddenly, an image flashed in his mind of a dark-haired woman passing a white bowl of green beans to a girl of five or six. The girl shook her head, but the woman said, "Victoria, don't argue with—"

"Now it's your turn to show off." Mr. Billings gathered the four men who were working in the shop, and led them out to the trucks. The talk turned to something Sam knew about: motors and tires.

❧

"I can take the train back," Sam said when Mr. Billings invited him to stay overnight at his house.

"Actually, you can't. The next train doesn't leave until one, tomorrow afternoon." He put an arm around Sam's shoulders. "As my wife always says, 'I won't take no for an answer.' Come meet my family."

They walked through the square that had a water pump in the middle. It was quaint and inviting. Children walked along a low sitting wall, pushing each other off, while old men leaned against their canes discussing whatever old men discussed. On one side of the square was a bakery next to a building that said, "The Summerfield Sewing Workshop", and across the way was the Summerfield Mercantile. There was a bench out front and lovely red flowers in pots that lured a person inside.

"You need anything, the Mercantile will have it or will get it for you. It's the heart of the village and is still run by the earl's family."

Earl not viscount.

They turned down another side street, to a brick two-story home. "Here we are."

They went inside. "Clarissa?"

A sixty-something woman came at his call. "You're ba—" She stopped as she saw Sam. "We have company?"

"We do. M'love, this is Sam Colyer, the man from London who's been working on both trucks for me. He was kind enough to drive one of them here. Sam, my wife, Clarissa."

Sam held his cap in his hands. "Very nice to meet you, ma'am."

"And you." She looked at her husband expectantly, as if she wanted to add, "And . . .?"

"Sam is staying for dinner and spending the night."

"Thank you very much for your hospitality. I'll leave on tomorrow's train."

There was a hint of imposition on her face, but just for a second. "Or course. Welcome, Mr. Colyer."

"Sam. Just call me Sam."

She raised a finger, as if remembering something. "Actually, we're invited to a casual family dinner at the Hall. But I'm sure Lila won't mind another setting at the table."

What was the "hall"? "Don't go to any bother, ma'am."

"Lila will never consider it a bother." She gave his clothes a once-over. "Timothy? Perhaps you could loan Sam a suit?"

Suit? *I have to wear a suit?* Sam's nerves kicked in.

"Not a problem," her husband said. "And you can come to church with us in the morning before your trip. Would you like that, Sam?"

"That would be nice." He hadn't been to church in a long time. He missed it. Which meant he was used to going.

"Gracious, Timothy," his wife said. "You certainly are giving our guest the full Summerfield experience — such as it is."

"We don't get many strangers staying over here. It will be nice to have some new conversation."

"I beg your pardon," she said with her hands on her hips.

"Just teasing, m'love."

Sam needed to tell them something. "Actually, I don't have much to contribute. For I lost my memory in the war."

"How tragic," Mrs. Billings said. "At least you remembered your name."

"Actually . . . no. I took the name Sam Colyer because it seemed close to right, but I don't think that's my name."

"Well then," she said. "I am quite sure you are the most unusual guest we have ever had." She took a step into another room and then instructed a servant to show Sam to his room to freshen up.

The maid nodded to the stairs. "Sir?"

A maid. Fancy. He nodded to Mrs. Billings before following. "Again, thank you for the hospitality, ma'am."

"It is our pleasure. Feel free to walk around the village if you'd like. Dinner will be at seven. I'll have Timothy bring up something to wear."

Dinner. In a dining room. That probably meant there would be napkins and china and goblets. He hoped his memories included manners.

❦

Sam washed the dust of the road off, then took Mrs. Billings' suggestion to explore Summerfield. He chose the mercantile first and was just entering when a slovenly-looking woman rushed out. Another woman rushed after her. "Agatha Wood, you bring that back!"

The woman hurried away.

"You want me to go after her?" Sam asked the shopkeeper.

"No need. It's a game we've played for decades. Agatha pinches something without paying, we yell at her, and she runs away."

"She's a thief?"

"She's our town thief."

"You have a town thief?"

"Every village needs one." She brushed her gray hair out of her eyes and put her hands on her hips. "But you sir? Are you just traveling through?"

Sam explained the situation. "I'm looking around. Seeing the sights."

She laughed. "Not much to see, yet it's the whole world to many of us." She held out her hand. "I'm Rose Wilson."

"Sam Colyer."

"Come in, Mr. Colyer. Let yourself be tempted by our wares."

Once inside Sam realized he did need a few things. He bought a comb, toothbrush and paste, and a razor. Rose gave him a ten-percent discount for being a friend of the Billings.

"In my short time to explore, what should I see?"

Rose thought a moment. "If you head east you can see Summerfield Manor."

"Sounds grand."

"Very. But if you walk out of town a wee bit in the opposite direction, you'll see Crompton Hall." She leaned forward confidentially. "That's my favorite of the two. Still grand and all that, but more . . . cozy." She laughed. "I'm sure cozy isn't a word most would use to describe the ancestral estate of a viscount."

Viscount?

Then he latched onto another word. "Hall? I'm going to dinner in a hall that has a woman named Lila as the hostess?"

Rose laughed. "That it! You're going to dinner at the hall? Aren't you the lucky one. Lila Kidd is the dowager viscountess."

"Excuse my ignorance, but what is a dowager?"

"Lila was the viscountess and her husband was the viscount, but when he died, her son became the viscount and his wife the viscountess. So she gets the title of dowager." Rose chuckled. "Which means still alive, but moved into the background a bit."

He shivered at hearing the titles and knew that somehow this would be a dinner he'd remember. He thanked her and left to explore.

As he walked across the square, he heard his name called. "Mr. Colyer?"

A young woman walked toward him. "Are you Sam Colyer?"

"I am." *Though I'm really not.*

"I just stopped at my parents' house to drop off my daughter and Mother told me the story of the trucks and how you're coming to dinner with us at the Hall tonight." She extended her hand to shake. "Penelope Billings Evers. People call me Pin."

"Very nice to meet you. Your parents are being very kind. I would have gone back to London straightaway but apparently the train doesn't run until tomorrow."

"Stranding you here. Poor you."

"From what I've seen it's a lovely town."

"Village. 'Town' gives it too much credit."

Her disparaging tone made him wonder why she lived here.

She flipped her own words away with a hand. "Don't mind me. Summerfield's nice enough. I only pretend to want to be somewhere else." She pointed at a building straight ahead. "I'm heading to the workshop. Would you like to come along? It's quite a unique place."

Sam looked past her to the Summerfield Sewing Workshop. "I don't think I've ever seen such a place."

She turned toward the low structure. "I'm not surprised. We like to think it's one of a kind." She led him inside where two women were sewing at machines. They stopped their work to look at him. An elderly woman sat near the window. Pin led Sam over to her. "Lady Summerfield, this is a friend of my father's, Mr. Colyer. Mr. Colyer, this is Lady Summerfield, the dowager countess of Summerfield."

Another dowager. He was glad he understood the term now. But countess? He didn't know the protocol for such a meeting, so nodded. "Nice to meet you, your highness?"

The woman grinned. "Not near that. Just call me Genevieve." She cocked her head. "You're American."

"I am." He'd heard an American accent to her words. "And you?"

"New York City, born and raised."

New York City . . .

"I didn't know an American could be a countess," he said.

"Though not usual, it can be arranged. Was arranged." She swept an arm to encompass the room. "How do you like our little sewing workshop. I started it over thirty years ago to teach local woman how to sew."

Sew . . . sewing . . . The words seemed to have roots in his memories.

He saw a pattern envelope on a cutting table and was drawn to it. "Butterick?"

"It's a sewing pattern," the countess said. "Paper pieces that you pin to the fabric and — "

With a glance he recited: "Pattern number 3558, a girl's coat in raglan style with an inverted or box pleat in back."

Mrs. Evers picked up the envelope. "He's right. That's what it says on the front, down to the description. How do you know that?"

He pressed a hand to his forehead. "I have no idea."

"It's unusual for a man to have knowledge of sewing," the countess said. "Especially such
specific knowledge."

Sam looked around the workshop. Suddenly he knew things. He touched a blue fabric. "This is chambray, and this . . ." he moved on to a floral fabric that had a glazed finish on it, "this is chintz."

The two women at the sewing machines stood. He pointed at what one was working on. "You're setting in a sleeve, and you . . ." He looked at the garment at the other machine. "You're sewing the facing for the neckline."

The countess applauded. "Bravo, Mr. Colyer. Why didn't you tell us you were involved in the dress trade?"

He shook his head. "Because I didn't know I was. I was injured in the war and lost my memory. I'm not even sure my name *is* Sam Colyer."

"Crikey," Pin said. "You don't remember a thing?"

"Pin. Don't pry," the countess said.

Sam strode around the workshop, feeling more and more at ease with the scene. "I get hints now and then. A word, a smell, a—"

"Sewing pattern."

He pointed to his ring. "I think I'm married too, but I can't remember her name."

"How tragic," the countess said. "You had a breakthrough today. That's encouraging."

"It's another piece to the puzzle. I keep praying God will let me remember."

"I'm sure He will at just the perfect time."

He realized all four women were standing, making him the center of attention. "I should go, but thank you for showing me what you're doing. I don't know how it all fits in, but I know it does."

"We will pray for you, Mr. Colyer—whoever you are."

❧

As her maid readied her evening dress, Lila read a new letter from Henrietta in New York. *"Please come to visit, Mamma. With the war, you've not even met our boys. They'd love to see you. Please come!"*

She carefully folded the letter. She would love to go for a visit. Yet to leave now might make Theodosia feel it was because of her.

Lila smiled to herself. Would that be so bad?

"Ma'am?" her maid said. "I believe it's time to get dressed for dinner?"

"Of course."

She'd leave the decision for another day.

❧

Sam looked at himself in the mirror. *Not bad.* The sleeves of Mr. Billing's shirt and suitcoat were a bit long—which was far more acceptable than the other way around.

He'd been offered a bath and had wallowed in its luxury. His boarding house in London had a tub in a bathroom shared by eight men. But it was always grungy and the hot water spotty and sparse. He couldn't linger in such a bath. At the Billings, he let himself close his eyes and felt his muscles relax in the steaming water. The soap smelled like flowers.

While combing his hair—he was thankful he'd thought to buy a comb—he'd wished for a haircut, but guessed the Billings would allow for such a lack. They were gracious people.

He was ready to go to dinner at Crompton Hall. What had Rose called it? Grand, yet cozy? He was curious to see such a place.

There was a soft knock on his bedroom door. "Mr. Colyer?"

He opened it to Mr. Billings. "My, you clean up well, young man."

"Thank you for the loan of it, sir. And for inviting me to come with you. I do hope it's not an imposition to the hostess."

"Clarissa already contacted Lila. All is well. You are expected and welcomed. Shall we go?"

♈

Lila heard automobiles on the drive. She peeked through the lace curtain in her bedroom and saw two vehicles carrying Clarissa's and Pin's families. She was late going downstairs, having misplaced one of her pearl earrings. She tried not to fret, knowing that Theodosia was the official hostess.

But she still hated being late.

"Found it!" the maid said, grabbing for it from under the dressing table.

Lila put in it, then checked herself in the full length mirror. She enjoyed family dinners where all could dress less formally. They'd all seen her ivory crepe georgette dress many times—and she didn't care. It was a favorite and had been sewn at the sewing workshop. It boasted a V-neck with a wide collar, wide horizontal panels of peach fabric, and vertical insets of lace. She'd had fun designing it and was so very glad that the fashion had changed during the last decade from nipped and tucked into a flowy linear silhouette. It was about time dresses were comfortable.

She heard voices below and made her way to the top of the stairs. *Nothing like making a grand entrance.*

Theodosia and Adam were greeting the guests, with little Robbie running between them all, making chugging sounds with a toy train. It was nice to see Pin and Jonathan again. Sophie was almost five, and was getting tall, though she hid from Robbie behind her mother's skirt.

I'd hide from Robbie's rough play too.

Lila noticed that Clarissa wore a new dress. It was expected, for Clarissa loved to show off her new clothes. Again, Lila didn't mind. Although they'd once been competitive—more on Clarissa's side than Lila's—middle-age had lessened the need, at least on Lila's end.

The group moved toward the drawing room and she saw the stranger, the guest.

Her heart stopped.

No! It can't be.

"Sean?" she called out.

Everyone looked up at her. She hurried down the stairs and pulled him into an embrace.

"I can't believe you're here! Why didn't they tell me you were the guest?" She stood back to look at him. "You're alive!"

He looked totally confused. "You know me?"

It took her a moment. "Don't you remember me? I'm Henrietta's mother."

His expression changed to one of panic. "I . . . What's my name?"

Your name? "I don't understand."

"Tell him, Lila," Timothy said. "He lost his memory."

It was a hard concept to understand. "You're Sean Culver."

He closed his eyes and opened them slowly. Then a huge smile passed over his face. "Sean Culver. That's me!" His face beamed. "That's me!" He pulled her into another embrace and they did a little jig together. When they stopped he blinked a few times, then said, "My wife is Annie. I have two daughters, Victoria and Alice." His eyes filled with tears. "I have a family!" He turned toward the door. "I need to go to them! They're in New York!"

Timothy stopped him. "Hold up, now. Give yourself a bit time to get your bearings."

Sean nodded slowly, looking disappointed. Lila led them into the drawing room where they all took a seat. Lila could see the wheels of his mind spinning.

"You truly didn't know who you were before now?" Adam asked.

"I was injured in the war and woke up in a British hospital. A nurse suggested I choose a name, so I chose Sam Colyer."

"The right initials," Theodosia said.

"The right number of syllables," Adam added.

Sean sat with his head bowed, his hands clasped under his chin. Lila couldn't tell if he was praying or just trying to sort it through. Probably a bit of both.

He looked up with an *aha* expression. "My wife is from Summerfield. She was your maid!"

"Yes, she was," Lila said.

Theodosia wagged a finger. "His wife is *that* Annie? The maid who ran away from her position when you were visiting New York?"

"She's the one," Lila said. "She became a pattern artist at Butterick Patterns—"

"I worked there!" Sean said. "I think I still work there as a salesman." He looked to Pin. "That's why I knew about the pattern and fabrics and dress construction."

Pin shared the circumstances at the workshop that had transpired earlier that day.

Clarissa had a question: "Didn't Annie open her own shop in New York?"

"Unruffled," Sean said. "They named it Unruffled: Fashion for the unruffled, unveiled, unstoppable woman." He laughed. "I remember the slogan!" He looked at Lila. "And I remember meeting you when Henrietta and Steven got engaged. You and your husband took all of us to Delmonico's for dinner." His face suddenly grew serious. "He was killed, wasn't he? In the early part of the war?"

"He was," Lila said.

"I'm so sorry."

Pin piped up. "Jonathan served too, as a doctor."

"I also served," Adam said.

Lila didn't like the air of competition. "Indeed, so many served, for which we are eternally grateful. She turned the subject back to Annie. "Your wife is an amazing woman. To go from being the daughter of despicable parents, to my maid, to a successful businesswoman is quite a feat."

Sean's eyes grew large. "I met a woman at the mercantile today. Rose called her Agatha Wood. She was stealing something and Rose said she was the town thief."

"That's Annie's mother," Clarissa said. "Her father's still in jail for killing Annie's little brother."

Pin made a place for Sophie on her chair to get her away from Robbie's teasing. "Before we were married, Jonathan and I helped Annie escape that awful household. We helped get justice for little Alfie." She nodded at her husband. "Jonathan and his father were the doctors in town and saw the abuse."

"Too late," Jonathan said.

"Too late, too late," mimicked Robbie.

Lila pointed a *behave yourself* finger at her grandson and he crawled under a table to play with his train. She changed the subject to happier times. "Annie learned to sew at the sewing workshop, which led to her position at the Hall."

"And a trip to New York City," Timothy said.

"Where she ran away and found you," Pin said. "How romantic!"

Sean sat there, shaking his head. "I need to get home. Right away."

And with that, Lila made her decision. "I will go with you."

"You?" her son asked.

"Etta has been asking me to visit for months now. Seeing Sean home is the perfect reason to go."

Sean stood. "When can we leave?"

They all laughed. "Tomorrow we can take the afternoon train to London, then board a ship at Southampton," Lila said.

"I'll take care of the arrangements," Timothy said. "I believe they sail on Tuesdays."

"We'll be off Tuesday then," she said.

Sean sighed. "Tuesday." Then his face showed a question. "How long does it take?"

"Six days," Clarissa said.

He nodded, his voice revealing his awe. "In a week I will be with my wife and daughters again."

"And I will be with my daughter and *her* family. I'll be seeing two grandsons I've never seen." *Thank You, Lord!*

Robbie climbed out from under the table. "I'm a grandson."

Lila motioned him close and wrapped her arms around him. "Indeed you are. I have three grandsons." She kissed his cheek and he rushed away to play. It would be hard leaving him behind.

"Can I send a telegram?" Sean asked.

"Of course," Timothy said.

But Clarissa had an idea. "Wouldn't it be marvelous for both of you to show up and surprise them all?"

Lila laughed. "You do have a flair for the dramatic. Sean? What do you think?"

He was nodding even before he answered. "Although it will be hard to keep the secret, I think that's a marvelous idea."

"It's set then. We shall go to America on Tuesday."

❧

It wasn't surprising Sean couldn't sleep. His entire world had changed—and expanded. Instead of being Sam Colyer with a few memories of the near past, he was Sean Culver, with a lifetime of memories to discover and cherish.

They were coming back to him a little at a time, as though he was turning the pages of his life's story—a familiar story, unread for a too long, with many blank pages yet to fill.

Annie.

He smiled at the thought of her. She was the dark-haired woman with perfect skin and a bright smile who had permeated his blind spot. Right behind the memory of his wife were memories of his other girls and an overwhelming feeling of love. Victoria and Alice amazed him every day with their antics and their children's view of life. Victoria clomping around their apartment in his shoes. And two-year-old Alice climbing up on the dining table, so proud of herself.

Yet, I've been gone two years. The girls are six and four now. Annie has had to raise them alone. I'm sure my family and friends have worried after me, they've been afraid. They've prayed for my safe return. They probably think I'm dead.

He turned over in the bed, looking toward the moonlit window. His family was waiting for him. Was it wrong to prolong their suffering another week so he could surprise them? Was it selfish to want to be in their presence when they found out he was alive?

Probably. Would God forgive him for it? Probably.

He closed his eyes and contacted the Almighty who had heard his prayers and the prayers of his family. He had much to be thankful for.

Chapter Fourteen

Sean sat next to Lady Newley and her family in the Summerfield church, in their pew near the front. Behind them were the Billings family, including Pin, Jonathan, and Sophie.

Before the service began, Lila leaned forward and nodded toward the pew across the center aisle. "That's the earl and his family," she whispered in his ear. "We're related. We're all related."

Sean nodded and caught the eye of the dowager countess who'd showed him around the sewing workshop yesterday. She offered him a smile.

It was strange to be in the church where Annie had attended services. She'd looked at the same altar, heard the same organ, marveled at the way the sunlight came through the same stained glass windows on the side.

He wondered if her mother was in attendance. He wanted to look behind him, but dared not. Would the "town thief" attend church?

He felt bad for thinking such a thing and remembered a verse his mother had taught him when he got cocky: 'For all have sinned, and come short of the glory of God.' *Including me.*

He briefly wondered if he should seek her out but quickly decided against it. Annie had shared details of her horrific childhood, the abuse, the fear, the oppression. Her parents probably didn't even know where she was. He assumed she wanted it that way. Introducing himself to Agatha Wood might be like opening Pandora's box. He set the notion aside.

His thoughts continued to have two lanes. In one, he thought about how thankful he was that God had arranged all this. In the other lane were expectant thoughts about how events would play out in New York when he saw Annie for the first time.

"You're smiling," Lady Newley said.

"I'm imagining what it will be like to see Annie again."

"It will be a very happy day. Praise God."

That was easy to do.

♪

Annie sat in a pew and stilled Alice's kicking feet with a gentle hand. The little girl made a face, but did as she was told.

Annie felt very blessed that the girls were so good. Thousands of families were having to deal with the loss of the male in their households. She was luckier than most for she had Sean's mother across the street and friends who were as close as family.

When the pastor said, "Let us pray," Annie began her usual prayer that Sean be brought home safely. Yet since she'd been praying it since before he'd even left for the war, and he hadn't returned . . . she was tempted to stop. Obviously God's answer was "No."

I still need to pray.

Suddenly some different words came to mind. *Father, You know how I'd like things to turn out. But now I ask that You use Sean and I however You see fit. I'm weary of making plans. I accept Your plans, whatever they are.*

She opened her eyes. The prayer felt right and good.

Amen.

ও

Maude wrapped the pastor's prayers around herself, spinning a cozy cocoon. She'd forgiven Dock. The hatred and pain had been eased in the release, its power dulled.

Antonio nudged her. "You're smiling," he whispered.

"I'll tell you later."

She hadn't told her husband about the meeting with Dock yesterday and had asked Gela to keep it to herself too. It had been such an emotional experience she needed time for it to settle. It's like she needed time to make sure it was real, make sure her hate was truly gone, and make sure her heart was fully lightened.

She smiled because all were true. Yesterday had changed her permanently. Today she would share with Antonio what *had* happened with Dock. And what she wanted *to* happen with Dock in the future.

How would he react?

He'd be upset she'd kept it from him. He would be very upset she and Gela had gone into a bad neighborhood to speak with him — and to that point, he had a right to be. Beyond all that, would he understand the easing of her burden — and Dock's?

She had to trust he would. God hadn't brought her this far to taint the forgiveness transaction with doubt or condemnation.

Then there was the fact that Maude wanted to do more for Dock. Much more . . .

The pastor's words interrupted her thoughts, "As we travel on this journey of life we must remember this, 'For unto whomsoever much is given, of him shall be much required: and to whom men have committed much, of him they will ask the more.' Have you been given much? God asks you to give more."

She smiled to herself.

≈

The pastor's words struck a chord in Edna's heart: "For unto whomsoever much is given, of him shall be much required: and to whom men have committed much, of him they will ask the more." She couldn't stop thinking about the little girl who lived in the storeroom. Edna had left some food, a few coins, and a blanket, but she wanted to do more, give more.

I've been given my son back. I have more to give.

She had a lot to think about. To pray about.

≈

Gela snuck looks at her mother. She was smiling. She'd smiled a lot since they'd gone to see Dock last week.

Could forgiveness—the giving and receiving of it—cause such drastic change?

Obviously, yes. She had never seen her mother so happy. But more than that, there was a lightness to her. As if a burden—

The pastor said, "For Jesus said, 'Come unto me, all ye that labour and are heavy laden, and I will give you rest.' Let Him remove your burdens. In Him your happiness is found."

All right. There it was.

Bravo God.

≈

The pastor spoke of burdens . . .

Henrietta nodded, her shoulders feeling heavy with them. But then she felt ungrateful. For God *had* lifted the heaviest of her burdens by restoring Steven to the family.

But now . . . her suspicions about Guy Ship weighed upon her, a different sort of weight. The weight of injustice.

Maybe it wasn't any of her business as it was between Guy and Olivet. In truth, Unruffled had benefited from his lies. They'd received deep discounts on the bridal fabric. To uncover his sins would cost them dearly.

Monetarily. Yet ethically, the truth needed to come out. And personally too. Annie had befriended Guy, thinking he was one sort of man when he might be a different sort entirely. If Henrietta didn't pursue this and Guy *was* a thief, Annie could suffer the heartache of being the victim of deception. The uncertainty of Sean's fate was heart-wrenching enough.

I have to do something. I have to see this through.

She repeated the verse in her mind, finding comfort there.

Come unto me, all ye that labour and are heavy laden, and I will give you rest.

❧

"I'm glad to get you alone," Maude told her husband after church.

Antonio drew her hand through his arm as they strolled through Washington Square Park. "Those are words every husband longs to hear." He drew in a deep breath of the August air. "It is rather sad that the children aren't children anymore and prefer to spend their Sunday afternoons away from us."

"Would we want it any other way?"

"No, I suppose not." He led her to a bench.

Maude nodded to other couples strolling by. How should she breach the subject?

As she scanned the path ahead, she saw a man, sitting on the ground, his hat outstretched, begging for coins.

Antonio must have seen the direction of her gaze. "It's sad, isn't it?" He sighed. "'For the poor shall never cease out of the land.'"

It was a perfect segue. "I believe the rest of the verse says we should help them."

"I believe it does." He got up and tossed a few coins in the man's hat.

"Thank you, sir."

Antonio returned to the bench. "Does that make you feel better?"

"It's not enough."

"You want me to give him more?"

She angled her body toward him. "I need to tell you about something that happened last Monday."

His eyebrows rose.

"Gela and I followed . . . wait, I have to back up." She looked across the park where happy people spent a summer afternoon. The subject of their conversation seemed out of place, a shadow in the sunlight. Best to walk through it as quickly as possible. "When I was at Port Refuge I saw the man who attacked me thirteen years ago."

Antonio blinked twice. "Are you sure?"

She nodded. "He recognized me too."

He took her hand. "I'm so sorry. Did he hurt you again? We should call the police."

"I've already been to two precincts. They can't do anything."

"Why not?"

"I never reported it and it was thirteen years ago. I have no proof."

He took her hand onto his knee. "What do you want to do?"

And here we go . . . "I . . . I already did it."

His eyebrows rose. "Did what?"

"A while ago Gela followed him and talked to him. "

"She what?"

Maude held up a hand to stop his words. "And Monday the two of us went to the alley where he lives and spoke with him."

He stood and faced her. "You shouldn't have done that. An alley? He lives on the streets?"

"He does. He had a job at the docks but lost it." All this was for another conversation. "Please hear me out. I want to tell you the most important part." She patted the bench beside her and he sat down. "He admitted what he'd done to me and told me he was sorry. And . . . I forgave him."

Maude could see an inner battle play out on her husband's face. "That's very magnanimous of you. But — "

"It was the right thing to do." She spread her hands. "More than that, it made me feel free. I'm free, finally free."

He studied her face a moment, then cocked his head. "I can see it. You *are* free, aren't you?"

Her eyes filled with tears and he wrapped his arm around her. "I didn't think it was still haunting me, but it was. The difference between now and before I forgave him is the difference between stepping outside versus viewing the sunlight through a lace curtain. Everything seems clearer now."

"For that, I am grateful. But it was dangerous, Maude. You should have had me with you. Whether it became clearer or not."

Clearer . . . It was the perfect transition to the next part of the conversation. She sat upright and dried her eyes with a handkerchief. "What also became clear is that this man — his name is Clarence Varner — has been living a self-imposed punishment for his crime against me. He couldn't overcome the guilt. He lives in a shack. He goes to Refuge to get a meal. He is destitute and hurting. And . . . I want to help him."

Antonio scooted a bit to the side so he could fully see her. "Help him? How?"

"I want to help him get a job somewhere and — "

"How are you going to do that?"

I have no idea. "His nickname is Dock because he worked on the docks. Surely with workers dying in the war and with the flu there is a need for manpower there, or in some other labor position. Construction?"

"Does he have a skill?"

"I don't know. But I'm sure he'd be willing to learn."

"Would he? I know your heart is in the right place but is he willing to take help?"

His question surprised her. "Why wouldn't he?"

"Because he's led a life beyond what we can imagine. I suspect the crime against you wasn't his only — "

"But it was," she said. "He said it was and I believe him. His crime against me broke him."

Antonio looked unconvinced.

"I have to try. When we do good for others we have no control over what they will do with our good intentions. That is not on our shoulders. We are asked to give. Period."

They watched a pigeon strut on the ground nearby. Antonio finally spoke, "I suppose I could try find him a place to stay for a decent price." He was quick to add. "It's a long shot. All apartment construction stopped during the war and more people moved to the city for defense jobs. The vacancy rate is almost zero."

"But you'll try. It doesn't have to be fancy."

"It wouldn't be." He stroked his chin, deep in thought. "There is one building where I know a tenant is leaving . . ."

"Grab it!"

"I'll do my best."

She kissed him. Maude hated to say the next, but had to. "You have to realize he'll have no money at first . . ."

Her husband nodded. "I suppose we could pay the rent for a few months, until he gets on his feet."

She gave him another kiss. "Gela and I could get him some decent clothes and household necessities. And make sure he's fed. He can't work well on an empty stomach."

He sighed deeply. "You amaze me."

She chuckled. "*We* amaze me."

"No," he said softly. "I'm talking about you forgiving the man who hurt you so horribly. And here you are, working to make his life better. Not many would do that."

"I admit when I first saw him, I wanted revenge. I wanted him to be arrested and rot in jail."

"A logical response."

"We should be proud of our daughter," she said. "Gela was the one who was compassionate, who forced me to meet him. Without her, I would still be suffering with the force of the attack still raw. So would Dock."

"Who knew she had it in her?" Antonio said. "So often she's this rebellious, selfish girl, but then she does something like this and surprises us."

"She's growing into a lovely young lady, inside and out." Maude needed to comment on her previous mention of revenge. "As I said, I wanted revenge. But when I spoke with Dock and witnessed the angst in his heart and the self-punishment he's inflicted upon himself because of the crime, God softened my heart. God made it possible for me to forgive Dock, as He forgives us. I've not forgotten what happened, but I have found a way to lessen its power on my life right now."

"How can I argue with that?"

"You can't." Maude felt as if the final weight had been lifted. Antonio was on her side. They were in this together.

"My, my, woman," he said. "You've turned a simple stroll in the park into a life-changing event."

She pulled his arm around her shoulders. "Finding you was a life-changing event."

"Don't expect me to argue with you."

CHAPTER FIFTEEN

Sean hesitated as he approached Crompton Hall. Should he go to the front door or to the kitchen entrance? It was true he'd been invited to spend the day there by Lady Newley, but he wasn't one of the family's friends. He was the husband of their former housemaid.

He decided to go the humbler route and went to the kitchen door and knocked.

A young girl answered. "Yessir?"

"I'm Sean Culver. Lady Newley invited me to spend the day here and—"

A portly woman stepped forward, wiping her hands on an apron. "You Annie's husband?"

"I am. Did you know my wife?"

She drew him inside. "Course I did. Annie was a sweet girl, she was. She'd even help out down here when I was shorthanded for a big event."

The young girl had backed away, but stopped and turned toward him. "Isn't Annie the one who went to New York with the mistress and Miss Henrietta and run away?"

"She is," Sean said. "Did you know her?"

"I, no. I's too young, but she's unfamous 'round here."

The cook shooed her away. "Infamous is the word you're looking for. Now go on with ya. There's dishes to wash." She turned to Sean. "Sorry 'bout that. Tis no disrespect against yer wife. It's just a good story, it is. 'Servant makes good' and all."

"It is a good story. My wife is an amazing woman. She risked everything and gained a new life."

"And you." The cook winked at him. "Would you like a scone? Fresh this morning."

"No, thank you. The Billings fed me very well. I'm not used to eating much for breakfast."

She shrugged. "The cook they have is good enough, but I'm better. Just saying."

He lowered his voice confidentially. "I believe you are. I was here for dinner last night. It was delicious. The mutton pie . . . Mmm-mmm."

She beamed. "Glad you liked it." She went back to kneading some dough on a long work table. "I heard you lost your memory and it came back to you last night."

Word travels fast in a small town. "That's true." He didn't want to go into details. "Lady Newley and I are sailing to New York tomorrow."

"To see yer wife."

"And two daughters."

"Ooh. That will be a glorious reunion indeed."

He spotted a clock on the wall. It was five after ten. "I should go upstairs. She's expecting me."

"If you don't mind me asking, why didn't you go to the front door?"

"As an American I'm not sure about protocol."

"If yer invited you go to the front." She called to a young boy, "Benjie, take Mr. Culver upstairs to the drawing room and tell Dowd to let her ladyship know he's here."

"This way, sir," the boy said.

"Thank you for the chat," he told the cook. "It's good to meet people who knew Annie."

"You tell her hey-di-ho for all of us."

"I will do that."

He followed the boy up some back stairs and thought about the hundreds of times Annie must have climbed these same steps. She'd told him the story of her getting a job here when she was fourteen. She hadn't come to the United States until she was nineteen, which meant she'd worked here five years. Five very important years in a person's life. Formative years.

As they passed through the front foyer, an extremely old butler appeared, and the boy handed Sean off, into his care.

"You came in the back way, sir?"

"I did. I'm sorry I'm a bit late. I got to reminiscing with the cook about my wife."

He nodded. "Annie was a good girl."

"You knew her too?"

"I did. She came from hard circumstances." He shook his head in disgust. "Despicable family. Despicable."

"I saw her mother yesterday."

"That's too bad. We can all thank God her father is still in jail."

The butler's words reinforced his admiration for his wife. "I'm glad Lady Newley took her in, gave her a new life."

"I hear you gave her another life," he said.

"She made her own life before I even met her. I'm lucky to have found *her*."

He smiled. "Very good, sir." He hobbled toward the drawing room, his back bent. Sean followed and wondered how long he'd worked there.

"I'll tell Lady Newley you're here," the butler said. "Please greet Annie when you see her. She was one of the good ones, she was."

"Still is. I will send your greetings. Thank you."

Before he left Sean, the butler added, "I'm thankful you're traveling to New York with the mistress. She's quite capable, but it will be nice for her to have the company." He looked to the floor. "We all miss Lord Newley — the elder. They were such a happy couple, so well-suited. The two together were far stronger than the two apart."

"I will make sure Lady Newley gets there safely. We will keep each other company."

"Very good, sir."

As soon as he'd left, Sean said aloud, "I didn't get his name."

"Who's name?" Lady Newley entered the room.

"Good morning. The butler's name, and the cook's name. They both knew Annie and I want to tell her that I spoke with them."

"The cook is Mrs. Dermott and the butler is Dowd."

"How long have they been here?"

"Mrs. Dermott has been here at least twenty years, and Dowd? He's been here since before I came into the picture." She looked to the ceiling. "Joseph and I were married in eight-one . . . Dowd was not young then. So I'm thinking he's . . ."

"Old."

She nodded once. "And very loyal. I'm not certain how many other servants were here when Annie was, but I'm sure as we progress through the day those who knew her will let us know. She always left a good impression."

"That's what I'm finding out."

"Would you like a tour of Annie's world?"

"Of course — if you're not too busy packing for our trip. We leave this afternoon on the train to Southampton?"

"We do. No worries." She waved a hand. "The benefit of having a household of servants is that they do the work *for* me, which leaves me time to spend with very important guests. Shall we?"

❧

Sean and Lady Newley walked up a narrow back stairway, two more flights. Lady Newley held onto the railing, taking each stair carefully. "I haven't been up here in years. My, the stairs are steep."

They reached the top where she stopped and caught her breath. "I have a new appreciation for those in our employ." She looked down a long hall with many doors on either side. "Oh dear. I meant to ask which room was Annie's, but forgot."

"I'll go back down," Sean said.

But then a young woman came out of a room, adjusting her cap. She looked at them, blinked, then bobbed a curtsy. "Your ladyship?"

"Oh good. Bessie, would you please show us the room where Annie Wood stayed when she worked for us?"

Bessie looked at Sean, prompting him to say, "I'm her husband, from New York."

Her eyes brightened. "We all heard about you, the story of last night with you rememberin'."

"Yes, Bessie," Lady Newley said. "I'm sure the entire household knows the story — or a version of it. Which leads toward wanting to show Mr. Culver where his wife lived. If you please?"

"Of course, ma'am." Bessie went to a room, knocked, and upon hearing no answer, opened the door. "Annie stayed in here the whole time until she sailed to New York with you and then . . ." She shrugged, revealing that everyone knew *that* story too. Or a version of it.

Sean and Lady Newley went inside, with Bessie staying behind in the doorway. "There used to be a chair in the corner where Annie would do her sewing. But they musta moved it when they put two beds in here 'steada one." She touched the one on the left. "This one was Annie's. I remember the white iron headboard."

Sean walked the perimeter of the room — which didn't take more than a few steps in each direction. There was a window that looked out over the rooftop. Hooks on the wall. A small bureau and nightstand with a lamp. He had an odd urge to lay down on the bed.

"May I?"

"Certainly," Lady Newley said, though she seemed confused with what he wanted to do.

He sat on the bed, then lay back upon it. His shoulders were barely supported. He looked up and saw a water stain in the ceiling that oddly looked like a rabbit's head.

Just like Annie described to me. He felt a warmth at the past and present melding together.

"Oh dear," Lady Newley said, following his gaze. "We should have that fixed."

"I think it's old, your ladyship. Remember in '05 when we had that awful rain?"

"That was fourteen years ago."

"The roof was fixed, but they never got around to fixing the ceiling part."

Sean stood, looking at Lady Newley, for "they" implied "her".

"Then I think it's high time," she said. "I'll speak to my son about it. Thank you, Bessie." She led Sean out and down the stairs to the family's bedroom level. He was shown various bedrooms—including Lady Newley's which was abuzz with packing.

Then they stopped in another room, this one more masculine. "I've had my husband's clothes moved in here," she said. "After his passing it was too difficult to see them every day in our room."

"Annie was very grieved when she heard of his death. She admired him very much."

"We all did." She moved to the dressing room which was filled with dark suits. She fingered a sleeve. "When war came, Joseph wanted to help. Everyone told him it wasn't necessary—at least not physically. He was sixty years old. He could help in other ways. But as the young men of the county left to fight—as Adam left to fight—he said he couldn't stay behind and do nothing. So he volunteered to drive army supplies to the coast, to ship to France." She dropped the sleeve. "On his third trip his lorrie overturned and he was killed." She shook her head. "I begged him not to go."

Sean wasn't sure what he should say except. "Would it have been easier to accept if he'd died in battle?"

She cocked her head. "Perhaps. Perhaps that's what sticks in my craw, that he died by accident."

"Helping the cause. Doing his part."

She nodded, then took a fresh breath. "The reason I brought you in here is that you are in need of some clothes. I do believe you are nearly the same size as Joseph."

"I don't want to take his clothes."

"What good are they doing here? He would approve of anything that would support our goal of seeing Etta and Annie. I know it." She moved down the racks to some black suits and grinned back at him. "Besides, Mr. Culver, as we are sailing first class, you will need formal wear." She pulled out a tuxedo.

"I've never worn such a suit in my life—nor did I expect to."

She draped the suit over her arm and her face turned pensive. "None of us expect what happens to us. Good or bad. Now . . . we need to take full advantage of this very good opportunity. "I'll send in Jennings, Adam's valet, to get you set up in full fashion."

He was overcome with gratitude. "Thank you, Lady Newley. I will try to do justice to your husband's attire."

"I'm sure you will. I need to deal with some correspondence in my room. Come see me when you're through."

Sean knocked on the doorjamb of Lady Newley's room. Amid the busyness of servants packing, he saw her seated at a desk, pen in hand. She looked up, smiled, then stood to give him a once-over. "Look at you. I knew you were Joseph's size. Turn around."

He felt foolish doing so, but gave her the full view.

"Annie will be so impressed. From dapper to debonair—though I doubt she'll even notice your clothes."

Sean felt himself blush, which made Lady Newley laugh.

"I have something to show you." She went into her bustling dressing room and returned with a dress that had beading on the bodice. "See this beading?"

"It's lovely."

"Annie did it."

He looked at it with fresh appreciation. "A housemaid who could sew. She told me about such projects."

"There were many—beyond my knowledge. Besides making beds, scrubbing bathrooms, cleaning out grates, dusting and whatever else she was asked to do from dawn to dusk, she showed amazing sewing skills. This is extremely out of fashion now, but I wanted you to see the fine beadwork she did on the bodice—in her spare time."

He could recognize quality work. ."

"The problem was," Lady Newley said, "I didn't know it was Annie's workmanship, which was one reason she ran away. A person can only be exceptional without credit so long." She sighed. "We had two lady's maids here at the time—who are no longer with us. They misused Annie by having her do the work I asked them to do, then passed it off as their own. In New York, Annie finally had enough and took a chance by running away."

"She said she realized she was stuck where she was in the hierarchy of the servants, no matter what she did."

"Now I understand why she would feel that way, but it's tragic."

"I know she felt bad about running away. She admired you and Henrietta greatly. And now, she and Henrietta are close friends."

"A happy result, for certain." Lady Newley put the dress back. "The truth came out when I got home and suddenly found the skill of the new handwork terribly lacking. The lady's maids finally confessed the truth. They were let go." She nodded once, as if putting an end to the thought of them. "Luckily, Annie and I eventually had a chance to make our peace."

"She's still a very hard worker," he said. "Sometimes it's difficult to get her to stop. A few days a week I will wake up and she's already at the workshop, or heading to the store."

"What of your girls?"

"My father died and my mother has rented a flat across the street from us. Mother comes to our place to stay with them every day—along with Henrietta's boys."

"Vesta. Yes. Etta has mentioned her so fondly, and we met her when we visited. I'm sorry about your father, but it brings me much joy to think that Annie's and Etta's children are growing up together." Lady Newley pulled a bell pull and a footman appeared. "We'd like tea please. And perhaps some of those delicious tea cakes."

He left to do her bidding.

They walked out of the bedroom and toward the stairs. "Seven years ago, when Etta traveled to New York on her own . . . it's still hard to fathom. I didn't know she had such gumption. She was betrothed to a family friend here and was not very happy about it. For her to run away without telling us was frightening. She only did so because your Annie inspired her."

"Annie inspires a lot of people to stretch their boundaries."

She adjusted the cuff of her sleeve then took the railing and descended the stairs to the foyer. "For the longest time we had no idea if Etta was all right or even where she was."

"She didn't write to you?"

"She did, but didn't give us details. We knew from the postmark she was in New York City, but beyond that . . ."

Sean remembered something. "Wasn't it Steven who contacted you and told you her situation?"

"It was. He told us about her questionable living conditions, and informed us she was out of money. He also told us he wanted to marry her." She smiled. "I will never forget the day he arranged for us to surprise her in Central Park."

"You enjoy surprising people, don't you?"

"I do. Even now I cling to the happy memory. That's what you and I will create when we have our reunions."

"In just a week's time." *That* was hard to fathom.

᪣

Matteo carried a short pile of clothes from his bedroom into the parlor. "Here, Mama. Good thing I've had a growing spurt. Hopefully some of these will work for your man."

"He's not my man." She started going through the clothes.

"He's our *project*," Gela said, helping her. She held up a shirt. "How about this one?"

Maude draped it against herself. Dock was shorter and bulkier than she was. "That's a good one. Pants will be the toughest."

Antonio sat at the kitchen table, eating toast and jam for breakfast. "When do you plan on bringing him all of these things?"

"I wondered that too," Matteo said. "You're not just going to show up in his alley and dump them by his shack, are you?"

"Of course not. We need to get him a job and then a place to live. We'll fill it with these clothes and other necessary items and have a big unveiling."

"You're going to surprise him?" Her son looked skeptical. "What if he doesn't want a job and a place to live?"

"Why wouldn't he?" Gela asked. "It's not like he's a stranger. Mama and I have talked to him. He knows us."

But Matteo's points were valid. Maude was making enormous assumptions about another person's life. Dock could reject everything.

So what if he did? She blinked at the inner question before repeating it. "So what if he does? We are helping a man in need. It is not up to us to soften his heart so he accepts them. That's God's job. Ours is to help."

Gela put her arm around Maude's waist. "Don't mind them, Mama. Like you say, we're doing a good thing."

Together. They were doing a good thing together.

Gela took the shirt and folded it. "Don't do anything without me. Remember I'm going to the fundraiser with Mack."

"Do I know about this?" Antonio asked.

"I told you . . ." Gela drew out her words. "A lot of performers are getting together to earn money to fund the new actors union. I'm an actor. I want to be part of it."

"Is anyone else going with you?" he asked.

"Just me and Mack."

"Oh."

She gave them an impatient look. "You like him. You trust him. We perform at Refuge all the time together. Surely, you don't object."

Maude looked at Antonio and he shrugged. "I suppose you can go. But come back right after."

She clapped her hands—making her look like a little girl. "It should be so exciting. I've heard famous people are going to be there."

"What famous people?" Matteo asked.

"I . . . I don't know. But I want to see them, whoever they are."

Steven stood before his wife, tugging at his suitcoat. "How do I look?"

"Like the best teacher in the entire city."

He made a face. "Not in the entire world?"

She went to him and pulled him close. "The world can't have you. You belong here with me."

He kissed her just as the boys came into the parlor.

"Eww," Lennie said.

Which caused Steven to kiss Henrietta again.

The boys covered their eyes. Steven took advantage and pinched her bottom.

"I'm off then," he said. "No students yet, but I'm meeting the principal and seeing my classroom."

"A classroom again," she said wistfully.

"I wasn't sure it would ever happen." He took his derby from the hat rack. "What do you have planned today?"

Not much. Just your usual, run of the mill espionage. "I have a full day. I'll see you tonight and you can tell me all about your day."

And I can tell you about mine.

꿴

As Henrietta took the El south toward the address on the invoice, her stomach rumbled with nerves. She wished Steven could have come with her, but she hadn't dared mentioned her plan lest he miss his first day of work.

Actually, she'd grown braver during the time he was incapacitated and staying at Edna's. Had good come out of bad? She had a new confidence in herself as an individual, and had reignited the pith and courage of the Henrietta who had sailed from England to New York City on her own, without even knowing where Annie lived. God had been with her and had brought them together — a miracle in itself. He'd been with her then, as He was with her now.

The train clattered along and she closed her eyes, letting herself sway with its movement. *Show me the truth, Father. Then give me wisdom to know what to do with it.*

She sensed the train slowing and knew it was her stop. She followed the crowd out of the train and down the steps to the street, but after that, she wasn't sure which way to go. She stopped a woman and asked directions, showing her the address.

Down two blocks, turn right, then left. She was surprised to see it was a residential area with neighborhood shops on street level. It wasn't near as nice as Greenwich Village, with smells that offended her nose, broken windows, crumbled walls, and garbage catching the whirl of the wind along the narrow streets.

Although it was morning, there were already many people outside against the stuffiness of the summer heat. Many women sat on stoops watching young children playing tag or ball in the streets. Lines of laundry were strung from building to building like flags waiting for a breeze. There was little of that and Henrietta wished she had brought along a fan.

She was close enough to check the addresses and finally reached the spot. She looked for Olivet signage, but found nothing but signs for a tobacconist and a pawn broker.

She accosted a mother with a baby slung over her chest. "Excuse me, but I'm looking for Olivet Fabric and Supplies?"

"What?"

"Olivet? They are a distributor of sewing fabrics and supplies."

The woman shook her head and adjusted the sling to give the baby more air. "No Olivet 'round here."

Henrietta had one more idea. "Do you know a man, Guy Ship?"

"Sure. He lives up there, middle, back." She chuckled. "He's a charmer, that one. Told me I was pretty as a Madonna. Pfft. We all can see that ain't true." She crossed herself. "Though he did give me a pretty length of a brocade, told me to use it as a shawl. Too hot for it now, but come winter, you'll see me flaunting it up and down the street."

Stolen brocade, no doubt.

Her eyes brightened. "You mentioned fabric? He's got that, for sure." She pointed to an upper floor. "He might be up there, if you want to see him. He'll give you a good deal on fabric."

"He's selling it from his flat?"

She shrugged. "I have no need, but I've heard he gives a good price. Go on up. He doesn't go to work early."

Henrietta considered it a brief moment, but decided no. She didn't want to confront Guy on her own. She was brave. But not stupid.

❧

Edna was at the workshop, but not at the workshop.

"Edna?" Ginny was standing beside her, a half-sewn dress in hand. "What do you want us to do with the facing here?" She showed her the neck facing of the V-neck.

Edna showed her what to do and Ginny started to go back to her sewing machine. But then she turned. "What's wrong with you today? It's not like you to stare out the window. What's out there?"

The question surprised her and she looked outside trying to pinpoint an answer. She saw the bedroom window across the street — the window of *her* extra bedroom. Her now empty bedroom. And then she knew.

"I have to go to the shop."

Gert got up from her machine. "We were going to check my dress one last time. I'm getting married tomorrow."

"Maude will handle it."

"Maude has been distracted as much as you." Gert huffed. "I need the dress to be perfect."

Edna put a hand on her arm. "It will be. I promise." She grabbed her hat and purse. "I'll be back."

She made it to the store in record time, her resolve giving her feet wings as it made her heart flutter with anticipation.

This is right, Lord. I know it. I feel it.

❧

As soon as Edna entered Unruffled, Annie rushed toward her. "I'm so glad you're here. We're very busy for a Monday. We could use your help on the floor."

Today of all days? "I'm sorry. I can't right now."

"But we need you." Annie's eyes were plaintive. "Please."

The girl needs me more. She placed a hand on Annie's arm. "I'm sorry. I can't right now."

"But—"

Edna knew it was rude. She knew she should help. But her thoughts were totally focused elsewhere. She rushed to the far corner of the storeroom, then paused and calmed herself. Scaring the girl with her zeal was *not* the way to do it.

She walked toward the back of the room, her heart pounding. *Please, Father, help me. If this is truly what You want me to do, let everything fall into place.*

She looked toward the crates and didn't see any feet. Was she in there?

She heard a sneeze and a sniff. She took a handkerchief out of her pocket and held it over the top of the crates. "Here."

Nothing happened.

"Come on," she said. "Take it."

There was a tug and Edna released it. She heard it being put to use, then a meek, "Thank you."

It was time. "Would you come out please?"

"No."

"It's all right. You're not in trouble. I promise."

After a brief hesitation, there was a scuffling, then a girl of about five or six stepped out of her hiding place.

Edna offered her a smile. "Hello there. We finally meet. My name is Edna. What's yours?"

"Lizzy." The girl leaned forward to scratch her leg. "You the one been leaving me stuff?"

"I am. Did it help?"

"Yeah. Thank you."

She was far too skinny, her clothes torn and ill-fitting, her face and hair filthy. "How long have you been staying here?"

"Dunno. A while. I don't like the streets." She shook her head. "They's scary."

Edna's heart broke. "I'm sure they are."

Lizzy pointed to the water closet. "You had a toilet and sink. I's not used to that."

Edna wanted to ask for details, but it wasn't the time. "I have a proposition for you, Lizzy."

"A what?"

"Would you like to come live at my house?"

The girl eyed her warily. "Why would I do that?"

Edna had to look beyond the obvious answer. "You'd be doing me a favor. My husband died a while ago and my son got married and moved out. So I have this extra bedroom sitting empty and sad, and . . ." She sighed deeply. "The truth is, I'm rather lonely. I miss having someone to care for. I could really use the company."

Lizzy scraped a scuffed toe across the floor. "Well . . . I suppose maybe . . . maybe I could use the company too."

"Splendid! We can help each other." She extended her hand to shake. "Is it a deal then?"

Lizzy wiped her hand on her skirt, then shook Edna's. "I guess so."

Edna's happiness was so intense she wanted to dance a little jig. Realizing that would surely scare Lizzy away, she restrained herself. "Shall we go see your room?"

"Is it far?"

"Not at all. Just a few blocks."

"Good, cuz I's afraid of the trains overhead. They're so loud."

"Indeed they are. Luckily, there are no trains involved today. Just walking."

"I need to get my things."

"Of course."

Lizzy stepped behind the crates and returned with some items wrapped with the wool scrap. The end of a loaf of bread was on top. "I got it this morning in the garbage."

Edna spotted mold on it and was tempted to toss it. Instead she said, "How resourceful of you. It turns out I just made fresh bread yesterday."

Her eyes grew large. "You got jam?"

"Boysenberry. And butter."

"Ne'er had that one. But I know I'll like it."

"I know it too. And you can have as much as you want. Shall we go?"

They left the storeroom and walked into the main part of Unruffled. Annie and a customer looked up, their eyes full of questions.

"Lizzy, this is Mrs. Culver and—" She looked to the other woman.

"Mrs. Brindle."

"And Mrs. Brindle. Ladies, this is Lizzy. She and I are going home now." They walked toward the door.

"Edna?"

Edna left Annie's question hanging in the air. She had enough questions of her own.

❧

Lizzy stood in Steven's room, hugging her bundle of belongings. She seemed frozen in place.

Edna didn't know exactly what to do to break the ice, so she gave a tour of the room—which was ridiculous, yet it gave her something to do.

"Here is your bed. There's extra covers in the trunk over there, but you won't need those until it gets cool again. Here's a lamp on the bedside table and in the parlor I have shelves of books you can read."

"I can't read."

Edna kept her surprise in check. "Then I'll teach you."

"I know my numbers though. Up to thirty."

"Excellent." She moved to the dresser. "These two drawers are empty and—" She remembered that Lizzy didn't have much to put in them. "We'll get you some new clothes and you can fill them up." Edna wondered if Victoria had any hand-me-downs Lizzy could have.

"New? I ain't never had new."

Nix the hand-me-downs. "I will sew you some clothes, just your own, but until then, we'll take a trip to Macy's and buy you everything you need."

"What's Macy's?"

Who didn't know about Macy's? "It's a huge store that sells everything from furniture to clothes to dishes." She thought of something else. "And toys. We'll get you some toys."

Lizzy broke out of her stance and put her bundle on the bed. She unwrapped it and took out a makeshift doll. "This is Susannah. I made her out of scraps from the store."

Edna studied the doll. It was crudely sewn, with two buttons for eyes.

"I stuffed it with other scraps, and found some needles and thread in the counter." She put hand to her mouth. "I weren't stealing. They's just scraps. And I put the needle back when I was done. I can take the buttons off and—"

Edna's throat grew tight. "You did a very good job with what you had. Do you like to sew?"

"Don't rightly know. It gave me something to do. After everyone left it gets really quiet." She reached in the bundle. "I made her a scarf and a blanket too."

The blanket was simply a rectangle, but the scarf had been made from a tiny triangle with a ribbon tacked to each end of the long side. While Edna held the doll, Lizzy tied the scarf around her head. "See?"

"She looks lovely. Shall we put her to bed?"

Lizzy took Susannah, placed her against one of the pillows, and covered her with the blanket. "She likes it here."

"I hope you'll like it here too."

Suddenly, Lizzy ran to Edna and wrapped her arms around her waist. "I knows I'll like it here with you. I knows it."

Edna held her close and said the same thing to the Almighty.

❧

Annie was exhausted and it wasn't even noon. They had enjoyed— at the moment a questionable word—a steady stream of customers, which had kept herself, Sara, and Eudora busy.

She was also starving and took a bite of her sandwich from her lunch pail beneath the counter.

"Success creates an appetite, doesn't it?" Eudora said. She glanced toward the door. "Don't mind if I do." She took out her own lunch pail and Sara followed suit.

"I thought Henrietta was coming in today," Eudora said.

"And what's going on with Edna?" Sara asked. "In one minute, out the next, taking a street urchin with her? Where'd the girl come from anyways?"

"I have no idea," Annie said, taking another bite. "Both Edna and Henrietta have been preoccupied lately."

"If we're being honest, Maude too." Sara nodded toward Eudora. "I, for one, am very grateful we have you to help us."

"I agree," Annie said. She realized she'd taken far too little effort in knowing her newest employee. "Are you liking the work?"

The peach of her cheeks blushed prettily. "I am, which surprises me more than you know. I am used to buying clothes, not selling them."

Annie remembered what Mrs. Sampson had said about her. "You were engaged?"

She looked at her sandwich. "In a way."

Annie wanted to ask more, but didn't want to pry.

"Oh, go ahead and ask," Eudora said with a sigh. "Do you really want to know what happened?"

"If you care to share . . ."

Eudora wrapped the rest of her sandwich in its waxed paper and took out an apple, shining it on her bodice. "As Eleanor stated, my family is rich. I am used to getting what I want."

"That's candid," Sara said.

Eudora shrugged. "Long story, short, I loved this man—I was thinking he might propose—and he lured me into having intimate relations with him. We were caught in the act by my parents—who were beyond angry. And then to add insult to injury . . . we found out he was married."

"Married?"

She raised her arms as if fending off an accusation. "Honestly, I had no idea. He was so charming and kind. I was a fool." She shook her head, then raised her chin defiantly. "George was a complete and utter cad."

"Absolutely." Annie felt badly that such a young woman would be taken in like that.

"My parents were furious with him, and then with me for . . . you know. They were livid." She took a bite of apple and chewed feverishly before she continued. "I endured a hundred sessions of them heaping guilt upon me, questioning my morals, my sense, and questioning their own method of bringing me up. They declared me a spoiled brat and said they were through with me."

"What does that mean?" Sara asked.

"It means I had to get a job and earn my own way."

"All in all, that's not a bad thing, is it?" Annie asked.

"I suppose not." She looked around the store. "That's why I'm surprised I enjoy it so much. I never worked a single day before this."

"You're doing a good job here," Annie said.

"Thank you." Eudora took another bite of apple, which filled the area with its luscious scent.

"What happened to the man?" Sara asked.

"He disappeared — with a good chunk of our money."

"How did he get your money?"

"He'd impressed my father with a business idea to buy old tenements and refurbish them to sell. He showed Father a property, shared his grand plans, and got Father to give him money for the renovations." She sighed deeply. "We found out later he didn't even own the place. He absconded with my virtue *and* my father's money."

"That's horrible — on both accounts," Annie said.

"Father wants him arrested for fraud or thievery or whatever crime is involved, and also for . . ." She lowered her voice. "*Flagrante delicte.* Having sex when one or both parties is married."

"I wonder if his wife divorced him," Sara said.

Eudora shrugged. "She should."

Annie was curious about this delicate crime. "What is the legal punishment for married infidelity?"

"Six months in jail and a five-hundred dollar fine."

"Gracious," Sara said. "I know people can be unfaithful, but I didn't think there was a law against it."

Eudora nodded. "Beyond the law, my heart was broken." Her face lost its edge and became vulnerable. "More than anything I hate that he duped me. I hadn't had a lot of experience with men — in any way, even courting — but he'd seemed so genuinely in love with me and my parents liked him too — they really did. But now I hate him for making me feel stupid, conning my father, and for changing my parents' opinion of me." She looked up, her expression pathetic. "How can I ever get them to trust me and think well of me again? I let them down dreadfully."

"It's not all your fault. Your father was taken in too."

She shrugged. "But I brought George into the family. If I hadn't . . . everything would be so different."

Annie offered her a reassuring smile. "You're changing their opinion right now, working here and being a responsible, independent woman."

Eudora nodded. "Thank you. I'm trying very hard."

"So you haven't seen the man since?" Sara said.

"I haven't. But if I do . . ." She made a fist. "You'll have to hold me back or else *I'll* be arrested."

They all laughed.

"It's good you can laugh about it," Sara said.

"Mark Twain said, 'The best way to cheer yourself is to try to cheer someone else up.'" Eudora nodded toward the store. "Working here is showing that to be true."

Annie gave her a hug.

❧

Gela had never been to the Lexington Avenue Opera House, but that night she and Mack squeezed their way inside with hundreds of other actors. There were no more seats so they had to stand. Mack found them a place along the right aisle, letting Gela stand in front to see better.

See what? All shows were dark because of the strike.

Finally the house lights dimmed and a man walked through the break in the center curtain. The crowd roared. She turned back to Mack. "Is that?"

He nodded, "W.C. Fields. In the flesh."

Wow.

"Ladies and gentleman. Welcome to the first night of many benefit performances, brought to you by our beloved Actors' Equity Association."

There was another roar.

He quieted them. "We are here tonight to show our support for the strike and the union, and to pick your pockets to fund the damn thing. Everyone performing tonight is doing so out of the goodness of their hearts."

"Try again!" someone shouted.

He shrugged. "If you can't dazzle them with brilliance, baffle them with bull."

A woman poked her head out of the wings. "Get on with it. We're ready to dance."

"And so, after fifteen minutes of rehearsal, I give to you Marie Dressler and her horrendous and hilarious hoofers." He stepped to the side and the curtain opened to 150 dancers.

Their production wasn't perfect by any means, but everyone laughed and clapped.

The comedian Eddie Cantor came out next and said that tonight he was making as much as Ethel Barrymore—who also performed the second act of *The Lady of the Camellias* with her husband, Lionel.

Gela felt ready to cry. All these actors who had made it, who had found fame on the stage. Would she be one of them someday?

Mack stood behind her and squeezed her shoulders. He must have been feeling it too.

One after another, famous actors performed: Eddie Foy came out with a bunch of children who did a skit, and an actress Gela had seen in silent movies, Pearl White, came out and brought the house down by saying, "I finally get to talk!"

Then the spotlight turned to the audience where Ed Wynn stood up from his seat in the third row.

He's in the Ziegfield Follies!

He turned to the crowd, quieting them. "Earlier today a judge issued an injunction against me, trying to prevent me from appearing here this evening. Apparently, the Shuberts own me and my talent exclusively."

There was derisive laughter and someone shouted, "No one owns you, Ed!"

"Indeed, they do not. Judge Lydon has forbidden me to appear *on* the stage tonight. I am very sorry this has occurred, but of course the orders of the court must be obeyed."

There were boos.

He held up a hand. "If I *had* been able to appear tonight, I had in mind to tell you a story…"

To everyone's shock and delight he performed his whole act from his seat.

The show went on and on, with numerous pleas for money. The Barrymore siblings each pledged $1000.

A young actress stood up and said, "I pledge $100!"

The man beside her said, "Sit down, Tallulah, you don't have that sort of money."

"My daddy does."

Gela wished her father had that sort of money, because she desperately wanted to give. Buckets were passed repeatedly, with everyone giving something. She put in the few coins that were in her pocket, feeling small for not having more.

Mack put in twenty dollars and whispered in her ear. "It's not the amount, it's the heart behind it."

She hoped he was right, for her heart was full to overflowing.

❧

Henrietta sat at the dining table with her family.

Steve admired the spread. "Roast beef, potatoes, corn, and applesauce? What's the occasion?"

"It was your first day at your new job—which you say was a success."

"The real test will be when the students come back."

"You'll be grand."

Willie pointed at the potatoes. "Can we eat? I'm starving."

The food was passed and devoured as if they hadn't eaten in weeks. Actually, they hadn't eaten like *this* in weeks. While Steven had been gone, the rest of them had subsisted on far simpler fare.

"I need to talk to you about something," she told Steven after the children had asked to be excused.

"It sounds serious."

"It is. It's about theft and deception." He looked skeptical as she told him about Guy Ship and her discoveries. "What do I do next?"

"Have you told Annie and the rest of the partners?"

"Not yet."

"You need to—before he pulls any more shenanigans."

"The thing is . . . we'll owe Olivet more money. He stole the fabric from them and we paid *him.*"

He contemplated this a moment. "Unfortunately, that can't be helped." He reached across the table and took her hand. "The police have to be involved, Etta. The ladies first, then the police."

She did not relish the thought. "I wish I'd discovered it earlier. The prices were far too good. I remember my father saying, 'You don't get something for nothing.' That should have sounded a warning."

"Good people don't expect other people to be bad. It's not your fault. It's—"

There was a knock on the door. Henrietta answered it and found Edna outside. She wasn't alone. There was a little girl with her.

"Can we come in?"

They came inside and Edna told them a fantastic story of the girl—Lizzy—living in the storeroom at Unruffled, and how she was living with Edna now.

Lizzy hid behind her, peeking out at Willie and Lennie. Lennie stuck his tongue out. To her credit, Lizzy did not reciprocate.

"Really, Mother? Isn't all this going a bit too far?"

"Just far enough," she said with a defiant lift of her chin. "Our immediate need is this: may we borrow a nightshirt? I will wash her things tonight and tomorrow Lizzy and I are planning a shopping spree at Macy's."

"It's a huge store," Lizzy said from behind Edna.

Henrietta had to smile. "That, it is."

Edna sighed deeply. "Here it is, plain and simple. Since you went off on your own, Steven, I have had an empty room. Over the years God has given me many wonderful people to fill it, first Annie, then Maude, and then even you in your time of need. But you are home now, making the room empty again. I do not believe it is a coincidence that God has brought Lizzy into my life at just this moment when I have a place for her in my home — and in my heart." She drew Lizzy out from behind and pulled her against her hip, putting a hand on her shoulder. "What God has joined together, let no man put asunder."

"That's a bridal vow," Steven pointed out.

"It's a vow. Now then. Can we borrow a nightshirt?"

After they left it took a moment for the room to settle. "What do you think?" Henrietta asked her husband.

"I think my mother is a good woman."

"You don't object?"

"Logically, yes. Emotionally, no. The girl needs a home and someone to love her. My mother needs someone to love."

"She has us." Henrietta heard how selfish it sounded. "Sorry. That wasn't nice."

"She *does* have us. So let *us* be there to help her."

Henrietta thought of the Guy issue. Edna was one of the partners. "What about Guy Ship?"

Steven considered this a minute. "Just tell Annie. Let her decide what to do next."

↩

Combing through Lizzy's hair after her bath was not an easy task. "Sorry," Edna said for the tenth time. "I'm trying to be gentle. Next wash it will be easier."

Lizzy nodded. "I's glad there will be a next time."

"Me too." Edna finished and they went into the bedroom — Lizzy's bedroom. It was such a special feeling to tuck a child safely into bed. "Comfy?"

"I ain't had a bed in a long ways."

She took Lizzy's hands and clasped them above the covers. "Let's say prayers. You've heard about God, haven't you?"

"A little. He damns things."

"What?"

"I's heard men yell out, 'God damn it!'"

Oh dear. "That's a bad thing for them to say. God created us all and loves us unconditionally."

Her forehead furrowed.

"Do you know what 'unconditionally' means?"

"Forever and ever, no matter what?"

Edna smiled. "I couldn't have said it better myself. Now let's thank Him for bringing us together."

"To love each other forever and ever, no matter what."

Edna's throat tightened. She could only nod.

CHAPTER SIXTEEN

Dressed in her newly washed dress, with her clean hair revealing its pretty auburn color, Lizzy's eyes grew large as she and Edna walked into Macy's. "I ain't never seen anything like this place." She looked everywhere, high and low. "I tried to go in big stores when it was cold out, but they shooed me away."

Edna believed her. "Do you want to see the department where I worked?"

"You worked here?" she asked with awe in her voice.

"I did. I sold sewing machines. Come on."

Edna led her to the department and introduced her to the clerks who all remembered her. They looked curiously at Lizzy, but Edna let them be curious. She was tired of explaining herself.

"Let's go up to the girls' department." She led Lizzy toward the escalator, but the girl balked at the moving stairs. "It's all right. They're safe. See everyone going up and down?"

But Lizzy shook her head. "They got stairs?"

"They have something better." She took Lizzy to the elevator. They'd be on the second floor before she had time to be afraid of the mechanical box.

Lizzy squeezed Edna's hand when the elevator started to move. There *was* an odd feeling to it when they were pulled upwards.

As the car slowed, the elevator operator said, "Trimmed millinery, youth clothing, glassware, pottery, card engraving, and ladies' restaurant. Watch your step."

As they walked to the department, Lizzy walked slower and slower. "What's wrong?"

She kept shaking her head. "I . . . I just never seen so many pretty things."

"Let's go make some of those pretty things *your* pretty things." As they entered the department, Edna realized this was the first time she'd ever shopped for girls' clothing. What a treat.

The next hour made Edna feel like Lizzy's fairy godmother, supplying everything the little Cinderella needed and deserved — from her undergarments, out.

Lizzy traced her finger along the neckline of her camisole. "There's lace on here, and nobody even sees it."

Edna laughed. "You see it."

"It's soft too. Not itchy."

"The mark of good undergarments is that they don't make you scratch."

Lizzy nodded seriously, as though she was storing away the information.

In the end they chose three dresses: one for every day, one a bit fancier for church, a skirt and blouse, a nightgown, three pairs of stockings, drawers and camisoles, two pairs of shoes, a lightweight coat for the coming autumn, and a straw hat with an artificial daisy stuck in its brim.

Lizzy looked in the mirror, swaying back and forth, making the skirt of her dress flow. "When I was hiding in Unruffled I saw the pretty dresses but never thought I'd ever get anything as pretty." She looked at Edna. "These are prettier."

"You make them prettier."

Suddenly, a cloud passed over Lizzy's face.

"What's wrong?"

"I can cook and clean, and do laundry for you. And maybe sweep the store too."

"You don't have to do those things."

She looked confused. "I has to pay for all this, and my room and the food."

"No, no, you don't." Edna knelt beside her, taking her hand. "You don't have to do anything to earn all this. It's a gift from me to you." *As you are a gift from God to me.*

"That's crazy."

"Forever and ever, no matter what, remember?"

She nodded. Hopefully she was convinced.

Edna stood. "We can stop by the sewing department on the way out and get hair ribbons to match every outfit."

"Really?"

"Of course. Then we can go up to the cafeteria and have some lunch."

"They have food here?"

"They have everything here." Edna pointed to their choices, hanging in the dressing area. "Which one do you want to wear home?"

Lizzy stroked the blue cotton she had on.

"A very good choice, mademoiselle."

"What's a madem-selle?"

"It's a French word that means young lady."

Lizzy preened in the mirror. "I feel like a madem-selle now." She turned around and rushed into Edna's arms. "Your madem-selle."

Edna cradled her head against her chest. God was so good. Forever and ever, no matter what, good.

≈

Annie was just getting the cash register prepared for the day when Guy came in. He carried his sample case.

"Annie! The best of the morning to you."

"And to you."

"I have some samples to show you that might complement the silks I sold you a few weeks ago. Shall we take them to the back table?"

Annie looked around for Eudora to man the register, but didn't see her. She wanted to introduce her to Guy.

Instead, Sara came over. "I'll finish up here."

Annie and Guy went in the table and he showed her samples for heavier silks that would do well for the colder weather. His prices were amazing and she ended up ordering six more bolts.

When they went back to the front counter, Eudora was still absent, so Annie bid Guy goodbye. They could meet another day.

Oddly, as soon as he left, Eudora emerged from a dressing room. An empty dressing room.

"You missed him. I wanted to introduce you to our Olivet salesman, Guy—"

"I know him."

"You do?"

Eudora sank into a chair. "He's George! The man who ruined my life."

Sara joined them. "He's *him?*"

Eudora nodded mournfully. "I never expected to see him again." She looked up, her face panicked. "I need to call my father! Or the police! He needs to be arrested!"

Annie's thoughts swam. "Are you sure Guy is George?"

"As soon as I saw him and heard his voice, I hid in the fitting room." She shuddered. "I don't want him to know I work here."

"That . . . that might be difficult. He doesn't come in often, but he does come in."

"He won't if we get him arrested," Sara said.

They heard the bell on the door and turned to see Henrietta. She joined them. "What's going on? You all look upset."

They told her about Eudora's connection to Guy. George.

Henrietta's reaction went above and beyond what was expected. "He's a cretin and a heel," Henrietta said. "And a thief and con-artist."

"What he did to Eudora is inexcusable," Annie said.

Henrietta shook her head. "He hurt Eudora and her family, but there's more." She removed an invoice from her satchel. "See the address here?"

"Yes."

"I sent payment for all the wedding fabrics to that new address."

"Guy said Olivet had moved."

"Only they haven't." She told about running into Mabel from Olivet. "Yesterday I went to this address to check things out and it's a residential area. There is not store there at all and a neighbor-lady said Guy lives there. He *lives* there. *And* he's selling fabric out of his flat."

Annie tried to grasp the implications. "You sent payment to this address? To Guy?"

Henrietta nodded. She took the invoice and waved it in the air. "Olivet probably knows nothing about this sale at all. I have no proof but I'm betting he nicked all this fabric and is selling it cheap because it's all profit. His profit."

Annie felt a wave of anger fight a wave of embarrassment. She'd been taken in by him in so many ways. *Though not as many ways as I could have been.* "Have you contacted the police? Or Olivet?"

"Not yet. I wanted to tell you first. What should we do?"

"Let's get him!" Eudora said. "Make him pay for all he's done."

It was an emotional response, and yet . . . "I think you're right." *In general.*

"I'm going to call my father, and then the police," Eudora said. "He needs to pay."

Annie was conflicted. "I'd like revenge as much as you," she said. "But is that up to us? Isn't that God's domain?"

She didn't like how they looked at her.

Henrietta broke the silence. "Annie's right. God said, 'Vengeance is mine. *I* will repay.'"

"What about 'God helps those who help themselves?'" Eudora said. "I want to get Guy. Now."

Annie took a deep breath. "I think a more appropriate response is that God helps those who help others."

"I'm an 'other'," Eudora said. Her pout was childish.

Annie knew they were treading a fine line. "I want to help you, help us, help Olivet, and anyone else Guy has hurt in the past."

"And prevent him from hurting anyone in the future," Henrietta said.

Annie agreed. "Above all, justice should be served, not revenge."

Eudora huffed.

"How do we do that?" Henrietta asked.

Guy's sins of the past . . . the future. The present? An idea formed in Annie's mind. She let it settle. It was plausible. Doable. She paused long enough to pray: *Is this what You want, Lord?*

"Annie?"

She felt an inner nudge. "To strengthen the case against him, we need to catch Guy in the act."

"How do we do that?"

She had some ideas, but wanted help. "We should go to the police, explain the situation, tell them the gist of my idea, and see what they think."

"I want to tell my father right away," Eudora said.

"You can. But tell him not to take matters into his own hands. We have to do this right. Let the authorities be in control."

"Catching him in the act *would* provide additional evidence against him beyond the fake bill," Henrietta said.

"Beyond my broken heart?" Eudora asked.

"Yes. To both."

Henrietta folded the invoice. "We need to tell Olivet. They are the key victim."

"Excuse me? I beg to differ," Eudora said."

So many crimes. *God, make this right.* "Here's my idea . . . "

Annie and Henrietta left work and went to the police station to share Annie's idea with professionals.

They paused at the door. "Do you think they'll want to listen to us?" Annie asked.

"They'll listen. But will they help us with our plan? I don't know."

Annie was having second thoughts. "If they say no, we should take that as a sign that it's not the right thing to do. All right?"

"All right."

"But if they agree . . .?"

"Then we have their expertise to support us." Henrietta bit her lip. "I will feel better when the police are involved."

"Me too."

They both took a cleansing breath. "Shall we?"

They were shown into an office, and thirty minutes later, the sergeant said, "I commend you on your idea, Mrs. Culver."

Annie let out the breath she'd been saving. "I'm so glad."

He used his pencil to point at his copious notes. "But I think it needs to be broken down into two parts."

"Really?" She was open to suggestions.

He tapped the pencil on his desk. "Olivet needs to be involved. Immediately."

"Because we're hoping he'll steal from them again."

"Indeed. But to catch him, we need the fabric to be specially marked in some way."

A good idea. "Tell me more."

A short time later the ladies said their goodbyes with the reassurance that Annie's original idea had been fine-tuned by someone who was used to dealing with criminals. "Step one will happen tomorrow," Annie said. "I'll contact Guy and ask him to come to the shop."

"Step two on Saturday," Henrietta added.

They reached the sidewalk and paused. Annie put a hand to her chest. "This is really going to happen."

"It appears so."

"What if Guy doesn't take the bait?"

"The sergeant said if that happens, they'll proceed with the evidence they have, both the invoice, and the testimony of the Mitchells."

"But what if—?"

Henrietta put a calming hand on Annie's arm. "The police have this. God has this. We simply have to do our part."

There was nothing simple about it.

Gela sang at Port Refuge with new confidence. After last night's fundraising extravaganza, she felt part of something bigger. She knew she had talent—talent she wanted to share with anyone who would listen.

"Sing 'Beautiful Dreamer' again!"

She put her hands on her hips in mock annoyance. "Charlie, if you had your way I'd only sing that song."

The old man shrugged. "It reminds me of me wife."

She curtsied. "And so I shall sing it again."

Mack played an arpeggio and the song was sung. Charlie closed his eyes during the singing.

To know that her music could reach a heart in need spurred Gela to let the song soar.

As she reached the last stanza, she spotted Dock come in. Their eyes met. He offered a little wave and she nodded.

She was glad the song was nearly over. She wanted to talk to him.

Her audience clapped, she bowed, then told Mack she'd be back in a minute. She found Dock sitting in his usual corner.

A woman brought him coffee. "Want a sandwich, Dock?"

He nodded. "It would be much appreciated."

The woman turned to get him one, then saw Gela. "You want one, Gela?"

"No thank you, Tilly." She stood on the opposite side of Dock's table. "May I?" They hadn't talked since Gela and her mother visited him.

"Any time." He stared at his coffee, holding the cup with two hands as the steam rose. "I wanted to thank you for bringing your mother to see me. I . . . you . . ."

"She and I were both glad for the chance."

He glanced up, then away. "She still forgives me?"

"Oh yes," Gela said. *And so much more.*

"I'm thankful for that. Such a gift."

"Have you forgiven yourself?"

He looked to the ceiling and sighed. "I'm trying."

Gela wished she had the arsenal of Bible verses that her parents could tap into when one suited the moment. She had to improvise. "You're sorry, Mama's forgiven you, and so has God. It's your turn."

He smiled. "You make it sound so easy."

"I don't know easy from hard, but I know you should do it."

He chuckled. "Then I guess I'll have to do it."

She felt herself blush. It was so hard to keep a secret. She wanted to tell him all that her family was doing to help him. But Mama had made her promise not to say anything until everything was in place.

Dock pointed to Mack, who was trying to get her attention. "They want another song. *I* want another song."

How could she refuse?

Gert's wedding day. Henrietta was glad for the distraction. After the drama of finding out multiple truths about Guy, coupled with the anticipation of bringing him to justice, Henrietta relished the chance to celebrate something positive.

At this evening's nuptials she wasn't just a guest. Gert had asked her to stand up with her and Simon. It was an honor. She owed so much to Gert. When she'd first arrived in New York—alone and ignorant of how much things cost—she had quickly learned if she stayed at the first-class Hotel Astor, her money wouldn't last. She'd had to find a flat that suited her limited and dwindling funds.

The flat had been an awful place with only two dilapidated rooms. But dilapidated or not, the hardest part had been Henrietta's total and utter inability to live by herself. She didn't know how to make a fire, didn't know how to cook, had never scrubbed a bathtub—that sat in a communal bath down the hall no less—and couldn't even get out of her clothes without help. That's when Gert had come to the rescue. She'd been on the outs with her husband and had addressed Henrietta's ignorance with kindness. She'd moved in and had taught Henrietta how to be an independent woman. Gert's father, Mr. Cody, had also stepped in. He had a bakery close by and was constantly taking pity on the poor little rich girl, giving her bread and sweets to keep her alive when money grew tighter.

They had needed each other and had formed a bond that had stayed strong. When Gert had asked her to be an attendant at her wedding—her only attendant—Henrietta had felt far more honored than she ever had felt back in Summerfield when she'd stood up at the weddings of her gentrified friends.

She took a moment to glance at her own new dress in the mirror. It was a simple design made of burnt orange charmeuse. The dress had unlined chiffon sleeves. Embroidery highlighted the sleeves and the waist. Underneath Henrietta wore a slim black mid-calf skirt. "I do like this dress," she told Gert and Maude.

"I chose the design so you can wear it other places," Gert said.

Actually, it was a possibility.

Now to the bride. Maude helped Gert slip a long crepe voile cardigan over her satin sheath dress. The bodice was covered in Chantilly lace, and the cardigan was edged with a satin trim. She helped her tie the self-belt and bloused the cardigan over it. "There," she said, stepping back.

"My pearls!" Gert said.

Henrietta hooked the clasp on the pearl necklace. "These are beautiful."

"Simon got them for me." Gert held out a hand. "I'm shaking."

"Wedding jitters," Henrietta said. "I felt the same way when I married Steven." She grinned. "He can still make me shiver."

"Better than *shudder*," Gert said. "My first husband did a lot of that. When he wasn't smacking me around."

Henrietta remembered. "When we shared the flat, you suffered more than a few blackened eyes and bruises."

"Best thing I ever did was leave Frankie."

"Did you ever divorce him?" Maude asked.

"As much as did, but without the paperwork. He'd show up at the odd here and there and make a bit of a ruckus. But then Pa would go talk to him and he'd promise to stay away. Actually, if the flu hadn't killed him, I think he woulda pushed Pa's hand enough to have *him* do the killing."

"Odd to be thankful for the flu," Maude said.

Gert shook her head. "I'm not saying that. Too many died. I'm not saying that."

"I know you're not," Henrietta said. "No more talk of the past. Today is a new beginning."

"Indeed." Maude stepped back. "I present to you, the bride." She pointed to the full-length mirror. "Take a look."

Gert gasped. "That's me?"

Henrietta stood behind her, putting her hands on her shoulders. "That's you, dear lady. Simon will swoon at the sight of you."

She put her hands to her mouth. "I'm so lucky to have him."

They indulged in a group hug.

๛

Maude studied Gert's dress as she walked down the aisle to marry Simon. There was a slight pucker in the hem back, which distressed her, and it could have used a bit more pressing, but she knew most people would never notice.

The service began and Maude let her thoughts wander . . .

Earlier, while they'd gotten dressed for the wedding, Antonio had told her he'd found a flat for Dock. One room. In Chelsea. He said it had a small bed with a headboard and a single upholstered chair with assorted tears, but otherwise was empty.

Maude needed to make a list of what to buy. She had a notepad and pencil in her purse and moved to take it out, but wisely stopped herself. She couldn't physically make a list during Gert's wedding, but that didn't stop her mind from making one.

We'll need a dresser, a table, and a bedside table. Dishes, cooking utensils, glasses –

Antonio hadn't mentioned whether it had a bathroom. Most flats nowadays did, of course, but some old ones still had a shared bath down the hall.

She felt her husband seeking her hand. He cradled it on his knee and smiled at her sweetly.

Oh. The ceremony. Maude smiled back.

" . . . to love and to cherish, in sickness and health . . ."

I need to make sure he has some basic medical supplies and a shaving kit. Toothbrush?

The list went on.

஦

Gert's wedding was beautiful, and her dress . . . Maude had done an excellent job bringing Annie's design to life.

Yet Annie was peeved – not of Gert, but of Henrietta. Seeing Henrietta standing beside her, standing up *with* her ignited a flame of bitterness.

They wouldn't even know each other if it weren't for me.

Their friendship was her doing. Henrietta wouldn't have met Steven either, nor would she have had the chance to discover her bookkeeping abilities. And she never would have been a part of a business like Unruffled.

Without Annie her chances to be a part of all those things would have been zero.

So there.

You did all this?

Annie felt the inner check as distinctly as she would have felt a punch to her gut. A wave a shame rushed over her.

Sorry, Lord. It's not my doing. It's Yours. Please forgive –

"I now pronounce you man and wife."

Oh. The ceremony.

Annie watched as a beaming bride and groom walked up the aisle. Married. Gleeful. Happy.

Their joy made her think of Sean.

Where are you?

She felt a gnawing of pain, but forced it back. Now was not the time.

❧

Lila took Sean's arm as they took an evening stroll around the ship.

"Did you like our first dinner?" she asked.

"All seven courses. I'm glad you schooled me in forks ahead of time or I would have flubbed it badly. Let's just say that this is far different than the troop ship which brought me over."

She patted his arm. "You held your own and if I may say, you look very handsome in your tuxedo."

"Your husband's tuxedo."

"Yours now."

He chuckled. "I truly doubt I will have reason to wear it again. Annie and I don't run with the tuxedo set."

"You never know." But she knew he was probably right. Lila looked down at her beaded chiffon dress. "Actually, I may not have a reason to wear an evening gown in New York either."

"You never know," he said.

"Touché."

"You might wear it. Your cousin lives in New York, correct?"

"Mary Friesen, Joseph's cousin. She married a rich American— though most British deem him *nouveau riche.*"

"Money is money."

"Very true, but in England old money has more clout. I feel badly that we haven't stayed in touch. We were both embarrassed when Annie left since she took two of Mary's servants with her. And then the war happened, and Joseph passed . . ."

"You'll have plenty of instant family with Annie and I, and Edna, and Maude and her family, and—"

She laughed. "I look forward to it."

"You will also have the joy of getting to know your grandsons."

"That, I will."

He hesitated. "Will you miss Robbie back here?"

She felt a twinge in her heart. "Deeply. It was a difficult decision to leave him."

Sean stopped walking. "I hope you didn't leave because of me. I could have sailed alone."

"No, no," she said, walking again. "I'd been contemplating it a good while as Etta's letters have been full of invitations. And pleas." She didn't tell Sean about Theodosia's disparaging remarks. There was no need. "Your sudden arrival in Summerfield was God's final nudge. It's quite amazing how it all worked out, don't you think?"

They stopped to look at the moon shining on the water. "It's a miracle," he said.

"I wouldn't go that far."

"I would."

Lila looked at the stars which twinkled more brightly than at home. "You're right. It is a miracle. There have been too many coincidences to be coincidences."

"I don't believe in such a thing," Sean said, gazing at the sky with her. "God's ways are mighty and mysterious. Everything has a purpose." He sighed. "I am in awe."

"You're going home," she whispered.

"Perhaps *we're* going home."

What a novel thought.

‍◞

Victoria and Alice were tucked safely in bed but Annie knew she wouldn't be able to sleep. She was angry and needed to walk and be outside.

Her mood started at Gert's wedding. Seeing her friend happily married had made her think about her own wedding and her own happy life with Sean.

She'd tried to lock the mood away, but mental screams of *It's not fair!* forced her onto the empty sidewalk. She didn't walk far, just up and back, up and back. She wished she could scream aloud, letting God hear all the horrid, angry words that were battling in her heart and mind.

You brought us together. You let us love and live and be partners in all things. And then You took him away? No! It's worse than that. because I don't know what happened to him! Where is he?

Shaking, she leaned against a railing to support herself.

She looked up at the building and realized who lived there. The Lawson family had lost two sons on the battlefields of France. Mrs. Wallin had lost a husband at Verdun. Mr. Smith had lost a wife and a daughter to the flu . . .

Annie turned to look up Leroy Street. Building after building, house after house had suffered loss and pain — were still suffering loss and pain.

At least you have hope.

She started to argue the point, saying that she had lost hope . . . but she didn't, because the inner voice was right. At least she had hope. Edna had shared a verse with her when they'd first realized Sean was missing: "Be of good courage, and he shall strengthen your heart, all ye that hope in the Lord."

She took a cleansing breath, looked toward the sky, and whispered, "Sean? Wherever you are, please know I would run across the ocean to be with you. Come home soon, my love."

◆

Sean couldn't sleep. It had been hours since he'd left Lila at her stateroom and entered his own. Yet sleep wouldn't come. His heart and mind were too full of gratitude and excitement. And so he'd gotten dressed to take a walk around the deck — which he had to himself.

It was an odd feeling to be so alone, a feeling intensified when he looked over the vast and endless sea which met with the vast and endless sky. God created them all as He had created this moment. He thought about the moments to come, when he would see Annie and run into her arms. It couldn't be soon enough.

"Annie?" he whispered. "Wherever you are, please know I would run across the ocean to be with you. I'll be home soon, my love."

CHAPTER SEVENTEEN

Annie and Henrietta visited Olivet together.

Henrietta realized she'd been doing all the talking. Mabel and her boss at Olivet just sat there, staring at her.

Henrietta showed them the invoice again. "This is the proof. Look at the address."

Mr. Romano motioned to Mabel. "Give me that list of items missing from inventory."

Mabel found it in a stack of papers.

He looked it over, matching it with the Unruffled invoice. "There it is. Bolt by bolt, what he delivered to you matches what we're missing — or part of what we're missing."

"We're betting he has the rest of it stashed in his apartment," Annie said.

Mr. Romano slapped his palms on the table and began to rise. "That's it then. I'm calling the police and — "

"We've already talked to the police," Annie said. She told them the plan.

"My, my," he said. "You've thought of everything."

"The sergeant came up with a lot of the details." Annie looked to Henrietta. "We think everything is covered."

"As much as it can be," Henrietta said.

Mr. Romano nodded and exchanged a look with Mabel. She nodded. "All right then. We will do our part." He stood and offered the ladies a hand-shake. "Well done, Mrs. Culver, and Mrs. Holmquist. We are in your debt."

After visiting Olivet, Henrietta stayed behind to work with them to mark the fabric while Annie went to Unruffled. Her stomach was fluttering with butterflies. Hopefully helping customers would get her mind off justice. Off Guy Ship. Annie was surprised to see Gert come into Unruffled with a garment bag draped over her arm. "Back from the honeymoon so soon?"

"One night at the Waldorf Astoria busted our budget a'plenty."

"Fancy," Sara said.

"We could get used to it," Gert said.

"It is fancy," Eudora said. "Father let Mother and I stay there when we had some water issues at our house."

Sometimes Annie forgot that Eudora's family was wealthy — until she made comments like this.

"How is married life — all twenty-four hours of it?" Sara asked, with a bit of suggestiveness in her voice.

Gert handled it in her usual down-to-earth manner. "It is wonderful, Simon is wonderful, and I know our life will be wonderful."

"You are a walking advertisement for the institution."

"I believe I am. But truth be told, Simon had to work today."

"But *you* don't have to work," Annie said. "We gave you the week off."

"I'm not exactly working. Hold this." She handed the hanger of the bag to Eudora and drew the bag up and over, revealing her wedding dress. "As requested," she said.

Annie felt badly. "I said I'd like to display your dress, but never expected you to bring it to us so soon after the event."

"Better here than in our apartment, which is quite chaotic with his things and my things every which way."

"Well, thank you. We'll display it proudly."

"When I get the wedding photo, would you like to display it next to the gown?"

"What a marvelous idea," Annie said. "How generous of you."

She grinned. "It's my one chance to show off — show Simon off too." They covered the gown again — for now.

"Don't you mind having people copy your gown?" Eudora asked.

"Not at all. They can't take away the fact that I had it first."

"We should call it 'The Gertrude'," Sara said.

"Consider it done," Annie said. It was a great marketing tool.

Gert laughed. "I can't wait to tell Simon I have a dress named after me. Speaking of . . . I'd better get home. There are crates and boxes to unpack."

They all gave her hugs and well wishes.

"I love seeing her so happy," Eudora said.

"Finally happy," Annie added.

"We're going to need to buy more of that fabric," Sara said.

"I'm ordering more today." She drew the ladies closer so the few early customers didn't hear. "In fact . . . " Gert's dress would play into the plan to catch Guy. "When Guy comes in today — "

"He's coming in?" Eudora asked nervously.

"I asked him to come in early this afternoon. I was going to tell you to take a few hours off so you aren't here. I'm sure he and I will be in the storeroom *and* out in the showroom, so there will be — "

"No good place to hide," she said.

"Exactly. Leave at noon and come back at three. You'll be paid for the hours."

Eudora nodded. "I appreciate you thinking about me in all this. But how is ordering more of Gert's fabric going to *get* him?"

"I was going to have him order more fabric — it might as well be the fabric in Gert's dress." She hadn't told them the plan yet. As the store wasn't busy, now was a good time. "If Guy continues doing what he's been doing with past orders, he will steal the fabric and bill us for it, wanting payment to be sent to his home address."

"And if he doesn't?" Sara asked.

"The police will proceed with what we have."

Eudora nodded. "I'd say a prayer for the plan, but praying that a man steals and steps *into* temptation seems a bit odd."

"Pray for justice," Annie said. "In whatever form God wants to provide it."

&

Annie was glad she'd sent Eudora home at noon, because Guy showed up at half-past. As usual, he swept in with a flamboyant greeting and a bow. "My dear, lovely ladies . . ."

It was effective, as even the customers smiled and blushed. No matter what else he was, Guy *was* a good salesman.

"How can I entice you today?"

She ignored his double entendre. Gert's wedding gown provided the perfect transition. "See this gown?" She lifted the bag enough to reveal the fabric. "We're going to put it on display, which will surely entice more customers to buy. In fact, I have a bride who's in a time pinch coming in Saturday at one. I know once she sees the yardage is available — in person — she'll want it."

He studied the fabric. "So you need more of this particular fabric."

"At least one bolt."

"Two would be better, don't you think?"

If you say so. "Two then."

"I'll bring them over Saturday morning."

No! Annie needed him to come at a specific time so the police would be there. "That won't work. We have appointments all

228

morning, so I need you to bring it by at one o'clock when I have the bride's appointment. You can charm her."

"That, I can do."

Unfortunately, it was true.

He offered the bow of a gallant. "I will come with bells on."

And hopefully go out wearing handcuffs.

ॡ

Edna paused outside of Unruffled to check Lizzy's appearance— and calm her excitement. Annie had not met Lizzy yet, though she'd most certainly heard about her through Henrietta.

"Are you ready?" she asked the girl.

"Are you?"

"I believe I am."

"I's never gone in through the front door."

"Then it's about time." Edna held out her hand. "Shall we?"

They walked in together and found Annie at the cash register. She looked at Edna, then at Lizzy, then at Edna again. And smiled. She came around the counter to greet them. "You must be Lizzy."

Lizzy nodded. "Are you Mrs. Culver?"

"I am. But you can call me Annie."

Lizzy looked up at Edna as if asking if it was all right.

"Yes, you can call her Annie."

"Now I know an Annie, a Henrietta, a Maude, a Ginny, a Myrtle, and a Mary."

"Very good."

Annie looked a little hurt, and Edna realized everyone in their circle had met the girl except her. "She knows everyone at the workshop because I've taken her with me the last couple days."

The explanation seemed to make Annie feel better. "Next, you will need to meet my daughters, Victoria and Alice."

"Ooh, Victoria . . . that's a fancy name."

"She may have a fancy name but she's not a fancy girl. She's six. And Alice is four. How old are you?"

"I think I'm six."

"You think?"

Edna explained. "She doesn't remember her birthday year, but knows the date is February third. We're going to hunt down her birth certificate so we really know."

"Ma died a while back."

"How long ago is a while?" Annie asked.

"I dunno. A couple a winters."

"Where's your father?"

She shrugged. "I don't know who he is."

"Perhaps that's best," Annie said, then immediately shook her head. "Sorry. That wasn't kind."

It wasn't kind, but Edna suspected the comment stemmed from Annie's family background.

"Welcome to our store, Lizzy."

"Oh, I knows the store," she said. She walked to a rack of green dresses. "This is one of my favorites."

"Of course you know it," Annie said. "You . . . lived here?"

"Part of the time. Some nights after everyone left the pretty part of the store I came in from the back and looked around."

"How did you get in?"

"The lock's not good on the door to the alley."

"Really?"

Edna nodded. "We'll have to get it fixed."

Lizzy sighed deeply. "There sure is lots of pretty stuff in here." She looked at Annie. "But I didn't steal anything and didn't touch the dresses. Much."

Annie knelt beside her. "I'm glad Edna found you and that you've found a new home."

Lizzy held out the skirt of her dress. "Look at what she bought me." She turned full circle, showing it off.

"Macy's," Edna said.

Annie stood. "You look quite fashionable and pretty."

"I got another one for church and undies and stocking and—"

"Yes, yes," Edna said. "You are now properly attired." She spoke to Annie. "We need to get her enrolled in school. Victoria's going this year, isn't she?"

"She is. And yes, that would be a grand idea."

Lizzy piped up. "I know my numbers to a hundred now, and Edna is helping me with my ABCs. I can write my name—the Lizzy name. The Elizabeth name is hard."

"You'll get it," Edna said. She looked at Annie. "She's smart."

Lizzy nodded, making Annie laugh. "Being smart is a very good thing," Annie said. "But school doesn't start for a few weeks. Do you want to bring her over to our apartment every day? Since Vesta is there she could watch Lizzy along with the others for a few weeks."

"That would be very nice of her." Edna looked at Lizzie. "Would you like that?"

Lizzy nodded vigorously.

Edna had a different idea. "Perhaps three days a week with Vesta and two days a week with me at the workshop."

Annie felt selfish for bringing it up but, "You have work to do. It's a busy time right now."

Edna moved to set her mind at ease. "We're on top of things. And when Gert comes back—"

"She's back. She stopped in to bring us her dress to display."

"That honeymoon was short."

"Simon had to work. Gert will be back to work on Monday."

"I get to meet a Gert too?"

"You get to meet a Gert too." Edna put her hands on Lizzy's shoulders. "I've been teaching Lizzy how to sew. I'd like to continue until school starts. We all know how advantageous it is to learn a skill."

"I can't argue with you," Annie said. "We can always use another seamstress in the family."

∼

Gela walked down the street feeling like a queen. She had money in her pocket and a purpose to her shopping: Dock.

Her parents had given her $15 to buy all the household utensils he'd need. She'd wanted to go to Macy's or even order from the Sears Roebuck catalogue, but they'd told her frugality was needed, because Dock needed so much. They were not wealthy people. Her task was to mine the second-hand shops nearby. Plus, she needed to be frugal because they didn't even know if Dock would accept their gifts. Yet why wouldn't he?

Gela had to shop today because they'd gotten news that the actors' strike was over. Rehearsals resumed Monday. She had so much to be excited about—and thankful for. And so much to marvel at. If not for the strike there was a good chance she wouldn't have gotten to know Dock at all as her time at Port Refuge would have been limited. Her parents were always talking about how God created good out of bad. This was a prime example.

She reached the Nearly-New shop and went inside. It was stuffed with items of every description piled high and even hung from the ceiling.

"May I help you?" came a voice from the back.

Gela snaked her way down narrow aisles, holding her purse close to her body so as not to knock anything off a shelf. She spotted an old woman sitting behind a counter that was also stacked with things to sell.

"You need help or just looking?"

"I need help to look." She pulled out her mother's list and showed it to the woman, who adjusted her glasses to read it, nodded, and then stood with a moan, as if knowing that Gela was a real customer gave her strength. She looked over her glasses. "You look too young to be starting up yer own place."

Gela took offense. "I'm sixteen."

"Like I said."

"It's not for me, it's for someone else. My parents trust my choices."

"Do they now?" She didn't wait for Gela to defend herself but walked to an area where there were stacks of dishes. "How many of each you need?"

One? That didn't seem right but Mama hadn't specified. "Maybe four plates, four bowls, four cups. Same with glasses and silverware."

The woman perused the stacks, moving this and that. "I don't want to break up a set of eight." She looked at Gela. "Unless you'll take more."

"Just four."

She pointed to a low stack. "There's three and you could choose one odd one."

Dock wouldn't care. But Gela would. "They need to match. And nothing too fancy. This is for a man's apartment."

Gela received another glance over the top of the woman's glasses.

"A family friend," Gela said. "If you please? There's a lot on the list."

Some more dishes were rearranged, and ivory plates brought out. "These are sturdier. And no flowers or frillies."

"They're perfect."

"Got a serving bowl and a big plate too," the woman said, rummaging around. "And a butter dish. You want those too?"

All would come in handy. "Depends on the price."

The woman considered this a moment. "A dollar for the lot?"

I would have paid two. "Done. Now to silverware?"

Four place settings were found for a quarter—with two sharp knives thrown in. Then four glasses for a dime.

"Now I need a few pans, a tea kettle, and maybe a mixing bowl."

"Mixing bowl's not on the list."

"I'm adding it."

The items were found and Gela added two lidded glass ice-box containers for leftovers.

She also found a lamp that would work well next to the bed for a quarter, some kitchen towels that looked nearly new, as well as a blanket. Mama had said sheets, a pillow, and body towels would be bought new.

The collection was growing on the counter, including a cast iron skillet. Mama loved hers, and babied it by wiping it clean and re-tempering it like it was a treasured object. Because of the skillet, Gela bought a pancake turner and a few large lidded jars for flour and sugar. She doubted Dock knew how to cook, but maybe having the ingredients at hand would inspire him.

She also bought him a clock so he could get to work on time.

She spotted a low bookshelf and immediately thought of the books she'd donate from her own library. Surely Dock would love reading about Robinson Crusoe—a man who also had to deal with survival. And Robin Hood was a rousing story too.

While looking around she saw a tall bureau, a bedside table, a small drop-leaf table, and two chairs that almost matched.

The apartment had an upholstered chair, but Gela had seen many tears in the fabric arms, so she found two rectangular doilies that could cover the worn spots. Plus a padded footrest, floor lamp, and end table. She carried each one to the counter, creating a moat of furniture around herself.

She took a deep breath, perusing her finds. "I think I'm through." But then she saw a painting of a port with ships, water, and docks. "And that."

"I always liked that picture." She got it down. "Your 'man' is very lucky."

"I hope he likes everything. It's a surprise."

"What, you say?"

She shouldn't have brought it up. "He doesn't know we're doing it."

"Who's doing it?"

"My family."

"Is he family?"

"No. Just an acquaintance who's run onto hard times."

The woman studied Gela a moment. "Doing all this . . . tis very nice of ya." She added up the total. "Comes to $15.85."

Uh-oh. "I only have fifteen."

The woman looked at the bill. "Fifteen it is."

"Thank you."

"What can I say? I's a sucker fer a do-gooder." The woman looked over the purchases. "You need this delivered?"

"I suppose I do."

"My son's in the back doing nothing but collecting dust. He's got an old truck. He'll do it."

She thought of her lack of funds. "How much?"

The woman winked. "He'll do it for free. He needs to do a little good too. You want to ride along and show 'im the way?"

God worked in amazing ways.

❧

Gela was having fun setting up house for Dock. Yesterday she and Mama had gone to the apartment and wiped things down so the messy part was done. In order to better do the work Gela had put on a pair of Matteo's trousers but had been told to take them off. Immediately.

"I'm cleaning a dirty apartment. Pants make much more sense than a skirt."

The vote had been three to one, against.

Gela hadn't really expected them to be okay with it, but it was fun to rile them every so often. One of these days women would get to wear pants. She'd bet a hundred dollars on it.

They'd taken the curtains home to wash and iron too. Mama was coming back to hang them. All Gela had to do today was put her purchases away.

They still needed to get clothes to fill the dresser, but that was her father and brother's assignment. Papa said he knew of a place that would give them a deal. And Mama said she'd run over to Macy's and get the sheets and towels. The last task would be getting some food, but that would have to wait until they knew the answer to the *when* question, as in *when* was he was moving in? Mama and Gela also wanted to make him some baked goods so he'd have something special right away.

She arranged the easy chair and end table with their back to the window to allow for easy reading. The doilies did their job and covered the flaws in the arms. She found an electrical outlet near enough that the floor lamp provided nice light for both reading and eating at the table with mismatched—but nearly matching—chairs. The bookshelf was placed by the door.

The kitchen items were set in neat stacks on open shelves and in drawers, with cooking utensils set in a small crock.

The last item to be put in place was the port picture. Luckily, there was a nail still in the wall of the parlor in the approximate center of the wall. She hung it, adjusted the square of it, then stepped back to get the full affect.

"It's perfect," she whispered. She scanned the space. "It's all perfect. Help him like it, Lord."

∾

Lizzy ran up the stairs to their flat then looked down at Edna. "I beat you!"

"You will always beat me, child." She held up the key. "But I have the key." She reached the top of the stairs.

"Can I do it?"

Edna relinquished it. With a little fumbling Lizzy got the door open. "I did it!"

Such simple pleasures. "I hereby assign you all locking and unlocking duties from now on."

"Really?"

Edna marveled at her lovely hazel eyes and had a premonition that she would succumb to them many times during their life together. Happily succumb.

They went inside and Lizzy plopped on a kitchen chair. "I'm hungry."

"Those who don't help, don't eat," Edna said.

Lizzy stood up.

"Wash your hands first."

Lizzy skipped off to the bathroom.

There was a knock at the door. Edna answered it. "Mack?"

"Long time no see."

"Indeed." She hadn't seen him in nearly two weeks, since her birthday. He'd invited himself to her birthday dinner but Steven had made the evening awkward.

"With your son living here, I didn't want to intrude."

"You didn't need to stay away for that."

He shrugged and leaned against the door jamb. "I heard he's all right now and you're alone again."

It seemed an odd distinction. They weren't close enough to want privacy — at least Edna wasn't.

He continued, "Would you care to go for a bite and then come with me to Refuge? I'm playing there tonight."

"I can't."

"Why not?"

Lizzy came out of the bathroom and Edna motioned her close. "Because I am *not* alone. Mack, this is Lizzy, Lizzy, this is Mr. McGinness."

"Hi," she said.

"Hi to you too." He looked totally confused.

"Lizzy has come to live with me."

"Live with you?"

"That's right."

Lizzy piped up. "I was living at Unruffled," Lizzy said. "This is way better."

His eyebrows rose.

"That's a story for another time," Edna smiled at Lizzy and pointed to the kitchen. "Why don't you wash some carrots."

"All right."

When Edna and Mack were alone again he asked, "How long is she staying?"

"I expect until she's twenty or so."

His eyes grew wide. "You've fully taken her in?"

"Fully. I'm going to adopt her."

"At your age?" He immediately backtracked. "I mean, you are a grandmother and she's —"

She closed the door an inch. "Perhaps another time, Mack."

He nodded, though half-heartedly. "Have a nice evening."

"You too."

She closed the door and stared at it a moment. He hadn't warmed to the idea of her having a child around. It was clear he was disappointed. Would he ever come around to visit again?

It made her sad to think he wouldn't.

Maude barely got in the door after work when Matteo said, "I found Dock a job!"

"Where?"

"With my company. Loading trucks."

Antonio must have recently gotten home too, for he was loosening his tie. "Doesn't it sound perfect for him, Maude?"

She hung her hat on the rack and tidied her hair. "How much does it pay?"

"Ten dollars a week to start."

"That's good." She turned to Antonio realizing she'd never asked a very important question. "I've been there, but I never asked how much the apartment costs a month?" *That we're paying.*

"Twenty-five dollars for one room — bath down the hall."

"Isn't that a little steep? It was grungy until Gela and I cleaned it."

Antonio shrugged. "Supply and demand. There is very little supply because construction stopped during the war. Since it's on the top floor it's less expensive than lower floors. More stairs, less rent."

Matteo grabbed a hunk of bread from the cupboard. "If he's loading trucks, he'll get strong real fast. You remember how sore I was the first few weeks." He showed off his biceps. "I'm strong now."

"That, you are," Maude said. "It all comes down to beggars can't be choosers."

They heard struggling in the hall, and Maude opened the door. It was Gela, carrying a small table. "Help!"

Antonio took it inside, but it couldn't sit upright as it was missing a leg.

"What are you going to do with this?" Matteo asked.

"Fix it and put it in Dock's apartment. It was sitting on the curb on Bleecker. I couldn't resist."

The men looked at the table. Matteo said he could get a piece of wood that would work. "It won't match the other legs."

"Doesn't have to." Gela bobbed on her toes, brimming with excitement. "You will never believe all that I bought for Dock."

She listed all the purchases. "You got all that for the fifteen dollars we gave you?" her father asked.

"Got it delivered too. And set up. It's beautiful." She stole a bit of bread from her brother. "I'm famished."

Maude got an idea. "Let's eat a quick supper then go to Refuge and tell Dock about his new job."

"You three go," Antonio said, sitting down to read his paper.

Maude snatched it away. "We'll all go. This is a family affair."

"We'll tell him about the apartment too?" Gela asked. Maude wanted to say yes, but looked to Antonio. "I think it's best to wait on that detail. Let's see if he even wants the job."

"Let's see if he *gets* it," Matteo said. "He needs to go to the shop and apply. They'll be there tomorrow."

Job first. Home second. Victory later.

❧

Gela was nervous as her family approached Port Refuge and had second thoughts about descending upon Dock together. She turned around and stopped them.

"What's wrong?" Matteo asked. "We're here. Let's go in."

"I think it's too much, all of us being here."

"Then why did you invite us?" Papa asked.

"I didn't. Mama did."

They all looked at Mama. "I thought it would be satisfying for all of us to be a part of it."

"We didn't think about Dock," Gela said. "He's still sensitive about you forgiving him and all that attention."

Mama threw her hands in the air. "Why didn't you say something before now?"

"I . . . I didn't think of it." She held her ground. "The lot of us going in there, surrounding him, telling him about the job when he hasn't had one in ages . . ."

Matteo put his hands in his pockets and turned to leave. "I'm going home."

She grabbed his arm. "No! You stay. I need you to give him the details." She looked at her parents. "But could you two . . . not go in?"

Mama gave a frustrated sigh and Papa pointed a finger at her. "What you say makes sense but you need to think things through, Gela."

"I know. I'm really sorry."

Papa offered Mama his arm and they walked away, with Mama giving her a backward glance.

"You bungled that one, sister."

"I didn't mean to. It *seemed* like a good idea."

Matteo looked toward the entrance to Refuge. Four men were milling around outside. "This is the place, huh?"

She realized he'd never been there. "This is it."

"I've seen places like it around the city. You sing here?"

"I do. With Mr. McGinness."

"And this Dock-guy just showed up?"

"He'd been coming here before I showed up. Then Mama came. She recognized him. And the rest . . ."

"Yeah, yeah. It's getting late and I have to work tomorrow. Can we do this?"

As they went inside, Gela had the awful thought that Dock might not even be there. There wasn't time to go to where he lived before dark — and it certainly wasn't a place she wanted to go to after dark. She looked towards his usual place and was relieved to see him.

"Come on."

Dock offered a little wave as she approached, but then looked warily at Matteo. She was quick to put him at ease. "Dock, this is my little brother, Matteo."

Dock smiled. "Ain't so little."

"Our dad's tall," Matteo said.

There was an awkward silence, then Dock said, "You sing too?"

"Not a note. I'm here because . . ." He looked to Gela.

"He found you a job with his company. He drives a truck, making deliveries, and—"

"And they need people to load and unload. You interested?"

Gela nearly panicked when he hesitated. "I ain't worked in a while."

"You willing to work?"

"Well, yeah."

"Then meet me at this address tomorrow at ten." He handed Dock the address. "You need to talk to the foreman, Mr. Walters, but I told him you were coming. I don't think you'll have any trouble getting the job."

Dock stared at the paper, then nodded. "I'm much obliged. I'll be there." He looked at Gela. "Thank you."

❧

"How many times do you think we've walked around this deck?" Sean asked Lila.

"Four hundred twenty-three?"

"At least."

"That's the trouble with sailing. No place to go. If we straightened our walking route, I'm sure we'd be to New York by now." He immediately felt bad for complaining. "Sorry. I shouldn't have said anything. I'm very thankful for the first class passage. I *have* enjoyed the food and the card-playing and—"

"You're getting very good at Whist. And you said Annie is better than you?"

"Much."

"I'll have to keep that in mind."

They nodded at another couple as they passed. "Can we count on your for cards tonight, Mr. Culver?" the woman asked.

"Of course, Mrs. Dobbins," he said.

"See?" Lila patted his arm as they continued their stroll. "You have a following."

"She's not very good."

"You can enjoy playing cards without being good."

"You enjoy it more if you win."

Lila pointed to the inner part of the ship. "Come with me. I want to send a cable."

He stopped walking. "To whom?"

"Not Annie," she reassured him. "To Maude."

"Why Maude? Why anyone? We want to surprise them."

"A cable is necessary *for* the surprise. We don't want to show up and have no one around, do we?"

"I guess not."

"I was going to contact Steven, but he'd have a hard time keeping it from Etta — and I want to surprise him too. And Edna is also family. So we're down to Maude."

"What are you going to tell her?"

"Just what you and I have talked about. We'll recreate the surprise Steven and I arranged before they were married. We'll be in Central Park at the Bethesda Fountain and Maude will make sure everyone is taking a stroll. And voila! Surprise!"

It was a good plan. "Let's send a cable."

Chapter Eighteen

Edna squeezed Lizzy's hand. "Don't be nervous."

"But I ain't never been to school."

Haven't ever. Edna left the grammar lesson for another day.

They entered the school building and went to the office. A woman greeted them, giving Lizzy a special smile.

"What pretty hair you have."

"Edna did it for me special today 'cuz I was coming here."

The woman's left eyebrow rose. "Am I to understand you are Edna?"

"Edna Holmquist, yes." She didn't offer more of an explanation, though she knew they wouldn't leave without her having to go into it. "We are here to enroll Lizzy in school for the upcoming year. She's six." *We think.*

"I've been learning my ABCs and numbers."

"That's very good." She looked at Edna. "What grade?"

"I'm not sure. I think first."

"You're not sure?"

And there it was, time for the explanation. "Lizzy is an orphan. I am adopting her."

"Do you have a letter from an orphanage?"

"She lived on the streets."

"I lived in the back of Unruffled mosta the time."

"Unruffled?"

"Our dress store. On Bleecker Street?"

"Can't say as I've been there."

Lizzy piped up. "It has really pretty dresses. You should go."

The woman chuckled, then held out her hand to Edna. "I'm Mrs. Granger."

Edna shook her hand. "Very nice to meet you." With the introduction she felt more comfortable laying things out as they were. "I found Lizzy living in the storeroom and have taken her in. We don't have a birth certificate yet, but I will pursue one, if you need it."

"It's preferable." She looked at Lizzy. "What's your last name, Lizzy?"

Lizzy bit her lip, then looked at Edna. "Holmquist."

Edna's throat grew tight while she nodded.

"Very well then. Lizzy Holmquist, we shall put you in first grade and see how it goes."

∾

Gela pointed at the painting of the harbor scene. "Do you like it, Mama? I thought it was appropriate since Dock worked at such a place."

Mama brushed a hair back after putting up the newly washed curtains. "It's very nice, Gela. Everything you've done here is spot-on. I'm very proud of you." She opened her arms.

Gela loved the feel of her mother's embrace and the familiar smell of lavender.

Mama held her head close. "We need to do this more often. You may be grown, but that doesn't mean we shouldn't hug."

Gela nodded against her shoulder. "Thank you for trusting me with all this. And for trusting me to have a job in 'Irene' and all that. I'm glad Dock's apartment is coming together before I start rehearsals again. Otherwise I wouldn't have had time to do it."

Mama let her go. "I've thought of that too. It was hard letting you buy the furniture and such on your own because it meant I had to admit you were old enough. And mature enough."

Gela felt a stitch as memories of past behavior returned. "I may have acted mature in this, but a lot of the time I've acted like I was ten. I'm sorry for being so difficult."

"The apology goes both ways." Mama ran a hand over the top of the small table. "Matteo's going to give Dock this address if he gets the job, then bring him here to meet us around noon, during lunch break. That is, *if* he gets the job."

"Matteo thinks he will. They need men to work."

"Beyond filling the spot, I hope he's a good worker — for both their sakes."

Gela was surprised at her doubt. "Why wouldn't he be? He worked at the docks until he got the flu. And yes, he stole a few things, but he was desperate."

Mama sighed and moved one of the chairs toward the table a quarter inch. "He may have developed bad habits being on the street, on his own, with no one to report to."

Gela waved the thought away. "Don't think like that. Give him a chance."

Mama looked down, then nodded. "You're right. We're offering him a fresh start. We have to trust God to make it work."

"In whatever way He wants it to work."

Mama looked up and smiled. "Who made you so wise?"

"I think it might have been you."

Two hugs in one morning. How amazing.

&

Maude paced up and back, stealing looks at the clock in Dock's apartment. *Tick tock tick tock tick . . .*

It was ten after twelve. Matteo had said he'd bring Dock over around noon.

Don't panic. It's only ten minutes.

Eleven.

"Are you nervous?" Gela asked.

"I'd like to say no, but yes, I am very nervous. What if he doesn't come? We would have done all this work for nothing."

"Not nothing. Papa could rent out this place to someone else, couldn't he?"

"I sup—"

There was a knock on the door. Gela and Maude froze, then exchanged a glance. Maude's stomach did a flip. She opened the door.

Dock's face was a mask of surprise. "Mrs. Ricci?"

"I didn't tell him a thing," Matteo said.

She stepped aside and the men came in.

Dock spotted Gela. "Gela?" He looked from one to the other. "What's going on?"

"We wanted to congratulate you on your new job," Maude said.

"Thank you. Matteo got me in."

You ain't seen nothing yet. Maude stepped further into the room so he could see it. "This is your new apartment."

He looked from left to right and back again. "What?"

"Papa got it for you," Gela said. "And I furnished it and got you dishes and pans, and new sheets and towels, and Papa and Matteo even found you some clothes . . ." She flit around the room, showing him everything.

He stood there, shaking his head. "I don't understand."

It *was* overwhelming. Maude stepped in with the final details. "We have paid two month's rent to give you time to get on your feet again. With your new job, you will be able to afford it. The rent is twenty-five dollars a month."

Dock squeezed his head with his hands, his face crumpling with emotion. "I don't know what to say."

"A simple thank you will suffice."

He shook his head. "It will not suffice. It's not enough." He lowered his hands. "Why would you do this for *me*? After what I did to you? I don't understand."

Neither do I — not completely.

Maude's throat was tight. She took a few breaths, in and out. "When I forgave you, I felt an enormous release. The hatred and anger I'd held onto for thirteen years was gone. When I saw how you were living and how you'd punished yourself . . . I—"

"God did it," Gela said.

Maude nodded. "God did it."

Gela pointed to the upholstered chair. "Try it out." As soon as he sat down she brought him a book. "You need to read this book. It's about two men shipwrecked on a deserted island."

He held the book, but was clearly still in shock.

Gela turned on the floor lamp behind him. "I positioned the chair to give you good light from the windows, and when it gets dark you can turn on this lamp."

Maude went to the cupboards. "We've stocked the shelves with some staples. And Gela and I made you some bread." She held up the loaf. "There's butter and strawberry jam in the ice box." She opened its door. "There's some fruit, pastrami, and a few potatoes and some lard. They're real good if you slice them thin and fry them in a pan."

"I got you a cast iron skillet," Gela said, getting it off a shelf. "You don't wash it, you just wipe it out."

Maude could tell they were saying too much. "What do you think?"

Dock seemed to realize he was holding a book. He set it on the arm of the chair. "I am humbled. And very grateful."

Maude saw Gela heave a sigh of relief. "We'll leave you then, to give you time to get settled." She handed him the key, and nodded at her children. They moved to the door.

Dock intercepted her and stood before her nervously, his hands keeping each other company. His eyes were full of angst, relief, and gratitude. "I will not let you down, Mrs. Ricci. I will not throw away this second chance you have given me."

"God has given you, Clarence."

He nodded.

She felt tears threaten and wanted to leave before she cried. "God bless you."

"God bless all of *you*."

As they went down the three flights of stairs, Gela started to talk, but Maude raised a hand, silencing her. "Wait."

They got outside and walked a full block before Maude turned toward her children and let the happy tears come. "We did it!"

"He really liked it," Gela said.

"I hope he sticks with the job," Matteo said.

She touched his cheek. "This is no time for pessimism."

He shrugged. "I gotta get back to work."

"Just one more minute." She squeezed his hand. "Thank you for finding him the job and the clothes. As you just saw, he's very appreciative."

"I liked doing it."

Giving can be joyful. What a good life lesson they've just learned.

Maude took her daughter's face in her hands. "You, my dear young lady, are an extraordinary human being. You were instrumental in healing two lives. God bless *you*, Gela."

Gela started to cry, and they fell into each other's arms.

"Stop it," Matteo whispered. "No crying on the sidewalk."

Maude grabbed a hunk of his shirt and pulled him into the embrace.

Annie and Henrietta waited impatiently in front of the police sergeant's desk while he spoke with an officer standing beside him. He'd contacted Annie that morning, asking them to come to the station. Annie was excited. It had to be good news. Didn't it?

He stopped his conversation and looked up. "I apologize. There are many logistics to work out for our plan on Saturday. Our sting.

Annie liked the term. "So it's happening?"

"It is."

"Guy has stolen the bait-fabric?" Henrietta asked.

"First thing this morning. We received word from Olivet."

Annie and Henrietta exchanged a glance. "This is really happening."

"It most certainly is," the sergeant said. He handed a piece of paper to the officer. "Here's the search warrant for his apartment."

"Yes, sir."

He spoke to the ladies again. "I've arranged for two officers to enter his apartment while he's at the store on Saturday. You arranged for him to come at one o'clock?"

"Yes. It's all set on our end."

"Can I be at his apartment?" Henrietta asked. "I'd like to see what else he's stolen—how much else."

Annie intervened before the sergeant answered. "Don't you want to be at the store and see him get arrested? He'll have the bait fabric with him."

After a moment's hesitation, Henrietta blinked. "Of course." She looked at the officer. "Never mind."

"We wouldn't have been able to let you enter his residence anyway. At best you would have had to stand in the hall."

It was settled then.

"What do you need us to do at Unruffled?" Annie asked.

"Our plan has two goals: Firstly, there is the thievery of the fabric and fraud for collecting the money due Olivet, as well as the real estate fraud he perpetrated against Mr. Mitchell. Secondly, there is the delicate offenses against Miss Mitchell. I would prefer we nab him on the theft and fraud first. Miss Mitchell will need to stay out of sight until we have him safely in custody."

Henrietta and Annie had already talked about this. "There's no place to hide in the store since Guy will probably want to take the bolts to the storeroom," Annie said. "But we'll have Eudora across the street at a friend's store waiting for our signal to come over."

Henrietta sighed deeply. "To see his face when Eudora walks in will make my century."

Annie thought of something. "Eudora knows him as George and we know him as Guy. Which is his legal name?"

"Neither." The sergeant pointed at the search warrant. "His legal name is Gilbert Scrubbs."

Henrietta looked at Annie, then the two let out a laugh. "No wonder he changed it."

"And he's married, though obviously estranged from his wife."

"Eudora said he had a wife. Poor thing."

"Beyond these recent crimes he has a long list of offenses from burglary to kiting checks to theft, and . . ."

He looked embarrassed. "And?" Henrietta asked.

"Miss Mitchell isn't the first women he's compromised."

He had their full attention. "What happened?"

He looked uncertain about the telling, but relented. "Back in '17 he seduced a married woman up in Albany and got her to give him expensive gifts and money. The husband actually . . . shall we say, caught them, and was going to shoot them both. Luckily, his wife talked him down and he decided it was more satisfying to bring charges against Scrubbs—before divorcing his wife. Scrubbs spent time in jail and is in debt for many hundreds of dollars in fines, plus lawyer's fees. While the United States was sending brave men to fight, he was safely incarcerated."

Annie let out a huff. "He implied he fought in the war."

"Not a day. He was let out just before armistice was declared."

Henrietta thought about the timing. "The war was over in November of last year . . . he must have gone after Eudora right away."

"He probably planned it while he was inside," Annie said.

"How did he choose her?" Henrietta asked. "Why her?"

The sergeant shrugged. "You'd have to ask him."

The standing officer interjected. "Pardon me, but the Mitchells are always in the newspaper either because of his bank or in the society section. Even *I* knew the name when you told me, Sergeant."

The sergeant gave him a look. "*You* read the society section, Officer Reynolds?"

He reddened. "My wife reads it word for word. Wouldn't miss it."

How interesting.

The sergeant stacked some papers. "Apparently, he's always looking for his next con."

Annie shivered. "He conned me," Annie said. She knew the officer thought she was talking about the invoices, but it was so much more— could have been so much more if she'd let him tempt her. She thanked God for saving her from his clutches. "He's very charming."

"A charm he uses for unsavory purposes." The sergeant pushed his chair back from his desk, stopping further discussion of Guy's character flaws. "On Saturday we will have officers in place near Unruffled at noon and—"

"He's always early," Annie said.

"We'll be in place by half-past eleven then."

She nodded.

"Once we see him go in with the bolts, we'll give him time to speak with you—to offer you the goods as it were—and then we'll come in and arrest him."

"Then we'll signal Miss Mitchell to come in."

"Exactly. Do you have any questions?"

They didn't.

He stood and shook their hands. "I want to thank you both for bringing this criminal to our attention."

"With pleasure."

ℒ

After Dock's big reveal, Matteo went back to work and Gela wanted to go back to Port Refuge. Both options were fine with Maude. She needed time alone to celebrate their victory.

If she'd been a child she would have skipped down the street toward home. She felt light and free, and full of God's love. The world was good.

As she got out the key to her front door, it opened. "Antonio? You're home?"

"For just a few minutes. I have a showing nearby." He pointed at her face. "It went well?"

"Perfect." She told him about Dock getting the job and showing him the apartment. "He loved everything. Gela did a marvelous job."

"I'm so glad it all worked out. It was a risk — still is. He needs to keep his job so *he* can pay the rent."

"I think he will. I really do."

He took her chin in his hand and kissed her. "I'm not going to argue with you. Not for a minute."

The clock on the mantel struck the hour. "I need to go." But as he was leaving he backtracked to the table. "This was slipped under the door when I got here."

It was a cable. "I can't imagine who would be sending me a cable."

"I would have opened it, but since it was only addressed to you . . . open it."

She unfolded the paper and read the words. Then read them again, unbelieving. "Oh. Oh my!" She put a hand to her chest. "Sean is alive!"

Antonio took the cable from her and read it. They he took her in his arms and they jumped up and down together. "He's alive! He's alive! Thank You, God!"

Antonio broke away first. "But why is Lila sending the cable? What does she have to do with Sean being found?"

"I have no idea." Maude's mind swam with a thousand impulses. She wanted to run and tell Annie, tell Edna and Henrietta and Steven. And Vesta! But the telegram said not to tell. She had to read that part again: *Arrive Sunday am. Please arrange for all to meet at Central Park. Bethesda Fountain, 1 pm. Big surprise. Don't tell anyone! Eager to see you. Lila Kidd.*

"It's reminiscent of the time Lila surprised Henrietta."

"She'd arranged it with Steven."

"And now, with Sean." He shook his head. "I can't believe he's all right. Annie has been waiting for so long."

Maude could easily imagine the happy reunion—which wouldn't happen until she set it up. "I have to go invite everyone to the park on Sunday."

She moved toward the door but Antonio stopped her. "You can't tell. You'll want to, but you can't. You need to calm yourself."

He was right. She took some deep breaths, trying to get her heart to stop racing.

He pointed at her face. "Ye, of the transparent face. One look at you and they'll know something is up."

He was right. "Tell me something horrible and bad."

"What?"

"So I stop smiling."

He nodded toward his daily newspaper. "I read that Joe Wilhoit didn't get a hit yesterday, which broke his 69-game hitting streak."

"Baseball? That's the worst thing you can think of?"

"It is for him and for Wichita."

She thought of something which would explain away her happiness. "I'm smiling because of what happened with Dock today."

He cocked his head. "It might work."

It had too. Maude realized there was nothing anyone could do or say to take away her smile. Or her joy.

❧

When Maude got to Unruffled she found Henrietta and Annie sharing details about the upcoming arrest of Guy Ship. She hadn't known they were going to the police station to arrange for his arrest, which made her feel bad. She'd been so caught up in the issues with Dock that she'd set herself outside the inner circle for this upcoming, very important, event.

There are all sorts of important events! Help me keep the secret, Lord. Please—

"What's got you smiling so much?" Annie asked.

She'd prayed the prayer just in time. With a fresh breath she told them about Dock.

It was Henrietta who summed it up so nicely. "We'll have a lot to be thankful for come Sunday."

You have no idea. It was the perfect segue into her invitation. "Why don't we all go to Central Park after church to celebrate? Meet at the Bethesda Fountain at one?"

They all agreed. Edna said, "I'd love to show Lizzy the park."

"All the children would love an outing," Henrietta said.

"That would be lovely," Annie said. "I should ask Vesta to join us."

Maude couldn't have said it better herself.

CHAPTER NINETEEN

Today was the day they'd all been waiting for.

Henrietta stood behind the counter at Unruffled, gnawing on a fingernail. *What if Guy doesn't bring the fabric here? What if —*

Annie pushed her hand down. "Stop it. You look as nervous as we all feel."

"Did Olivet put some red ribbons in the bolts before they were stolen?" Henrietta asked. "That's what the police said to do to mark the bolts."

"I assume they did," Annie said.

"What if they aren't there anymore?"

Annie took her hands and squeezed. "Stop it."

Henrietta curled her fingers under. "I just wish we could make an announcement and tell all the customers to leave. Put a "closed" sign on the door until this is over."

"You know that won't work," Edna said. "We need everything to appear normal."

"I'm glad Sara and Eudora are here to help the customers," Henrietta said.

Annie looked in Eudora's direction. "She shouldn't have to work. If we're nervous she's got to be doubly so."

"I'll go take over," Maude said. She paused to say, "By the way, Antonio said he'd go to Guy's place to watch what happens. Be our eyes."

"That's wonderful," Henrietta said. "Mr. Romano and Mabel are going to be there too. They'll be able to confirm what goods are stolen."

"All of them," Henrietta said.

Eudora came over, her face flushed with nerves. She looked at the clock above the door which read eleven o'clock. "How is that time goes fast when you don't want it to and snails by when you want it to hurry?" Her attention moved to the door. "Mother!" She ran to her mother, then her father — who were accompanied by Mrs. Sampson.

Mrs. Sampson joined the other ladies. "Forgive me but I had to come."

Eudora took solace under her mother's arm, as her father spoke to Annie. "I want to thank you for arranging all this, Mrs. Culver." He glanced at his daughter. "A father longs to protect his family. Unfortunately, I was unable to keep them from pain."

"Oh, Papa . . ." Eudora wrapped her arms around him.

He kissed his daughter's head. "We will be forever in your debt. For this, and for giving Eudora a job."

"She's a wonderful asset."

He looked down at her face. "I was wrong to make you go to work. You don't have to work anymore."

She left his arms. "But I want to. I like it. I like having my own money."

"I will give you an allowance again."

She shook her head. "It's not the same. I earned this money. I'm looking forward to getting a small apartment nearby."

Mrs. Sampson agreed. "She's right, Abel. Your daughter is a modern woman. You've let her enter the workforce. You cannot snatch her back again."

He looked sad. "We'll talk about it."

Annie realized time was passing. "Not today."

He nodded.

"It's time for you to all retire across the street to Meindorff's until we signal you. Guy is known to come early to appointments."

Mrs. Sampson herded the Mitchells across the street.

The other three ladies took a communal breath at the same time, which made them chuckle. "We have to remember to breathe," Edna said.

Easier said than done. Henrietta regretted eating this morning. "Do you want me to be standing with you when he comes in?"

"Not necessary — or well advised."

Henrietta was disappointed, yet agreed. Her nerves might give her away. She'd never been a good actress.

"Actually, I asked Gloria to come in and play the part of a bride."

"Gloria?"

"She was one of our original models? Works at a printing company. And she *is* engaged."

"Is she a good actress?"

"She's a bride-to-be playing the part of a bride-to-be. It won't be difficult."

"Does she know what we're doing?"

"I felt obligated to tell her. With police storming in and all . . . Don't worry. She'll be fine." Annie put a hand on her shoulder. "It will all work out. I know it." Annie bowed her head. "Lord, watch over us this day and use Your mighty power to bring justice. Amen."

They heard the bell ding on the door and looked toward it. It wasn't Guy. It was Officer Reynolds—the one who'd been in the office when she and Annie had talked to the sergeant.

He came up to them. "Just wanted to tell you we're all in place." He pointed outside, to the left, and the right. "We have men in both directions in case he gets spooked and tries to run."

"Thank you," Annie said. "We're nearly ready in here too." The door opened again and Gloria entered. "The final player has arrived. We're all set."

"Very good, ma'am." He retreated outside.

Gloria's eyes were wide as she watched the officer leave. "This is so exciting. Thank you for letting me be a part of it."

Annie chuckled at her enthusiasm. "You're welcome? All you have to do is act normal, a bride looking for a dress. Guy will bring in some fabric."

"I'm supposed to like it?"

"You are."

Annie took out some sketches of wedding dresses, placing them on the table next to the counter. "Why don't we look at these to get started, and when Mr. Ship comes—"

"Oooh," Gloria said. "They're gorgeous." She was totally engrossed.

Annie gave Henrietta a nod to go find something to do.

This would work. It had to.

&

As expected, Guy was early. He swept into the store carrying two bolts of luscious silk—*the* silk, as much as Annie could tell.

He spotted Gloria and leaned the bolts against the counter so he could greet her. "And this must be the lovely bride?" He took her hand and kissed it.

She looked flustered. Hopefully, from his effusive attention. "I . . . yes, I'm the bride."

He bowed. "Guy Ship, at your service. And your name, Miss . . .?"

"Aston."

"Though it won't be Aston for long, eh?"

Annie recognized his usual line. So much of what he said were "lines." She stepped beside the fabric. "You brought it. Thank you."

"I aim to please."

And steal. And con. And deceive.

Gloria glanced nervously at Annie as though uncertain what she should say next. So Annie took control. They needed to get done with this *now*.

She began to lay one of the bolts on the table. Guy rushed to help her.

"I think this fabric would be perfect for the design you're looking at, Gloria," she said. She pointed to the strips of muslin, tied around the bolt. "Guy, would you undo it so Miss Aston can see the drape of it?"

"With pleasure." He set the fabric loose, pulling out a three-yard length.

A red ribbon floated to the floor. He bent to pick it up. "This is odd."

Annie nodded to Henrietta, who hurried outside and motioned in both directions.

"It *is* odd," Annie said, trying to keep him diverted. "Almost like it was placed there on purpose. As a marker perhaps?"

Three officers came inside. Gloria stepped back.

Annie felt a surge of strength. "The ribbons were placed there by Olivet to prove you stole these bolts from their warehouse. What do you say to that, *Mister* Ship?"

Guy saw the police, looked at the ribbon, then bolted toward the storeroom. Maude cut him off and shoved him down.

The police quickly pounced, dragging him to his feet, putting handcuffs on him. "You're under arrest for theft and fraud," Officer Reynolds said.

"You can't prove anything," Guy said.

"We can prove everything," the officer said. "We're searching your apartment for more stolen property as we speak."

Guy looked at Annie, imploringly. "Annie? You know me. You know this isn't true."

Annie saw Henrietta's chest heave with emotion. "I'll let Henrietta have a turn at you."

Henrietta stepped in front of him and removed an invoice from her pocket. "See this? This is not Olivet's address, it's yours. I've been paying you money for goods you stole from them. That's fraud."

For a single moment he looked nervous. But then his face cleared. "I bought those bolts at a deep discount. They are mine to sell at whatever price I choose." He looked at Annie. "I gave you a very good price for very expensive fabric. You know I did."

"I know you did." Annie was calmer than she expected. "We should have known it was too good to be true. *You* are too good to be true."

"Or too bad," Maude said.

Officer Reynolds looked to Annie. "Would you like to continue the rest of this now?"

Eudora! "Henrietta, get the others."

She ran out the front.

"Others?" Guy said. There was a slight stitch in his voice.

"You'll see."

"The cuffs are too tight," Guy complained.

"Stop resisting and they won't hurt," an officer said.

Suddenly, in a flurry, Eudora rushed in the door. She ran to him, pounding her fists against his chest. "How could you do that to me? I hate you! I hate you!"

"What? Eudora?"

She pushed him back and glared at him. "Yes, Eudora. Happy to see me?"

Guy looked at the policemen, as if wanting to be saved.

Mr. Mitchell stood by his daughter. She crossed her arms defiantly. "I hate you for what you did to me," she hissed.

Officer Reynolds stepped up. "Gilbert Scrubbs, aka George Shipman, aka Guy Ship, you are charged with theft, fraud, infidelity, and attempted misappropriation of the funds of Olivet, Unruffled, and Mr. Abel Mitchell, among other charges I'm sure will be added to your list of offenses."

"Gilbert Scrubbs?" Eudora said. "Really? You didn't even use your own name to seduce me?"

Guy smirked, revealing more of his true self. "It didn't take much, Eudora. You're the easiest mark I've ever met. Just a few sweet nothings and you were mine."

Eudora charged at him. Her father pulled her back. She turned to Officer Reynolds. "Can I testify against him in court?"

"You'll be asked to do so. And give a full statement at the station."

"Good," Eudora stood in front of him and got in his face. "I want this no good, lying lecher put away forever." She pegged a finger into his chest. "You will never hurt anyone again."

When the two officers led him out, the whole of Unruffled erupted in applause.

Everyone in the shop hugged each other — even the customers who had no idea what had just happened.

Then Antonio rushed in. "You got him?"

Maude rushed toward him. "We did. We surprised him with the ribbon in the fabric *and* Eudora." She looked around the store. "We got him!"

More shouts of joy.

"How about on your end?" Annie asked.

"We got him there too."

More cheers.

"What did they find?" Henrietta asked.

"Twenty-four bolts of fabric and dozens of other supplies, all stolen from Olivet. Mr. Romano and Mabel confirmed it. Guy Ship — or whatever name is really his — will be put away for a long, long time."

Annie was overcome with relief and gratitude. She held out her hands to her friends and customers, and they all formed a circle right there in the middle of Unruffled. Then she offered a prayer. "Dear God, we thank You . . ."

ہے

They closed Unruffled early. Facilitating justice was exhausting. Everyone went on their way, their conversations popping with the events of the day. Tomorrow they would celebrate in Central Park.

Annie was the last to leave. She turned the OPEN sign to CLOSED and pulled down the shade on the glass door. She turned out the lights, letting the daylight choose where to shine.

She retied the bolts of bait fabric and set them near the front door. They'd get them back to Olivet on Monday. Then there was the issue of paying Olivet for what Guy had sold them, which would mean they'd lose money on the deal as they'd be paying twice. She knew getting their money back from Guy was never going to happen.

She closed out the cash register, putting the money in a safe in the storeroom. They'd worry about tallying the sales tomorrow. Today hadn't been about sales, but about truth winning over lies, right conquering wrong, good overcoming evil.

Her duties done, Annie was suddenly struck by the silence. It was a stark contrast to the voices, cheers, and activity that had filled the store just minutes before.

Before everyone left with their loved ones, happily sharing the day's dramatic events.

Leaving me alone to share with no one.

Annie fought the urge to sink into a chair, draw her knees to her chest, and wallow.

She'd done enough of that.

Instead she opened her arms wide and looked to the heavens. "Thank You for personally saving me from that man, and bringing him to justice. I have much to be thankful for."

The sudden image of Victoria and Alice entered her mind.

"Exactly," she told God.

Annie locked the door and went home to her girls.

CHAPTER TWENTY

Maude didn't hear much of the minister's sermon Sunday morning. She was too full of the private worship service going on in her heart: Dock, Guy, and later today, the reunion of Annie and Sean. And Henrietta and her mother too.

She hadn't received any more cables so assumed everything was on schedule. She marveled at how easily everyone had agreed to go to Central Park. That was also God's doing. This was His show. Maude had no reason to worry.

Some words from the pulpit reached her. "Our Bible passage for today is Psalm 100. It's the shortest Psalm in the Bible and is complete in five verses — five very important verses that sum up our relationship with our God." The pastor took a new breath and raised his hands and face toward heaven. "'Make a joyful noise unto the Lord, all ye lands. Serve the Lord with gladness: come before his presence with singing. Know ye that the Lord he is God: it is he that hath made us, and not we ourselves; we are his people, and the sheep of his pasture. Enter into his gates with thanksgiving, and into his courts with praise: be thankful unto him, and bless his name. For the Lord is good; his mercy is everlasting; and his truth endureth to all generations.'"

Maude smiled. She couldn't have said it better herself.

❧

Annie held Alice's right hand while Vesta held her left.

"One, two, three jump!"

They lifted her off the ground to the accompaniment of squeals and giggles.

"Again!"

They did it again, but then Victoria wanted a turn. Vesta called a halt to it after two more lifts. "You're wearing me out, girlies. I'm too old."

"Nonsense," Annie said. "You're the most youthful grandmother I've ever known."

Vesta smiled. "You flatter me. But perhaps being around the children every day *has* kept me younger than I would be without them."

Actually, Annie could see that Vesta had aged in the past year. Worry about Sean mixed with grief for Richard. She knew *she* had aged. There was a crease between her eyes and furrows in her forehead where none had been before. She'd tried special creams but had resigned herself to the evidence of her tribulations. She'd heard other women say that each wrinkle told a story and was earned. It was a silly rationalization, but partly true. The real truth was, it couldn't be helped.

The girls skipped on ahead with Willie and Lennie. And Lizzy. Gela and Matteo ran after them, starting a game of tag.

Edna pointed at them. "I'm so relieved to see Lizzy playing like a child should play."

"She's doing well, yes?" Maude moved one of the picnic baskets to her other arm. Antonio held a second one.

"She's doing very well. She's enrolled in school and I have a meeting next week with an agency to help me with the adoption."

Steven touched his mother's arm. "I admit it will be strange to have a sister nearly the same age as my boys."

"She'll be their aunt," Henrietta said with a laugh. "Imagine that."

They neared the Bethesda Fountain and joined hundreds of other New Yorkers who'd decided to take advantage of the late summer afternoon. Some children tormented pigeons while others leaned over the edge of the fountain and splashed in the water. Families carried model sail boats toward the lake nearby.

"Antonio, remember when the children used to race their boats?" Maude said.

"That's where we found you the last time we all gathered here."

"I was sitting on a bench, pouting."

"Why were you pouting?" Edna asked.

Maude cocked her head. "I believe it was because I was alone and the rest of you had someone."

I can relate to that.

They heard a child's cry. Alice had fallen down.

Annie rushed to help.

≈

Sean heard a child's cry. He spotted Alice on the ground, nursing a skinned knee. When he'd left she was only two, a toddler. Now she was a little girl. And there was Victoria! She'd grown so tall. He'd missed so much.

Then Annie came into view. Sean put a hand to his mouth, fighting back tears.

Lila touched his arm. "Go on. They're waiting for you."

"And you?"

"I'll let you have your moment. Then I'll have mine."

Sean took a deep breath, trying to calm himself. He'd imagined this moment a thousand times since remembering who he was. But those images were nothing compared to the real moment.

He left Lila behind and walked among the crowd toward his family. Annie had knelt at Alice's side, patting at the scrape with a handkerchief. Victoria stood beside her.

Suddenly, Sean knew exactly what to do. What to say.

He stopped ten feet away, then said, "There's my girls."

Annie turned her head. She gasped. She stood and ran into his arms. "Sean!"

They held each other as if trying to fuse their two into one. She sobbed. He cried. *You're here! You're here!* blended with *I'm back. I'm back!*

Sean let go enough to take her face in his hands. "My dear Annie-girl." Then he kissed her again and again. He never wanted to stop, but was interrupted by his daughters grabbing his legs, calling out the most important title in the world. "Daddy! Daddy!"

They each picked up a child and wrapped their free arms around each other, a bond of four that was finally together again.

"Sean?"

He looked up to see his mother, her face incredulous

He set Victoria down and opened his arms to her. More happy tears were shared.

Then he saw his friends, their hands at their mouths, or hugging each other, waiting their turns.

He pumped his fist into the sky and yelled, "I'm home!"

They all surrounded him, sharing their joy. Passersby looked on, smiling at the contagious joy.

As the joy set in, the questions started. "Where have you been?" "Are you all right?" "What happened?"

Then he remembered: *Lila is waiting.* He held up a hand, putting their questions on hold. He went to Henrietta and took her hands in his. "Close your eyes." He stepped aside.

Lila stepped out of the crowd and everyone gasped. Sean put a finger to his lips and they let the surprise play out.

As Lila walked forward, she said, "Open your eyes now."

Henrietta smiled at the voice and opened her eyes. She ran into her mother's arms. "You came!"

Steven, Willie, Lennie, and Edna all had a turn before the rest of them greeted her.

Then more questions began.

Maude held up a picnic basket. "Hold the questions. Let's go find a place to enjoy a picnic celebration."

"You knew about this?" Annie asked.

She deferred to Lila. "Maude knew. I cabled her, wanting to surprise you in the same way we did years ago."

Henrietta linked her arm with her mother. "What a great surprise. I couldn't be happier."

"Who wants a picnic?" Antonio asked.

While the others left to find a place on the grass, Annie and Sean held back.

They found a bench and sat close, not speaking. Yet they *were* speaking in ways that didn't have to be voiced aloud.

Annie found her special place beneath his arm, her head leaning against his.

"How?" she whispered.

"God."

She nodded and took a deep breath as Sean did the same.

They let out their breaths together, forever synced, two become one.

EPILOGUE

Three Months Later

Lila was in a predicament.

She stood at the door of Unruffled carrying three pumpkins which meant there was no way she could open the door. She feared if she tried to put them down they'd splat on the ground.

She looked inside, but there was no one close by to see her.

"Gracious," Mrs. Sampson said, hurrying up the sidewalk. "Let me help you."

"The door, if you please?"

Once inside, Mrs. Sampson took the smaller pumpkin, allowing Lila to set down the larger ones.

"Thank you. I nearly lost them."

"You're quite welcome. But what, may I ask, are you doing with pumpkins in a dress shop?"

"I've just created a new window display with some fall-colored dresses and it needed a few props to finish it off."

Mrs. Sampson stepped over to the window, taking a look. "You gathered the scattering of leaves yourself?"

"With the children's help. We went to the park and they gathered enough for two bushel baskets." Lila took the largest pumpkin and set it on the right side of the display, then went back and added the other two. "There," she said. "Groupings always look better in odd numbers."

"You learn something new every day," Mrs. Sampson said. "Annie said you used to create displays at your family's mercantile back in Summerfield?"

"I did. My mother didn't think much of my efforts, but Father appreciated it because our sales increased on whichever items I displayed."

Mrs. Sampson pointed at her eyes. "We are visual. What we see, we want."

"That's the plan."

A customer left — with a nod of approval at the display — leaving Annie free to join them. "Sorry. I saw you through the door, but a customer was talking and — "

"Never fear!" Mrs. Sampson said with a fist in the air. "I was here!"

Lila noticed the sash across her chest. "Votes for Women? I thought that was a law now."

Mrs. Sampson adjusted her sash. "It was passed in June but has yet to be ratified by all the states. We need thirty-six out of the forty-eight states."

"Back in England, I voted," Lila said.

Etta walked over to the discussion. "Really?"

"Last November." Lila looked at Mrs. Sampson. "We received the right in February."

"Women over thirty received the right," Etta said.

"You're over thirty," Lila said. "Did you vote?"

She shook her head. "I was here, not there."

Annie shook her head. "You and I became citizens when we married Americans. We'll both be able to vote."

"Good," Etta said. "I didn't know."

"Now you do," Mrs. Sampson said. "It will be your right and your privilege."

Lila agreed. "It made me feel very powerful to finally have a voice." She raised an arm in the air. "Votes for women!"

"Votes for women!" Mrs. Sampson said.

"You should run for president," Annie teased.

"Nah. I'm too bossy."

"A president has to be boss. They're in charge."

Mrs. Sampson shook her head. "They are forced to deal with Congress." She shuddered. "Trying to get all those people to agree on anything is nearly impossible."

"Someday they'll be a woman in Congress," Annie said.

"There already is," Mrs. Sampson said. "Jeannette Pickering Rankin is a representative from Montana—has been two years now. The first woman to be elected to a federal office."

"Why didn't I know that?" Annie said.

Mrs. Sampson leaned in close. "Ignorance does not become you, Annie. Someday I predict there will be a woman president."

"I'd love to see that," Annie said.

"One day you will," Mrs. Sampson said. "But one step at a time."

❧

Sean carried his sample case into Macy's, heading straight to the sewing goods department. Out of habit he put on his salesman-smile — though in the case of visiting Macy's, it was genuine.

He greeted the clerk. "Good morning, Mildred."

"Morning, Sean."

She looked a little pale. "Are you feeling all right?"

"As right as I ever feel when another one's on the way."

Unfortunately, he didn't catch himself before he glanced at her midsection. "Congratulations. This is number three?"

"Four." She sighed deeply and secured a stray strand of hair behind her ear. "The youngest is only one, but God gives blessings on His timetable, not ours, eh?"

"A blessing to be sure." He nodded toward a chair. "Would you like to sit while I show you the new patterns?"

She shook her head vehemently. "After seven years I may have seniority, but sitting has never been allowed." She pointed to the counter. "But I *can* lean."

He took out the newest Butterick patterns, then checked her stock drawers while she helped a customer.

They finished at the same time. He packed up his case. "I'll bring over the stock tomorrow."

"Very good." She got a pensive look on her face. "Just like old times, eh?"

"In some ways, yes. I'm very thankful Butterick gave me my job back."

"I didn't like the man they put in your position. An old codger who didn't know a peplum from a godet."

"With so many men gone, they had to make do. Luckily, he was just as glad to have me take over as I was to step in."

"Like you hadn't even been gone?"

He shook his head. "I wouldn't say that. Couldn't ever say that."

She got the gist of his words and gave a serious nod.

"The world is different now," he said. "To ignore all that happened cheapens the sacrifice."

"I don't like to remember."

"But we must. Remember and never repeat the mistakes again."

"I'm not sure humans are capable of that."

He agreed, but couldn't let the conversation end on a down note. "Rejoice! Times are better. The war-to-end-all-wars is over. We're all starting fresh." He nodded toward her midsection. "New life is always cause for celebration."

Edna finished sewing a hem, then checked her watch. School was out. Lizzy should arrive any minute.

She heard energetic footfalls on the stairs outside. As expected, Lizzy burst into the workshop with a flurry of youthful exuberance. She kissed Edna's cheek.

"How was school?"

Lizzy set a pile of three books on the table and unbuckled the book strap. "Look at these. Mrs. Union said I could take them home. I can't read 'em yet, but you can read 'em to me."

Edna looked at the books. *Baby Ray's and His Pets, Andersen's Fairy Tales,* and *The Tale of Peter Rabbit.* "Our evenings will be full."

Lizzy nodded, but had already moved on. She stuck her head in the sewing room. "Hi, Gert. Can I sew?"

"Let me finish this seam and I'll set you up."

Edna was thankful to Ginny and Gert who always took extra time after school to teach Lizzy. She was a quick study, already making her hand stitches straight and small.

"Come out here and wait," Edna said. "Let the ladies finish what they're working on."

Lizzy collected the basket of *her* sewing and sat at a bench near the window. She got out the doll's dress she was working on. Edna never tired of watching her sew, her face so intent and serious. She was such a good girl.

Gert came to help, taking a seat next to Lizzy. "Let's see where you are." She studied the dress. "One side-seam done, now do the other. Remember to pin it first."

Lizzy took the dress to the worktable and carefully pinned the front and back together.

Gert stood nearby but spoke to Edna. "Simon and I are excited about seeing Gela's play tonight."

Lizzy looked up. "You know her too?"

Gert flicked the tip of her nose. "She used to work here, silly. She was a seamstress too."

Lizzy nodded. "I forgot." She set the dress down. "Mama says we're going to a Great White place and we get to dress up."

"The Great White Way," Edna said. "It's what they call Broadway because of all the electric signs."

"It lights up the sky almost like daytime," Lizzy told Gert.

"You don't say." She shared a smile with Edna.

Ginny came out of the sewing room to join them. "We're going too. It's special to actually know someone in a play."

"Are you going to see Mack?" Gert asked with a wink.

It was an awkward subject, one she'd avoided all fall. "He's in the orchestra so I'm sure we'll see him."

"You haven't talked about him much since summer," Ginny said. "I thought he was coming around."

"He was," she said, making a small nod toward Lizzy.

"Oh," Gert said.

"Oh," Ginny said.

Lizzy went back to pinning. "She has everything she needs." She pointed at herself. "With me. Right, Mama?"

Mama.

"I sure do."

♆

Lila left her apartment—which was in the same building as Vesta, Edna, and Etta—and could hear her grandsons arguing even from out in the hall. She knocked.

Her daughter opened the door. "Welcome to the chaos."

"How can I help?"

The boys stopped their shenanigans and ran to Lila, wrapping their arms around her legs.

Etta nodded. "Perfect. Keep them entertained. Steven and I are nearly ready."

Lila spotted some wood blocks scattered across the floor of the parlor. She removed her coat and set it aside, then scooped up a few. "Let's make the tallest tower *ever.*"

The boys took the challenge and began building one that reached a good two-foot. Lila prepared to add her two blocks to the top.

"Careful, Nana," Lennie said.

Lila made a show of calming her nerves, then set one, then two blocks on the tower.

"We did it!" Willie said, jumping around.

Lila joined Lennie in a little dance. Then she caught sight of Etta and Steven standing in the doorway to their bedroom and stopped. They stared at her. "What?"

With a glance to Steven, Etta answered. "We're counting our blessings."

Lila blew them a kiss.

"Come boys. Let's go see Auntie Vesta. You get to sleep at her apartment tonight."

~

Gela sat in the greenroom, putting on eyeliner. Her hand shook.

"Nervous?"

Gela looked up to see Edith Day – the star of the show. Gela took a deep breath. "Are you?"

"Always – until I get out there. Then the nerves go away."

"I hope you're right."

Edith pointed at the eye-liner. "Want me to do it?"

Gela was shocked.

"I'm an expert. Let me give it a go."

"All right." Gela closed her eyes and let Edith do the work.

"Wait a minute for it to dry now."

Gela nodded, keeping her eyes closed. "Thank you."

She felt Edith's hands on her shoulder. "I'll see you soon."

To think that Edith Day had helped her with her makeup. Even though Gela had met her many, many times during rehearsals, she was still star-struck.

There was a knock on the door and she heard her mother's voice as it opened. "Gela?"

"Over here," Gela said, keeping her eyes closed.

"Ooh, look at you," Mama said.

"Is my eyeliner dry yet? Miss Day helped me and I don't want it to smudge."

She smelled Mama's perfume as she moved close. "It looks dry."

Gela opened her eyes to see not only her parents and Matteo – as expected – but Dock.

He handed her some flowers. "These are for you."

She was moved. "Thank you. How sweet."

"And these are for you too." Papa gave her another bouquet and kissed her cheek. "Good luck tonight."

Matteo batted his arm. "You're not supposed to say that. It's bad luck."

Papa looked baffled. "What should I say?"

"You're supposed to say 'break a leg.'"

"Why?"

Matteo looked to Gela. "I have no idea."

Papa shrugged and amended his well wishes. "Break a leg then. Only please don't."

"You're such a father."

Mama nudged Dock. "Share your good news with Gela."

He shook his head vigorously. "It's not the time."

Her interest was piqued. "Please?"

He looked around as if making sure no one beyond their circle was listening. Then he lowered his voice. "I finally forgave myself."

It took her a moment to let the words register. She took his hands in hers. "I'm so glad. How does it feel?"

He cocked his head and smiled. "It feels like an opening night."

Break a leg, Dock.

※

That's my daughter!

Maude stared at the stage, totally enthralled. When Gela sang in "Talk of the Town", she grabbed onto Antonio's arm. Gela was a natural, her voice pure and true.

I'm so glad we allowed her to pursue the stage and helped her find her calling.

During the applause she leaned toward her husband, "She's wonderful."

"Yes, she is."

Maude stole a glance in the other direction and smiled at Dock sitting next to Matteo. He looked very nice tonight. Obviously, in a new suit—that *he* had paid for.

When they'd picked him up and she'd seen how nice he looked, she'd commented on it.

"I'm a new man," he'd said.

And then he'd explained that he'd forgiven himself for his sin against her. "All thanks to you," he'd said.

She'd set him straight on that one, and in the remembering, set herself straight on taking the credit for helping Gela find her calling.

It's Your calling, Lord. And Your forgiveness. It's all thanks to You.

Bravo.

※

The play was a success—at least in Henrietta's eyes. She'd attended a few productions in London as an ingénue, but had been more interested in the social aspect of the evening than in the performance.

She, Steven, and her mother headed home in a taxi, but the traffic was horrendous.

"Remember when your Aunt Clarissa was on the stage?" her mother asked.

"I've heard. But I was a baby."

"Of course," Mamma said. "Your father and I accidentally saw her once. She was performing under the stage name of Clara West. None of the family knew about it until then."

"I can imagine her doing such a thing," Henrietta said. "She always had a flair for the dramatic."

"Still does."

Henrietta noticed a wistful tone in her mother's voice. "Do you miss Summerfield?"

"I do. I miss Adam and Robbie. And even Theodosia."

Steven adjusted a blanket over their laps. "Do you miss being Lady Newley, mistress of Crompton Hall?"

Mother considered this a moment. "A little perhaps. But that baton has passed to Theodosia—as it should."

"You haven't received many letters from them."

"I think I miss them more than they miss me."

"Nonsense," Henrietta said, though she wouldn't be surprised if it was true. Her brother was rather self-absorbed, and now that he was lord of the manor, she expected he was more so. Theodosia always had a kiss-my-ring attitude that rubbed Henrietta wrong. Plus, she'd only acted marginally polite to Steven when they'd come for Henrietta and Steven's wedding, as if Theodosia deemed him lesser because he worked for a living.

Personally, Henrietta was glad to be away from Summerfield and its titles.

"What about you, Etta?" her mother asked. "Do you miss Summerfield? Will you ever return home?"

She took her husband's hand. "I *am* home."

❧

Sean was mesmerized as their taxi drove through the traffic to get them home. He'd experienced such traffic in London and even here in New York before the war, but this was different. Even though it had been three months he still marveled at the fact he was safe. He knew exactly who he was and exactly how much God had played a part in bringing him back to Annie. *I'm so thankful, Lord.*

"A penny for your thoughts?" Annie asked.

He took her hand in his. "It's hard to explain."

She drew his arm over her head and around her shoulders then leaned her head against his.

Annie held open the door of her apartment for Henrietta and Lila. "Shh!" She lifted a hand, freezing in place.

The other women froze, then laughed. "Silence is a rare commodity," Henrietta said. "It was so nice of Vesta to take them overnight."

"It was so nice of you to ask us here," Lila said, taking off her coat, hat, and gloves. "What a brilliant idea to suggest the women have some time in your apartment — "

"While Sean and Steven play cards in ours."

Annie was glad she'd thought of it. "I bet Maude and Antonio are having a grand time celebrating with Gela."

"She did so well."

"Such a talent." Annie removed her shoes. "It's nice to just be the three of us here."

Henrietta slipped off her own shoes. Annie was glad she felt that at ease.

"Would you like some tea?" Annie asked. "I also have biscuits."

"Yes to both," Lila said.

"Biscuits . . ." Henrietta said. "We are the only three English women in our group, the only ones who know that biscuits are actually cookies."

Annie filled the kettle and took out a tin of biscuits, plus some napkins and small plates.

"No need to dirty plates," Lila said. "I'll set mine on my napkin."

"Me too," Henrietta said. "Though I'm not sure it will make it there." She popped a butter cookie into her mouth and closed her eyes in culinary ecstasy. "There is nothing better."

"I agree," Lila said.

"Have you tried brownies?" Annie asked.

"I haven't had the pleasure," Lila said.

"Edna makes them." Annie moaned. "It's like a cake, but also a cookie. Very chocolaty."

Henrietta bobbled her head. "Brownies are a close second."

Annie took a seat, eating her second biscuit. She was feeling tired, but didn't want to waste this chance to be with her friends.

Henrietta read her thoughts. "I wish tomorrow wasn't a workday."

Lila nodded. "Is it usual to have an opening night on a Tuesday?"

"I don't know," Annie said.

Henrietta helped herself to another biscuit and smiled at Annie. "Work we must, but at least we know the boss."

"That *is* handy," Lila said.

They ate their cookies. Then suddenly Annie gasped. "Oh my."

"What?" Henrietta asked.

"Do you realize how odd this is, that you two used to be my mistresses? *I* worked for *you*. And now — as you say — I am your boss and you both work for me, *and* you are my dear friends."

They shared a moment of silence, making Annie fear she'd said too much.

Then Lila laughed and Henrietta joined in.

"Only in America!" Henrietta said.

Only in America.

THE END

"Now to him who is able to do immeasurably more
than all we ask or imagine,
according to his power that is at work within us,
to him be glory in the church and in Christ Jesus
throughout all generations,
for ever and ever! Amen."
Ephesians 3: 20-21

Dear Reader:

I hate to end a series. The characters are more than my friends, they are my family. Who knows? Perhaps Annie, Edna, Maude, Henrietta and the others will show up in a future book.

I chose to move forward six years between Book #2: *The Fashion Designer* and Book #3: *The Shop Keepers* for two reasons. One, I didn't want to write about World War I—or any war. And two, I thought it was more interesting to write about after the war, when the country was rebuilding.

One note about the hard issues of rape and PTSD. I am no expert, and I'm sure I've made mistakes in the portrayal. Please forgive me. My heart and prayers go out to those of you who have suffered. But the biggest fact I wanted to portray is that God is with us in the pain and in the recovery.

As usual, I have included a lot of real history in my story. Here are some facts:

- World War I was responsible for nearly 40,000,000 civilian and military casualties, resulting in 10 million military deaths, and eight million civilian deaths, making it one of the deadliest conflicts in history. The Spanish flu pandemic was responsible for a third of the deaths. The war involved 4,000,000 soldiers, including nearly 117,000 American military who died from combat and the flu. Over 200,000 were wounded. There were 744,000 British soldiers killed. Doing the math, the military deaths equaled nearly 6000/day.
- Though the war started in April, 1914, the United States did not get involved until 1917. This was the point in history when the US became a world power.
- I fudged the date of the victory parade in Chapter 6. General John Pershing presided over the parade on September 10, 1919, though there had also been parades on March 25, May 6 . . . whenever another regiment came home. The September parade traveled from 107th down 5th to Washington Square. The earlier parades went through a temporary Victory Arch near Madison Square. The arch was built of wood and plaster for a cost of $1 million in today's money ($80,000 then). It was The Victory Arch was torn down by the summer of 1920. Washington Square arch also started as a temporary structure, but was made permanent with marble. A few days after the September parade, a new rank was created for Pershing by Congress: "General of the Armies," a unique rank,

making him the highest-ranking military figure in the country. I grew up in Lincoln, Nebraska and attended many school and city functions at our own Pershing Auditorium.

- The Spanish flu/Influenza Pandemic: 500 million people became infected with the flu virus — that was one third of the world's population. Fifty million died worldwide with 675,000 deaths in the United States. There was no vaccination. The way to control it was to keep people apart by limiting public gatherings, staggering work shifts, and through quarantine It was spread through the air or by touching an infected surface and then touching your mouth.

- Barbetta's, mentioned in Chapter 7, is still a family-owned restaurant in the Theatre District. It was opened in 1906 and is the oldest Italian restaurants in New York, and in the Theatre District. And yes, they are known for their risotto and the porcini mushrooms that the owner Sebastiano Maioglio hand-picked in the Connecticut woods.

- The Great White Way. The theaters along Broadway and 7th had colored lights on their marquees, but they burned out too fast, so they replaced them with white lights. The area *glowed*.

- Edna and her Quaker oats: The iconic round box made its first appearance in 1915. Later that year, Quaker offered the first cereal box premium to buyers. By sending in one dollar and the cut out picture of the "Quaker Man" customers received a double boiler for the cooking of oatmeal.

- Grace Godwin's Garret near Washington Square Park was a real place. Bohemian. A bit scandalous. There's a photo of Grace sitting in the upper window, inspiring me to make her to do so when Guy and Annie walked by.

- Leroy Street . . . in the first two books I didn't pay much attention to exactly where the ladies lived. But this time, I happened upon modern pictures of apartment buildings on Leroy Street and was so charmed by them, that I decided to claim the street by name. BTW, if you'd like to purchase one of the apartments, you simply need to can shell out $1 million.

- "Irene": The original Broadway production, directed by Edward Royce, opened on November 18, 1919 at the Vanderbilt Theatre where it ran for 675 performances, which at the time was the record for the longest-running show in Broadway history — a record it held for nearly two decades. A song you might know from the play is "Alice Blue Gown", which was inspired by Teddy Roosevelt's daughter, Alice who loved blue dresses. It was performed by Edith Day. The show made a star of Day, who left the cast after five months to recreate her role at London's Empire Theatre, where it ran for 399 performances. Other songs you might know are "You Made Me Love You." and "I'm Always Chasing Rainbows."

- Vanderbilt Theatre: The Vanderbilt Theatre was designed by architect Eugene De Rosa for producer Lyle Andrews. It opened in 1918 and was located at 148 West 48th Street. The theater was demolished in 1954. In the mid-1920s, the 780-seat theater produced several Rodgers and Hart musicals.
- Actor's Strike: In 1919, Equity called the first strike in the history of the American theater, demanding recognition as the performers' representative and bargaining agent. The strike lasted 30 days, spread to eight cities, closed 37 plays, prevented the opening of 16 others, and cost millions of dollars in lost revenue.
- The actual strike was August 7 to Sept 6. I moved up the resolution date by a few weeks for the purpose of my story.
- The Actor's Fundraiser evening. The actors and acts I mentioned were real. Caught up in the moment, a teenage unknown named Tallulah Bankhead pledged $100 she did not have. Her grandfather wired the money soon after. "The enthusiasm of the players for the cause went right across the audience and we got immediate return from them," remembered Ethel Barrymore, "just like a ball being tossed back and forth; you threw it out to them and they threw it back to you; regular team play." Most of Ed Wynn's speech are actually his words.
- Votes for women: The Suffrage movement was voluntarily put on hold during the war. In May, 1919, Congress got the necessary two-thirds vote in favor of the women suffrage amendment. The proposed amendment was sent to the states for ratification. By July 1920, all the states had passed the amendment except Tennessee. It looked like it would come down to one vote. Twenty-four-year-old Harry Burns cast the winning vote after receiving a letter from his mother saying, "Don't forget to be a good boy" and "vote for suffrage." Women had the vote!
- Housing conditions: Because American industry had to focus on defense needs, construction of housing virtually stopped during the war. After the war only 1481 apartments were built in 1919 – a 94% decrease from 1915. Prices soared as the vacancy rate fell to .36 percent.
- The quote from Miss Pruitt who was a streetcar conductor applying for a job at Unruffled, was from a real woman. Mrs. J.E. Barry, a conductor on the Broadway line said, "There is no more

reason why a woman shouldn't stand on her feet than anyone else. I have to stand up every little while on these Broadway cars. Sitting all the time is not good for you; you don't exercise your muscles." The "candy and orchid" quote from the law, was real. There was an outcry regarding the unfairness of limiting hours for women, which eventually inspired the Lockwood-Caulfield Bill. It was signed into law in April 1920. It prohibited limiting hours to women who worked on transit lines. Yet it was too late. With men returning from the war, there were few positions open for women. "With a strange sense of irony, the law enacted to protect women's working rights in transportation, ensured they would be excluded from it. It would take many years for women to gain another foothold in New York's transportation industry."

- The elevated train stop where Gela gets off at 50th & 6th, is near where Radio City Music Hall and Rockefeller Center were built in 1933.

- Brassieres: In 1913 the modern bra was created by socialite Mary Phelps Jacob. She'd bought a sheer evening gown and found that her usual corset stays showed through. So she took a couple of silk handkerchiefs and some ribbon and voila! A bra. She had it patented.

- In 1917 the U.S. War Industries Board called on women to stop buying corsets to free up the metal in the boning. 28,000 tons of metal were freed up—and women breathed deeply for the first time in centuries!

- When Sean is in London, a Butterick store is mentioned. These pattern stores were also in Vienna, Paris and London.

If you'd like to read Annie's pre-story, how she came to work at Crompton Hall in 1906, read my novella, *Pin's Promise* in the anthology *Christmas Stitches*.

If you'd like to read more about Lila and Henrietta, and their home in Summerfield, England, read The Manor House Series: *Love of the Summerfields, Bride of the Summerfields,* and *Rise of the Summerfields.*

As you see, I like to interweave the characters in my books.

Enjoy! And let me hear from you.

Nancy Moser

DISCUSSION QUESTIONS

for *The Shop Keepers*

1. Chapter 4: Edna allows her son, Steven, to move into his old room. What do you think about her decision?

2. Chapter 7: Maude and Antonio gave their permission to let Gela join the company of "Irene." They worried about temptation. Despite promises from those in charge, "The brunt of the situation would fall on Gela. Was she strong enough for it? Unfortunately, there was no way to find out except by letting her do it." Do you think they made the right decision? Why or why not?

3. Chapter 7: Annie lives in limbo, not knowing if Sean is alive or dead. What do you think of her ways of coping? What do you think about her going out to dinner with Guy Ship?

4. Chapter 9: Now the dowager, Lila feels displaced in her own home. Have you ever lived in a home with three (or more) generations? What are your experiences with this situation?

5. Chapter 10: Henrietta is rude to neighbors who are gossiping. She returns their wrong deed with her own. But then she apologizes. How has your temper or your words caused harm? How did you right your wrong?

6. Chapter 12: Lila overhears her daughter-in-law say she wants Lila gone. Lila gets an inner God-nudge to call her on it. Although it was against her non-confrontational nature, Lila heeds the nudge and stands up for herself. To good results. What do you think about "God-nudges"? Have you had a few yourself? Have you ignored them or followed them? What was the result?

7. Chapter 14: Annie is in church praying about Sean. But instead of her usual "Bring him home safe" prayer, she changes it: *Father, You know how I'd like things to turn out. But now I ask that somehow You use Sean and I however You see fit. I'm weary making plans. I accept Your plans, whatever they are.* Soon after her surrender, God answers both prayers. Name a time when God has answered a prayer after you've surrendered to Him.

8. Chapter 14: Maude wants to help Dock. "I have to try. When we do good for others we have no control over what they will do with our good intentions. That is not on our shoulders. We are asked to give. Period." Do you agree with her? Has this attitude affected your charitable giving?

9. Chapter 15: Henrietta realizes she's grown stronger because Steven was incapacitated. Name a time in your life when you had to take charge for someone else. How did it change you?

10. For fun: In Chapter 16, Gert tells her bridal attendant, Henrietta, that she chose her dress so Henrietta could wear it other places. Did a bride ever tell *you* that? Or did you tell your bridesmaids that? Does anyone ever wear their dress again?

11. Chapter 16 & 17: Annie, Eudora, and their friends long for revenge against Guy. This contradicts God's call to leave vengeance to Him. The women work with the police to gain justice. What is the difference between revenge and justice? What do you think of the scheme to trap Guy? Was it the right thing to do? The God-thing to do?

12. What do you think about Edna rejecting the possibility of a relationship with Mack McGinness for the sake of orphan Lizzie?

13. Do you think Lila will stay in New York City?

FASHION of *THE SHOP KEEPERS*

ANNIE'S DINNER DRESS

Perry, Dame & Company, 1919

Chapter 7: (left dress) Annie chose a yellow silk she'd made for Easter. It was a maize-colored silk chiffon with embroidered medallions in the same color. It fell into three ruffles at the bottom, had elbow-length sheer sleeves, a scoop neckline, and a wide satin cummerbund She'd wanted a pretty dress to wear when Sean got home—for she'd expected him in May. Or June. Or . . . and now it was August.

Eudora's Dress

December 1919 issue of "The Woman's Magazine."

Chapter 10: (lower, middle dress) "The rust color of her [Eudora's] ensemble brought out the hues of her hair. Her slight build was evident even while wearing a loose sheath that formed a knee-length overskirt, covering a straight skirt beneath. A long string of pearls draped down to her midsection over a self-tied belt... the short sleeves and overskirt were edged in a wide ruched trim that spoke of couture. She wore a gold asymmetrical hat, sweeping high on the left, and dipping low over her right ear."

EDITH DAY in "IRENE"

Chapter 7: Suddenly, there was applause from the back of the theater. A woman with bobbed hair covered with a pink cloche walked down the aisle toward the stage. "Bravissimo."

Mr. Starling greeted her by kissing the air above her cheeks. "Edith, come meet the newest member of the Irene company. Miss Angela Ricci. Angela, this is Miss Edith Day, our star."

SEAN in SUMMERFIELD

Chapter 13: With a glance he recited: "Pattern number 3558, a girl's coat in raglan style with an inverted or box pleat in back."

Mrs. Evers picked up the envelope. "He's right. That's what it says on the front, down to the description. How do you know that?"

He pressed a hand to his forehead. "I have no idea."

LILA'S DINNER DRESS

Drawn by Florrie Westwood (Victoria & Albert museum)

Chapter 13: (dress on the right) "They'd all seen Lila's ivory crepe georgette dress many times — and she didn't care. It was a favorite and had been sewn at the sewing workshop. It boasted a V-neck with a wide collar, wide horizontal panels of peach fabric and vertical insets of lace. She'd had fun designing it, and was so very glad that the fashion had changed during the last decade from nipped and tucked into a flowy linear silhouette. It was about time dresses were comfortable."

GERT'S WEDDING DRESS

Chapter 16: Maude helped Gert slip a long crepe voile cardigan over her satin sheath dress. The bodice was covered in Chantilly lace, and the cardigan was edged with satin trim. She helped her tie the self-belt and bloused the cardigan over it. "There," she said, stepping back.

NOTE: This photo is of my grandparents, George and Ruth Swenson. They married in March, 1920. The pearls Grandma wore were worn by my mother, my two sisters, and myself on our wedding days. By the way, Grandma's maiden name was Holmquist.

HENRIETTA'S BRIDESMAID DRESS

October 1919, "The Delineator" magazine

Chapter 16: (middle dress) She took a moment to glance at her own new dress in the mirror. It was a simple design made of burnt orange charmeuse with unlined chiffon sleeves. Embroidery highlighted the sleeves and the waist. Underneath Henrietta wore a slim black mid-calf skirt. "I do like this dress," she told Gert and Maude.

"I chose the design so you can wear it other places," Gert said.

Actually, it was a possibility.

ABOUT THE AUTHOR

NANCY MOSER is the best-selling author of nearly 40 novels, novellas, and children's books, including Christy Award winner *Time Lottery* and Christy finalist *Washington's Lady*. She's written seventeen historical novels including *Love of the Summerfields*, *Masquerade*, *The Journey of Josephine Cain* and *Just Jane*. *An Unlikely Suitor* was named to Booklist's "Top 100 Romance Novels of the Decade." *The Pattern Artist* was a finalist in the Romantic Times Reviewers Choice award. Some of her contemporary novels are: *The Invitation, Solemnly Swear, The Good Nearby, John 3:16, Crossroads, The Seat Beside Me,* and the Sister Circle series. Nancy has been married for over forty years—to the same man. She and her husband have three grown children, seven grandchildren, and live in the Midwest. She's been blessed with a varied life. She's earned a degree in architecture, run a business with her husband, traveled extensively in Europe, and has performed in various theaters, symphonies, and choirs. She knits voraciously, kills all her houseplants, and can wire an electrical fixture without getting shocked. She is a fan of anything antique—humans included.

Website: www.nancymoser.com
Blogs: Author blog: www.authornancymoser.blogspot.com
History blog: www.footnotesfromhistory.blogspot.com

Find Nancy Moser here:

Excerpt from *Where Time Will Take Me*
Book 1 of the Past Time Series

Enjoy this novel of time travel, justice, and romance.

Prologue
1868 Piedmont, New Hampshire

"I'm dying."

Granny's words caused ten-year-old Justine to take a step back from the bedroom door before showing herself.

Granny couldn't die! Granny was always there. Granny was . . . Granny.

Justine heard her mother's voice and stepped forward again, peering through the crack in the doorway.

"You are not dying," Mother said. Commanded. She fingered a perfume bottle on the night stand. "Don't be so dramatic."

So Granny isn't dying?

"I'm the one who knows whether I'm dying or not, so I'd appreciate it if you'd stop arguing with a dying woman."

Granny sounded feisty. She sounded normal. Justine let herself breathe again.

"Are you going to let me speak my mind or are you going to argue with me all morning?" Granny asked.

Mother sighed. "Go on. Though I know what you're going to say, and the answer is no."

"It can't be no. You must take up our gift after I'm gone. You must continue with the Ledger. And after you, Jussie will continue our legacy."

"I am not moving back here to Piedmont."

"But this is where it begins."

Mother removed the stopper of the perfume, smelled it, crinkled her nose and put it back again. Justine loved the smell of honeysuckle. It was Granny's scent.

Then Mother said, "I left this town eleven years ago. Good-riddance was what I said then, and good-riddance is what I say now."

"Don't be rude, Mavis. Your roots are in Piedmont, it's the place where the Tyler ancestors first settled back in 1800."

"I have no interest in the past, only in the present and the future." Mother extended her arms out, as if putting herself on display. "Do you see this dress? I ordered it from Worth in Paris. It's crêpe de chine."

"It's as practical as a parasol in a downpour."

Mother huffed and sat in the chair beside the bed. "The point is, I've moved on from Piedmont. I don't belong here—if I ever did."

"You could have belonged."

Mother shook her head. "I'm weary of this. Say what you have to say and let Justine and I get back to New York."

Granny closed her eyes and a ridge formed between them. Was she hurting? Justine wanted to comfort her, but she'd been ordered to stay out.

Finally Granny's ridge eased and she opened her eyes, but her voice was raspy. "I don't know how to say it any stronger. It's imperative you do what I ask, Mavis. Past secrets must be revealed, and wrongs made right."

Mother's head shook once right then once left. "I am aware of what you went through. The condemnation, the threats. I will not put myself through all that—any of that."

"But there are truths that need to be shared," Granny said. "I regret I wasn't strong enough to follow through. But you *are* strong. You can do what I could not."

"Your neglect is not my problem," Mother said. "None of this is my responsibility. You chose your way and I chose mine."

"But the gift—"

Mother rose from the chair, forming fists at her side. "I didn't choose the gift. And as such, I refuse to—"

"'For unto whomsoever much is given, of him shall be much required: and to whom men have committed much, of him they will—'"

287

"'Will ask the more.'" Mother plucked a thread from her sleeve and let it fall to the floor. "I know. I *know*. Aren't you getting weary of spouting that verse at me? I'm not listening."

"But you should. You must." Granny sighed, then pointed at a dresser. "There's a letter in the top drawer for Jussie, for her to open when she's twenty. Promise me you'll give it to her."

"If it's full of this claptrap . . ."

"Mavis. You must. The Ledger and the gift can't die with me."

"Some things are better off dead."

Granny's chin quivered. "Some people you mean."

With a sigh, Mother touched Granny's hand. "Don't go getting dramatic again. I'm not rejecting you, I'm simply rejecting — "

"Our legacy. The legacy of all those who are depending on us to — "

"Enough!" Mother shuddered as if the discussion had pushed her to her limit. She went to the dresser and took up the letter, slipping it into her pocket. "There. I took the letter."

"Good. Thank you."

"We're leaving. Can I get you anything before Justine and I head back to the city?"

"I've told you what I need."

Mother turned toward the door, then shook her head. "Justine? *Tsk. Tsk.* Naughty girl. It's not polite to eavesdrop."

Justine pushed the door open. "Sorry."

"Come in here and say good-bye to your grandmother while I finalize our luggage."

Justine moved to the bed and Granny held out her hand. It felt so cold and smooth, like a pillow slip left in the night air. "Bye, Granny," Justine said.

Granny squeezed her hand and pulled her in. "You heard what I said?"

"I didn't mean to listen."

"You heard?"

Justine nodded.

"It's up to you to carry on what your Mother rejects."

"I don't understand."

"The gift will come to you when you're twenty. What you do with it then is your choice. A very important choice."

"What gift?"

"Be open to it. Then use it to carry on the Ledger. Learn from it. Add to it. Then pass it on. 'Ye shall know the truth, and the truth shall make you free.'"

Suddenly, Granny bolted forward in a fit of coughing. Justine thought it would pass, but when it didn't . . . she didn't know what to do. She put a hand on Granny's back, then poured her a glass of water.

Granny spilled it all over the covers, the glass crashing to the floor. She was having trouble catching her breath.

Justine ran into the hall. "Mother! Goosie! Come quick!"

The housekeeper got there first, took Granny's hand, and started rubbing her back, saying, "Slow. Slow now. Take a breath. Slow."

Granny gasped. Her eyes got big.

Then she fell back upon the pillows.

Her eyes closed, her mouth hung open.

There was no sound.

"Mrs. Tyler? Breathe! Mrs. Tyler!"

Justine heard feet on the stairs and ran out in the hall a second time. "Mother! Granny had a coughing fit and now she's not moving. Hurry!"

But Mother didn't hurry. She walked down the hallway at her usual pace. When she finally reached the room, she stopped in the doorway.

"Help her!" Justine yelled.

Goosie turned around, crestfallen. "She's gone! My dear Jesus, she's gone."

"No!" Justine ran to the bed and flung her arms around Granny. "You can't be dead. Come back. Come back!"

It felt strange to hug Granny and not be hugged in return. "Granny, don't go!"

Goosie stood nearby, crying. "I've been here sixty-eight years. What to do? What to do?"

Mother stepped into the room. "Oh, hush, Goosie. Stop thinking of yourself." She peered down at Granny, then sighed. "I suppose this means your father and I will miss the opera at the Pike this weekend."

Justine couldn't believe her ears. "Is that all you care about? Granny's dead!"

Mother stabbed a finger into Justine's chest. "Don't you ever talk to me like that again! Ever."

Justine knew she should be sorry for her words but wasn't sorry at all. If anything, she felt brave. "What is this gift Granny talked about? And what is the Ledger"

"None of your business."

"But it is my business. Granny said so."

"Your grandmother is dead. I'm in charge now, and I say the subject is as dead as she is. Let it die."

"Let what die?"

Mother pinched Justine's cheek until it hurt.

Justine didn't say any more. She didn't argue. But in that moment she made herself a vow.

She *would* use the gift. Somehow she would fulfill Granny's wishes.

Whatever they were.

@ Nancy Moser 2019

Coming in late 2019:
Book 2: *Where Life Will Lead Me*

CPSIA information can be obtained
at www.ICGtesting.com
Printed in the USA
LVHW030114030720
659626LV00003B/894

9 781733 983013